DANDELION DAYS

NOTE

THE FOUR Books (of childhood, boyhood, youth, and early manhood) making the work called *The Flax of Dream* are

The Beautiful Years
Dandelion Days
The Dream of Fair Women
The Pathway

DANDELION DAYS

BY

HENRY WILLIAMSON

'I hope in the days to come future thinkers
will unlearn us, and find ideas infinitely better . . .
let us get a little alchemy out of the dandelions.'

RICHARD JEFFERIES, in *Nature and Books*.

'Shock-headed dandelion,
That drank the fire of the sun.'

ROBERT BRIDGES

LONDON
FABER & FABER LIMITED
24 RUSSELL SQUARE

First published in 1930
by Faber and Faber Limited
24 Russell Square London WC1
First published in Faber Paper-covered Editions 1966
Reprinted 1969
Printed in Great Britain
by Latimer Trend & Co Ltd Whitstable
All rights reserved

SBN 571 06755 7 (FPCE)
SBN 571 06690 9 (Cloth)

TO
ANDREW DAKERS

CONTENTS

ONE PETAL OUT

'There is nothing in books that touches my dandelion.'
RICHARD JEFFERIES, in *Nature and Books*.

Chapter 1

THE beeches of Rookhurst Forest have grown to the sunlight of centuries, their tap roots deep in the chalk and flints of the lower southern slope of the downs. In early spring the winds sing shrill in the topmost boughs, and the rooks sway aloft, or hop sideways flapping about the nests. Boisterous are the winds from the south-west—from the sea far beyond the corn-fields of the plain of Colham—when the sun is bright and the clouds are swift and white; boisterous as they swirl the leaves of the old year out of the drifts in the mossy hollows, scattering them, brown and crisp-curled, on the ancient swine-paths.

Caw! Caa-aa! krok-krok-krok! Ca-ca! Wing-flaps and chortles of greeting, soft cries of contentment, harsh squarks of suspicion and anxiety, loud caws of excitement—the wind rushes away with the immemorial rookery noises. Lisp and flick of leaves against the massive grey trunks below, while twigs fall aslant among the bare branches, and to the ground strewn with white splashes and the split covers of beech-mast.

Then shadow takes the scanty colour of the early April woodland; raindrops hiss and patter on the leaves, and cease as suddenly before the light and heat of the sun sweeping through the trees again. Caw! Caw!

When *Doomsday Book* was made the rooks were in the tree-tops; for therein it was named Rookhurst Great Forest, where roamed the tall red deer, with wolves and wild boars, and beavers in the stream that flowed to the mere called the Long-pond. In the village of Rookhurst it was said that the swine which routed in the autumn beech-mast—an ancient right of fattening—were bred from the wild pigs of olden time.

13

During the centuries the Great Forest grew less; the axes rang in the wood, and the ploughs turned the brown loam against its flanks, until but a narrow strip of its olden depth remained. Very beautiful were the massed trees, under the grey-green downs which rose along the length of the northern sky.

One windy April morning towards the end of the im-memorial life of Rookhurst Great Forest (it was thrown during the third year of the Great War), two boys were walking along the lower swinepath near the brook. Both wore black caps with identical silver badges sewn above the peaks; one cap was set with a red button, the other with a buff button, de-noting that they belonged to different Houses of Colham School. The boy wearing the red buttoned cap was con-siderably larger than his companion. He walked with a good-natured, loose-shouldered slouch; his cap had been carelessly pulled over his yellow head, with the peak over one temple. He was listening to the smaller boy beside him, sometimes saying 'Ah' in a man's voice, and grinning as he hitched up a worn leather satchel tighter over his left shoulder —a satchel half undone, showing the battered corners of books.

The smaller boy, whose books were held by a canvas strap, was taking long strides in order to keep in step with his friend; the strides appeared to be longer than his thin legs. He walked upright, and his cap was set straight on his small, dark head. He wore a threadbare norfolk suit of cheap material. A large Eton collar, showing much-mended stud-holes above an old tie of his father's, rested stiffly on the top of his shoulder blades, and emphasised, ironically—for he wore it outside his coat collar in order to hide the defect—his small size. The wind had given him much animation; often he hastened to the left or right of the path, to wade through a drift of leaves and kick them up before him; but his friend slouched along, with for-ward bent head and rounded shoulders, one big fist bulging in his shrunken trousers.

14

The rooks cawed over their heads, swaying on the fine bare branches, or hurtling down to a treetop perch with wings crooked back against the air-blasts.

'How about if it's like this 'is afternoon, Jack? Shall we try it then?'

'Easy! You'll be all right, Willie.'

'Do you think they will attack our eyes?'

'Get out! Don't you worry. Rooks never have attacked men yet!'

'Well, I was only wondering, you fool!' replied the smaller boy, in a sharp treble voice. Instantly his voice softened, and he said, 'shall we just go and have a look and see if the jackdaw's laid yet?'

Without waiting for an answer, he led the way up the slope to the jackdaw's nesting tree. The bigger boy followed; he seldom went first.

At the higher edge of the wood was a loamy field, scattered with whitish flints. A pale green mist lay low over the field; the young corn-blades glistened before their feet. With big strides the small leading boy crossed the field, walking up a draining furrow, which led over the slope and down to another part of the wood. The beeches of Lower Side, as it was called, had grown under the main rush of the prevailing winds: and the trees at the edge of the field had spread themselves wider, finding more sunlight. One tree was more dispread than the others, with branches growing regularly almost from the ground to its head. Seeing the boys underneath, the rooks rose cawing from their high dark nests.

'They're like inkblots against the sky,' said Willie, gazing up at the swaying black nests. How thin were the branches; how could anyone climb up there?

'I'll climb to the jack's nest,' he said, and started to climb quickly, before his friend had time to volunteer.

About twenty feet from the ground was a hole in the tree-trunk, the rain-rotted socket of a bough that had long since broken off. As the boy climbed up, a bird with a slate-grey pate peeped out of the hole and flew rapidly away.

He looked down to cry the news to Jack; and immediately allowed the fear of height to overcome him.

Trying to master the fear, he looked up at the hole above him. Supposing he fell? The thought seemed to glue him to the trunk. Before he could reach the hole, he must cease to hold the bough on which he kneeled; and with only finger-tips pressed against the yard-thick trunk to steady himself, to rise slowly to an upright position. Had the bough been his own height from the ground, he could have risen with un-thinking ease, without using his hands; but now he crouched as though all but his main joints were rigid. He tried to force away the dilated visions of falling, the blurring rush to earth, the jagged flash of death; and the effort absorbed most of his strength, leaving him with parched throat and quivering muscles.

'Hurry up, man, or we shall miss the motor,' called out Jack from below.

'I can't move!'

'All right, I'm coming!'

A few moments later Jack's complacent face appeared above the smooth grey bough.

'Stand up, man. It's easy as pie! You can't fall.'

'Shut-up, you fool!'

Seeing his friend's face, Jack said, 'I'll help you,' and swinging up easily behind him he put his hands on his friend's shoulders; and thus steadied, Willie got astride the branch, and clung to the trunk.

'By God, I am a cursed fool. But I can't bear heights.'

'Get out, it's no height at all.'

'That's right, jeer at me because I get giddy. I suppose you think I'm frightened!'

'Don't get ratty. I know some chaps can't stand heights. Shall I see if there's an egg in the jack's nest?'

'Yes. But leave it if there's only one.'

'All right.'

Rapidly Jack's head and forearm were thrust into the hole. Leaning against the trunk, his other hand by his side, he held out a greyish-blue egg, speckled with black and brown.

'Only one. Warm. Just laid.'

'What's the nest made of? Be careful not to disturb it too much, or she'll forsake.'

'Feels like string. And bits of paper, too.'

'Right. I'll put it in my Diary of Observations'

Jack began climbing higher. 'It won't take me half a mo to get to the rook's nests. Then we shall have to sprint for the motor.'

'We'll go like the wind!'

He watched Jack's clambering from branch to branch; and then he began to swing himself down from branch to branch, hardly using his feet. The fifteen feet to the ground was accomplished with the effortless ease of one who was not consciously thinking of what he should do. My arms aren't weak, he thought, looking up at the jackdaw's resting hole and measuring the distance with his eye. I must do my morning exercises again: and this time I swear I won't ever stop doing them! I will become beefy, I will!

Many times before had he undertaken exercises of an almost fanatical violence in order to become beefy: swung Indian clubs and did belly-grinders off the floor until his back ached: and rubbed vaseline into his upper lip and lower belly in order to hasten the envied change into manhood. As it was, he was half ashamed to go bathing in the river-baths above the gas works at Colham, lest the chaps notice that he, an Upper School man, had not come to puberty—puberty being a term he had discovered looking through a *Popular Medical Directory*.

Willie Maddison was older than most people would have judged him to be; he would be fifteen in less than a month. At the end of the previous term—the Christmas term—he had put weights in his pockets before taking his turn on the official weighing machine of the school: even so his report had shown only 4-stone 12-lbs. Although he had considerable powers of endurance, he was not physically robust. His friend Jack Temperley, whose forebears had been yeomen for many centuries at Rookhurst, was a year younger, a hefty lad, with hairs on his upper lip and cheeks; Willie Maddison was small and thin, his face smooth, his voice still unbroken, and these disabilities, as he had come to regard them from various remarks made to him at different times, caused him to feel inferior when he remembered them.

He had grown slowly; scarcely at all since the age of twelve years. He felt that everyone was conscious of his insignificance. 'And a little bit of a boy like you, too!' was a phrase occassionally used by his father when Willie was being reprimanded for one of his frequent misdemeanours: a phrase that caused him, in occurring retrospections—generally in bed at night—acute feelings of mortification. He was conscious, too, of his unmanly appearance. A year previously he had attracted the notice of a certain senior boy, who had told him how pretty he was—a pleasing experience at the time. Both boys had fallen in love; there had been a few secret meetings in the alley behind the woodwork shop, and in the lavatories —known generally as The Bog—which fascinated Willie at the time, but shamed him now in reprospect; meetings of a mutual furtive seeking. The phase had passed; the Sixth Form boy had, the previous term, gone up to Cambridge.

Although long girlish lashes could be cut with scissors in his bedroom at night, brown eyes could not be changed, unfortunately, into a more manly blue. Studying his face in a mirror, during the operation on the eye-lashes, he had realised that his mouth was too large, his cheekbones high, his brow narrow and his head small—sure signs of no brains! Well, he didn't want brains. Hair a common mousy-colour and very thick. Jack was nearly twelve inches taller than himself, and nearly double his weight. Jack's face was ruddy, not pale brown like his own; his hair bright and fair, his hands large, his wrists thick; while his own wrists were slight, with long thin fingers. And his awfully small knees. How he longed for big knees and hefty thighs, like the full-backs in the First Eleven.

'I'll do some belly-grinders!' he said aloud.

Clenching his teeth, he stretched himself on his back and placed his hands behind his neck. Slowly he raised his stiffened feet above his head, and slowly lowered them. He would raise them twelve times. The second raising was not so easy as the first; the third was completed only with stopped breath; the fourth was achieved only by the help of hands pressed to the ground by his side. The fifth ceased when his feet were over his head, and there they remained, while he watched Jack swaying under a nest, very small between the instep arch of his boots. The rooks were flying above the trees, high in the air, flapping against the wind, almost still; then, as though tired, gliding downward and beating slowly up again.

Watching the birds, Willie decided to test his power of endurance by keeping his feet in that position until Jack came down. His feet remained over his face for several minutes; but gazing at the shine of the sky he imagined swallows and swifts wheeling there, and the midsummer hum of insects over the wheat. Soon his heels were on the grass; and with shut eyelids glowing red against the rays of the sun, he dreamed backwards into vanished days of his life, seeing a boy who once was himself, who drifted, as a gossamer on the sun-wind, over meadow-scenes gone for ever and ever.

His heart ached with unaccountable longing for the past to come again. Nevermore those hawthorn leaves so green at opening, the green mossy nest of the chaffinch—the first chaffinch. Nevermore the same shining water; nevermore the summer wheat waving in the wind. The wraith of himself drifting over grasses and by trees became tenuous, and slowly vanished in remote and everlasting sunlight.

He remembered himself again; and he remembered how, at HER Christmas party, when sitting with her by a window where he could see the stars, he had tried to tell her: and had asked her if ever she felt like that—and she had—she had— ah!——

He dug his nails into the grass and leaves, trying to hurt himself, writhing inwardly at the memory of the rebuff. Oh, oh, what a soppy fool she must have thought him; she had laughed, and said, 'No, I should hope I jolly well didn't!' He tried to injure himself, but stopped immediately when he felt a sharp pain in one finger-tip.

Sitting up, he examined a nail broken on a flint. Blood welled out of the earth on the nail. Taking a knife from his pocket, he pared off the broken part, afterwards scraping the earth from the other nails. Then kneeling by the tree, he pressed the point into the bark and drew down the blade, making a long cut. Another scooping out with the point, and a slip of pinkish rind fell away. He was regarding it longingly when a shout from above made him stand up. Jack shouted down the news that the motor was slowing up at the Halt.

'Hurray!' yelled Willie, wild with sudden excitement. 'Damn the Old Bird! We'll mitch to-day!'

The thought of mitching, or staying away altogether from school, caused a thrill of fascination in the muscle between his legs; and with bright eyes he knelt down by the trunk again. Boldly, almost rapturously, he drew the point of the blade down the bark, until her initials were cut above his own. When she saw them, surely she would know that he— that he—what he had meant to tell her a hundred times, but never dared to say: looking forward all the week to Sunday morning Church because she would be there: recreating from a smile or a glance of those lovely eyes a thousand smiles and a thousand glances filling the secret darkness of his bedroom as he lay with face pressed in the pillow, the clock striking the long hours of night: praying to dream of HER whose gaze filled all his sky and all his earth, to dream so that the heavy-sweet feeling, which glowed with all ancient sunlight, might fill his breast.

Jack was beginning to descend, his cap held in his mouth. Quickly Willie gathered the pinkish-green chips, and threw them away. Leaf mould rubbed into the cuts would hide the newness of them, but even so they were easily seen. Quick! Jack was climbing down steadily, growing bigger and bigger. Oh! Quick! The boy stood still, the exquisite feeling between his legs holding him as an anemone in a sea-pool holds a little fish; until in panic he ran to the border of the field, picked up a clod, broke it in his fingers, and with spittle in his palm mixed it into mud. The mud clung to the cuts in the bark, and being smeared over the place, hid the outline of the be-traying heart and the initials.

When Jack dropped to the ground from the lowest branch, most of the mud on Willie's hands had been transferred to the seat of his knickerbockers. Jack's face was redder, smudged and sweating; he spat, and knuckled his eyes, in which frag-ments of the bark of dead branches had lodged. He took the cap from between his teeth, and handed it to Willie.

'I got a few,' he said casually, and looked at his friend for approval.

'Good old Jack! Won't we score off Clemow and Hoys! And Bony Watson! They haven't any rookses in their col-lections!'

He knelt on the grass, and lifted out the eggs, which were of all shades of grey-green and blue-green, spotted and speckled with brown and black. Some were long and pointed at one end, like small unripe pears, others were more rounded. He laid them out in a row, counting seventeen.

'You can have them,' said Jack, standing still above him.

'What, all of them?'

Jack nodded.

'But don't you want any?'

'You can have them.'

'But you got them. Let's divide. You have first choice.'

'Righto!'

When they had chosen, Willie said doubtfully,

'Do you think we'd better mitch, after all? The Old Bird would play hell if we're copped. If we catch the 9-53 motor we would just about be in time to slip in as the chaps were leaving Taffy's.'

'Good bloater. I haven't done my Physics homework. Oh darn it, the next hour is with Rattlethrough!'

'Bloody old Rattlethrough!' said Willie. '"One before two, two before three, three before y, y before en. Stop sniggerin'! Stand out there, stupid fool."'

Jack laughed so much at the imitation that Willie felt bold again, and dismissed the Old Bird's face from his mind.

'Jack, shall we mitch, and go on the downs? I can get Biddy to write me an excuse. Won't your mother write one for you?'

Jack shook his head and grinned, 'Not her!'

'Well then, we'll risk slipping in at second bell, shall us? Righto!'

They shook hands.

'I don't care a dam for the Old Bird!' yelled Willie, springing to his feet.

'I don't care a damn for Rattlethrough either!' bawled Jack.

They selected two eggs each to show the chaps; and having concealed the remainder between a root-crevice of the tree, and covered them with earth and leaves, they went down to the Longpond, to look for moorhens' nests.

Chapter 2

As they walked up Colham Hill an hour later they agreed
that it had been a grand expedition, and the swim in the
Longpond the finest thing of all. And what a joke it would
be when Useless, taking out Cigars or Nuts,—otherwise the
Colham Grammar School Natural History and Field Botanical
Club—on one of its Saturday afternoon rambles, discovered
four young rooks in a moorhen's nest in the rushes!

They talked less when the School buildings showed through
the trees. At the Lower Playground gate, they hesitated.
Should they climb over, and slip in that way? Willie whispered
that it was too risky : they would never reach The Bog without
being spotted either by Rattlethrough or Bunny, or Hoxygen
Horace, or Old Scratch, or Soapy Sammy, the porter. On
the other hand, if they crept in through the Masters' Entrance
just as the boy from 5c classroom was swinging the bell at the
end of the second hour, the only danger would be from Soapy
Sam appearing out of the Bowels—as the school kitchens
were called. And yet, Willie whispered, it would take at
least a minute after the bell, for 4a to file out of Taffy's; and
meanwhile the Old Bird might look out of the Sixth, and
catch them as they were waiting for the Physics Lab. door
to open.

'Listen,' hissed Willie, feeling the anemone of fear gripping
him again as they stood indecisively by the tall iron gate
worn by many boots, 'Our half of 4a is with Taffy in the
Physics Lab. The other half is in the Stinks Lab. with Hoxy
Waugh. If we can get to the Bog through Little Hall we can
wait there and join them as they come out. Hoxy usually

stands there, by the fountain, and he won't know that we haven't had permission to go to the Bog.'

'Good idea!'

'Here's the plan. We slip in together into Little Hall.'

'What if its locked? Last time we did it, the Bird told Soapy to lock it at nine o'clock in future.'

'My God, yes. Oh Lord. Hell. I know! If it's locked we'll slip down here and chance it.'

'Right. How goes the time?'

Willie looked at his gun-metal watch.

'Quarter past ten. Better be on the trail now. Come on, man!'

He walked lightly up beside the wall and railings, above which, through the shrubs and trees of a sloping embankment, they could see the western windows of the school. They crept past the room of the drawing master, Mr. Worth, nicknamed Useless; past 3a classroom, and Mr. Worley's sing-song voice with its inevitable 'You boys pay attention to me!'; past 3c classroom and Mr. Ellison's high-pitched rapid talking, coming through the open window; past the Physics Lab., where Mr. Croodrane, called Taffy, was at that very moment moving among the benches, inspecting the experiments of their half of 4a. In his mind Willie saw them all, experimenting with magnets, compasses, vulcanite rods, iron filings, Wheatstone bridges, galvanometers, voltmeters, pith balls, and Wimshurst machines. If only they could slip in through the floor! What a fool he was to come so late. Better if he'd mitched altogether!

Uphill round the bend they crept, the big boy behind the small boy like a led bear. Ssh! warned Willie, turning round, his face strained, his arm rigid from raised finger to shoulder. They were passing the Prefects' room, where some of the Sixth form might be working. They stopped and listened. Yes, the Prefects were there! They heard the murmur of voices, a laugh, the sound of a mild scuffle. Now was the terrible moment—before the great iron gates.

ONE PETAL OUT

They passed between the high, wide iron gates of the Masters' Entrance, and on tip-toe crept over the gravel path. Below were the basement windows, but to their relief no pale, sulky face of Soapy Sam was looking up at them. Carefully they stepped over the clean grey hearthstoned step on to the big mat, pausing to wipe their boots, unconsciously treating it with deference. With an alarmed glance at Jack, Willie turned the worn brass handle and pushed gently.

The door opened noiselessly. Jack grinned at Willie. He grinned although his throat was dry. Pushing past Willie, who was standing on tip-toe listening fearfully and breathing fast, Jack touched his hand, 'Come on,' he whispered.

Willie strained against the noise of their boot-nails as they tip-toed over the gleaming, tessellated floor. How dreadfully loud they were! Klick-klack, klick-klack, past varnished doors that were dimly realised in shadow; klick-klack, klick-klack, past the glass-covered model of a steamship whose details few small boys had seen, since always it had stood in this high, chill, twilight, awe-ful place. Klick-klack, klick-klack, slowly, very slowly, the pink, glass-shiny length of the steamship sailed behind them. The mahogany door of Mr. Rore's study (Willie dared not even think of him as the Old Bird in that terrible twilight) seemed to make negative their efforts to pass by it. Klick-klack, klick-klack, towards the open half of the door leading to Big Hall beyond, with its glimpse of the familiar and half-friendly desert of its wooden floor.

They stopped just inside the door. Willie peered into the Big Hall, with its many classroom doors, its dusty silence, its gymnastic apparatus, its long rectangular framework of window high up by the raftered roof. Jack's head craned round the door above his own; Jack's hand rested heavily on his shoulder. Willie braced himself, for Jack was heavy; it gave him confidence to think that he was supporting Jack's envied weight so easily. The way was clear; thirty swift steps, and they would reach the safety of the upper playground door; and the lobby beyond was halfway to the sanctuary of The Bog.

'Ready?' whispered Jack.

'Yes.'

'Come on.'

But Jack's weight, partly against Willie's cube of books slung on his shoulder, had pressed the cube into a parallelogram; and as soon as the pressure was released, the books clattered on the tiles of Little Hall, directly outside the mahogany door of the Headmaster's study.

With a stifled laugh Jack ran past the parallel bars and ladders of the gymnasium and reached the shelter of the lobby, followed by Willie, who dangled the empty strap in his hand.

'Quick, quick, what shall I do? Oh, Jack, don't laugh, you cad!'

'Lumme!' laughed Jack. His face became serious. 'My God, your name's in them!' he said.

'Of course it is, you damn fool! Quick, quick, I must get them. You go! Quick! Quick!'

Jack looked at the clock, which was above the doorway leading into Little Hall. It was nineteen minutes past ten. At twenty past ten a boy coming out of Old Scratch's class-room would ring the bell which stood at the corner of the platform by the piano. One minute to go.

'Yes, you go,' said Willie to Jack. With anguish he knew he was an utter coward. 'No, I'll go.'

Before he had realised what was happening he was running past the parallel bars and the rope-enwound ladders, and the dreaded Sixth Form on the right. As through glass he saw himself stooping down, and clawing together the books scattered on the green-and-white tiles of Little Hall. Then from the Headmaster's study a voice rang keenly:

'Now, sir, how did it happen?'

A mumbling noise followed.

'Very well, sir, I'll give you that cane! 'Tis the price you pay for your folly! You are a pauper spirit, sir! Wasting my time like this!'

He heard Mr. Rore walking quickly across the carpet, heard the rustle of a cane being selected from the cupboard in the corner. A chair scraped upon the wooden border of the floor. Now was the time to slip across Big Hall to the lobby where Jack was waiting; but held by his imagination, Willie stayed near the door. He heard the thwacks, and the murmurous chant of the Bird's voice; the scrape of the chair again; the kinder voice of the Bird. Then footfalls sounded behind him, and his arm was gripped just above the elbow.

'Now then, Maddison, what you doin' here, eh?'

'Nothing, porter, really,' he gasped.

'Nothing, eh? What's the game, then? Sent in, that's about it? Eh? You can't kid me with your lies, you know!'

'No, porter, I know I couldn't. I was just picking up my books.'

'Sent in to Mr. Rore for misbe'avour, eh? Wondering if you'll go in or not, eh? Or slip back when the bell rings? We'll soon see about that, young fellow.'

'I wasn't sent in, please porter. I came to tell you that I wanted to stop to full lunch. I forgot to hold up my hand when you came round during first hour, to the Physics Lab. I beg your pardon, porter. Please may I stop? I hope I haven't inconvenienced you at all.'

'Oh you do, do you?'

'Yes, porter. Is it too late for me to stop, please?'

The little liveried porter of Colham Grammar School had a pale face and a sullen expression, which was probably due to ill-health and an unhappy growth to manhood. He rarely spoke to the boys unless to check them. His characteristic attitude was standing with his hands behind his back, but never looking at any particular boy. Sometimes he was to be seen in the lavatories after school hours, prowling round silently in order to detect boys in any of the various by-actions of covert adolescence, one of which was the etching of crude words and pictures on the walls of the building known as The Bog.

Soapy Sam, as he was called, still held the thin bone of the boy's upper arm, and waited. The door opened, a boy came out, closing it behind him. He grinned fixedly at Willie, then hurried away into Big Hall.

'Now we'll go to Mr. Rore,' muttered the porter.

He gripped Willie's arm harder, and turned so that the boy turned with him. He rapped on the door.

'Come in!'

The door opened.

'Well, porter?'

'If you please, Sir, I caught Maddison listening at the door, and when I asked him if he had been sent in, he told me that he wanted to put 'is name down for full lunch, 'aving missed me morning round. Well, Sir, on Saturday there is no luncheon.'

'Very well, porter. Maddison, come in!'

Willie went in, closing the door after him.

'Well, sir? What have you to say?'

Willie gazed up at Mr. Rore, looking at him steadily in the eyes. He stared fixedly, hoping that Mr. Rore would know he was honest, able to look anyone straight in the eyes. He did not blink.

'Answer me, sah!' blared Mr. Rore, shifting his gaze sideways.

His keen glance was on the boy, he towered above, his eyes cold as blue-green water flowing under ice. All his great power and personality seemed to be in those eyes, and to enter the brain of the thin brown-eyed boy in front of him, numbing it and searching every thought that came, that flurried and died in it, leaving him, with his paled cheeks, with his fixed, motionless stare. Mr. Rore felt scorn for what he considered a lazy and indolent boy, one hypocritical and without any

sense of honour: one who later in life would be not only negative to any community in which he might dwell, but a
hindrance. He knew him to be a slacker, and a liar; a boy
who had ability, but who would not develop his mental
powers—a mental prodigal, a pauper spirit, furtive and
without moral backbone.

It was perhaps ten seconds before Mr. Rore spoke again, in
his voice scorn and almost a loathing of the boy before him
who stared him straight in the eyes. Ten seconds only, but
in that time he saw the opposed positions and his own right-
eousness in their naked simplicity. He was trying to mould
character and make men: almost in vain he tried to break the
bars of brass binding a complacent humanity; indolence and
sloth must be fought by every means at the disposal of the mind!

'Were you sent in for misbehaviour?' the keen voice cried.

'No Sir.'

'How came you here?'

'Please Sir, I missed the train at Rookhurst Halt.'

'Have you just arrived?'

'Yes Sir.'

'You know that it is forbidden to steal in at the Masters'
Entrance?'

'Yes, Sir.'

The voice stormed coldly and keenly.

'Be careful, sir, be careful! You will have to leave the school
sir! Why were you late?'

'I looked at some birds in the forest, and forgot the time,
please, Sir.'

'You what? I can't hear! Use your lips and teeth, sir.'

Mr. Rore turned his ear down to the boy.

'I went a bit longer way round, Sir, to see some birds. I
forgot the time, please, Sir.'

The voice rose in scornful anger, and all in the Sixth Form
room, behind the closed door, were listening, many were
grinning.

'Good heavens, the boy's ill! Fancy giving me that excuse! Pauper spirit, sir! Supposing we all forgot the time and lingered under trees, eating the lotus! You are a savage, a Black Man! To lie on your back and let ripe bananas drop into your mouth, that contents you, sir! And where is the Black Man now, sir? Degenerate, flabby, a pauper spirit! It's absurd! Absurd, I tell you! And why do you carry your books in a strap? You know it is against the rules! Come along, sah, come along, I'll give you that cane!'

Willie stood before the desk, while Mr. Rore, with an angry and impatient swish of his gown, went swiftly to the cupboard, to choose from a rustling bundle a cane about three feet long and half an inch thick. Now the Headmaster spoke softly but concisely, as if intoning a personal and confidential prayer; only those near the door connecting study and classroom could distinguish the words—the well-known words.

'Now sir, don't let it happen again. Think!'

He drew out a yellow wooden chair, and placed its four legs on four worn patches in the stained border of the wooden floor.

'Over—hands right over.'

Willie knelt over the chair. He felt the back of his coat being lifted up, oh, why had he left off his pants that morning?

'Now think—it must not occur again.' Pause. 'You must not waste my time like this.' Pause. 'Now think.' Pause. 'Eyes shut.'

A long pause.

'Think—it shall not happen again. Quite still.'

A swish, and a sudden sharp pain. The shapeless idea came again to the boy that only that morning, owing to the sunshine, he had left off his woollen pants. O why, why?

'You've got to get that mental power. Think.'

A sharper pain, just where the first stroke had fallen. He stopped his breath, and pressed his elbows against the chair in an effort to make rigid his whole body and so spread away the agony. Pants—wear them always. Think of pants, then he wouldn't cry, perhaps. Mr. Rore struck again, unexpectedly without his usual admonition to think, with the result that the air in the boy's throat was forced out of his mouth, and the chair jarred on the floor.

'One more for wriggling,' murmured the Headmaster.

'Don't let it occur again. It is all for your good. Think hard now! Quite still.'

Down cut the cane. The boy flinched, for his eyes had been open, and he had anticipated the stroke.

'I told you to shut your eyes. You opened your eyes. You must do what you are told. One more. Say to yourself, I will do what I am told.'

The voice was now not unkind. The boy made a small sound which the man did not hear; a sound of a half-hysterical sob. Followed a stroke immensely heavy and hurtful on the same place.

'Now go back, work hard, and don't let me see you in here again! Double back to your desk, and hard at it, hard at it!'

Willie opened the door and closed it behind him. A blurred and hasty glance around told him, to his relief, that he was alone. He waited by the model steamship until his sight and breathing were normal. Then he went through the door into Big Hall, dreading lest he be noticed, and be greeted with grins. He tried to put an expression of careless scorn on his face.

Chapter 3

Doors were opening and streams of boys emerging; boys with satchels slung over shoulders, boys with books held under arms. Files of boys of all sizes, the little ones walking sedately, the bigger ones traipsing slowly, the biggest boys coming singly and in small groups. Boys in breeches and trousers, flannel collars and Eton collars, serge suits and tweed suits. Obedient files of little boys in little jerseys. Seventeen year olds, eight year olds. Some of the middle sized boys slid on the iron grating, some stamped. A subdued hum filled the Hall.

Masters passed through open doors while the incoming classes filed into the rooms, and exchanged a word with their neighbours. Slowly the straggling files wove and interwove. One boy, coming from the classroom of Mr. Rapson, the French master, managed to knock the bell from the corner of the platform. Another kicked it along the floor with a metallic protesting sound. A master named Worley cried, 'Stop that!' and the bell was restored.

Willie waited until the other half of 4a, from the Chemical Laboratory, came into Big Hall, then he walked forward carelessly and joined them as they filed into the French master's doorway. His own half, from the Physics Laboratory, was already seated.

The French master, known as Rattlethrough, stood at the door, irritation on his oval face. He was a man of medium height, about forty years of age, and almost invariably he wore a blue suit, shiny at the elbows and the seat of the trousers, which were short, creaseless, and baggy, with frayed bottoms turned up and showing a permanent exhaustion of fringe. He made a point of wearing his gown whenever he left 4b classroom, and always referred to Mr. Rore as the Head Master, emphasising each word with staccato abruptness. His eyes were a very light blue, set in inflamed rims, his cheeks were threaded and mottled with little red veins, his mouth hidden by a ragged brown moustache which he alternately gnawed and fingered.

'Hurry, that boy, or I shall keep you in! Stop talkin'!' he shouted irritably to the seated boys, instant silence following.

He walked to his desk and sat down.

'Close that door after you, you stupid fool!' glaring at the last-comer, who darted back and closed the door loudly in his eagerness not to displease.

'Stand out there, miserable midget.'

The last-comer, a boy who sometimes stuttered named Clemow, stood with his back to the class, and forthwith commenced to gaze absently at the lists of irregular French verbs, conjugation tables and other dusty dreariness chalked with a painful neatness upon brown paper and pinned with meticulous accuracy in one straight line upon the wall before him.

'I won't have this talkin',' said the French master, leaning back in his chair, fingering his ragged moustache and vibrating his right knee. 'Never have I met such an unruly lot of hooligans in my life. There is no discipline in the school. Why were you late?' glaring at Clemow.

'Mr. Rore detained me, if you please, Sir.'

'Who?' shouted the French master. Irritation caused him to gnaw his moustache savagely.

'The er-er-er-er Headmaster, Sir.'

'That's better! The Head Master! I never *heard* of the Head Master being called by his name in any other school. Certainly not at my public school. Why did you see the Head Master?'

'If y-y-y-y-you please, suker-suker-suker-Sir, the Huh-huh-the Headmaster cur-cur-cur-caned me.'

A change came over the face of the French master. His knee ceased to vibrate; he smiled frankly and charmingly, regarding Clemow with amiability.

4a, unable to appreciate the frankness or the charm, knew that Rattlethrough was going to make a joke, and prepared to make the most of its chance.

'Then perhaps, Clemow, I acted under the direct influence of a benign Providence in orderin' you to stand out in front.'

Clemow grinned widely, and 4a sniggered obsequiously.

The French master chuckled, looking round at the boys.

4a hoped that he would continue to make jokes, so that the dreaded reading-aloud of *Le Roi des Montaignes* before translating would be postponed as long as possible.

'Who says that there is no direct intervention in human affairs?' inquired the French master, stroking his moustache. 'Here a miserable boy is caned by the Head Master, and acting under an unseen force, I order him to stand out there. I did not know that a certain portion of *le miserable*'—the word was uttered with the most painstaking enunciation, and Mr. Rapson's face beamed with joviality—'had received an undue attention recently. Never rail against Fate, Clemow'—the master shook his head waggishly—'or you will show yourself to be an ingrate. Yes, an ingrate. What? Huh! Huh! Huh!' he chuckled.

4a as a class was sophisticated. It knew that to take advantage of the French master's lax attitude—he was leaning back in his chair, sucking a finger, and swaying gently backwards —would be most disastrous. With other masters it was not a case for the strictest attention and response to their quips and humours. In the French master's classroom during these rare lapses, no boy allowed his attention to wander; no boy attempted a clandestine conversation; no boy attempted to pinstick his neighbour or flip paper darts by means of elastic bands and the teeth. Indeed, the idea of any such action would have made 4a aghast. No one dared even to cough or sneeze, lest the slow rumbling of the French master be changed entirely into a volcanic eruption, and there followed the awful ordeal of reading aloud amid a molten flow of scorching criticism, upon whose tumbling rush there rode like uprooted trees and houses such hissed epithets as 'stupid fool', 'idiot', 'depraved lunatic', 'abandoned wretch', and (as a semi-humorous reference to his specialised profession) *sans culottes* and *gamin*.

The French master swayed backwards and forwards, appearing several times to the class as though he must crash over backwards into the wall, but always just managing to save himself. 4a watched the pensive manipulation of his moustache change to an absent-minded nibbling of a thumb nail, and knew by that sign that the crisis was approaching. Either the French master would become irritable and order an immediate resumption of work (angrily, as though 4a were responsible for its idleness) or he would meander into digressive reminiscences of an autobiographical nature. Sometimes he told them of his own boyhood 'at my public school'—but 4a could not possibly imagine Rattlethrough as a schoolboy.

4a held its breath. Two boys who owned watches covertly glanced at them. Willie, waiting at the bottom of the class, was muttering a rehearsal; it was he who would begin to read out a few sentences in French, and then render them into English.

Since the beginning of the term he had not moved many places above the inside seat of the desk at the extreme right-hand front of the classroom. This place was ignominious, yet coveted. Its advantages included the security of the knowledge that its occupier would begin the translation; he could therefore render his probable turn word-perfect. As soon as his turn was done, he could cease to dread that he would mix up the words, or pronounce them wrongly: he could sit still, as though intent on his book, but really thinking of all things that he and Jack were going to do during the summer—on the Longpond, in the forest, on the downs, and round the tall whitethorn hedges.

The boys above Willie were working out their approximate turn, but no reward for their labour was guaranteed, owing to the fact that a boy lower down might muck his turn, and be ordered to stand out in front. When this happened, his lower neighbour had to bear the double and ironic burden of translating a part unfamiliar to himself and later to hear his own exquisitely prepared sentences mucked by a higher boy.

Very quiet and still in the bottom form, Willie waited. 4a waited. Then a boy coughed, with a booming sound in his handkerchief. Several heads quarter-turned his way: several heads held thoughts of bashing the cougher afterwards. The French master looked up, stared vacantly at 4a, who perceived that he was fingering his moustache and not gnawing it. There was hope after all.

'Huh-huh-huh,' gurgled the French master, and 4a swayed after the tension. 'I remember a boy at my public school being caned by the Head Master so often that he wore permanently in school a leathern satchel sewn on the inside of his trousers. Huh-huh-huh.'

4a sniggered, but not too loudly. Willie licked his lips, and wondered how much longer it would last; how far away was eleven o'clock? Drip-drip-drip, he felt the sweat under his right armpit.

'You, Clemow,' continued the French master, turning to the boy standing in front, who smiled nervously and attempted for some obscure reason to balance himself upon one leg. 'You have not yet distinguished yourself sufficiently to warrant the bestowal of the Order of the Leathern Shield. Huh-huh-huh. Bazeley was a curious boy. He seemed to be possessed of a fatal faculty of attractin' attention to himself. It was Bailey, I think. No, no, it was Squire. No, no, my memory is failin' me. Let me see, eighteen eighty-five. Longbottom was captain of the school, or was it Heygate-Gardner? No, no,

Longbottom. Longbottom it was—What are you sniggerin'
at?' he thundered suddenly to Effish, who at the mention of
the name Longbottom, had started a giggling fit with his
friend and neighbour Beckelt. 'STAND OUT THERE, STUPID
FOOL!'

Effish, his eyes looking like watery blue soap bubbles and
thin lithe Beckelt, eyes small and shifty and weasel-bright,
walked out beside Clemow. The French master got up and
banged their heads together.

'I shall keep you all in,' he fumed, glaring round the room.
'Who's that sniffin'? You, Macarthy! Stand out there! Sniff,
sniff, mornin' noon and night. I've never known such an
unruly lot of hooligans in my life. There is no discipline in
the school. At my public school one never had this appallin'
sniffin'—have none of you heard of the existence of handkerchiefs at Colham School? I assure you they are in general use
elsewhere.'

'Bet he used blottin' paper at his public school,' whispered
a boy called 'Bony' Watson, out of the corner of his large
mouth. Bony's nickname exactly expressed his appearance.
He wore glasses with steel rims; his face was long and white
and gaunt; his head, with its close-cropped hair, was shaped
like an acorn. His ears and teeth protruded, and his shoulders
appeared only a trifle broader than the width of his head and
ears, so tall was he. His nose was big and bony, and as he
peered above the lowered heads of the boys, he looked like a
vulture that had lost all its feathers seated among a flock of
sparrows.

'*A qui est le tour?*' enquired the French master suddenly.

'*C'est à moy, mersewer,*' promptly replied Willie; and swallowed the spittle in his mouth in preparation. '*Lorsker les—*'

'STOP COUGHIN', I SAID!' suddenly bawled the French
master, to a boy named Farthing—whose nickname was
'Money Bags'. Farthing went red, then white, as he held his
handkerchief ready to smother the next cough.

'Coughin' and sniffin' is what I have to put up with,' groaned the French master, gnawing his moustache, glaring, and vibrating his right knee furiously. 'I've never met such an unruly lot of boys in all my life. *A qui est le tour?*' he asked, abruptly.

Willie promptly raised a hand, and cried, '*C'est à moi, merseer.*'

'*Eh bien, continuez, s'il vous plaît!*'

'*Lorsker lays mees avaye—*' he commenced rapidly.

'Page, page,' cried the French master. 'How many more times am I to tell you that it is the duty of the boy occupyin' the gutter of the class to tell the page and line? What? Stand out there, *malheureux!* Next boy! Temperley, *continuez, s'il vous plaît.*'

Jack had prepared for this. He had done twice as much translation as Willie had the night before; that is, he had prepared the first eight lines instead of the first four.

'*Page soixante sept, line onze,*' he said. '*Lorsque les emmikness—*' he was declaring, when Willie, pushing out past him, upset his satchel spilling the contents on the wooden floor.

One of Jack's habits was to carry within his satchel a considerable number of pens, pencils, and rulers. In fact he collected these badges of servitude with a fervour nearly equalled by that of Willie for birds' eggs, Farthing for stamps, Macarthy for nuts and bolts, Effish for silver cap-badges, Beckelt for cigarette pictures of the *Famous Boxer Series*, and Bony Watson for wings, claws, talons, and bleached skeletons of hawks, jays, and stoats filched from various keepers' vermin poles. Fifteen or sixteen pencils, half a dozen yellow rulers, twenty or twenty-five pens, most with broken nibs, some converted into darts with paper elevators wedged into split ends—they were scattered under his desk.

'Pick them all up,' cried the French master, 'stupid careless fool. Throw them in the waste-paper basket. All of them. *Continuez,* next boy.'

'*Page oixante sept, line onze, lorsker lays—*'

'WAIT, you depraved wretch, will you? Page sixty-seven, line eleven. *Nous y sommes. Continuez, enfant terrible!*'

'*Lorsker lays emmy knee—*'

'*Gamin!*' yelled the French master. 'Go on, next boy. Go on—*Lorsque les ennemis.*'

The next boy faltered. He said *avic* for *avec* instead of the master's meticulously enunciated *arvec*. Such a mistake, repeated to the French master many thousands of times each term, called forth the usual irritability. Falteringly the lesson proceeded along the bottom row of the class, and along the second row, each boy being subjected to alternate tension and the flaccidity of the reaction. Then the turn reached a boy called Rupert Bryers.

Bryers, who was interested in the lesson because he had spent three weeks' holiday on the coast of Brittany the previous summer, read half a dozen lines in his soft voice.

'Splendid,' cried the French master. '*Continuez, mon cher ami.* The wilderness has blossomed. Bryers is an oasis in the parched desert of my existence at Colham School.'

Almost gaily he twisted his moustache; almost happily he swayed backwards. The tension in 4a eased off along the third and back rows, reaching the best boys—among them being Swann, Lonsdale, Manning, Shephard, Walton, Lucas and Fitzaucher. (There were thirty-two boys in 4a form, occupying sixteen desks). Very quietly stood the boys by the cupboard; very still the boys in the front row whose turns had been passed. At last, with a vast sigh of relief 4a heard the preliminary tinkle of the bell in Big Hall, as it visualised the boy out of Old Scratch's classroom holding it in readiness for exactly eleven o'clock. A long space of time dragged by; and then the swinging peals announced the end of the lesson. Now for the BREAK, ten minutes of freedom!

But the French master ignored the bell. Shephard, next to Manning, congratulated himself prematurely on his luck.

Frenziedly he searched under the desk among the flimsy pages of his *French-English Dictionary*, but it was too badly printed for an easy discovery of a word.

Half a minute passed. Bony Watson looked almost openly at his watch. Rattlethrough was curtailing their liberty. They were entitled to ten minutes' break at eleven o'clock. Yet none dared to show upon his face the bitter thoughts within his mind.

At four minutes past eleven o'clock, the French master closed his book, and the boys rose all together, closed books and filed out irregularly. 4a cared no longer now that there was some justification for ignoring Rattlethrough. He had diddled them of part of their Break—he was a dirty swine! Just before reaching the bell on the corner of the platform opposite 5c classroom, Willie and Jack began to shove; others shoved too, cling-a-ling—klash! went the bell. 'Quietly there', thundered Rattlethrough; and amidst laughter the gutter of the class made a rush for the playground.

Chapter 4

THE sunlight absolved them of all hatred. They continued their rush down the steps into the lower playground, yelling joyously as Burrell released a semi-skinned tennis ball for a kick about.

'On the pill, boys! On the pill! Pass, man! Oh, *pass!*'

Sides were hastily formed, boys rushed anywhere; no goal-keeper occupied the chalked posts upon the woodwork shop at one end and a netted railing on the other. The exhortations to pass were ignored, since every man was for himself. If one swift individual dribbled the worn dirty ball, a score pursued him, bumping, charging, and shouting. Bony was there, kicking ponderously with legs that resembled those of a young colt; head and shoulders above every one else and pushing them away with his huge hands as they butted him like goats. Willie was there, running swiftly but rarely seeming to kick the ball; Jack was more skilful; Effish and Beckelt charged each other upon every possible occasion and ended up by having a wrestling match, cheered by the others who prodded the writhing contestants genially with their boots.

Four boys were playing fives in the court. Three were watching them from above, one of them, a fair-haired boy named Macarthy, throwing orange peel at them and receiving alternately threats of extinction and plaints of 'Stop it, I say, man.' Clemow and Hoys, the rivals of Willie and Jack, were discussing the possibilities of tracking the two that afternoon and discovering their nests. Rupert Bryers, whom everybody liked, was testing himself on the passage of Shakespeare's *Midsummer Night's Dream*, set by Mr. Kenneth, the English master, to be learned during the previous night's preparation. Rupert Bryers was a simple nature, incapable of retaliation. He was one of the few boys in 4a who did not dislike poetry, although several had been known to compose verses; but they were either about unpopular masters or sent to girls at the High School with whom a few of his friends were in love. Willie had asked him one day to write a valentine to a 'Golden-haired Blue-Eyed Fairy Queen', and he had written three verses, and made a water-colour painting of grass, water, trees, and cows—which Willie had signed with his own initials. Rupert liked 'Mad Willie' almost as much as Bony; friendship had begun when they had sprung the jay traps in Brogborough Wood nearly five years previously. Seeing him, Willie cried out 'I've got something for you. Lumme, I hope it isn't bust,' and ran to the Upper Playground.

Bryers thanked him for the rook's egg, and after admiring it, put it carefully in his handkerchief. 'I say, Mad Willie, do you mind testing me?' he asked afterwards.

'Beastly muck, this Woggledagger,' said Willie, taking the book. 'Here's Old Bunny coming.'

A tall man was striding, hands in pockets, down the asphalted Upper Playground. Reaching the railings he called out, 'Fall in 4a!' turned round and walked back, gown sailing out behind, gazing upon his highly polished brown boots.

Willie tested Rupert, having to prompt him only once; then he began furiously to try and learn the speech set for homework the previous night.

Several minutes later 4a was standing more or less in line with one of the iron pillars supporting the covered way between Big Hall and the Chemistry Laboratory. The boys were breathing hard, talking, laughing, pushing each other with their shoulders, while the English master waited nearby. He knew they had left Rapson's classroom five minutes late, and so he did not hurry them.

The late stragglers lolloped in from the Lower Playground,

42

some of them making for the iron mug chained to the drinking fountain by the Chemical Lab., for a gulping drink.

By the fountain, it so happened, a foul smell of sulpheretted hydrogen was straying, and 4a made the most of it. The boys already lined up made an exaggerated action of holding their noses, and uttered loud cries of 'Poo, most beastly sniff—Poo, what a ponk—I say, Poo!' while Effish, the clown, pretended to faint drolly into the arms of the never-still Beckelt.

The last stragglers came in fast; Bony lumbered up to the fountain, was sternly called to the line, and turned away, looking with an injured expression at Mr. Kenneth. Then Willie and Jack ran in at top speed, the last but one—the last boy being Burrell, the owner of the tennis pill, which Manning, the strongest boy in the class, had rooted, or kicked, so high at the end of the break that it had fallen out of the playground and run half-way down the hill into Colham.

'Come on,' urged Mr. Kenneth, looking up from his brown boots. 'Where have you been?'

'To get my pill, Sir—I mean—ball, Sir,' gasped Burrell.

Mr. Kenneth held out his hand.

Burrell made much business of pretending to try and squeeze the ball out of his pocket.

'Don't hurry, will you?' rang a keen ironic voice from the lobby doorway.

4a jumped into life. Silence fell upon the boys. Effish, who had run behind the line to pinch Willie's behind, darted back to his place and stood to attention.

'Mr. Kenneth!'

The English master hurried towards the Headmaster. A whispered conversation, short, terse, the tail end of which 4a managed, by straining its ears, to hear.

'Always keep them hard at it, hard at it! Play a good servant, a bad master!'

The spirit of 4a groaned, and the Headmaster disappeared behind the black floating skirts of his gown.

4a filed through the Hall, past the crouching Specials waiting for the VIθ form door to close, and into Mr. Kenneth's classroom. Several heels stamped on the loose iron grating stretching towards 4b classroom as they darted into the lobby. Effish came last, and having closed the outer door, threw down half a dozen caps from the pegs, and joined the others looking solemnly virtuous as he went to his seat. 4a took out copies of *A Midsummer Night's Dream*, and prepared to be mildly bored by Shakespeare, otherwise Woggledagger, Tremblesword, or Quiverspoons, until ten minutes to twelve o'clock, the end of the fourth hour.

A habit of the English master was the keeping of a stub of chalk in his right-hand coat pocket. This at times he brought forth and tossed into the air, and caught it, repeatedly, speaking very softly the while. Invariably he produced it when he was annoyed by a boy; and if the boy were wise, he would act upon the warning of the rising and falling chalk.

He was tall, wide-shouldered and partially bald. His face was lean, and the lower half would have been described by a Victorian novelist as lantern-jawed. He seemed permanently unshaven, and was often seen making long strides up Colham Hill towards the Masters' Entrance by those boys who avoided being late by a small margin of time themselves. His eyes were kindly, gray, set rather close together; he wore high starched linen collars, known to his pupils as brain-starvers, and a big ginger-coloured moustache that sprouted out and at times seemed to cover the lower part of his face. He looked through pince-nez spectacles, rimmed in tarnished steel and with a rusted centre-spring. Upon the third finger of his left hand rested a large gold wedding ring which he spun quickly with the finger and thumb of his right hand, at intervals as he walked and talked before the English, History and Geography classes.

A vague noise came from 4a. Effish and Beckelt were playing noughts-and-crosses; Macarthy was polishing, beneath the

desk, a large nut and bolt he had picked up on the road.
Clemow and Hoys were reading, conjointly and furtively, a
copy of White's *Natural History of Selbourne*. Bony was chewing
an American gum, of the four-ounces a penny variety, which
he had found in the chipped, bored, and rutted desk at which
he sat. Willie was drawing a rook on the flyleaf of his Shakespeare, and Jack was watching him. The other boys were
whispering, making last minute attempts to learn the speech
set for homework, or slacking. One boy, sallow of face and
with a long pointed nose, had settled down to sleep with
his head pillowed in his arms upon the desk.

'Well, Cerr-Nore major,' said Mr. Kenneth, after looking
up from his wide brown boots, 'What's the matter with you?'

Cerr-Nore major did not move. His neighbour seized the
opportunity to prod him hard in the ribs. Cerr-Nore major
remained as somnolent as before. He frequently pretended
to be asleep with his head on his arms. He had a sharp tongue,
and was not liked by most of the masters.

'Cerr-Nore!' cried Mr. Kenneth, a note of anger in his
voice. His neighbour prodded harder. The boy looked up
sleepily. His red hair was ruffled, and his long nose
quivered.

'Were you calling me, Sir?'

'What's the matter, Cerr-Nore?'

'Matter, Sir?' drawled Cerr-Nore. 'Nothing, Sir. I was
trying to visualise revengeful words sucking fogs from the
sea, Sir.'

'You are not yet in the Sixth Form,' replied the English
master. 'You are in my classroom. Bestir yourself.'

Charlie Cerr-Nore smiled lazily.

'Now then,' commenced the master briskly, 'this is one of the
most poetical passages in the play. Let us have therefore a
decent recitation from some one. Some one with intelligence.
Effish, for example!' He smiled—they liked Bunny.

Effish looked up quickly from his game of noughts-and-crosses, put his tongue in his cheek, and with an assumption of droll surprise, answered quickly, 'Me, Sir?' and then gazed round at his neighbours with an expression of exaggerated astonishment.

'Yes, you,' replied Mr. Kenneth grimly, taking a piece of chalk out of his pocket.

Effish cleared his throat, stood up, and after moving his tongue round and round his mouth, fixed his eyes on the ceiling and commenced in a dramatic manner.

'These are the forgeries of jelly and never since the middle summer's spring—'

'The forgeries of jelly?' asked the master.

'Jealousy, Sir,' corrected Effish, with a surprised air, and simpering.

'Go on.'

'And never since the middle summer's spring met we onhillindale forestormead.'

'No, no, no!' cried Mr. Kenneth, 'you've got no idea of rhythm. If you were an actor, I tremble to think what you would do for even the price of a crust.'

'I don't want to be a nactor,' reproached Effish, enjoying the sniggers of 4a. 'Father says they're a wicked lot.'

A shout of laughter came from the class.

'Oh really?' inquired Mr. Kenneth. 'Well, come here.'

Effish went to him, and Mr. Kenneth put out a hand to catch him by the hair, Effish dodged, a look of exaggerated terror in his eyes.

'Pauper speerit,' whispered Bony.

The class laughed.

'Come along, Effish,' called the master lazily.

Effish's head was smacked, twice deliberately, and each time he cried out, 'Oh, oh.'

'Effish, of course, will repeat the passage to me at half-past twelve. Go on Watson. Don't trouble to remove that acid drop from your mouth.'

'You've guessed my secret,' muttered Bony, spitting it into his hand.

4a tittered, and Mr. Kenneth looked down at his boots, then looking up, tossed the chalk-stump into the air, and deftly caught it.

Bony began canorously, paying great attention to the metre.

'These are the forgeries of jealousy.

And never since the middle summer's spring.

Met we on hill in dale forest or mead.

By paved fountain or by rushy brook.

But in the beached margent of the sea.

To dance our ringlets—'

'Apparently word perfect, but otherwise uttered as intelligently as a fire-watered aborigine! Go on, Maddison, where he left off.'

Willie stood up and stared at the desk.

'To dance our ringlets to the whistling wind,' urged Mr. Kenneth.

'To dance our ringlets to the whistling wind,' Willie repeated, frowning.

'But with—' suggested Mr. Kenneth, softly.

'But with—' said the boy, staring at the ceiling, and frowning harder.

'—thy brawls—'

Willie's face lightened.

'But with thy brawls thou has ruined our sport, therefore—'

'Disturbed our sport, Maddison.'

'Yes, Sir. But with thy brawls thou hast disturbed our sport, therefore the winds calling to us without result have sucked up mist and fog revengefully on account of the moon overbearing its continent—'

'No, no, no!' cried Mr. Kenneth, 'You're all at sea. You don't know it. You're a slacker. Come at twelve-thirty Maddison. Go on, Bryers.'

Bryers bobbed up alertly and without falter went on:

'But with thy brawls thou has disturbed our sport:
Therefore the winds, piping to us in vain,
As in revenge have sucked up from the sea
Contagious fogs; which, falling on the land,
Have every pelting river made so proud,
That they have overborne their continent;
The ox—'

'Splendid,' beamed Mr. Kenneth, pitching his chalk stump
into the air, catching it, and dropping it in his right-hand
pocket. After a critical regard of his toe-caps, he told Temperley to continue.

Jack was about to begin, having taken a hasty glance at the
open book, hidden on the seat between himself and Willie,
when from the adjoining room came the muffled blare of a
voice. The wall was thick; like a ghostly sound it came, and
4a chuckled.

Watson whispered '*Arvic*, not *avec*'; but apparently Mr.
Kenneth, in no wise disconcerted by the action of bending
his neck over his tall stiff collar, was so preoccupied that he
heard nothing.

'The ox hath therefore stretched his yoke in vain—' began
Jack.

'The ploughman lost his sweat,' whispered Willie.

'The ploughman lost his sweat—'

'And the green corn hath rotted.'

'And the green corn is rotted—'

'Ere his youth attained a beard,' mouthed his friend silently.

'Fair is youth's brained beard.'

'The fold stands empty.'

'The fold stands empty—'

'In the drowned field.'

'In the brown head killed.'

Several boys, led by Burrell, laughed out loud.

'Shakespeare, thou should'st be living at this hour,' said
Cerr-Nore, loud enough for the English master to hear.

48

Mr. Kenneth looked up and said:

'Twelve-thirty, Temperley. And write it out twenty times.'

'Oh, Sir,' said Jack.

'Twenty-five times, Temperley.'

Jack muttered.

'Did you speak, Temperley?'

Jack muttered again.

Mr. Kenneth became angry.

'Come out here,' he cried. 'I can stand anything but insolence.'

The English master smacked his head; once, twice, thrice. Jack stood still, red in the face. 'Go on, you can't hurt me,' he muttered.

Swiftly Mr. Kenneth swung round on his heel. 'Go on reading and learning the speech,' he said very quietly, 'until I return. And if I catch any boy playing the fool while I am away, I will return with him to Mr. Rore's study.'

'The Headmaster's study,' Bony said audibly.

'Watson will come with me too,' said Mr. Kenneth. 'Come along, you two.'

Putting on his gown, he opened the door and walked out, followed by Jack and Bony, now quiet and grinning skull-like. The door closed behind them. Immediately a hum arose in the classroom.

'Ha, ha,' said Cerr-Nore. 'Some people seem to invite the whack. Oh, what fun to be a farmer's berhorhoy, to be a farmer's boy!'

Willie turned round and flung Jack's satchel at him.

Immediately the books flew from it, and the boys seized upon them and threw them about joyously. In a rage Willie leaned over Swann's desk and grabbed Cerr-Nore's long hair. Effish seized the opportunity given in the disturbance to lift an inkwell out of its socket and secretly jerk it across the room. Unhappily for Macarthy it hit his forehead and belched over his face a black slime with which rotted blotting paper pills, dead flies, and old rusted nibs were mingled. Macarthy swore, the class laughed. Four gym shoes whizzed through the air and were returned immediately. Books followed. The noise attracted one of the Special Class—known as the Special Slackers—from Hall, who opened the door suddenly and cried:

'Come along, come along! Saw your eyes, sir! I'll give you that cane!'

4a sank to silence, then laughed with relief. The Special Slacker flung a couple of shoes, hitting Cerr-Nore, who was whacking Willie with a ruler; and the scrimmage recommenced with such abandon that the Special went back to his seat in alarm, but fiercely glad inside and gloating at the inevitable consequences. Cunningly he closed the classroom door, but left the lobby door open; then flinging a gym shoe against the French master's door, he sank over his desk, pretending to add up a column of figures, and waited.

It was unfortunate for Beckelt that when he saw the door opening again he should think that the Special Slacker had returned to repeat his joke. For Beckelt flung a burst indiarubber shoe and almost hit the French master, who had left the French-stewed boys of 5c in order to ascertain the meaning of the thump on his door. It was unfortunate also for Willie that he should be trying to rend over the head of Cerr-Nore a satchel that had somehow come into his hand. The French master noted that Beckelt had flung the shoe that smacked the wall three inches away from his left ear and that Maddison was apparently one of the worst offenders, before silence and stillness brooded over 4a. Macarthy ducked his head to hide the blotch that had given one side of his face the bloom of a grape, and continued to scrape stealthily with the blotting paper he had taken from Mr. Kenneth's desk.

'Oh, so this is how you behave when left upon your honour to work, is it?' cried the master. 'I have never met such an unruly lot of hooligans in all my life. Maddison and Beckelt stand out there! I shall report you all to Mr. Kenneth on his return from the Head Master! The disgraceful noise of your brawlin', illiterate sweeps, could be heard in Colham.'

He glared round, encountering surreptitious glances that on meeting his eyes of forget-me-not blue looked away guiltily but swung back again as if drawn by a ghastly fascination.

'Get on with your work,' he ordered sharply, looking quickly from one falling glance to another, which seemed to infuriate him. 'Cerr-Nore, DON'T STARE AT ME, YOU GRINNIN' FOOL!'

Cerr-Nore bent low over *A Midsummer Night's Dream* and stared intently at nothing, while his lips scarcely moved with all the swear-words he knew.

When Mr. Kenneth returned with Jack and Bony, the French master went forward, his glasses held elegantly in his left hand, and said, with an earnest punctiliousness:

'Oh, Mr. Kenneth, a thousand pardons for my trespassin', but I was so disturbed by the noise these boys were makin' that it was impossible for me to hear my own voice. *This-s-s* boy'—pointing to Maddison—'was brawlin' with an inoffensive lad, and jammin' a satchel over his head, and *this-s-s* boy'—pointing to the lean, swaying, jerky figure of the fair-haired Beckelt—known as the Weasel—'*this-s-s* boy threw a shoe, which might have done serious injury had it struck me. A thousand apologies, Sir, for my trespass, and . . . er . . . '

Mr. Kenneth bowed, taking a swift glance at his boots as he did so.

'I am sorry that you should have been disturbed, Mr. Rapson. I will deal with them severely.'

Mr. Rapson looked at his taller colleague with an almost piteous expression of earnestness; the spectacles in his left hand quivered.

'I *must* ask your pardon for my . . . er . . . my . . . er . . . trespassin' Mr. Kenneth . . . '

The French master hurried out, the baggy seat of his blue-serge trousers shining dully as he went through the door. A hum was coming from his own classroom, but it died suddenly a moment later. Willie felt sick. He knew he would be caned. Bony looked at him, winked, and held up two fingers. The skull-like look had left his face.

'Come here, Maddison and Beckelt,' ordered Mr. Kenneth abruptly.

He gave Willie and the Weasel two sharp cuts with a ruler on each hand. They bore it stoically, because it did not hurt excessively; and Effish whispered, 'Oh, oh,' as though he himself were being struck, looking round in mock anguish and licking his lips and rolling his eyes.

'Come on,' said the English master, and gave him six sharp cuts. But Effish did not mind; he had raised a laugh, and been prominent in the eyes of the class.

Five minutes later 4a was being bored. The morning was nearly over, and they had the delights of Saturday afternoon, and the lesser but welcome delights of Sunday, between them and next Monday's school. The English master explained the notes at the end of the school edition of *Midsummer Night's Dream* to an uninterested audience until the bell sounded the beginning of the last hour. Alertness immediately spread over 4a. The last hour would be enjoyable; they would be able to do what they liked, for they were going to Useless for drawing.

Chapter 5

MR. WORTH, the drawing master, nicknamed Useless, had
the temperament of a minimus poet, which found outlet in
drawing and design and an interest for natural history, neither
of which was great enough to be communicable as an enthusiasm. Having, like the other masters, no real contact with
the boys who came under him for lessons, and being possessed
of a frail physique and a shy demeanour, he was unable to
control a class, even of the smallest boys of the Lower School.
He stooped a little wearily towards the end of a school day, when
usually his face was wan, his dark eyes sunken and more woeful.

The impertinent Cerr-Nore once said after a visit to London
that he had seen Mr. Worth's double. Certainly a pronounced
pallor of cheek and forehead, intensifying the jet of his eyes and
the wisps of thread-like hair upon the small head, increased his
resemblance to one of the great glaring dolls grouped together
in the underground chamber of Madame Tussaud's; one of the
places of delight and horror to London visitors from the West
Country.

At some former period a boy had discovered his first name
to be Eustace, and since then the master had borne the nickname of Useless. At times a violent temper would possess Mr.
Worth, a temper lasting but a few moments. On these occasions he was apt to do unusual acts, such as emptying a boy's
satchel out of the window, breaking a drawing-pointer on the
desk, or tearing so violently at a boy's collar that it parted
company from his shirt with a rending noise. Invariably when
he did these things he would cry, between a bellow and a moan,
' I won't have it, I won't have it.'

His passion apparently blinded him to the humour of a situation wherein he said, 'I won't have it,' when dropping the satchel or hurling the collar into the wastepaper basket. But these occasions were infrequent, and Mr. Worth was usually apathetic and dolorous as he moved among the hollow wooden shells of his cubes, spheres, rhomboids, pyramids, and other figures the likenesses of which a million times had been reproduced, distorted, caricatured, or disguised entirely, according to the skill of the multitudes which had sat before them with pencils, rubbers, papers, and (not a few times) concealed rulers and compasses.

4a sat lazily at the desk in Mr. Worth's classroom, happily conscious that twelve o'clock had been passed, and that in another half an hour the class would be free till Monday morning. Boys thought that no homework need be done on that Saturday evening, and were content. The two twin brothers, named Golding,—dark curly hair and prominent noses—were learning the next speech in *A Midsummer Night's Dream* in order to store it up for the future.

Mr. Worth moved from desk to desk, handing out photographic copies of old classic statuary, such as *Themistocles* (*from the bust in the Vatican*), *Roman schoolboy in the Toga Praetexta* (*from a statue and a terra-cotta bas-relief*), *A Hemicyclium* (*Pompeii*), and *Marking out Boundaries with a Plough* (*from a coin*), which the boys had to reproduce on the paper before them. Three members of 4a had a natural gift for drawing; they were interested in their work, and Mr. Worth had once praised them; and while the others talked and slacked till final bell, they worked steadily. Neither Willie nor Jack could draw, so they made a pretence of copying *Statue of Ianus* whenever Mr. Worth looked their way, lest he might project at them the dreaded order to 'go into Mr. Rore.' Had such a calamity fallen upon them they would not have gone, as it was the last hour; but would have spent the time skulking in The Bog till half-past twelve, whence on hearing the bell they would have slipped into 4a classroom.

'I say,' whispered Willie, 'I votes we don't go with the Cigars or Nuts this afternoon. Bony isn't going, nor Rupert, and I know that Clemow and Hoys are going on their own. Let's mitch!'

'We mitched last week, man!'

'Doesn't matter. Let's climb the rookery. Useless won't report us.'

'Right!'

'I swear I will climb to a rook's nest this afternoon!'

Willie's imagination sent a colour to his cheeks. He drew what was meant to be a rook in the corner of his paper, but it resembled more a beetle that had fallen into an inkwell and was struggling on its back.

On Saturday and Wednesday afternoons, membership of the C.G.S.N.H.A.F.B.C.—otherwise 'Cigars or Nuts,' otherwise the Colham Grammar School Natural History and Field Botanical Club—provided an alternative to the playing of games, and the rambles of the Club were conducted by Mr. Worth. In giving his consent to the formation of the Club, Mr. Rore had insisted that its members should remain together and take notes of their observations. For this reason chiefly membership of 'Cigars or Nuts' was considered a poor escape from more strenuous forms of exercise, and too much like work. The club suffered from a paucity of members that was more or less permanent except for a transitory swelling at the commencement of term, when new boys were wont to join with the spontaneity of newly-hatched flies blundering into the most hoary spider's web in the corner of a potting shed.

'Jack, I swear I will climb to the rooks' nests this afternoon! I won't think while I climb, I swear I won't!'

'Stop talking, stop talking,' Mr. Worth turgidly commanded. His face took on a lilac hue. No one paid attention to the command. Through the wall could be heard the fumings of the French master, for the classrooms were separated by a wooden partition that could be rolled back, thus making the two classrooms into one upon the historic occasion of Speech Day in the summer. Everything therefore that was said loudly could be heard in either room, and 4a listened with joy to the halting translation of a wretched youth on whom Rattlethrough in eruption was showering his usual stones and cinders.

Two boys in the back row turned round and stared through the holes bored in the cracks of the partition. One of them, Effish, placed his lips on a crack and blew suddenly. Rattlethrough's chair grated; there was the sound of an opening door, and Effish commenced to draw with a perfervid desire. 4c door opened, and Rattlethrough came in, spectacles held poised in his left hand.

'Oh, . . . er . . . forgive me, please . . . er . . . Mr. Worth', he began nervously, entreaty in his light blue eyes, 'but . . . er . . . a . . . er . . . boy is blowin' through the . . . . er . . . partition. I distinctly felt a cold draught on the back of my neck. May I find the culprit?'

'Yes, yes,' murmured Mr. Worth, his dark eyes woeful, his voice feeble and thin.

Willie whispered to Jack, 'Useless looks as though he were being embalmed against his will.'

'Effish, I think it was you, what?'

The French master glared at Effish, who looked up as though unable to believe that Rattlethrough could credit him with such an action.

'Me, Sir?' he asked, moving his head in feigned utter surprise.

'Yes, you!'

'Me, what Sir?'

'WAS IT YOU BLOWIN', BOY?'

'Blowin', Sir? I never felt any blowin', Sir.'

'Don't argue! Answer my question. Did you . . . or did you not . . . blow through the compartment?'

'The compartment, Sir?' asked Effish, frowning and holding out his pencil in apparently unconscious imitation of Rattlethrough's spectacles.

'WITLESS WRETCH!' enunciated the French master, 'were you blowin' through the compartition?'

'The compartition, Sir? What is that, Sir? I heard wind rattlin', Sir, rattlin' through somewhere near here, Sir. I've been drawin', Sir! Look, Sir, I can show you my drawin'!'

'Don't stare at me, you grinnin' fool!' cried the French master, who, unknown to all except Mr. Worth, was suffering in anguish.

Cerr-Nore hid his head. The class chuckled. Effish felt an immense and sensuous feeling of great fear and thrilling nervousness between his legs. That was one reason why he delighted in dangerous encounters with various masters, although his feigned air of innocent insolence occasionally led him into the Headmaster's study. The masters knew that behind a barrier of buffoonery that was almost second nature to him by reason of its constant assumption, lurked a clever and cunning brain.

'Was it you, Beckelt?' almost implored Mr. Rapson of the Weasel.

'No, Sir, not me, Sir, no Sir.'

Effish began to cough violently. 4a was enjoying itself. Mr. Worth sat still and said nothing.

The French master asked every boy in the back row if he had been blowing, and received from each a denial. He turned with a fretful expression to the drawing master.

'I . . . er . . . am sorry, Mr. Worth, to have disturbed you. The boy will not own up. He . . . er . . . is apparently without a sense of honour. I am . . . er . . . afraid that we must leave it at that!'

'Yes, yes, Mr. Rapson,' mumbled his colleague.

The French master withdrew. The hum in his own room

ceased, and in silence 4a heard him walking to his seat, calling out:

'Whose turn is it? Go on, then, and try and remember that *avec* is pronounced *arvec* and not *evick*. *Continuez*, miserable wretch.'

A weak voice commenced to read aloud.

4a went on lazily with its drawing, until Bony occupied its interest by stretching out a long claw-like hand over two desks and rapping Burrell on the head.

'Sit down, sit down,' fluted Mr. Worth.

Bony rubbed his ear. Burrell had shot a pellet at him.

'Oh, oh,' lamented Effish a moment later, 'oh, oh, water some one.'

'Quiet, you boy,' piped Mr. Worth who was losing his temper.

'My head, my head,' groaned Effish, rolling his eyes and grinding his teeth.

'Old Useless doesn't half get ragged,' grinned Jack to Willie.

'It's rather a shame Jack. He's decent really.'

'Come out HERE, boy, I won't HAVE this nonsense,' shouted the master. He leapt from his desk, went up to Effish, who immediately wrapped his hands round his ears and head and ducked under the desk. Mr. Worth clawed his back, but could get no grip. Effish called out 'oh, oh,' in a dull voice, 'oh, oh, I can't get my breath.'

'Go into Mr. Rore,' cried Mr. Worth.

'The Head Master,' said Cerr-Nore, wearily. 'Always at my public school it was the Head Master, I assure you, Sir, and Colham is very nearly a public school, Sir. Not quite, t'ough.'

Unknown to 4a, Cerr-Nore had been expelled from the big public school of Overborough, some miles away eastwards under the downs.

Effish got up with a dazed look, put his hand to his brow and moaned incoherently.

'Go on,' ordered the drawing master with quivering voice.

The door opened suddenly, and Mr. Rore himself appeared. For a moment he stood looking keenly over his semi-circular glasses, his pink face, with its smooth glow and white drooping moustache, gazing at Effish. For a moment only, but every boy had sunk in fear to his desk. For a moment only, but it seemed as if the room were charged with some force. Every brain responded with awe to the vibrant energy of the big man, black-gowned, standing absolutely motionless on the threshold of the room.

'What is the matter, Mr. Worth?' he inquired, the keen voice striking the alarums of boyish minds. His eyes under the frosted brows looked at Effish, who lowered his hand.

Mr. Worth mumbled that Effish was misbehaving.

'Well, Sir?' inquired the Headmaster coldly.

'Headache, Sir,' muttered the boy, now frightened.

'I'm sorry,' replied Mr. Rore, in low and courteous tones. 'Perhaps that explains it, Mr. Worth? One cannot be too careful in adolescence, you know.'

'He cried out, Mr. Rore.'

The Headmaster's eyes were sternly fixed upon the drooping figure of Effish.

'I suffer from neuralgia, Sir,' said Effish piteously.

4a admired his temerity in ecstatic silence.

'What a lad he is!' whispered Willie to Jack.

'I am sorry if you are ill,' condoled the Headmaster. 'Do not attempt to do any work to-night. Are you playing football this afternoon?'

'Yes Sir,' lied Effish. He was one of the few boys who managed to elude both games and its alternative of expedition with 'Cigars or Nuts'.

'Good, good,' the Headmaster approved. 'Sport is necessary in order to rid the body of its waste tissues, to stimulate the mind. Boys, I cannot urge that fact too emphatically upon you. Work hard and play hard. Let that be your motto. But sport is not all. A good servant, a bad master. And never forget, *What should be, shall be.* Master your difficulties! What boys agree?'

4a showed its hands promptly, certain boys well hidden behind others looking at one another and winking.

The Headmaster called Mr. Worth outside, and spoke to him briefly in earnest tones. Then he was gone, and thereafter his personality hovered in spirit over the classroom so that almost in silence the boys continued to await the bell.

When its peals shivered in Big Hall ten minutes later, the drawings were collected hurriedly and roughly into heaps. Desks were slammed by a few impulsive boys for joy at the termination of the week's work. In Big Hall classes were hurrying towards their different form rooms. No boy stamped upon the iron grating that bordered the floor. A stream of boys headed for the playground, bumping and scrambling in their eagerness. The sun shone brightly outside the school.

4a waited impatiently for another form to quit its own room, then rushed in, deposited books in desks, took homework slips, glanced at them, assorted books and crammed them into satchels.

'Goodbye, chaps!'

'Tata, Mad Willie. Get that power!'

'Hard at it, hard at it!'

'Phippy, give us a lift on the carrier of your motorbike to footer this afternoon?'

'Who's pinched my blasted Latin dictionary?'

Gradually 4a room was empty.

Seven minutes later Willie and Jack were seated in the train on their way to Rookhurst Halt, each smoking with enjoyment a Woodbine cigarette. Jack had sold one of his rook's eggs to Hoys for a penny, the price of a packet of five.

Chapter 6

'WELL, and how did you get on at school to-day?' asked Mr. Maddison, at mid-day dinner.

'Oh, all right, thank you, Father.'

'What did you do?'

'Do, Father?'

'Yes, Willie.'

Willie looked at his plate.

'Well, don't tell me if you don't want to,' said Mr. Maddison, inevitably.

'I don't know what you mean, Father.'

How much did Father know? Who could have told him that he had got the whack for being late?

'I meant what I said, of course. What lessons did you do this morning?'

'Oh, I'm sorry, Father! I thought you meant something else! We did Physics, French, and then Shakespeare, then Drawing.'

'Which do you like best?'

'Drawing. But Physics is decent, too.'

His father said, 'Ha,' and for two minutes there was silence. Then he asked,

'Are you playing football this afternoon, or going out with the Natural History Club?'

Willie looked at his plate and began a long and invented explanation about Mr. Worth being ill and unable to take them that afternoon.

'Mr. Rore said we could go on our own, if we promised not to spend the afternoon indoors, but we must write up notes of what we saw.'

'And are you going to do it?'

'Yes, Father,' replied the boy, feeling relieved that his father had not suspected. He spoke hurriedly and a faint colour came into his cheeks. He felt uneasy, lest the lie be detected and punished. Actually, he kept a *Diary of Nature Observations*, but it never occurred to him that this was anything but wrongful; since he wrote as he wanted to in it, in his own way and not the correct English Essay way taught by Mr. Kenneth. His *Diary* was a very secret and private account written in a purloined school exercise book.

'Well, you are lucky to be a boy,' said Mr. Maddison. 'I don't suppose you realise how these are the best days of your life.'

'Yes, Father, I do!' replied Willie looking through the window at the sun in the fields. A shadow covered them swiftly.

Father and son continued to eat their dinner—the principal meal of the day. At night they had supper, not a sit-down supper, but Mr. Maddison had his carried into his study on a tray, and Willie ate his when he felt inclined with Biddy, the cook and housekeeper, in the kitchen. He enjoyed supper, especially when Big Will'um was there, sitting always in the same chair with his legs stretched out in front of him, because Big Will'um could make any kind of trap, snare or spring, and could successfully noose a jack in the brook.

Willie began thinking of the tree he was going to climb that afternoon. He would climb up, straight up without thinking about height, or about falling. After all, there were branches all the way up, and the beech tree was trusty, unlike an elm tree. The trusty beech, the crafty elm, the sturdy oak—he must write that in his *Diary*, under the heading *Thoughts and Observations of Trees*. And an account of the climb, for climb he would!

'Don't bolt your food, Willie. I've told you that before. You must control yourself. That is one of the first lessons a man has to learn in life.'

'Yes, Father,' replied Willie, looking forward to the end of the meal.

Outside in the open freedom of the country the sunlight rushed suddenly from behind a great cumulus and washed with light the fresh greenery of spring; inside the room the dull wall behind was lit instantly, showing the flatness of the oil portraits hung there in their tarnished gilt frames.

'Shall I pull the blind down, Father?' he said, in his inner exultation wanting to please Father.

'Good heavens, no! What ideas will you have next? Sunlight is what we all want, my boy.'

Willie felt a surge of gladness from his heart that nearly closed his throat. He thought of the coming joy, of the cuckoo soon to arrive, of the romance in the fields as the meadow grasses waved in the wind and the blossom opened on the hawthorns.

He looked at his father quickly, and was embarrassed by meeting the full look of his eyes. He always avoided doing that if he could, unless Father wasn't looking. The sunlight showed Father's beard, straggly with gray, and his long and clean and pink fingernails. In a burst of comradeship Willie said,

'Do you know what happens if you rub a vulcanite rod with catskin and hold it near a pithball, Father?'

Mr. Maddison went on eating.

'Do you, Father?'

'Do I *what?*'

'Do you know what happens when you rub a vulcanite rod with a catskin, or a glass rod with silk, or sealing wax on your coat?'

'I should imagine that a charge of static electricity is induced. That is common knowledge, I believe. Why?'

Willie felt foolish.

'Oh, I only wondered,' he said.

'Have you been doing Physics this morning?'

Willie hesitated, and then admitted that he had.

'Oh, I see; you want to unload some of your recently acquired knowledge upon me?' inquired Mr. Maddison.

The boy chewed the uninteresting cold mutton, longing for the time when he could dash away to Jack.

'No, Father.'

'Then why did you ask?'

'I just asked, Father.'

Conversation ceased until the housekeeper came in to clear away the plates and to remove the exhausted mutton bone that Bob, the old terrier, was awaiting anxiously in the kitchen. She was a short, stout woman, with a circular face and shiny cheeks upon whose rounded curves existed permanently the hue of a ripe Victoria plum. Her eyebrows were dark clusters of hair, which were liable as the years went on to increase in thickness and texture, proportionally as their immediate predecessors were blown off in her biennial attempts to clean the flue of the copper with gunpowder. Although she was over sixty years of age, her hair showed no grayness, and she accounted for this by the lavish use of mutton dripping applied to the scalp regularly every Saturday night since she was thirty. Otherwise no signs of youthfulness lingered with her; every part of her was stocky and plump, from her small feet amply encased in elastic-sided boots, to her enormous shoulders.

'Well, Mas' Wullie, ban't ee going to eat your meat?'

He shook his head.

'Thank you!' warned Mr. Maddison.

'No, thank you,' he repeated.

'Triccle tart be coming, zur,' she announced to Mr. Maddison.

He did not answer, but Willie said, 'Ha!' and Biddy's face beamed.

When the plates, knives and forks, vegetable tureens and the mutton bone were placed on the tray and carried jinglingly to the kitchen, his father said:

'I've told you again and again, I won't have you speak to
Biddy in a disrespectful manner. I never heard such a thing,
a bit of a boy like you, too. Why, your voice hasn't even
broken, and how old are you, almost fifteen? Lord knows
when you're going to bring a prize home. You're rudeness
personified. Are you listening?'

'Yes, Father.'

'Very well then, don't let it happen again. I don't want to
have continually to be telling you. It's time you grew up. Now
you understand, don't you?'

'Yes, Father.'

'Very well, then, remember in future—please! I won't have
it. You don't think it gives me any pleasure to continually
reprove you, do you? And there's another thing I want to
speak to you about. And that's about bird-nesting. I've told
you again and again, but it makes no difference apparently.
I may as well speak to a stone wall. You'll get me fined by
your wretched hobbies one day. You know very well that outsider Isaacs has got his knife into me and you ever since that
affair of the jay traps. Well, my boy, I don't want *you* to get
into trouble, can't you see that?'

'Yes, Father.'

'Very well, then, I'm glad you take a sensible view of it. I
am going to ask you, upon your honour, not to go bird-nesting.
You are too old for such things now. Will you give me your
word?'

While he had been speaking, the father had not looked once
at the son. When no answer was given, his voice grew more
impatient.

'Are you going to give me your word or are you not? 'Pon
my soul, you are a most extraordinary boy. I wasn't like you
when I was your age. I was full of fun, not moony and miserable. How often do I hear you laugh? Anyone would think
that you were a squirrel by the way you wish to destroy your
clothes climbing about. Besides, it's wrong to take eggs.'

'I don't take all the eggs we find,' said Willie, a quaver in his voice. 'Jack and me only want one of each kind. We like visiting our nests and seeing how they get on. Not like Clemow and Hoys who rag and have a dummy camera where they hide the eggs.'

'Oh, you can't deceive me! I've been a boy myself. You'—he leaned forward and pointed at his son who looked sullenly at the table cloth, a blaze of bitter thoughts within him—'You try and tell your grandmother to suck eggs. Well I've warned you. Since I cannot expect you to behave like a gentleman's son and act honourably up to your promises, you must be treated otherwise. Very well then. Now, listen to me; if I catch you with any eggs, or bringing young pigeons into the house, or squirrels, or badgers, or anything else, without asking me first, I shall smash all the eggs you have now and punish you severely. Mr. Rore said on your report last term,"His standard of honour should be raised." Think what that means! But do you care, I wonder?'

Not a bit, thought Willie to himself.

'It would hardly surprise me to learn that you did not,' went on Mr. Maddison. 'Well, as I have said, people who are not amenable to the ordinary codes of conduct must not expect to be privileged. I should dislike very much to forbid your going to Skirr Farm, but that's what it will come to unless you improve. That Temperley boy must have a bad influence on you, I fear. Yes, you can sulk, my boy! You can sulk, but you will thank me when you are older that I checked your wilful ways.'

Mr. Maddison shifted in his chair, breathing deeply. He had been much irritated recently because his son, for some reason of his own, had been taking the chisels of his carpenter's bench—carpentry was one of Mr. Maddison's hobbies—without permission, and returning them in a damaged state, without even mentioning what he had done. He dreaded any sort of scene with the boy, and for this reason he seldom spoke what was in his mind, until, irritated by the mental repression he said much more than he intended to say. Also, the cold mutton scraps had given him indigestion.

He went to a cupboard in the sideboard of blackened oak that filled half one wall, and took out a bottle of tablets. He dropped two in his glass of water, watched them fizzing, then swallowed the liquid.

Biddy came in with a large tart on a white plate, which she placed almost lovingly before her master. That done, she withdrew two steps to watch the effect upon the boy's face when he should taste it. Although a servant nominally, she was in charge of the house. On the many occasions that Mr. Maddison had given her notice to leave, she had refused absolutely to go, as she considered it her heaven-approved duty to look after the child of her dead mistress. Mr. Maddison had given way on the many occasions, and had long since abandoned any attempt to remind Biddy that it was his house. Nor indeed was such reminder necessary except upon those occasions. Under a rind of life-weariness was an affection for the old countrywoman, based on the memory of her regard for his wife, and her kindness to himself when, that night, nearly fifteen years ago, she had held him as he sobbed in the kitchen —although he disliked remembering such old happenings now.

'Tart, Willie?' asked his father, wishing that he had not spoken so harshly to the boy before him.

'No thank you, Father.'

'I thought you liked treacle tart! Let me give you a small piece? It looks beautifully cooked, Biddy!'

'It be,' replied Biddy, in a satisfied voice.

'I don't feel hungry, thank you, Father.'

' 'Tis a proper tart, Mas' Wullie,' urged Biddy.

'A small piece, Willie? Come on!'

He shook his head.

'I made it for 'ee,' came from Biddy.

'I'm not hungry, thank you.'

His father said, between his teeth, 'As you wish. I'm damned if I'm going to pander to your moods.'

When the meal came to an end, the boy said nervously, 'Oh, Father, Jack says can I go to tea with him and supper as it's Saturday?'

'You mean to ask permission? Then why not ask outright, "May I go to Jack's for supper?" I don't like the round-about way you phrase your requests, but I suppose it's in keeping with your creepy-crawly nature. Yes, you may go. Be back by half-past eight.'

'They have supper at eight,' the boy faltered.

'Very well then, half-past nine.'

'Oh, *thank* you, Father.'

'Don't thank me. I don't want to be thanked!' replied his father gruffly. 'Now run along and don't get into mischief.'

'No, Father.'

Mr. Maddison went upstairs. Willie got his cap from its peg in the hall, listened, then slipped back into the room, cut a large segment of the tart, and, in his own phrase, hared off towards Skirr Farm.

He met Jack along the road, and they set out for the beech forest, speaking only at intervals. Nine years of intimacy had formed a friendship of such grandeur to themselves that perfect understanding existed in everything they did together.

In a corner of the meadow a kestrel hawk was leaning on the breeze, brown pinions swaying in the gust, tail depressed and raised to maintain balance. Had Willie been with some-one else, he would have said: 'I say, look at that mouse-hawk in the gust,' but to call Jack's attention to it (since it was a most important sight) he jerked his head in its direction and knew that his friend was thinking the same thoughts as him-self.

The hawk swung round and swept down the torrent of the wind, coming into its rush again and hanging poised a quarter of a mile away. Up the smooth dull green of the downs beyond the cloud-shadows climbed slowly, the yellow light following after and bleaching small chalk-line objects that were sheep feeding on the sward of the slopes.

The wind billowed past them, blowing their trousers against their legs, his own so much thinner than Jack's, he noticed, as he had a hundred times before. The wind came from the south-west, lingering in the hollows of the woodlands where grew primroses and wind-anemones, stirring the young green corn and swinging the bines of honeysuckle, swaying the beech-trees where the rooks nested, and onwards, through the hedges and the nut woods. Charged with sunbeams, it brought once more the message to the old earth.

They passed through the meadow, crossed over the brook by a log footbridge, and came to the roadway. Hearing a shout, they turned, and saw a figure waving to them from a garden gate about a hundred yards away.

Willie waved back, and hesitated.

'Oh, come on, man,' said Jack.

'Half a minute, Jack. I must—I ought to—just a minute.'

He turned round, and walked slowly back. After a few steps his pace increased, slowed again; then he went forward quickly, not straightly, but veering out of his line to kick a stone or snatch at a tall dry grass by the roadside. As he came near the gate he glanced up, took the sweetness of a face to his heart, and looked on the ground.

'Hullo, Willie,' she said, in a clear, frank voice. 'It's simply ripping to be back home again. How are you?'

'Oh, all right, thank you—Elsie.' He spoke her name with difficulty. 'I didn't know you were here.'

'I've been staying with Mary in Devonshire. We only came back last night. She's staying with us until we go back to School next Wednesday.'

He tried to think of something to say to her.

Another girl came down the path, and stood beside her.

'Hullo,' said Willie.

'Hullo,' she replied.

'We're just going to climb up to some rooks' nests,' he said, kicking a stone with his boot.

'What now?' said Mary. 'What fun! I haven't got a rook's egg.'

He wanted to hear what Elsie would say. She said, 'Perhaps Willie will give you one, Mary.'

'Yes,' he replied, hardly daring to hope that Elsie would say she would like to go with him. If she did, it might mean that she—

Even in his mind he could not formulate the word love.

'Do you mind if we come with you?' asked Mary, eagerly.

Looking up at Elsie's face for a moment, Willie said, with a growing alarm and anguish within him, 'I'll bring an egg back here for you, shall I?' Why did I say that, he inwardly cried.

'Don't bother,' said Elsie. 'We were going for a walk in the forest, weren't we, Mary? I'd rather like to watch you both climbing.'

'Come on then!' said Willie, with a boldness and joy that made Mary smile at him.

'Just a minute—we'll get our hats.'

'I'm ready,' declared Mary. 'I don't want a hat in this lovely wind.'

In the lane they found Jack, who barely raised his cap and said, 'How do,' before vaulting over the stile, leading into the Big Wheatfield.

After waiting for Elsie and Mary to get over, Willie tried to vault, but owing to his small height he failed to clear the top bar, and landed in a heap on the other side. They laughed, not knowing that he had banged his ankle. Pain and mortification caused his sight to become misty, and he thought that they were laughing because he could not do what Jack could.

He got up, smiling fixedly, and they saw that he was hurt. Mary offered an arm, which he refused, and Elsie said, 'Poor

Willie,' in a tone of voice that made him wish he had broken his ankle. Had he done so, he wouldn't have told, he thought, no, he would have walked on until he fainted!

Five minutes later they were laughing and talking together. Willie wondered how Jack could possibly treat Elsie so indifferently. He never looked at her once. If only he dared ask her to be his sweetheart—but oh, he would never dare. He would climb straight up, without once looking down! He might get dizzy all that height up, but no matter.

They kept to the lower edge of the field over which lapwings were falling and twirling, crying with wild sweetness to their mates below. The loam field stretched away up to the sky-line, where the spinney of dwarfed hornbeams and beeches grew with the fire-trees. Sometimes the echo of one of the crowstarvers' 'hulo-o-o-os' came to them when the wind ceased and left quiet sunshine on the lee-side of the hedge by which they walked. Sometimes the clanging of wood on the suspended length of rail was faintly borne across, then the clacking of the clappers. A boy called Bill Nye was employed to scare the rooks and jackdaws who came to uproot the sapling corn, and paid sixpence a day to remain there all day and every day, from the sowing till the time when the wheat was fully rooted.

When, alone, Willie heard the plovers and the cries of the crowstarvers he felt a lovely sadness; once he had composed a poem which he repeated to himself, inducing a lovely feeling,

> 'Over the fallow field crieth a lapwing
> Wild and plaintive, pee-weet, pee-o-weet.'

Now, walking beside Elsie, he thought what a fool he had been ever to think like that. O, it was a glorious walk! Elsie's cheeks, seen in quick stolen glances, were so beautiful. It was like being in a dream with her. Yes, she loved him, loved him, or else why were her cheeks so sweet and smiling? He picked up a clod and hurled it into the air with a shout.

They branched off from the Big Wheatfield, crossed the brook again, and went along a high hedge of hawthorn that led to the fringe of the beech wood.

A vast flock of rooks was drifting and swinging in the wind, over the trees. Here was the main colony. As they walked under the trees a cawing uproar commenced, and those birds who had been brooding on eggs or perching near the nests, head to breeze, rose with a soughing of wings that overbore the noises of the wind.

Under the beech trees their feet crushed the split mast-covers and brown leaves, while directly below the nests the ground was covered with crooked oak-twigs brought from a mile away.

'They always break off oak twigs,' said Willie. 'And look!'

He pointed to the blue, black-speckled shell of a thrush's egg, the remains of a young wood-pigeon, and many signs that the birds pilfered the corn. 'Dirty old robbers!'

'I say, you aren't going to climb right up to the top of those trees, are you?' asked Elsie, her eyes wide open.

Willie nodded. 'Not here—at the other end of the wood.'

'But you'll fall, both of you. It's so high, and look at the wind!'

'Pooh, that's nothing,' answered Jack over his shoulder. He would not walk with girls; but slouched on in front.

When they had come to the top of the slope, Jack went away along the field-edge to look at other trees. Willie went after him and said, 'I don't think I can climb these ones. I think I'll climb the one I nearly got up this morning.'

'Right ho, I'm with you, man.'

They went back to the tree, under which the girls were sitting.

'What muscles you have, Jack!' said Mary, as Jack took off his coat and threw it on the ground. Jack drew up his arm, grinning, and shook his fist in her face. Willie thought it would be best to keep his coat on, and determined that when he got home he would do dumb-bell exercises until his biceps were as swelling as Jack's.

'The wind's getting up,' he remarked, wetting his finger and holding it up.

'What's that for?' asked Mary.

'The side that's coldest is where the wind comes from,' he told her, 'and the Ichiargo Indians can tell if a cyclone or hurricane is coming by a tingling feeling in the finger nail. I was just wondering if a cyclone would be coming, because if so you must go home, for then all these trees will be uprooted and carried for miles.'

'But you're not an Ichiargo Indian,' said Elsie.

Willie smiled in a superior way to himself.

'Perhaps I've learnt some of their secrets,' he hinted.

He saw that Elsie was puzzled.

'It was supposed to be a joke,' he said.

'Are you sure you're strong enough to climb so high?' replied Elsie. 'You don't look strong, you know.'

'Sometimes the wiry men are the strongest,' declared Mary, but her words did not allay his mortification.

'You can only be killed once, and *I* don't care when.'

'Oh, Willie, you naughty boy, to speak like that!'

'Its the truth. Jack and I are fed up with life. You just go and take a squint at the Old Bird, and have a chat with Rattlethrough, and you just see what we have to put up with. I can tell you, one day we are going to sail into Rattlethrough and knock his conk off.'

'His what?'

'His conk—snout—sniffler—nozzle—nose.'

'I expect you're naughty boys, that's why you don't like your masters.'

Jack and Willie exchanged superior glances.

'Come on, Willie,' said Jack.

'Won't you tear your coat, Willie?' asked Mary.

He frowned at her.

The spaniel was leaping around and barking at the rooks, who had formed a circle and were sailing in cartwheel formation high over the trees. Suddenly their cries ceased, for the boys had begun to climb.

The first part, thought Willie, was easy. The branches were so numerous that even if he slipped he would bounce from branch to branch and manage to get a grip somewhere. Jack climbed rapidly. Far down below Willie could see the upturned face of Mary. And yet he was only on the branch under the jackdaw's nest.

'Shall I get you an egg, Elsie? he shouted.

She looked up and nodded.

Raising his hands from their grip on the branch he was straddling, Willie gripped the main trunk and lifted one foot into the socket between bough and trunk. Looking upwards, he raised himself slowly, heavily, painfully. He daren't move higher! In this cramped position many thoughts and images beat like wings in his mind. He dared not do it, he could not do it! And yet he was raising himself higher and higher: now his fingers were just under the hold of the jackdaw's nest. Sweat broke out over his body, and felt instantly cold. He trembled; reached up slowly, and gripped the edge of the hole with all his strength; drew himself upright.

'Good man!' Jack shouted down, from where he was resting fifteen feet above him. 'It's easy now!'

Laboriously Willie climbed higher, branch by branch.

'Ain't it ripping, man?' shouted Jack, in the wind.

'Not half!' quavered Willie.

'I say, man, you aren't funky, are you?'

Willie's hands, legs, arms, and voice were quivering. He looked down, and saw with a sickening clutch in his stomach that they seemed about a mile above the earth. He forced himself to shout back,

'No, only you know I'm not much good high up.'

'You're all right, Willie. You can climb no end!'

'Can I?'

'Of course you can. Besides, it's an easy tree. Isn't the wind fine? Good as the Fair swings, ain't it?'

'Better,' mumbled Willie, but his voice was lost in the wind.

Just by his face hung the bedraggled skeleton of a dead rook. The branches were splashed with birds' droppings, and covered with the evidence of grain-plundering. Looking up, Willie saw that the nests were not far above their heads; and how they were swaying!

He could not realise how he had climbed so high. He was gripping a branch so tightly with his hands that the muscles of his forearms were aching. And Jack wasn't even holding! He was leaning on a branch against his chest, chewing a sweet.

'Have one?' he asked, putting his hand in his pocket.

'No, you fool!' yelled Willie, gripping the branch tighter.

They climbed higher. The wind had been disturbing on the main trunk, but its fury seemed increased a score-fold against the outgrowing branches. It was necessary to grip with the knees to prevent the body being swung outwards like a belly-ing sail. At first Willie had to fight against an impulse to let go; but this went suddenly and took with it all sense of fear. Looking down he saw a tiny figure staring upwards. One egg? He would get her a capful!

Up he went. It really was very easy, with plentiful branches like a ladder. Swish! The wind cried shrilly through the thin branches. How big were the nests. Three feet wide at least. He was two yards under one nest. Wedging his foot in a miniature fork he looked across the downs, at the nearer vil-lage with its lime-washed, thatched cottages. A flight of pigeons was wheeling about Skirr Farm, fluttering and white in the sunlight. Turning round, he could see the Longpond through the trees. Nearer, the spinney in the Big Wheatfield. How small it looked from up here! The ploughed field far away looked small as a broken gramophone record.

He climbed again, reaching the next. Stretching his arm up

and over the platform of twigs he felt his fingers seized by warm things and sucked. A hoarse squawking and gabbling came from the mud-plastered crater. The blind young rooks were stretching up their necks and trying to swallow what they imagined to be worms. He lifted one out, saw that its skin was black, and its throat yellow, and dropped it back again.

He looked across to the other end of the tree, and saw that Jack had placed his cap between his teeth and was putting eggs into it. He descended a few feet, and crept up another branch. The wind swayed him smoothly. Lovely, not to be afraid any more! Reaching across the wide platform of twigs he felt warm eggs. One by one he put them in his cap. Another nest was quite near, and he emptied it as well. Then he started to descend, feeling a triumphant glow in his body.

With easy confidence he reached the fork. Jack was still climbing about in the summit of the tree. Willie rested, confident and happy. He tested himself, letting go his grip while leaning on a branch; he slipped, and his heart throbbed and his knees started shaking. He scrambled down further, taking the jackdaw's egg and putting a rook's egg in its place. The rest was easy. He descended not using his feet at all, except to steady himself, swinging by his arms, feeling very strong in Elsie's eyes.

On the ground he was amazed to find how his whole body was trembling. He was very hot, and his hands and shirt were grubby. His palms were blistered, too, where he had gripped hard.

'Jolly fine climb!' said Mary. 'Oh, and isn't your face just covered with blacks and dust!'

'Is it? That's nothing,' he replied, smiling, removing the cap, wet with saliva, from his mouth.

'What lovely eggs, Willie,' said Elsie, looking in the cap.

'You can have them,' he said shyly.

He looked at her swiftly. He felt that he was smiling in a dream. Then, feeling awkward, at the silence, he said,

'Those birds up there making all that row are the mothers and fathers. I say, give me your photo before you go back, will you?'

As though in reproach a broken croak floated down. He looked up and saw that a rook was flapping near its looted nest.

'I wish I'd left her some,' he said, looking up.

'Oh Willie, think of the poor mother without her eggs,' exclaimed Elsie. 'What must she think when she finds the nest empty?'

'I dunno'—he shook his head.

'Oh, hark at her! Poor thing!'

He took the eggs from the cap and began to place them carefully on the ground, in a line. He did it slowly, to prolong the exquisite feeling of being near Elsie. How kind she was about the rooks!

'I hope you're not doing it for me, because I don't want them,' said Elsie.

He stared at her face. 'But I got them for you, Elsie.'

'You told Mother you only took one from a nest,' persisted Elsie.

'So I do usually.'

O, was his voice going to get shaky? 'Would you like them?' he said to Mary, hoping to hear Elsie say she wanted them.

Mary hesitated.

'I'd like one if you can spare it, Willie,' she said. 'The rooks will lay again and forget all about these eggs.'

'Huh,' said Willie. 'I don't want them,' and with eyes on the ground he walked away.

Chapter 7

HALF AN HOUR later Jack found Willie in the spinney, sitting over the fire of Bill Nye, the crowstarving boy.

'What's up with you?' he enquired.

'Nothing.'

'What made you clear off like that? Elsie cleared off too. When I got down that other girl was there alone, and told me where she'd put your eggs for safety, then she cleared off too, after Elsie.'

Willie said nothing.

'Is it anything I've done, Willie?' asked Jack, after a while.

Willie shook his head.

'Then I know what it is,' asserted his friend. ' I told you you were a blinkin' idiot to have anything to do with girls.'

'Shut up, fool!'

Bill Nye, the bare-legged crowstarver, who looked about seven years old, so little and thin was he, puckered up his face in a grin. Jack caught his arm, but the boy hoarsely whined, 'Nunno, Mas' Temp'ly, doan't 'ee hit 'im, for gordsake, Mas' Temp'ly, doan't 'ee do that.'

'You mind your own business, d'ye hear?' warned Jack, twisting the small boy's arm.

''Ess, Mas' Jack, ess ee wull.'

He sprang up, pattered over the ground with bare feet, ragged trousers flapping round his thin calves, seized a clapper, whirled it vigorously and yelled: 'Ull-oo-oa, Ull-oo-oo-a.'

For an hour Jack and Willie sat over the fire. Sometimes Jack spoke but Willie did not answer, and soon he too became silent. The white, brilliant sun swung across a wind-washed

78

sky of blue, the larks climbed into the heaven singing their songs the while, and the afternoon grew older.

In silence they left the spinney to Bill Nye, with his clappers, his tins, and his plovers' eggs baked in the fire. The wind had left the earth; silently the high white clouds drifted towards the distant downs.

Halfway down the right-of-way they passed an oddmedodd erected to scare the rooks, made of an old torn coat stuffed with straw, and an ancient chimney hat. The erection of these figures of desolation was one of the duties of Bill Nye, himself a diminutive human scarecrow. Willie looked at it a moment, lost in reverie, for Jim Holloman used to make the oddmedodds for the Big Field, and Jim used to live in the spinney.

'I wonder where Jim is,' said Willie, half to himself, half to Jack, as he picked up a length of bone discoloured by fire. 'This may be part of him, for all we know.'

While he spoke Willie was half-convinced that it was true. The bone was long and round, about as big as a drumstick of one of the Cadet Corps drums at school. 'Damn funny bone,' mused Willie.

'Dog,' said Jack.

'Very long-legged dog.' He pitched it on the flinty earth, along the young blades of the rising wheat.

The lapwings were crying over the skyline of the bare rising field: wild and lonely were the cries, as though seeking that which would never be found.

Jack recited,

> 'Over the fallow field crieth a lapwing
> Wild and plaintive, pee-weet, pee-o-weet.'

Willie said casually, 'What does that rot come from? Beastly old Woggledaggar?'

'Woddledagger!' snorted Jack. 'You don't catch me out. No, a chap at school called Mad Willie wrote that poem, a funny sort of bloke he is who writes things in a secret diary that he sometimes lets me read. Awful rot, of course, most of it!'

Disregarding Jack's banter, Willie said, staring at the sky, 'Yes, it is awful rot. I'm no good at anything.'

'Get out! You're a jolly fine poet—Rupert Bryers said so, and he knows. Wasn't one of his poems in the school mag. last term?'

Willie felt pleased that Jack should remember his poem about the lapwing, although he was slightly apprehensive, since poetry was a thing to be held in scorn in 4a. The poem occurred in an entry in Willie's *Secret and Official Diary of Observations, as Supplementary to Pocket Diary* (*fuller account herein.*)

Only special friends were allowed to read this *Diary*, which, contrary to one of the many rules of Colham School, was written in a school exercise book; special friends such as Bony Watson, Rupert Bryers, Macarthy and Jack. Willie wrote in his *Diary* usually at night, when he was supposed to be doing homework. The entries were all concerned with the 'Happy expeditions and rambles I have had with my friends, to which I may want to refer to when the leaves fall, and only memories remain.' In moments of affectionate confidence the book was surreptitiously passed to a friend. Some entries were laconic, such as,

'Wednesday afternoon, raining, so I did not go anywhere to-day.'

against which Macarthy had pencilled a note, 'Took return ticket.'

The last entry, containing the poem which Jack had remembered, was dated March 6th, and like all the others, was in Willie's neatest handwriting.

6 March. Bicycled in afternoon to Wickham Court woods, where Father got me permission from Sir John Shapcote. I saw the head-keeper there, who does not in any way come up to my expectations as a keeper. I asked him what birds were here. 'Only your common sorts, thrushes, blackies, and robins.' He has a white stubble of hairs on his chin, and his face is reddened with long exposure to the winds of heaven and the elements of the universe, and, I fear me from his glowing nose, a too frequent application of the bottle.

These keepers here have two main vermin poles. The first one consisted of a pair of sparrow-hawks, several rats, jays, kestrels, weasels, stoats and *three brown owls*. All the bodies were, I should think, put up there last year.

It seems to me funny that he should kill kestrels and owls, and, perhaps we may include in this category the crafty weasel. For this reason:—

He shoots rats. Truly, they are cunning and great egg-poachers, and killers of young game birds. Now the keepers can only shoot about one per cent. (1%) of the rats in the wood. But yet quite fifty per cent. (50%) of them are killed during the year. How?

Why, kestrels and owls manage to exterminate the remaining percentage, and they are ably helped in this cause by the crafty weasel. Then why shoot both the murderer and the policeman?

A keeper sees a kestrel hovering on pointed wings over a place where pheasants are fed. As it swoops down on something, he fires. The beautiful bird is tied, anyhow, among the beastly rat and cunning stoat and crafty weasel. He (the keeper) does not stop to consider that there is a possibility that the kestrel was only after a rat or mouse.

Again, he sees a tawny owl sitting on a coop in the bright moonlight of a May night. He kills it. He does not think for a moment that the food at the coops attracts rats, and rats attract owls. Most keepers are terribly conservative in their ideas, as well as pig-headed and childish in their opinions of birds of prey.

Jack and I saw several gins there, besides three beautifully constructed traps for pheasants, made out of hazel sticks to form a kind of spring-fall coop. The hen pheasants are then taken to the wire netting aviary, and made to lay.

We found an old shed in one corner of a field with many ripping things (all old and rusty) in it.

Among other things it contained two old sporting guns of an obsolete pattern (percussion cap), cartridges, shot, bird-food, wire, wad-punchers, tins, traps, snares, cages, etc. I brought home several 'reminiscences' from the shed, as well as from the vermin pole, e.g., two stoats tails, kestrels wings and feathers, and two skulls of sparrowhawk and kestrel, and one sparrowhawk's foot.

Went on afterwards by myself to have a hasty look around Gardebone coverts. Everything was the same.

I found a cunningly hidden path running down to a larger ploughed field of loam (bigger than Big Wheatfield) so that the keeper can watch any one on the broad acres of the furrows without being seen. Doubtless this hidden path is to watch for hare poachers.

On the horizon of the field several male lapwings were flying about, twisting, turning, and suddenly pitching.

A poetical thought struck me as I listened to his mournful, and yet wildly-free, plaintive cry.

> 'Over the fallow-field crieth a lapwing,
> Wild and plaintive, pee-weet, pee-o-weet.'

As I gazed over the vast expanse of brown fields with the red sun disappearing beneath a mountain of pearly-ash cloud, a sense of the solitude of the world stole over me, only broken by the wild cry of the lapwing.

After leaving the coverts I rode home, arriving at 7 p.m. Fortunately, however, a certain person was out, and so all was well. I am writing this in the kitchen, before a bright fire, as it is bath night.

Chapter 8

'LETS go and have tea with Bob Lewis,' suggested Willie, when they had arranged and gazed at the rooks' eggs for the last time before hiding them in the hole in the trunk. Willie and Jack had gone back to the tree they had climbed, and were lying on the grassy landsherd at the edge of the cornfield, warm in the western rays of the sun.

The way to the old keeper's cottage led past the Longpond. At the end of the long sheet of water Colonel Tetley's coverts began. A swarded ride led beside the brook through the brakes of ash, hazel, oak, alder, and willow, crossing other green rides marked with hob-nailed boot-prints all leading in the same direction. At most of the cross-roads stood a tree hung with stoats, weasels, hedgehogs, and crows, and an occasional jay and hawk. The oldest weasels and stoats hanging there were black and shrunken and dry; on the noses of the last killed the blood was still crusted brown. From some all but the head had fallen, suspended on green string. Only the teeth were unchanged, whether of blackened, eyeless skull or drawn-out, sun-stiffened corpse. The teeth were set in fixed snarls, beautiful, strong, and white.

The main ride led through a plantation of spruce and larch to a cleared space where stood a cottage in half an acre of garden. In the garden were apple and damson trees, surrounded by a wall of limestone. In the south wall, sprigged by apricot branches, were six alcoves, in which stood six straw skeps for bees. Starlings whistled and wheezed on the chimney pots, shaking their wings. Four white fantail pigeons flew about a cot nailed to the tarred kennel-shed where setters and retrievers were barking.

83

The waters of the brook ran murmuring behind the garden, among the willows and alders. High up by the chimney was a small window, about a hand-span square. Many hundreds of times the long barrel of the 8-bore gun had waited in this open window for the winter sunset flight of wildfowl.

An old man sat under the skeps, facing the sunshine. His cap lay on one knee, and his hands were clasped upon the nobbed end of a great oak stick, polished with age. Sometimes he nodded his head gently. Since dinner time he had been sitting in his high-backed, yew-wood chair. From the pine wood came the drooling of ringdoves, near at hand the soft cooing of the fantails, the sipping talk of finches in the apple trees; and in an undertone the slumbrous hum of tame bees, and the burring of bumble bees at the wallflowers.

Long had he lived there; but now his beloved rearing-field was guarded by another. Old Bob Lewis had served the Colonel, his father and grandfather, for nearly seventy years. His own father had been keeper before him; neither had been to London. Now age and feebleness had compelled him to give up his work in the woods, and a continual house life pressed upon him. Whenever possible, he was out of doors; otherwise he fretted. He was simple as a flower itself, for so long had Old Bob lived among them, breathed their scents and loved their colours. He felt stifled in a house, and longed for the open. A simple old man, without wife or child, only the thoughts of flowers and birds and the dreams that they give to fill his mind.

After the blusterings of the wind, the sunshine and the murmur of bees made the garden in the wood a place of tranquillity. His head drooped forward till it nearly rested on his clasped hands. A woman came round the wall and called softly to him. He did not hear her. She walked nearer, faced him, thinking that he was asleep. A pity to wake him, but tea was ready. Then two magpies flew over the garden, uttering their harsh cries of *chack-chack-chack*. The old man raised his head and stared vacantly at her.

'Is that Harry?' he said.

Harry was the name of his son. Often he spoke of him as though he were not dead.

'Tea be ready, my dear,' said the woman. 'Will ee come now? The boys be come to see ee. Willie and Jack.'

Her voice was low and sweet.

'Young Mas'. Will'um? Hey? Proper boy, young Will'um. Where be'n to?'

'Inside the house. Tea be ready.'

'Proper boy. Tell'n goldypinks be in the apple trees. Hark 'ee, do ee hear'n singing now?'

He turned his head sideways and listened. The far-away sipping notes of the goldfinches rose and fell, coming reedy and wistful above the burring of the bees. The lichened forks of the apple trees were a favourite place in which to weave the fragile nests of moss and hair and dandelion flock, and building would soon begin.

Dolly waited for the old keeper to lift himself from the chair —he would have no help—and the sunlight revealed the faded and frayed hem of her skirt, the stockings patched and worn-out at one heel, her hands chapped and roughened by work. She had put on a print blouse in preparation for Sunday. Her clothes were adapted from old coats and skirts given her by her former mistress at Skirr Farm, and the shoes never fitted. They were too big. In her box she had a pair of patent leather shoes, which she had not worn since the disappearance of Jim Holloman.

Always Dolly's skin had been soft and smooth, and of that rare quality that is enriched by wind and sunshine. Her bosom was firm, with a simplicity of girlish outline. She had fastened her blouse with a pin, which had loosened and exposed the sun-tinged flesh moving with her breathing. Her face had altered during the years of yearning, especially the expression of the eyes. Their child-like wonder—so exquisite a loveliness of brown eyes—was gone, the thoughtless maidenly wonder drowned deep within those mournful depths. Her face was thinner, the cheek-bones more prominent; the lips were not so full—in girlhood they had been parted and expectant, but now too often they were closed in bitterness.

About her feet the wind stirred the wallflowers, the bees hummed their chant of nectar and sunshine, and from the orchard came the notes of the finches in reedy whispers of song.

'Hark ee, midear,' said the old man, raising a finger.

'There be great-grammer calling that kettle be boiling,' said Dolly. 'A proper old toad her's getting.'

The old man heaved out of the high-backed chair, and walked with his great thick stick to the porch round the corner, followed slowly by Dolly.

Inside the room a very old and decrepit woman was huddled in a yew-wood armchair stuffed with patchwork cushions. She was over a hundred years old, and liked nothing so much as a visitor to whom she could state this important fact. Some days before each birthday, a young man from Colham was wont to call upon her, and ask a number of questions, receiving a mass of irrelevant replies from which the staff-reporter of the *Colham and District Times and Advertiser, with which is Incorporated Smellie's Weekly Argus* managed to write about Mrs. Nye's 'hints for the maintenance of a serene longevity ' and what he imagined she thought about civilisation generally. It was impossible to report her views accurately, for those that were rendered intelligible through reiteration were toothless remarks about 'they steam-ingins', ' they teeth of mine brukken dwenty-voor year agon', and 'that grand-darter wot left li'l slaverer fur poor old grammer'.

Regularly at her birthday Mrs. Odo Cerr-Nore, the wife of the Vicar, and, as she remembered with satisfaction at least once every Sunday when looking at the wall-memorials, a cousin-in-law to the Earl of Slepe, paid a visit with a basket containing such delicacies as port wine of the fine old tawny variety stocked by grocers and manufactured during the current year, minced chicken and ham, bramble jelly, cream, a new nightcap, and a pair of bedsocks.

In temperament and in habit Mrs. Nye differed from her nephew, Bob Lewis, who had just entered. Although it was his cottage she refused to have a window open. She was as active as he was, but rarely went out of the house. Her head was bald and small, and when she removed her woollen cap, it resembled a sun-withered wurzel. Mere shrunken slits were her eyes, and her nose hooked downwards and her bearded chin curved upwards till they appeared almost to touch.

'Ke'lls byling,' she complained, in a thin knaggy voice, pointing at the kettle. 'Ke'lls been byling long time.'

'Hullo, young Mas' Willie,' said Bob. 'Hullo, young boys. How be it, midears?'

'Fine Bob,' they replied.

'You'll take a cup of tea?' said Bob.

'I should think so, Barb Loos!' cried out Mrs. Nye. 'Ke'lls been byling this 'arf hower!'

Jack and Willie exchanged hand-hidden grins.

'Ah,' replied the old man.

'Aiy, aiy, that it has, Barb Loos. You been mooning around, you can't keep no reck'ning o'time.'

'Ah,' said Bob.

Dolly knelt down and poured the water from the black iron kettle that had just sent its first soft vapour into the chimney. Willie watched it falling from the notched spout, gurgling an ascendant and hollow scale in the teapot as it rose higher with the swirling tea-leaves. Then he noticed the curve of Dolly's breast as she leaned forward; he looked away quickly, lest Jack should notice too; and then, as though casually, his eyes returned to the mysterious and thrilling sight of a woman's breasts.

Dolly rose, and putting the teapot on the table, covered it with a woollen cosy. She smiled at Willie, and asked him why he had not been to see his old friend Bob Lewis for such a long time. 'He's beginning to talk wandering, poor old man,' she said in a low voice, and looked into the boy's eyes, sadness and longing concealed behind her smile. 'What big brown eyes you've got,' she said.

'No sugar, thank you,' exclaimed Willie, hastily lifting up his cup to meet the teapot spout, to try and hide Dolly's remark about his eyes.

They were drinking and blowing on their tea when footfalls shuffled on the stone threshold outside, and a double knock came at the door. Dolly frowned.

The door opened and a big heavy man dressed in a suit smelling of moth ball, and a cap peaked excessively, came into the room.

'Evenun, Mrs. Nye. Evenun, Mr. Lewis. Evenun, Dolly,' he said, standing by the door with his cap on his head. 'Evenun,' he nodded to the boys.

'Evenun,' shrilled Mrs. Nye, and immediately started to eat a piece of bread and butter, munching at a quick rate, and making considerable noise in the process of mastication without the aid of teeth.

'Ullo, young feller,' greeted Bob. 'How you been keeping?'

'Nicely, thank you. How be you Dolly?'

'Well, John Fry. Cup o' tea, will you?'

'Aiy, I could do with a cup of tea.'

He removed his cap, and looked round for a place to hang it, as the nail behind the door, whereon it was usually left, was occupied by Willie's cap. He seemed disconcerted by this, and after hesitation, put it on a bowl of waxen fruit.

Then, moving slowly round the room, he drew up a chair near Dolly, and stared at the floor.

John Fry was a man who quoted the Old Testament more often than he laughed. He was reckoned by the villagers to be a hypocrite. He had a regular but small audience in the corrugated iron chapel. By trade he was a buyer and seller of horses and cattle. He owned several cottages in the village.

Nearly every Saturday for the past month he had been coming to the cottage, to read from the Old Testament to Mrs. Nye; and before, during, and after the reading he had been thinking of Dolly, who was obvious and downright in her attitude of dislike for him. The effect of this negation of his desire was to increase his religious intensity; and his hopeful passion afterwards. Sometimes, coming upon her washing up plates and cups in the backhouse, he had attempted, in his dejection, to embrace her; she had always sprung away, angrily.

Once she had taunted him about his religion, which taunting immediately restored his religious earnestness.

He felt dumbly distressed because she would never listen to him reading and explaining about God's Word; he could never understand why she did not love him. One day, he thought, she would lose her stubborn pride, and truly repent of her sins; and in that day, he believed, she would yield and love him.

To Dolly, John Fry was entirely repulsive. Often she said things to him that she regretted afterwards, until she imagined his sandy eyebrows and hair, his red face, his thick cold hands, the celluloid collar round his neck with the grey rubber covering worn and frayed where his chin scraped, and the dirty mark round the edge. Then she was set against him again.

John Fry blew and sucked at the teacup. Old Mrs. Nye munched a great quantity of bread and butter. Before she had swallowed the last mouthful of one piece she made shrill requests for more. She drank a lot of tea, her brown seamed throat showing every laboured gulp.

Jack sat on the horsehair-stuffed sofa beside Willie. Dolly listened to Willie as he imitated Rattlethrough taking 4a in French. ' "Ar key—ay ler toor? Sayta moy mersewer." Then he jigs his knee as though he's nursing Baby Rattlethrough and chews his ropey moustache, his cheeks like bottled cherries and his eyes like two blue chips off an enamel saucepan. "The Head Master," he hisses through all the cough-ses and sniff-ses——'

At this point in his imitation Mrs. Nye uttered a long wind-noise through her mouth, and gulped some more tea.

' "Coughin', sniffin', and gurkin'," ' muttered Willie, and started to laugh beside Jack, who joined in until the two were rolling against each other helplessly.

'Bad little boy!' said Dolly, lovingly, when their merriment was over. 'I'd whip you if I were your master. I expect poor Rattlethrough is too lenient with you.'

Willie shifted uneasily, disliking being thought a small boy.

'Aiy, that's about it. "Spare the rod and spoil the child".' said John Fry.

In his pocket John Fry had a small Bible, worn at the leathern binding and with grimed pages. He was going to read a chapter of Isaiah to old Mrs. Nye (and he hoped in his heavy desire that Dolly would not go out to the backhouse), as soon as those bliddy boys cleared out. He looked at Willie with dislike and hostility.

'Well, I think we'd better be going now,' Willie was saying, when there came a hesitant fumbling at the string of the door. Dolly looked up quickly, and saw that old Mrs. Nye had not heard. She went to the door, lifted the wooden latch, and whispered; then she came back for some bread and butter which she lumped hastily together with a slice of lardy cake, and took to the door. Outside stood Bill Nye, the crowstarving boy. He grinned at Willie, ragged fringe of lustreless hair over narrow forehead, black eyes quick as a bird's, wide mouth grinning.

'My God, baint I just hungry!' he said, tearing at the food, no longer furtive now that he was full-handed.

'You shouldn't take the name of our Oly Feyther in vain,' reproved John Fry, turning round.

'Oo be yim, mister?' grinned the boy. 'I ain't never seen yim!'

Suddenly the old woman levered herself with skinny silk-smoothed arms from the armchair, saw him, and cried querulously, 'Be off with you! Drive'n out, the young heller!'

The crowstarver slipped out of the door, frayed trouser-ends and oversize coat flapping round him. Mrs. Nye had never forgiven her dead grand-daughter for having had a child out of wedlock.

'Pauper spirit,' laughed Jack.

Willie listened to the heller's whistle as he went out of the garden. It died away, and faintly through the window came the song-talk of the goldfinches among the apple trees, reedy and wistful as they made their love.

'I can't breathe in this house,' muttered Willie. Bidding good-bye to Dollie and Old Bob, he went quickly out of the cottage.

'Jack,' he said, outside the gate, 'I've been thinking. I don't believe in God!'

He felt, a little anxiously, that he was very bold to declare his disbelief so definitely. 'Jack, do *you* believe in the Bible? I believe it's just made up by what men have thought in the past.'

'You oughtn't to say such things,' said Jack, seriously. 'You might be struck dead for it.' He added, 'Then I should never, never have another friend.'

'Jack,' said Willie, putting his hand on his friend's shoulder. 'I'm sorry I was such a swine in the spinney.'

'That's all right, Willie old man. I'm your friend, and I understand you.'

'Jack, its lovely being friends, isn't it? All our lives we'll be friends, won't we?'

'Willie, you know I'd die for you,' said Jack, looking away.

'I would for you too,' said Willie; but he was thinking of a face that was slowly drawing his heart out of his breast.

OPENING OF THE FLOWER

'It grows, ah, yes, it grows! How does it grow?
Builds itself up somehow of sugar and starch,
and turns mud into bright colour and dead
earth into food for bees, and some day perhaps
for you, and knows when to shut its petals. . .'

RICHARD JEFFERIES, in *Nature and Books*.

Chapter 9

SHINING lines of ripples drew out slowly from the pointed wooden floats of the catamaran, the flat green leaves of the water-lilies seemed to be gliding slowly past. The Longpond lay silent in the summer morning; the sun-splashes in front, seen through the lashes of lids closed in dreamy contentment, were like glittering birds in flight. A wood pigeon was cooing in a fir tree on the distant shore, and a family of blue titmice wheezing and saying, *chitter-chee, chitter-chee*, as they flitted among the willows leaning out of the bank. So peaceful was the shining water, with the faint haze of the summer morning not yet cleared by the sun high over the beech trees: the blinding spiky sun into which the swallows flew and vanished. So far in the blue air were they flying that the boy sitting still on the cracked wooden seat above the two floats could hear no sound of their twittering. It must be like this after death, he thought, seeing the blue of heaven in the water beside him.

The pigeon ceased its cooing. He could hear the beats of its wings as it rose over the trees. Silence and the bright flicker among the placid lily-leaves; only the last drops from the paddle across his knees striking, each with a tiny musical note, on the water. How happy I am, he thought; and looking into the water, watching the drops running silvery down the green broad leaves of the lilies, he smiled sorrowfully to himself. The holidays had seemed to lie away in everlasting summer on the last afternoon of term, so everlasting that with a slight feeling of void he had said goodbye to his friends of 5b on that golden afternoon. And lingering behind, how quiet and empty had appeared the lobbies and the classroom. Even the porter had spoken nicely to him, finding him wandering around. Going away anywhere particular Maddison? Yes Porter, I'm going to Hayling Island with my London cousins for the first fortnight. Well, I hope you enjoys yourself, and don't get into mischief, that's my tip. Now if you've done I'll lock up the classroom, young feller. Goodbye, Porter. I hope you have a nice holiday. Huh! My work begins now! What with the roof being done, and the painters coming along. Oh, I'm sorry. Well, goodbye, Porter. Ages and ages ago that had happened; all the bright, prolonged happiness of August lay between.

August—the long long golden days, that once had seemed everlasting—August was already past! The holidays were nearly over, and soon the summer would be gone. Another summer almost gone, he thought blankly. And he was sixteen—sixteen—so very old!

Where were those other summers now? Each with its happy, happy memories, and all ended now for evermore. He was growing up, and he wanted never to grow up; never to stop making fires in the spinney, and on Heron's Island with Jack, or wandering with Jack in moonlight and sunset, in the frosty star-light of winter evenings coming home from school.

One more term, and Jack would be leaving school; only one more term! To call for him on his new three-speed bicycle at Skirr Farm, to set off together along the Colham road, and race against the motor: to rush down Colham hill after school, or on half-holidays to the playing-field, for footer in winter and cricket in summer: to the swimming bath beside the river. No more, for Jack was leaving at Christmas.

O water, shine always—O trees, be green forever with these same leaves—O summer cornfield, wave with wheat forever and ever as thou wavest this morning when Jack and I walked through you, and I was nasty to him, and we quarrelled—O summer sun, shine on our homes forever like this, and shine on our friendship.

The points of the floats were now held by the lily-leaves, and the catamaran was very still. Through the trees, far away as though from another country, came the whirring of the reaper, cutting the corn in the Big Wheatfield.

Two dark eyes gazed at him steadily from the dark water between the floats, seen between his knees; the eyes became dim, and vanished slowly, and tiny musical notes were struck between his bent head and the faithful water-wraith beneath. He sighed, and felt happy, and said out loud,

'Well, if Jack would rather go after rabbits, let him go. I don't care. I will race by myself.'

It was lovely to be all alone on the Longpond!

With an involuntary shout he seized the paddle lying across his knees, and dug one blade into the water, then the other. The pointed floats of the catamaran dipped into and sheared the surface, the fore and aft cross pieces creaked, and the wooden seat swayed. Since the floats were half-rotten, and the securing screws rusty and loose in the woodwork, the catamaran was an unsafe vessel, and its use was forbidden: therefore it was a thrilling feat to navigate it. Even more unsafe was the birch-bark canoe resting on the black mud by the ruinous boathouse, for, besides being equally ricketty, it was bored by beetles, and in use was a seive which slowly filled. It was agreed between them that the catamaran was Willie's, while the canoe belonged to Jack; actually they were the property of Colonel Tetley, but that old squire had never been to the lake since the suicide, years before, of his young wife.

Sometimes the two friends had races in their craft. Jack was usually the winner; but the previous evening Willie had challenged him to a race up the eastern shore and down the western shore, a race which he was confident of winning, since the canoe would travel slower and slower as more water poured through the beetle-holes. Jack had agreed, and shown keenness; but in the morning he had wanted to stay in the Big Wheatfield, to hunt rabbits with a stick. Willie had accused him of selfishness, and Jack had retorted, 'Well, I like that! Considering we always do what you want to do. Mother says its you who are selfish, and I'm not sure she isn't right!'

'Well, if you like to get out of your promises like that, by appealing to what your mother says—'

'But think, Willie. We can race in the Longpond any old day, but we don't often get a chance of hunting rabbits.'

'You can murder little rabbits if you like, I'm not going to.'

'Don't talk so mazed. You're usually keen on rabbiting, and don't mind catching fish on hooks. Besides, who trapped the owl to stuff last winter? Not that I object, but—'

'Jack, did you mean I was selfish?'

'Well selfish was wrong, perhaps, but you *are* self-centred a bit, you know, man, aren't you? What the Old Bird calls an eg—egosist—'

'Pooh, you can't even pronounce it! Anyone would think you had swallowed a directory!'

'Ha, laugh at Mad Will! "Swallowed a directory!" Any fool knows that it is dictionary! You make me laugh,' replied Jack bitterly.

'It was a slip of the tongue. I meant to say dictionary.'

'Well, keep your wool on.'

'I am keeping my wool on.'

'Liar!'

'Liar! Lout!! Thick-skulled farmer's boy!!! '

'Maddison,' said Jack quietly. 'My mother says you're the rudest boy she knows. And now I agree.'

'Temperley,' said Willie, in a quiet voice, 'do you mean to say that you back-bite your friend like that, and talk about him behind his back—'

'Now don't be silly, Willie. You know—'

'Very well then, Temperley, I will go away. I apologise for

my rudeness. And for my ego—egot—my selfishness. Good-bye, Jack. I wish you jolly good luck in the world. Sorry I'm so rude. Good-bye.'

He had walked slowly away. Jack followed urging him not to be an ass. Why couldn't they have the race another day? But Willie went on without speaking.

'I say, man, I'm sorry that I annoyed you,' said Jack, making another effort as he followed his friend along the right-of-way. 'But I didn't mean to. I'm a silly fool to say such things. Mother didn't mean it to be nasty, you know that. Look here, let's make it up; its so silly to quarrel. Look here, I'll come and have the race.'

'I'm not interested in it now. I'll get my bike and go into Colham, I think. I know who would like to come and navigate the canoe.'

'Who?'

'Bony Watson,' replied the other.

Jack stopped. Willie looked at him. Jack had gone pale. A pain was in Willie's heart, but he joyed in it.

'You mean that?'

'Yes. I can rely on Bony Watson.'

Jack had turned away; and Willie had soon returned, but to pass his friend in silence over the new stubble. He had passed along the lane a few minutes afterwards, riding his bicycle, as though going to Colham; but at the junction of the turnpike road he had turned in the other direction and pedalled until he came to the woods. Hiding his bicycle behind the tall hazel hedge, he had crossed the fields and coverts and rested by the tree on which he had cut the initials more than a year ago. He had looked at the cuts for a while in silence, and then gone on down to the Longpond. For an hour he had wandered around the lake, and then he had taken out the catamaran.

Willie sent the catamaran along with steady racing thrusts, and soon he had crossed the belt of water-lilies called the

Sargasso Sea, and come to the shallow water before Heron's Island. The island was about a quarter of an acre in extent, with willows and alders growing on it. On the south-west side was a small stony beach strewn with sticks, feathers, shells of fresh-water mussels, and almost enclosed by sedges and reeds. A heron rose up flapping as the catamaran came round the south side; a flight-feather fell spinning and gliding under its long thin hanging legs.

'Good morning, old heron! Bags I your feather!' cried Willie to himself as gingerly he stepped on a float, and so to the beach. 'Many thanks. It will make a ripping float for roach.'

It was much nicer being alone, he thought, lying on his back on the dry beach stones, his coat and shirt flung off for the sun to burn his skin. He felt himself spreading into the sunshine, which seemed to suspend his body in its warm, yellow-red power beyond his shut eyes. The swallows must feel like that in the height of the sky, only they would feel themselves colourless, like the air. Ah, that was the best thing in life, to let yourself spread into the sunshine until you were part of it.

'But I am part of it!' he said aloud, and sat up, astonished by his thought. 'The sun makes all things out of itself, and therefore all life is sunshine!'

Delighted with this idea, he stood up, and began hurling stones into the water with all his might. Then fastening his braces round his waist, he pushed through the undergrowth of willows and wild parsnip to explore the island. Jack and he had landed there many times, but he had never yet looked at it carefully: he must make a map of it, putting in the mud-shoals and the sunken branches—no, a chart was the correct word. A chart with soundings, like the one he had seen in the parlour of the public-house on Hayling Island a fortnight before, when spending a holiday with his Aunt Ellen and his London cousins, while his father had gone to Ireland fishing.

The chart had been lined all over like the grain which stood out on the oak table in Skirr farmhouse after the hundreds of years of scrubbing, each line numbered with the depth of water in fathoms. And that steam pinnace, with its polished brass funnel, beside the floating pier at the North End of the Island, bringing the naval officers to play golf. What a glorious life, to be a naval officer! Plenty of time to go looking for nests in the Spring, and you could explore all the creeks along the coast if you wanted to. If you were a captain of a ship you could go away for weeks fishing in your pinnace, with no one to stop you. Lovely to be in the Navy.

During the first week of the holiday Willie and Phillip had been very keen to become sailors, after watching the searchlights of the battleships on night manœuvres off Spithead, the flashes of the great guns beyond the Isle of Wight, and hearing the mighty reverberations tumbling in from the sea. He and Phillip had talked about running away to Portsmouth and joining the Royal Navy, for the war that one day would start between Germany and England. Glorious to fire the big guns and blow the tin-pot German Navy out of the sea!

Willie and his cousin had gone fishing in a small boat, and the day had been breezy, and both boys had been sick, and that had been the end of their plans for running away.

A blackbird fluttered away before him, shrilling an alarm. Elderberry trees, planted by birds, grew thickly in the middle of the island. Among the elderberries stood a hut, roughly made of branches and roofed with bracken. Black circles of old fires were before it, and the charred carcase of a moorhen in baked clay, among half-burnt and broken potatoes scattered about—the remains of previous expeditions.

Down by the edge the willows grew out, some of the mossy trunks level with the surface, others partly submerged. The shadows of the leaves made a soft maze in the water, like many moths fluttering dim wings among the weeds. He peered for perch, but the fish were idle and out of sight; no use fishing until the evening.

A noise like a kiss sounded over the bright and level water, and looking out, he saw a brown fin among the flat oval water-lily leaves. The fin glistened as it slowly moved. As he watched, there was another sound like a kiss, and another fin glistened near the first. He saw ripples, and a blunt brown snout; and heard the noise again.

The carp were sucking some grubs or insects from the lily-leaves! Here might be a chance to catch one! Father had said once that the way to take a carp in summer, when they were basking on the top of the water, and idly sucking at insects or caddis-grubs, was to throw with a fly-rod a brandling worm on a small hook and a light gut cast, so that it dangled over the edge of a leaf. If only he had a fly-rod there, and if only Jack were with him! The scores of times they had fished in the Longpond for the giant carp, and never had a bite!

He must rush home and take one of Father's fly-rods: it would be no good asking Father to lend it, because Father would say no, as he did nearly always; and when he did lend a thing, it was usually only after so many questions and conditions, and telling him what a careless boy he was, that he preferred not to ask. He would put it back in the gun cupboard afterwards, and Father would never know.

A moorhen was paddling near the catamaran as he rushed back. On seeing him it flew in heavy flight, legs trailing in the water, to the shelter of the reeds, into which it scuttled. Forgetting his shirt and coat, Willie pushed out his craft, and crept aboard. With controlled excited strokes of the paddle —lest the carp be disturbed—he made for the boathouse. About ten lengths from the shore he heard his name urgently called, and turning round he saw Jack beckoning him from behind an elder tree.

'Quick! Hurry! I've got some frightfully important news!'

The catamaran was almost upset by Willie's efforts to reach the shore. Twin waves curled under the sharp bows of the floats. So fast did he travel that he hit the mud before he realised he was inshore, and fell backwards into it. Floundering and splashing to his feet, with rotting leaves and mud stuck to his neck and the back of his head, he asked what had happened.

'The Old Bird is coming! I saw him as I came down past the rabbit warren!'

Willie stood irresolute.

'What shall we do?' asked Jack.

'Quick!' replied Willie, 'take the catamaran! To the Island! I'll follow in the canoe!'

'But—'

'Do what I say!'

He leapt into the mud to his knees, and lugged at the stranded canoe.

'Willie, I'll—'

'Go on, I say!'

'Right.'

Jack clambered on board the catamaran.

'My God, I'm stuck!' gasped Willie, trying to pull out one foot, and wrenching a sinew. 'Oh damn, damn, damn, is he coming? I've got no shirt on. What will he say?'

'Pull yourself up by the branch overhead!'

'I can't reach it. Yes I can! If he says anything, swear a tramp stole my shirt!'

'Perhaps he isn't coming this way after all,' said Jack.

But Willie had wrenched one leg out, and was already stepping into the canoe. Pulling steadily, the other foot came out with a loud *plop!* he hung to the branch, and poising, he dropped suddenly into the canoe, balancing his weight with his hands on the gunwales.

'Good man!' cried Jack, as Willie picked up the paddle and dug into the shallow water.

'Quick, for God's sake,' cried Willie in a quavering voice. 'Fast as hell!'

They arrived at Heron's Island together. Now laughing in the greatest excitement, they abandoned their craft and dashed into the undergrowth.

'Spiffing adventure!' cried Willie, flinging himself down behind the hut. 'I wish I had my catty!'

Chapter 10

THEODORE WILLIAM RORE, ESQUIRE, M.A. (LOND.), B.SC.,
F.R.H.S., F.R.G.S., Headmaster (as he was described in the
Prospectus of Colham Grammar School)—Master of Arts and
Bachelor of Science of London University, Fellow of the Royal
Historical Society, Fellow of the Royal Geographical Society
—made it a duty to walk at least eight miles every day during
the vacation.

He loved trees, and frequently exceeded the minimum of
eight miles in his walks out to Rookhurst Forest. The thick grey
trunks gave him a sense of calm strength and endurance, akin
to that inspired in him by the ancient cathedrals of France.
Sometimes he walked on the downs, always alone; the pressure
of the immemorial turf underfoot tauntened his mind for the
problems, chiefly of a mathematical nature, he set himself for
his pleasure. He was sixty-four years old, but a reasoned and
ordered life after (he told himself) the illusions of youth and
the scorpions of Rehoboam's young men had given way to
saner estimates and the tranquillities of maturity, had kept
him in bodily and mental perfection. 'Work is the greatest
good' was often in his mind and discourse.

With an even tread, and head held high, and holding his
hard black hat—between a bowler and a tall hat—in his hand
to bare his temples to the morning, Mr. Rore walked along
the old swine-path leading through the fields from Colham to
Rookhurst Great Forest. As a duty to his body he breathed,
for the first half mile, deep draughts of the air not yet charged
with the heat of the harvest sun. He felt his heart respond to
the exaltation of the early morning. After the prescribed

distance he breathed more naturally. He had tauntened his body like a bow, and his head was clear as the æther. Mr. Rore looked around him benevolently.

After an hour and a half he reached the western end of the forest, sat down on a fallen trunk, and took a volume of Plato from his pocket. Certain marked passages of this he read swiftly, sufficient to stimulate his fixed ideas. So effectual was his concentration that all sounds around him disappeared. He was communing with the philosopher and Socrates his friend; listening to their talk, as calmly and with measured words they expounded their doctrines and their thoughts, while the sunlight beat on the temples and the doves fluttered about the marble columns. From afar came the murmur, as within a phantom shell, of a cerulean sea lapping the Phelerum Bay. Young and ardent men with fearless eyes and noble brows were listening to the discourse upon the Martian Hill, learning that life was beautiful if controlled by the mind, that virtue was knowledge. Then the condemnation and death of Socrates; the flight of Plato; his escape from slavery in Syracuse.

Mr. Rore read on, sitting on the thrown tree in ambient sunshine and shadows gently blown. A little bird came to the log calling, *sip-sip-sip*, taking no heed of the still figure who looked up and smiled at it. Reading the *Phædrus* he was strengthened once more in his belief that it was more important to teach than to write. He thought of the *Symposium*, and Plato's interpretation of the love men were gradually led to contemplate in its highest form, in which it appeared as an exalted and spiritual yearning for a super-sensible beauty that could be found only in an ideal world.

He laid the book on his knee, and closed his eyes. He thought of the centuries that had gone, of the centuries of labour and toil all passed into nothingness; the earth so beautiful, with its gifts for the human mind to accept; and still the mentality of the masses was unchanged. More than two thousand years since Plato died, and the thoughts still not acted upon. Greatheart after Greatheart misunderstood and bludgeoned. Hemlock, the cross, the stake—ah! The cultivation of a mentality to enable all to perceive the wisdom of the teachers, to understand the essential sanity of Jesus of Nazareth—the genius that was an absolute balance of mind and sane clarity of vision— and of all those lesser Others, was the highest ideal of Man!

Softly the wind rustled the veined leaves of the beeches above; wild pigeons flew from their hidden loftiness to drink in the shallows by the lake below; from afar came the cries of boyish voices and the whirring of the reaping machines. Slowly the bright-blurred shadows slipped over the ground, obeying the sun burning in unfathomed heaven as when Plato pondered and wrote. The summer morning went on, the boyish voices down by the water and the distant clatter of the reapers ceased. He looked at his watch. Remained twelve minutes before he need commence the return. It took him, he had found, ninety-seven minutes to walk back from the lake. He never ate in the middle of the day. He mapped out all his day, and rarely varied his programme.

He took a pencil from his upper right-hand waistcoat pocket, a pencil in a silver case worn smooth by long contact with a small pair of round-headed scissors. At the commencement of the Christmas term he intended to address his staff in the Common Room, and to give each a copy of a pamphlet setting forth the abstract ideals of Education. He began making notes, using a sort of shorthand he had invented for economy and rapidity, and writing in a very small hand:—

Boy's mind sown indiscrim. seeds ' heredity. Traits ' character raise blossom early or late. In field seeds ' charlock sprout centuries after burial by plough. Poppy, thistle, dock, ragwort, bindweed, etc. Whereas weed-seeding limited, boy's mind has impulses, traits, characteristics to nth, struggling for mastery. Poppy symbol ' sleep and darkness. Wild wantons take nourishment ' civilised grain. If unchecked, enfeeble soil

for *all*. ?Cf. harlotry. ?Stealthy roots ' thistle. Like ideal '
cultivator free soil good grain for mankind, so ideal ' teacher
enrich soil eventual power ' intellect: to *eradicate* weeds of
sloth, wh. if *allowed* to remain result mental pauperism.

Pursuit better than attainment. Happiness but bye-product
of useful activity, as down on peach, or bloom on grape.
Sphinx remains immutable as ever. Riddle' Universe remains
unread. Time increases grandeur of Life's Mysteries. Coper-
nicus displaces Ptolemy in Spiritual World as in stellar
Universe. Light enough for those who *care* to see—about wh.
Tennyson's Ulysses sounds no untrue note.

Danger too much introspection. Witness tragic genius
Francis Thompson. Objective life has its claims. Hardy's
Dynasts a Promethean effort.

The little bird flitted to the edge of the log, and glanced at
the seated figure, still except for one hand, before opening its
long slender beak and pouring out a startlingly loud song.

'Charming,' said Mr. Rore, and at the glint of his spectacles
it flew away. He wrote:—

Nature speaks with many fluted voices. Ours the loss if we
stop our ears. Fitzgerald most musical, most hopeless. *Gather
ye rosebuds while ye may* cannot satisfy. Yet a useful vision' one
facade ' Nature opening up instructive vistas.

Bernard Shaw provocative ' thought. In vain he breasts
bars ' brass. Authentic power contorted.

He slipped the pencil in his pocket, and glanced at his
watch. One minute remaining. He might relax.

Drawing a deep breath, he glanced upwards, and saw the
sky through the green shadowy arches of the topmost branches.
The topmost towers of windy Troy, he thought, and an exaltation filled him. The new term must bring forth greater good!
What should be, shall be!

Rising from the log, he realised how cramped he was; and after stretching himself, he set out briskly for his home in the Old Rectory beside the river Cole. He returned by way of the Big Wheatfield, walking up the slight slope through the tall and rustling cornstalks among which he had noticed the docks and thistles, with their big broken glossy heads, on the outward walk.

In the far corner by the road he saw, as he came over the central ridge of the field, the horses and the reapers, having their dinner. Virgilian pastoral, he thought, seeing one of the men standing with his head well back and drinking out of a two-gallon wooden firkin. Yes, it might be a scene from the Georgics—the ragged children, the binding women sitting in the circle, the beasts tossing their nosebags.

He climbed over the stile into the lane, and saw two boys before him struggling in the dusty roadway. One of them wore the Colham black cap and silver badge; the other wore nothing on his head save a bunch of hair that in an alleged civilisation responsible for the invention of hats was of an unnecessary length. Mr. Rore as he approached stared at them keenly; the one who had no cap saw him and immediately sat down in the dusty roadway. His companion immediately squatted on his stomach, and spread out his arms.

'Now, do you give in, Mad Willie?'

'Cave-cay-cay-vee!' gasped the other. 'Cay-vee, you fool! Cave, I say!'

His adversary commenced to massage his ribs. Willie's eyes seemed to bulge from his head like bottle-stoppers, but Jack continued with his enjoyment.

'Cave! The Bird! Quick!'

'What bird? Shall I put salt on its tail? You don't get me like that, my boy!'

'Mr. Rore, I mean! The Headmaster!' Willie managed to gasp.

Jack paused and looked round. Mr. Rore was standing

behind him, smiling. Jack leapt to his feet, pulled his cap from his head, displaying equally long hair as he did so. His jaw fell and he looked at the ground, then at Mr. Rore, rapidly and many times. Willie continued to lie on his back. He groaned slightly; then seeing that Mr. Rore was smiling, he rubbed his forehead with his hand, and sat up. Realising that all was well, he jumped up.

'Good morning, Temperley. Your hair is very long. Get it cut by a barber sometime, will you?'

'Yes, Sir.'

'Maddison, I perceived that you were groaning. Temperley was perhaps a little rough? The instinct for individual domination is still manifest in us. Evolution is tardy. We must not depend upon evolution solely. Otherwise we follow the mastodon and the brontosaurus to extinction.'

'We were only playing, Sir,' said Willie.

'Ah, yes,' smiled Mr. Rore. 'I would recommend you also to go to a barber and get your locks shorn. Unlike Samson, you would be in no danger of losing energy. But really, boys, you should not play about in the roadway like this. Remember that you belong to Colham School. I trust that you are enjoying your vacation?'

'Yes, Sir, thank you.'

Mr. Rore continued to speak to them as though they were his equals.

'Remember that nothing but play is injurious.'

'Yes, Sir.'

Gravely the Headmaster inclined his head, and continued: 'Make the most of your boyhood. Life is ever fleeting. Happiness haps! Seek for happiness, and we lose it. But you are young now, and should always be happy.'

'I am happy, Sir,' said Willie.

'Of course, of course!' smiled Mr. Rore.

'So am I, Sir,' said Jack.

'Nevertheless there are sharks and tigers in the world boys, as you will find. The pathway to righteous happiness is beset with difficulties. But time passes on swift wings. Well, I must return homewards. Give my compliments and best wishes to your fathers, will you? Good morning!'

'Good morning Sir!' they replied together. Jack raised his cap, and Willie tried to raise a cap that was not there. Fortunately The Bird did not notice. Walking rapidly to the style, they jumped over, to collapse inside the hedge and roll about with helpless laughter.

'You—you—you tried—you tried to raise—you—tried—raise—cap!' gurgled Jack, and collapsed again.

'Sharks and tigers and Old Birds! Happiness haps! Samson! Temperley was perhaps a little rough!' gurgled Willie.

'Stop it!' gasped Jack, aching with laughter.

O, what a glorious morning they had had! Wouldn't he tell the chaps at school about the day when Mad Willie went arse over tip into the mud, and their dash to Heron's Island, and, best of all, The Bird coming out of nowhere, and Willie raising a cap that wasn't there!

'Duck for dinner!' said Jack when their merriment was played out in weakness.

They ran to Skirr Farm with all speed.

Chapter 11

MR. TEMPERLEY did not linger over his dinner. The summit of the year was reached with the reaping of the wheat in the Big Wheatfield, and he was restless to get back to his work. Willie and Jack ate so quickly and heartily that a feeling of surfeiture overcame them before the pudding was brought on the table. But it happened to be merely rice pudding, and unrelieved by jam, so they asked to be allowed to leave the table. Jack's sisters, who in the opinion of Willie were of less importance than the most crumbled oddmedodd—much less so indeed, since wrens' nests had been found in the pockets of those figures of solitude—asked if they might go with the boys; but their mother restrained them, saying that they must wash their faces and brush their hair before going out; and this gave the boys an opportunity to slip out of the house.

They kept behind Mr. Temperley for no reason except that as a parent he was to be treated warily. The sun tremble-glittered high in the sky, and the glare of the white loose dust of the roadway made them screw up their eyes.

'Listen, did you hear that? That was a twelve-bore going off! Probably Big Will'um's gun.'

'Come on!'

Mr. Temperley turned round, saw that they were following, and waited for them. Willie noticed how his face was tanned by the sun, and his eyes a very light blue, like those of Jack.

'Hot work, running!' he remarked, and was silent till they reached the gateway.

In a corner of the field sat two groups of people. It being Saturday afternoon there were, besides the school children, several other men and women in the field. Some of the older men touched their hats to Mr. Temperley, who was a District Councillor and a Vice-Chairman of the Rookhurst Liberal Association. For helping with the tying they would be asked to the Harvest Supper at Skirr Farm, to eat the bread of the 'opening-up the Big Field'. Ever since Skirr Farm was built in the fifteenth century by John Temperley, an old reformed wrecker—that is to say, he became honest and retired inland from, his sea-haunt when he had stored enough money—the first sheaves had been cut with scythes before the reaping began. The grains from some of the sheaves were knocked out with flails upon the oaken floor of the threshing barn, ground by Andrew, the miller, and made into loaves for the harvest feast; everyone tasted of these special loaves and so swallowed the corn's virtue. It was still believed by some old men that the eating of the first corn brought luck for the next year; health to work, and good weather at sowing and reaping— which meant work, and food for their children. Time had seen the decay of the custom, but it still remained at Skirr Farm. Likewise all the water-mills had fallen into disuse save that worked by Andrew Fowler, the miller, in whose pond Big Will'um one evening had shot an otter.

The horses harnessed to the machines had finished their oats-and-chaff, and were tossing empty nose-bags into the air and breathing shudderingly into them. Sometimes a horse stamped ponderously, when one of the long grey flies had pierced its skin to draw its blood. Big Will'um the bailiff, stood by the firkins of ale and cider. On seeing Mr. Temperley he shouted, 'Get on with it,' and touched his hat. They had been friends since boyhood, and often crowstarvers together in the spinney. The old men looking on, who were enjoying an Old Age Pension each of five shillings a week—not long instituted —touched their hats, then went on with the smoking of pipes and spitting.

About a dozen other men, women and boys had come to

look on; among them a mason named George Davidson. He had a prematurely wizened face, and was usually in an intoxicated condition on Saturday nights, when he was liable to sing in a stentorian voice an old song, called, *Why I had to marry the Miller's Widow*. Near him stood Tom Sorrell, the young quarryman who was said to be courting Dolly. Tom Sorrell had been seen talking to her on several occasions when he had come to till Bob Lewis' garden.

Willie saw Bill Nye, and went to him to look at his flintlock, with which he was supposed to be starving the sparrows and finches. The barrel was thick and rusty; the walnut stock, which showed the tool-marks of its fashioning, was riddled with worm-holes. The heelplate was of nicked and dented brass; the ramrod a seasoned ash-shaft. Loaded with a charge of black powder well rammed down and wadded with paper, with half an ounce of dust shot, it was fired into flocks of sparrows and finches settling on the shocks behind the binders. More than once a howl of rage had succeeded the bang of the flintlock, when a reaper had turned round holding his behind, to see a bird-starving boy running away swift as a mouse in rags among the corn stocks. The dust-shot scattered wide, but did no injury beyond thirty yards range.

Bill Nye's pockets bulged. 'I've got two score of chaffbobs', he grinned, producing a dead chaffinch from his pocket, 'I'll eat'm, too, I will!'

What fun, thought Willie, to take the gun to school on the opening of the term, and blow a hole through the school weathercock! Also, to shoot the carp in the Longpond with!

'Lend me your gun, will you, Bill Nye?' asked Willie.

'Aw, 'tes Big Will'um's gun,' grinned Bill Nye.

'Well, you can get over that, surely! Look here, I don't want it immediately. When they've carried the corn will do. I'll give you a penny, and a tart if you call to-night.'

'Noomye! Bailiff will trim me up if he knows I've lent'n.'

'Rot, of course he won't. Be a sport, Bill Nye. We're friends, you know.'

'I daren't do it, maister!'

'Not for twopence?'

Bill Nye showed his teeth and shook his head like a dog.

'Threepence, and that's all you'll get!'

'Aw darn, but I oughtn't to lend it.'

Jack caught his arm.

'Come behind the hedge,' he ordered. 'Now look here Bill Nye, you've got to lend us the gun and the powder horn and shot, see? And what's more, you'll get nothing if you're not careful. And if you split I lick you, see?'

'No, Mas' Jack, Bill won't tell.'

'Right! When they've carried the corn, we'll come for the gun in the spinney, see? You'll hide it there, and if Big Will'um asks where it is, say you can't find it, see? It will be quite true, because you won't be able to find it. See?'

'Yes sir.'

'And you'll tell no one?'

'No sir.'

'Right, now hop off.'

Jack kicked him half-playfully, and Bill Nye slipped through the gap in the hedge.

'Poor little devil,' said Willie, reflectively.

'Don't you believe it! That's the way to treat them, Willie! He's a damned grawbey, and nothing more. Anyhow, we'll get the gun; that's the chief thing!'

They went through the hedge gap and joined the others, noticing that Dolly was sitting there, and also John Fry, standing near her. His dog-cart stood by the gate, the pony's bridle hitched to the post.

'Old Bob be coming this afternoon,' said Dolly to Willie.

'I wonder if parson will be coming, too?' said George Davidson, one of the King's Arms wits, glancing round at Dolly and then at John Fry.

'Aiy, he may, there's no knowing,' replied Dolly, understanding what he meant. 'And then again, he may not.'

'Be Ould Gramma Nye coming?' asked George Davidson, as though seriously. Dolly's straight reply had abashed him.

'Aiy, if she bean't broke in two,' replied Dolly.

They cackled with laughter, and George Davidson wiped his beer-stained moustache with the back of his hand. He felt rather nervous of Dolly's tongue, but was in a reckless mood.

'Then the parson will bury 'er in a couple o' boxes!' he remarked.

An instant shout of laughter from wide and open mouths, which revealed rows of rotten teeth and brown stumps. 'Then perhaps her feet will go upwards, and her head downwards!'

The wizened mason felt flattered by the guffaws that followed his four jokes.

'Reckon Jim Holloman will come back?' said one of the women.

There was immediate silence. Heads moved quickly as they looked at one another. Dolly was holding in her lap an old straw sun-hat, around which that morning she had twisted some purple scabious; and when the name of Jim Holloman was mentioned she went pale and looked at the flowers before her, which were drooping and beginning to wither. Slowly her fingers pulled a flower-head to pieces.

'What be that to do with you, Lizzie Boon?' she said, looking up suddenly.

'I were only asking. Time Jim Ollomun come back to you, ban't it?'

'Shut your rattle,' growled Tom Sorrell, the lime-burner, suddenly. He lived by himself in the tin-roofed cottage in the quarry beside the Colham road. The cottage was cold in winter and hot in summer, but it could not be thatched owing to the danger of fire when the kilns were pouring out their flames. His clothes and hair were generally covered with fine lime-dust, which made his blue eyes permanently inflamed—a thing which had aroused the sympathy of Dolly when first he had come to work in the garden.

The woman called Lizzie Boon was one of the daughters of the landlord of the King's Arms, and John Fry used to walk out with her until about eighteen months previously.

'Well, 'tes true!' declared Lizzie Boon. What was true was not clear to Willie; but he knew that Lizzie had been jilted by John Fry.

'I don't trouble!' she added, bitterly. 'Her can have 'n for all I care, the dirty troll, that's all she is, and I don't care who hears me say it!' Like some of the others in the field, she had been drinking.

Dolly got up and smacked her face. Lizzie Boon, screeching some obscene words, which caused Willie secretly to flinch, hearing them spoken by a woman, clutched the younger woman's hair. The others laughed and got out of her way. Tom Sorrell interfered, and she spat in his face. He pushed her away, and John Fry, who had been watching and listening nearby, ran up to him.

'Don't you touch a woman!' he cried.

'You be withered to flames,' shouted Tom Sorrell.

Both John Fry and Tom Sorrell were big men. The scar on Fry's head, where a horse had once bitten him, glowed livid. Willie saw a vein knotting itself on his temple.

'Now just you be off!' said Tom Sorrell, in the loud voice of one controlling himself not very easily. 'I don't want no interference from your sort of man. Just you be off, while you can, John Fry, preacher or no preacher.'

The tone of his voice made Willie realise, to his disappointment, that a fight was unlikely between them.

'I'm a better man than you be, anyway,' declared John Fry, in a shaking voice. His nostrils and eyes were opened wide.

'May be, may be not,' said Tom Sorrell. 'Now just you take yourself out of it. Us knows all about your sort, John Fry.

And you too, Lizzie Boon. If you please. I'm asking civil, now. If you please.'

Tom Sorrell took the briefest glance at Dolly, and then turned his back on John Fry and walked away.

John Fry, after staring at Tom Sorrell's back, also turned and walked away. He reached the gate, snatched at the reins, jumped into his cart, and lashing his cob, went down the road at a canter. After a minute's pulling and jerking at the mouth of his horse, he went on at a trot, regretting savagely that he had interfered on behalf of one who knew not God's Word. He groaned as he thought of Dolly as a woman of Babylon. 'For by means of a whorish woman a man is brought to a piece of bread. Can a man take fire in his bosom, and his clothes not be burned?' So he went home, where a little old and shrunken woman, who cooked for him and cleaned his house, took upon herself the weight of his misery. A flush came to the old woman's cheek as he cursed her, and her eyes that with the years had shrunken into their sockets grew shiny with her anguish. But she continued to mend the sock she was darning; the house was clean and fresh, for all the love in her heart went in work to make John Fry happy. She forgave him everything he said and did, and believed in him with a passionate faith that nothing disturbed; and nightly she prayed to the Dear Lord that He might spare her many years to work for him; for she was John Fry's mother.

Chapter 12

No more the rustling yellow grain in the Big Field bowed and returned to the wind. Morning gossamers strung with dew like silvery dust-shot tangled the stubble, and weighted the clover leaves growing between the stalks. It was beautiful and calm in the morning, when the sun stood over the beech wood in a mist of its own blinding fire, and the sounds from far away farms came distinct on the September air. From the autumnal light and air, from first discolouration of leaves and the passing of the corn, from the early withering of long grass in the hedges and the red berries of the bryony, the boy made a mood of sad tranquillity and resignation which he enjoyed as he lingered on the way to meet Jack every morning. And the days of the holiday lapsed slowly, and yet so swiftly, until the last day came.

'We must do something extra special to-day, man,' said Willie to Jack as they left the farmyard, their pockets stuffed with apples. 'Hullo, there goes Bony Watson! Bony! Hi! Bony, where be goin', midear?'

'Hullo,' said Bony, languidly swinging an immensely long leg over the saddle of his tall squeaking bicycle, and dismounting. 'I buzzed over to see how yu chaps were getting on.'

With his be-spectacled, skull-like grin, he leaned over them, appearing almost to sway on account of his height and thinness.

'Here, I've got something to show you chaps,' said Bony. 'Only we must go in a dark place first.'

Mysteriously he led the way into a linhay, and, in the dimness of the tallat, or loft, Bony pulled a young owl from his pocket, kicking with feathered legs and snapping beak with displeasure. However, it appeared to know him, as it sat upon his shoulder and stared at them with dark and solemn eyes. Its master made a weird noise with his lips, explaining that he was talking to it, and a shrill chirping came from the owlet's beak. It was asking for food.

'Here you are, Clarence,' crooned the boy. 'Here's his little mousie, then.'

He took a dead mouse from his other pocket, and held it up before the owlet, who gulped it into its crop.

'Owls are the loveliest birds. Let's form an Owl Club,' said Willie, suddenly. 'Just us three, and perhaps Rupert Bryers.'

'Poor old Rupert's got diphtheria,' announced Bony. 'So feeling lonely with only Clarence for company, I thought I'd look you chaps up. He won't come to school on the fourteenth, of course!'

'Lucky old Rupert!'

'I don't know so much. He's had a hole cut in his neck. He nearly pegged out .'

'Good Lord.'

They whistled at the thought of Bryers almost dying. Whoever would have thought it? Bryers! Good Lord!

'About the Owl Club,' said Willie, after a pause, as he stroked the soft head of the owlet, finding that although it looked enormous, in reality the owl had a small body, 'Let's have one. I vote that Jack and me, you and Rupert be in it. And in after life, when I'm known as the Birdman of Britain, and you, Bony, as the—the—the—oh, I fail to guess your secret.'

Bony grinned.

'I shall be the authority on stuffing animals and dissecting bodies at the British Museum.'

'And Jack here is the most famous angler, having caught an eighty-pun' pike after two hours' fight in one of those great sullen lakes in Ireland'—Jack whistled softly at the romance if it—'and Rupert is the Poet Lorry—you—know! Well, when all that's done, and we're famous, then we'll meet in this very linhay once a year and have a picnic!'

'Rather,' yelled Bony, 'and I shall have a house full of owls and hawks and jays.'

'We'll train an army of them to tear Rattlethrough and The Bird to pieces!'

'And Taffy!'

'And old sarcastic Hoxy Waugh.'

'Not Old Scratch though!'

'No. Nor Bunny.'

'By the way, you haven't done any holiday task, have you?'

'You've guessed my secret. Beastly old muck, Southey!'

'Nor have we. Good!'

Southey's *Life of Nelson*, with Book VI of Vergil's *Aeneid*, had been given to 5b as a holiday task by the Headmaster.

After they had smoked a Woodbine cigarette each, the more enjoyable since Jack's house was so near, Bony said he must be getting on. The owlet called Clarence, with protesting snaps of beak and silent flaps of tawny wings—not long sprouted from bluey-gray quills—was urged into Bony's pocket, and that six-foot youth, his face tanned by the sun, shook their hands and heaved away on his fixed-wheel bicycle, turning round many times to wave to them before a corner hid him; and long after a view of him was possible, they heard the shrill squeaking of his machine—or as Willie suggested, it might have been Bony and Clarence singing to each other.

The hollow, unreal next morning arrived. Willie, in reply to his Father's questions at breakfast, assured him that he had had a fine vacation. Mr. Maddison asked him if he had done his holiday task.

'Yes, Father.'

'That is curious, for I notice that the dust is still on your satchel, which is in the same corner you flung it in when you came home at the end of last term. Why *must* you lie to me?'

'I did look at the books,' mumbled Willie, uncomfortable and longing for the meal to end.

Afterwards he picked up his satchel, emptying out several rulers, wooden penholders with nibs crossed or broken, two darts made of pens, a broken pencil, and some small withered apples nibbled by mice. And the beastly books. Putting the things back again, including the apples, which would do to bung at the fat little porter at the level-crossing gates, he slung the leather satchel over his shoulder, picked up his cap, and prepared to leave the house.

'Well, I shall see you to-night, I expect. Don't be late. And by the way here is something for you. There's Jack coming, looking like a wet week. What a big chap he is! Good-bye,' and Mr. Maddison, after placing something in his son's hand and waving loosely to Jack, shuffled into the hall again in his slippers. Willie saw that his father had given him half-a-crown.

'Good lord,' he said to Jack as they went out of the gate, 'whoever would have thought it? He's a rum devil. I'm damned if I understand him. Curses me one moment for stuffing him up and then tips me.'

They bought two packets of Woodbines at the tobacconist's with twopence of the money, and determined to purchase catapult elastic and gunpowder with the remainder; and half a pound of broken biscuits every day till the small change was exhausted.

The Cerr-Nores were waiting at the Halt for the motor. This vehicle, driven by steam, had a variety of names, the most usual of which was Lazy Lizzy. It was a wheezing vehicle with a high funnel and black oblong narrow body, drawing two coaches each fitted with two long wooden cane-covered seats, one of either side. It was invariably driven by an ancient man with a peaked cap and a long white beard, who had endured stoically throughout the years the taunts of schoolboys and their sarcasms about his personal appearance and the welfare of his motor. Since the installation of the locomotive, innumerable remarks had been addressed to its driver, such as:—

'When's she going to have a baby, Daddy?' apparently sure of the sex of the Great Western Railway Company's property.

'Ma-aa-aa, old Nanny Goat, where's your licence for a performing flea?'

'Mind she don't bust herself with coughing, Grandad!'

'Poor old lady, give her a drop o' gin and she'll fall over.'

'Turn Lazy Lizzie into the fields and she'll sprout horns.'

All of which the driver allowed to pass with an expressionless face, as he saw no humour in their remarks, and "tidden no odds to me what they young limmers rattle'.

Willie and Jack left the sizzling motor at Colham Station and joined the stream of boys flowing along High Street and up the hill to the school. Everyone of 5b whom they met agreed that it was rotten to be back again; that he had had a spiffing time; that his Report had been bad, thank goodness, and he hoped he would not be moved up into 5a.

Soapy Sam, the porter, stood by the main gate to welcome them, wearing his black and red uniform and a cockaded top-hat. With a lucky shot of one of the mice-nibbled apples Willie managed to knock the hat from his head when Soapy was not looking; and Effish, lingering near, managed to be reported to Mr. Rore for the offence. While the classes were assembling for Prayers in Big Hall, Effish stood on the platform, facing the wooden movable wall of 4c classroom, while Mr. Croodrane, tanned of face after his annual muriation at Ilfracombe, thumped out *The War March of the Priests*.

Years before, Mr. Croodrane, nicknamed Taffy, had admitted, when a junior master, that he played the pianoforte and ever since he had been responsible for *The War March of the Priests* while the boys trooped into Hall at nine o'clock, and for the melody of the Latin Hymn, composed by the late Dr. Bullnote, D.D., when they were formed up and Mr. Rore gave the signal. The piano was a strongly-built one, having been made in Germany, but no piano could have withstood for long the assault of Mr. Croodrane's hands. Those hands and fingers, covered with long black hairs, would have been more suited to play the musical logs with the wooden mallet which lay along one wall of the School Museum, gift from some Old Boy who was said to be converting the heathen in a South Sea Island. Several of the strings that Mr. Croodrane banged were mute; a few twanged among pieces of paper, old books, and orange peel thrown inside the piano alongside ancient and split gymnasium shoes.

Mr. Croodrane played the *War March* thrice, continually looking over his shoulder to see if the classes were assembled, and glancing at the Headmaster, standing behind the green-baise table, for the signal to cease.

The Headmaster gave him a swift glance. The *War March* ceased abruptly. A pause, and then the first preparatory bass of the School Hymn in Latin, composed by the late Dr. Bullnote, D.D.

The Headmaster raised his hand: there was a pause: and then the whole school broke into song.

> 'Lum dum dum lum lulu dum dum
> Dum dum lum lum buhu bu rum
> Bahu luha rumrumrum mum mum
> Rum lum lum hum lum lum lum lum.'

they appeared to chant, while the face of the late Head, Dr. Bullnote, D.D., seemed to beam upon the assembly from its portrait in oils above the clock. The little boys with gentle eyes and fresh soft faces in 2c and 2b piped in thin trebles; some of those in middle school sang in a falsetto bass, as though endeavouring to effect a premature break in voices that were still high; boys with recently broken voices squeaked like bats, and boomed like bitterns alternately; the seniors made a vague lip motion, considering it undignified to sing with the rabble, while the Ishmaelites of the Special Class sang a parody composed by a former Special Slacker.

> 'The Old Bird is a moulted crow
> And he will reap as he does sow,
> Hour by hour he cries, "More Power,"
> But when we get it the sun will snow.'

Dr. Bullnote's hymn and its accompanying parasite came to an end; and the Headmaster, closing his eyes and inclining his head, led off the Lord's Prayer in a voice curiously meek and unlike his own. After the *Amen*, he opened his eyes. Three hundred and fifty-seven boys, twelve masters, and one cat called Colham Charlie, who existed to catch mice and eat the scraps of school luncheon, gazed at the pink satiny face with its high domed forehead and thin white hairs; at the drooping moustache hiding the mouth; at the broad shoulders, rounded by the gown; at the large hands placed on the green-baise table before him as his voice, incisive, terse, and resonant, urged the need of hard work and hard play in order to cultivate mental power.

'The holidays are over. Some of you will be sorry, more of you will be not unhappy. Now to work, boys. The only thing of value in this world is work! Why!'—the voice lowered as though scorning imaginary hecklers—'Why, without work, where would we be? Lying on our backs in the jungle, waiting for ripe bananas to drop into our mouths! Some of you no doubt would prefer such a life; an ideal of a soft snug job after leaving school. Boys, don't be pauper spirits! All your days, boys, I urge you to cultivate that mental power. Mind you, the brain won't keep going without sport, so I say to you, when the half-days come, play hard, hard at it, all the time! Then home again, sit at your study tables, and *master* your difficulties. *Ad astra per aspera*,' he apostrophised sublimely. 'Only pauper spirits would fail to be moved by such a thought. Now to your classrooms: make the most of every moment!'

He glanced at Mr. Croodrane, who brought down his hands on the notes for the opening chords of *The War March of the Priests*.

With a sudden movement that caused his gown to swirl about him, Mr. Rore turned round and regarded intently the face of Effish, whose soap-bubble eyes regarded him woefully.

'Well Effish, I am sorry to see you here. A bad beginning, Sir!'

'Yes Sir.'

'Why are you here, sir?'

Effish continued to look him in the eyes. 'I don't know, Sir,' he said, dolefully, moving his hands, and letting them fall by his sides again. 'A hat, Sir—Sir—it rolled at my feet—Sir. Porter, Sir—'

'Can't hear! Use your lips and teeth, sah!' cried Mr. Rore, turning his head sideways and listening keenly.

'If you please, Sir, Porter—'

'Foolish boy, foolish boy!' said the Head, facing him again, and chiding with stern gravity, 'to begin the new term so inauspiciously. But you know your sin, apparently, that it is something. You realise you are a pauper spirit.'

'Please Sir, Porter—'

'I heard you before,' replied the Head, earnestly, 'But do not despair. Cease to be a pauper! Now be off, and don't let it happen again!'

'If you please, Sir, Porter—'

'Is the boy ill? Banana mentality, sir. Be off, sir!'

The Headmaster swept off the platform, gown trailing behind him, head held slightly in the air, and his tall, big body moving swiftly and evenly as though floating over the floor. Willie, passing through the door into 5b classroom, turned to stare at him as he passed down the centre of Hall, under the horizontal bar of the gymnasium, past the ladders enwound with the rings and ropes, and so into Little Hall with its model steamship encased in glass, standing on the tiled floor.

'Come along, bor, close the door,' said Mr. Croodrane, 5b form master, genially. 'Ah, Effish, back again from your exalted position, what? Well bors, stop talking. Hullo, the desks have been varnished during our absence. Now'—his mouth opened, and his tongue curled upwards: 5b knew a joke was coming. 'Now there will be no excuse for any bor not sticking to his work this term, ahha, wha'?'

5b roared with laughter. Willie, taking advantage of Mr. Croodrane turning round to conceal how he was laughing at his own wit, flung one of the little apples at Bony and hit him on the head. The wizened apple bounced off and rolled at the feet of Mr. Croodrane.

'That's enough of that sort of thing,' said Taffy, kicking it towards the waste-paper basket. 'The holidays are over, Maddison. Now until the removes are announced, we'll have a few questions on holiday tasks. Maddison shall tell us his opinion of—er—what was it, now? Ah, hum. Southey's *Life of Nelson*. Well, Maddison, what was your opinion of its literary merits?'

'A Classic, Sir,' suggested a boy called Sheppard.

'I was asking Maddison. Well, Maddison? Tell us your opinion of *Nelson*.'

'One-eyed, Sir,' replied Willie, and 5b yelled with laughter. Mr. Croodrane's tongue curled upwards in his open mouth as he regarded Maddison, trying not to laugh. 5b waited. Suddenly the door opened, and Mr. Rore came in, a paper in his hand. 5b froze, Mr. Croodrane's mouth closed, his lounging attitude stiffened.

On the paper were the names of those who had been given their removes to 5a. Every boy heard his own heart beating as he sat quite still in a dark brown new-varnished desk.

Chapter 13

AFTER the dismemberment of the old 5b, Willie remained at his desk, laboriously scratching the varnish with his pen as he traced the outlines of birds, fish, and animals, or deepened the initials and grain-lines gouged by the pressure of hundreds of hands before his own had rested there. After the first day the new arrangement of faces at the desks of 5b was accepted; on the second day it became the usual scene. Jack was gone, sitting in Big Hall in the Special Class, among youths considered by the Headmaster to be the mediocre half-failures of life, and therefore left more or less alone while supposed to be fitting themselves as future wage-earners by learning shorthand, book-keeping, business letter-writing, and a subject which every boy disliked intensely—Commercial French—the instruction of which was given by the dreaded Rattlethrough.

At the end of every hour, when the bell on the corner of the platform opposite 5c classroom was vigorously swung by the bottom boy of the class that happened to have gone to Old Scratch for Latin, Willie trooping with the rest of 5b through Big Hall on the way to the next lesson usually managed to have a word with his friend, or to pass to or receive from him a note. Lucky devil, Jack, sitting there with the Special Slackers, doing nothing. However, Willie was fully happy with Jack before and after morning and afternoon school.

Thursday mornings were the best-liked in 5b. From ten o'clock until half past ten, they had gym under Sergeant-Major Featherstonehaugh, known to the boys as Wheelbarrow. The climbing of ropes and ladders, the turning inside-out on the rings, the exercises on the vaulting horse, the parallel and horizontal bars, made the half-hour as enjoyable as anything done in freedom.

Thursday mornings, in addition, were spent with those masters who were considered not bad, even decent. After gym. 5b went to Mr. Croodrane, who, standing by the door of the Physics Laboratory, always murmured, apparently to the rafters, 'Come along there—don't lag behind you bors— you're always late Maddison, Watson, Macarthy, Sheppard— hurry up, close the door.' The incoming class took a lazy notice of his words, and continued to trickle in the doorway. Some indeed, paused to inspect the pinned sheets of *The Sphere*, *The Illustrated London News*, and *The Graphic*, which Mr. Kenneth, the English master, considerately brought from the Common Room, after three weeks or a month of casual perusal by the Masters; thus the boys were enabled to know what had gone on in the Great World Outside seven or eight weeks before.

Those who paused did so fully aware of the risk they ran of being rapped on the skull by the knuckles of Mr. Croodrane's large and heavy and hairy hands. Mr. Croodrane was burly and dark, an old Rugger Blue, with a moustache like a small furze bush on his enormously long upper lip.

'Come along there d'you hear—don't prevaricate you bors —hurry up close the door Maddison—take out your homework and stop talking. No Effish you can't have another window open—what d'you suppose the Guv'nus of Colham School supply hot water-pipes for—to heat the air outside with, ahha, wha'?'

5b in a long line fumbling at satchels, laughed easily. Mr. Croodrane, pleased with his wit, opened his mouth and curled his tongue upwards into the cavity. This queer habit had been formed by continual repressions of a desire to laugh naturally before a class.

'No, Sir,' moaned Effish, 'only my head feels rather close in here, Sir.'

'Ahha, um', mumbled the Physics master, 'very probably, um. Very probably'—he looked up and down the line of boys, and 5b knew that sarcasm was coming—'very probably, um. So, I should imagine, would an egg feel when the mother hen is sitting on it. It means that it is getting addled, Effish. Your head feels close, you say, Effish, ahha, wha'?'

5b rippled a forced laugh.

'Yes, Sir, I feel just as if an old hen was trying to addle me.'

The line of boys shook with laughter. Mr. Croodrane's tongue uncurled, resumed its normal position, and then retired into obscurity behind his shut mouth. He frowned, took off his spectacles, wiped them, perched them upon his hairy nose, and frowned again.

'Ah yes, Effish. Little boys should not be impertinent. Come here, little bor—no, no, Effish, don't wriggle away—now then —just remember that you mustn't be—rude—or call out like a craven when retribution overtakes you—now go back to your place. Bors, show up homework!'

Effish returned to the line and held his head, exaggerating the effect of the six clumps he had received from Mr. Croodrane's hand. Nevertheless, his head hurt, for besides having a hand like a foot, Mr. Croodrane wore upon his little finger a big gold signet ring, and even the deep engraving of a heraldric crest with motto did not disguise its potentialities as a knuckle-duster. Everybody hated the ring, and once an Irish boy called Terence Dove had attempted to remove it in the belief that its owner would not notice his action, since he was looking away and his hand was spread out on a bench beside him. On that occasion Dove's head had resounded hollowly to repeated knockings and the pain had made him butt his tormentor in the stomach. Dove had been taken to the Headmaster, and caned; and the next day had been found at Southampton, trying to sign on as a cabin boy. The following day, however, he was back again at school, harum-scarum as before. Taffy had asked the Bird not to punish Dove, it was rumoured; and ever afterwards Taffy was secure in the estimation of the boys.

The Physics master moved down the line of boys, collecting sheets of ruled paper defiled by various diagrams and written explanations which purported to represent an hour's study the night before. He passed quickly from boy to boy, saying— 'Yours?'—'yours?'—'yours?' as he did so. Always he began at the left end of the room, and by a previous arrangement, the top boys, Power, Sheppard, Lonsdale, Manning, Fitzaucher, Walton, Swann, Macarthy, and others who usually had something to show up, gathered at that end. Competition for place was usually intense at the other end among certain boys who usually had nothing to show up.

Mr. Croodrane had passed the tenth boy, and iterated 'yours?' for the eleventh time when Beckelt and Effish, by crawling with silent speed on hands and knees round the benches, appeared suddenly among that section whose work had been collected. Yeates followed, and again the line obligingly shuffled to fill the gap. Dove and Bony came next, and a thin dark boy with brambly eyebrows and piercing eyes called Barnes, whose facial resemblance to a stuffed female sparrowhawk was often commented on by the members of the 'Cigars or Nuts'. 'Yours?—yours?—yours?' grunted Mr. Croodrane. 'Hurry up, don't keep me waiting, Maddison.'

Mr. Croodrane held out his hand, and absently looked away.

'Cannot the star-turn of 5b find his homework?' he enquired.

A few boys tittered.

'You have no examples of the taxidermist's art in your satchel to-day, I presume?'

'Not to-day, Sir!'

'Ahha, but you have your homework instead, no doubt?'

'Yes, Sir.'

Mr. Croodrane passed down the line, holding out his hand,

taking papers and adding them to his sheaf. If a boy fumbled in his haversack he passed on, returning later if he remembered or cared to remember.

When he had passed to the bottom of the line, he returned to Maddison who had recommenced, a moment before, an apparently diligent search for the missing papers. Under the eye of Mr. Croodrane he turned out his satchel on the bench before him, and his catapult with it.

'Ahha!' cried Mr. Croodrane, picking it up, 'our friend Maddison is of a mechanical turn of mind. Now we know how he lays low the fauna of Rookhurst.'

Willie laughed at the humour, not because he thought it funny, but because it was wise to laugh. As he hoped, the tongue curled up in the open mouth; but Taffy drew back the leather sling on the rubber thongs and made playful flips at his head. Willie pretended to be ruefully stung, and therefore chastised, for a catapult was unlawful, and was supposed to be reported to the Headmaster. Meanwhile he searched through various books, until Mr. Croodrane said, 'Well, where is that homework, Maddison!' when he shook the satchel again, opened exercise books, Latin and French grammars, Shakespeare's *Twelfth Night*, and a heavy text book on *Electricity and Magnetism*. At last he made a clucking noise with his tongue, and looked up frowning.

'I'm afraid I must have left it at home after all, Sir,' he said apologetically.

'How careless of you, Maddison,' mocked Taffy. 'But perhaps you brought this instrument instead as an example of your constructive skill, wha'?'

'No, Sir,' replied Maddison in a low and serious voice, 'I brought that entirely by mistake. The cats were howling all last night outside my window, Sir.'

5b shouted with laughter, and Maddison giggled nervously.

'Um,' said Mr. Croodrane, shutting his mouth.

'Honestly, Sir, they were disturbing me so that I couldn't

concentrate as I was doing my homework, Sir,' exclaimed Willie, alarmed.

'Very well, don't waste my time any longer, Maddison. Look for your homework after morning school, or produce its equivalent there, in my room. Perhaps one of your elephants swallowed it in error! Meanwhile, I will add this horrible thing to the Common Room fire at the first opportunity.'

The class tittered, but Maddison had an expressionless face. Taffy's mouldy jokes! Poof! He had nothing to gain by grinning now.

'Put out apparatus,' said the Physics master, laconically.

Golding and Clemow seized various apparatus that rested upon a shelf, and commenced to place them on the benches directed by the master.

Soon upon the mahogany-varnished benches lay Wimshurst machines, Leyden jars, bar magnets, iron filings, rods of steel, brass, vulcanite, glass, and wood, moulting catskins of various shades and patterns, silk and satin rubbers, pithballs, compasses, wet cells connected in series, galvanometers, voltameters, ammeters, and a cumbrous affair of tarnished brass that every boy tried to avoid, called a Wheatstone Bridge.

5b assorted itself into pairs, each pair attaching itself to one end of a bench. Work began. Notes were taken. Conversations were subdued but insistent. Mr. Croodrane continued to stare into eternity, or it may have been the flies on the ceiling. He came out of his trance only when Effish, having persuaded his partner Beckelt to hold the two nickel nobs connected with the tinfoiled glass cylinders of the Wimshurst machine, turned the wheel suddenly with the result that Beckelt yelled with the shock and fell writhing upon the floor.

With stoical indifference their heads were clumped and then banged together, and Mr. Croodrane passed from pair to pair explaining the principles of Electricity and Magnetism. These Physics hours were, with Chemistry, the most liked hours in the week, because there were interesting things to do, space to walk about in, and one could talk. After a quarter of an hour the pairs moved round to the next bench, and Willie and Bony exchanged the rather dull study of magnets and magnetic fields with research among the interesting cat-skins; interesting because by rubbing vulcanite rods violently, and then holding them near the hair of other boys, it drew the hairs down and made the victim's head itch.

Before Bony and Willie left the heavy bar-magnets, Bony placed one on the neck of Aunt Sally, thus giving him a surprise. Of course it was observed and his head clumped. Bony went back grinning that his secret had been guessed. Trying to outshine this ingenuity, Effish emptied some iron-filings down Fitzaucher's neck and was sent to the Headmaster. This casualty produced a remarked if temporary change in the stuffy atmosphere of the laboratory.

Then the third bell sounded, reminding them that another three quarters of an hour with the ten minutes break remained before the welcome visitation to Mr. Zimmermann for Oral French must be made. Quickly the time passed, while the room grew hotter and the plane trees outside loosened their leaves against the water-flawed window panes, and the sparrows in the gutter chirped indistinctly. Effish returned after half an hour, limping almost imperceptibly and with his right hand pressed to his seat as though he suffered pain. He stared pathetically at Taffy, who opened his mouth, curled his tongue, and grunted sardonically. 5b guffawed, not at Effish, but at Mr. Croodrane, for it knew that he had been nowhere near the Sixth Form room.

'Ahha, the penitent returns, Effish, wha'?'

'Yes, Sir.'

'A warning, bors, that we must not play with fire, wha'? Little bors that play with iron-filings, um, around a candle, wha'?—must expect to get their hides tanned, ahha, wha'?'

'Yes, Sir.'

'Of course,' went on the humourist, pausing while he opened

his cavernous mouth the wider, in order, Willie whispered to Bony, to allow more freedom for his tongue, 'of course, our friend, Maddison'—Willie started—'little knows how he plays with fire. Or, shall we say, um, the Siamese Twins, um, Clemow and Hoys. Fire burns, little bors—a good master, but a bad servant, um—as they say. What do you think, Effish?'

'Sport, Sir, surely?' asked Effish, dolefully, holding up his head.

'What were you pleased to say, Master Effish?'

'Sport, a good servant, a bad master, Sir. I fancy you said "fire", Sir.'

'Are you meaning to be impertinent, Effish?'

'No, Sir, indeed no, Sir. The Headmaster, Sir, just this moment remarked those very words to me, Sir.'

Effish took one limping step forwards. The cunning step saved him; for Mr. Croodrane's mouth opened, and the tongue curled up.

'Poor fellow, he can't help it,' said Taffy, with mock compassion.

'Did you really go into The Bird, man?' whispered Willie, when the interlude was over.

'No,' sniggered Effish. 'I've been waiting out in The Bog, and I've hidden the chains of six of the plugs!'

Chapter 14

NOISILY 5b settled in the forms while Mr. Zimmermann awaited them just inside the door of 3c classroom. On other days, the room was usually occupied by a junior master named Ellison, while he took his little boys of 3c class; but Mr. Zimmermann was an intermittent visitor to the school, coming only on Tuesdays and Thursdays to instruct the senior classes in conversational French and German. So, while Mr. Ellison watched his little boys in the workshop reducing with blunt tools small pieces of wood to chips and shavings, his room was filled with senior boys, and Mr. Zimmermann's rasping voice.

Invariably Mr. Zimmermann began his address with a brisk query about whatever French book the class before him was supposed to be reading, but after a minute or so his eyes would lift from the page at the sight of a raised hand, and his voice, earnest and rasping, would enquire what was wanted. To every kind of question he would reply willingly and seriously, unless it were too obviously a ragging question. Many many times had he explained that he had a Bavarian father and a French mother, but no connection whatsoever with what he called *les sacrés prusses*. Every boy in 5b knew what *les sacrés prusses* meant; every boy knew how to roll it off his tongue, with the Zimmermann rasp.

Zimmy was short and spare, with big brown moustaches like one of the lesser swinging oddmedodds, seen on allotments, made of two brown hen's feathers stuck in a potato on a string. His face was shrunken and lined, like an allotment field-track over which many carts had passed. Deep and dark ruts were impressed in groups upon his forehead, his cheeks, and his chin.

He wore, with very tight trousers and a sack-like coat, yellow leather boots that buttoned up and resembled the skins of over-ripe Canary bananas. With the cracked and pointed toecaps of these he sometimes beat a rhythmical tattoo upon the platform of the desk.

5b under Zimmy had an air of luxurious indolence. Some boys fell back upon the old pastime of noughts-and-crosses; others read bloods under the desk or talked with their neighbours. Zimmy was harmless, only feared for his one power, that of ejecting rowdy boys into the 'Eadmaster.

The reading in French and then the translation of prepared extracts of *Lettres de mon Moulin*, would have been a combined problem practically insoluble by 5b, suffering under the double handicap of a full interest in their own boyish lives and not the least interest in the French language, had not Mr. Zimmermann possessed a gratifying habit of doing both beforehand. Perhaps a philosophy bred from his gallo-teutonic blood enabled him to perceive both the futility of all attempts to render the average schoolboy bilingual, and the utility of the salary that such inanities involved.

'Now then,' he began briskly, 'let us get on with our work. Let us see, what page is it? One hundred and one. Ah yes, I have made my mark in pencil. Who must commence, eh?'

Effish raised a hand.

'Ah yes, that's all right,' assented Mr. Zimmermann, and forthwith began to read aloud, while Effish followed.

After a while Macarthy asked permission to speak.

'Please, Sir, would you call this book a prose poem?'

'Ah!' replied Mr. Zimmermann, laying down his book, removing his spectacles, folding them, and holding them in his two hands.

'Ah, that is a question that needs some consideration. Now what is poetry? I think we will all agree that it is more than the mere pretty-pretty. How then shall we judge prose-poetry?

By the massed effect, I think. You will agree with me there, no doubt.

'So far so good. Superficially, the Russians, with the exception of perhaps Tourgenieff, are farthest removed from prose-poetry in their works judged as a whole; nevertheless, I venture to think that by the effect on the spirit they can justly be included in the category mentioned a moment ago by Macarthy. Tolstoy, Tourgenieff, Tchekoff, Dostoievsky—'

'Please, Sir, Poppoffquickski?' asked Effish.

'I read 'im not. Look here. We have Dostoievsky, Tolstoy, Tourgenieff, what prose-poems flowed from the pen'older of that great serene man! *The Torrents of Spring!* And in my mother's country, what men 'ave we? Look here, Molière, Flaubert, the Goncourts, Dumas, Zola. Watson, did you throw that book at 'im? What you mean, I have guessed your secret? Go into the 'Eadmaster! Go on, out of it. Whose turn to continue?'

In an instant the glasses were back on Zimmy's nose; his face rutted and furrowed again; his face sunken into his shoulders.

Effish again interrupted.

'Oh, Sir, we're going to learn *Tannhäuser* for next Speech Day, so I have heard.'

'Ah! Now there is every relationship between the vast sound-dramas of Wagner and the prose epics of the mighty Russians. And, since the spirit of man, as exposed in its greatest artists, is unchanging, at least in our European civilisation, I think we will all agree that the Greek tragedies are correlated with our modern art, literature, music—'

'Do the Germans read Greek and Latin, Sir?' lisped Fitzaucher, tying to be daring.

'The good Germans, yes. But you must take care about differentiation. The good Germans are in the South. The bad Germans are in the North. They are without culture, heavy-minded, superior, stupid, brutal, powerful. The Prussians—'

'Lay sacray proose,' growled Effish.

'Pig-dogs,' chortled Cerr-Nore.

'Ha, yes,' exclaimed Mr. Zimmermann, 'they have not advanced out of brute strength. A hard core, the scoriæ of our Western fusion of ideas, has remained unaffected in the North. But in the South, we are milder, more imaginative. Well, what do you want, Effish?'

'Please, Sir, may I go out? I feel rather faint, Sir. My head hums peculiarly, Sir.'

'Certainly, my boy, certainly.'

'Thank you, Sir.'

Effish shuffled out, coughing dismally.

Zimmy's addresses appeared to 5b as being utter rot, but nevertheless welcome on account of their time-wasting value. Very few of the boys learnt German, which was an additional subject. Fitzaucher, sitting quietly in a desk with a bespectacled and pale boy named Swann, was the only boy who listened to the master's sincere attempts to answer the questions. Sincere: but Mr. Zimmermann had been talking like that, at minor lectures and at other schools, for many years. Art was his chief interest in life.

The lesson continued. Bony Watson returned, with his usual grin. Effish came back ten minutes afterwards licking his lips, and whispered to those near him that he had climbed the lower playground gate and slipped down to Old Mother Vandenbergh's at the bottom of Colham Hill.

Towards the end of the lesson Cerr-Nore's head was in his arms upon the desk and supporting a miniature hat of paper perched grotesquely upon his hair by the boy behind him. Slowly the reading reached the top of the class, Mr. Zimmermann always ready to lead. He believed that to lead was better than to let boys puzzle to remember, which he considered was bad; that to lead them was to familiarise them with the language in its less unnatural form. Fitzaucher and Bryers, who had spent most of the summer holiday together on the coast of Brittany, were the only boys who regretted the interruptions. They wanted to imagine that they were back again in the fishing village above the white cliffs.

During the latter part of the hour, Willie quietly wrote in his *Official Diary of Observations*, exchanging it afterwards, in spite of its advertised privacy, with Bony's briefer *Notes*. Underneath this seeming act of indiscretion existed rivalry, for both wrote paragraphs specially to bluff the other. Thus Willie read in Bony's exercise book:

'I wish I could trust a certain dark chap. But I can't. I would like to take him into partnership next Spring, to share my preserves, as his great friend is leaving. But I daren't. Is he honest, I wonder. Perhaps he would rag my nests. God preserve me from any disillusion. Years ago this chap sold me a carrion crow, young, saying it was a jackdaw. Unclean canine. Also some hen's eggs painted, saying they were peregrine falcons. Dirty dog. But I wish we could be friends. Sometimes he is quite a decent bloke. Wow-wow!'

Willie read this with a pleased feeling, and was sorry he had not been kinder to Bony. Bony would perhaps be hurt by his own entry.

'To-day I found an old magpie's in an ash, unsuspected before. I must mark the place in case a Kestrel's in there next year. Certain fellows in my class are decent, others are rotten. I prefer a certain man to another tall one, because the tall one wrote last year to Colonel T———y asking for a permit. Also to the Dowager Countess of S———e for fishing. These are my preserves. However. It is my opinion that a tree-creeper will nest in a certain rotten tree in a certain spinney next Spring. But I will tell no one, since I can unfortunately trust only Temperley. It is a pity, because I like a

certain very tall chap rather well, and he is in the Owl Club.
I must write no more now. More to-morrow.'

Soon after the surreptitious returning of manuscripts had
been made the bell rang announcing 12-15 p.m., the end of
Morning School. Mr. Zimmermann closed his book, removed
his glasses, and less than a quarter of a minute afterwards had
gone quietly out of the room.

5b draggled back to its own classroom, flung satchels and
books in desks, and rushed out into the playground, to discover that rain was falling and that no football was possible
in the lower playground. Luncheon not being ready until
twenty minutes to one, Willie suggested a quick game of fives.

There was no chance of playing in the fives court, as the
Prefects and senior boys of 5a had the privilege of turning out
boys of the lower forms. Any smaller boys who were there
when any of the mighty Sixth came down, or whose pill happened to roll in while a game was in progress, were liable to
have their pill rooted out of the playground into the road.
Sometimes a ball would be lost like this: it was a standing
grievance which had to be suffered. Some of the smaller
boys therefore, preferred to play against the school walls in
the upper playground, although it was forbidden, masters
objecting to dirty marks and splashes on their windows above
the red brickwork.

Willie was certain that Mr. Rapson had gone home to
luncheon, and so they decided to play against his wall. Jack
served to Willie, who, proud of a smashing stroke he had
perfected, returned it so violently that it entered 4b classroom
with the greater part of the pane. Almost immediately a
casement was opened and an object was poked out—the
well-known object of two bottled cherries glued to a piece of
frayed rope, with eyes like twin chips off a blue enamel
saucepan. The dismayed Jack was thunderously commanded
to be outside the Headmaster's study at two o'clock. Willie

crouching under the window was unobserved. At luncheon—cold beef and mashed potatoes, followed by a slice of spotted dog pudding heaped with white sugar—Jack insisted on pretending that he had broken the window: it would mean not more than two whacks, and since Willie had had the whack only the day before, wasn't it right that, as they shared all pocket money, homework, birds'-eggs, and everything, that they should also share the whack?

Willie made up his mind a score of times to be outside the Headmaster's room at 2 o'clock, to confess that he had broken the window; a score of times the mental vision of Mr. Rore's face dissolved his determination.

At 2 o'clock Jack was standing there alone, unconcerned and smiling. Indeed, he enjoyed the thought of saving Willie from the whack.

Chapter 15

Aт 2-2 p.m. Jack went before the Headmaster; at 2-3 p.m. he was in the study; at 2-4 p.m. he was rising off the yellow chair; at 2-5 p.m. he was leaving 5a classroom.

'Ah, Temperley,' said The Bird. 'My compliments to Mr. Croodrane, Mr. Beach, Mr. Kenneth, Mr. Rapson and Mr. Waugh, will all members of the first and second elevens assemble outside 5a room immediately. The captains of the first eleven to report when all present. Double!'

At 2-10 p.m. the twenty-two boys were lined up outside 5a door, the 1st XI in front, the 2nd XI behind. 'Nosey' Fortescue, the captain of the 1st XI, knocked, went in, and said, 'First and Second teams present, Sir.'

Mr. Rore came out and said, 'There are two vacancies for Colours in each team. Close your eyes, and show hands for your votes. Only one vote each boy. I will call out the names.'

Jack was one of the chosen. The Bird smiled as he congratulated him. At centre half, the pivot of the team, Jack was the admiration of the Lower School. He ran at the ball when rival forwards were advancing; he clashed; he emerged with the ball at his feet. He never flinched.

When Willie played for his House or in inter-form team matches, he rarely, in the words of Taffy, the rugger blue, 'established his superiority over his opponents'. He was a swift runner, and usually played on the left wing; when he had the ball before him, he would go through with it, trusting to his quickness to dodge the weight of the half-backs and backs; but he always avoided a clash if he could. He considered himself a coward, because he always remembered and dreaded

143

the pain of being hacked on the shins, as he had felt two years previously. He would charge a bigger boy with his shoulder; but he flinched from a possible kick.

During his last year at Colham School, Willie did things, however, that confirmed his nickname of 'Mad'. One of his exploits was to lash Bill Nye's flintlock to the railings of the upper playground during one luncheon hour, loaded with a double charge of powder and shot, with the muzzle pointing at the weathercock of the school turret, while more and more boys gathered near in a state of excitement that gave the operator a feeling of daring and coolness.

'One must make one's mark on the school somehow,' he said casually. Sheppard suggested that the flintlock might burst, and wouldn't it be better to tie a string to the trigger and let it off from the comparative safety of the lower playground?

As the mass of boys was moving away who should stroll on his flat feet out of the entrance to Big Hall, but Old Useless, the master on luncheon duty?

'Cave! Cave!' cried the scouts, and made off.

Crying, 'Look out, I'm going to fire it,' Willie ran away with the others, and jerked the string, but nothing happened.

Mr. Worth sauntered towards the railings as though it were the usual thing for a blunderbuss flintlock to be tied there with a knotty mixture of string and rope, pointing at the roof of Colham School. In silence he approached it, and bent his head to peer down the barrel.

'Oh, my God,' moaned Willie, from behind the back wall of the fives court, by the steps to the lower playground. Murder —Policemen—Hanging! He took another glance, and felt stuck to the wall in dread.

'Tell him, someone!' he gasped.

Useless put on his spectacles, and peered more intently.

Then Useless took a penknife from his pocket, and cut the string; and, watched by scores of eyes from various places of semi-concealment, he lifted the flintlock off the railing, and carrying it at the trail, he sauntered back the way he had come, splay-footed, round-backed, ragged-gowned, mournful-faced. They watched him disappear into Little Hall, still carrying the gun.

Willie was in a panic during the remainder of the time before afternoon school. What excuses should he make to The Bird? Trying an experiment about the force of gravity? It seemed a feeble excuse. That he had noticed some rats on the roof, which might be gnawing the fabric—that seemed a good word —the fabric of the Old School, and that he was trying to kill them for the sake of the Governors? That seemed a bit far-fetched. What then?

'Think out something, chaps. Jack, Bony, Hoys, Mac, quick tell me something to say.'

'Say you wanted to present it to the school museum,' suggested Bony.

'And the corpse of Useless with it,' added Macarthy.

'Oh lord, it may go off any minute. Shall I go and warn him? And apologise?'

It was considered the best thing to do, so Willie went off to find Mr. Worth. He could not see him in Hall, so he returned to his friends, dreading any moment to hear a loud report, a crash of glass and a scream, and then—

During the first hour he waited and listened for the Headmaster's step on the grating outside: the dread appearance: the question, 'What boy knows anything about a most serious attempt to blow up the school (founded in 1562)?' Why the reference to foundation he could not tell: but so The Bird's imaginary question took form in his head. An excuse, an excuse! If only he got out of this, he would never touch another gun.

The second hour was rung in by Bony, who sat nearest the door and the platform-bell. 5b cleared away from Old Scratch to 4c classroom—Drawing and Design under Useless. Willie went in quietly, hidden behind Bony, and sat with eyes on the desk before him. A sensation made him look up. Woefully Mr. Worth was balancing the flintlock on two cubes of wood, to be drawn by the class.

'Do not be apprehensive,' his thin voice piped, 'It will not go off. It has been well soaked in water.'

Another sensation in 5b. Willie did his best to draw the flintlock. He rubbed out much, frowned much, almost felt like weeping at the result as Mr. Worth came nearer and nearer the desk where he sat with Bony. Overlooking his shoulder Mr. Worth said, 'I can see you have been trying, Maddison; but your talent will be for music or literature, I fancy. If you come to my classroom after half past four, you can have your weapon back; but do not load it on the school premises or in the streets of Colham.'

Mr. Worth moved on.

'No Sir. Thank you, Sir.'

'I'll never rag Useless again,' declared Willie fervently, as 5b filed out of 4c classroom on the way to Mr. Kenneth for History. 'And the Owl Club will slosh any chap who does.'

Chapter 16

COMING into the dining-room one dark evening after returning home from school, Mr. Maddison said to his son:

'Would you like to have Cousin Phillip to spend Christmas
with you here?'

'Phillip, Father?'

'Yes.'

'Yes, I would, thank you.'

'You don't seem very glad.'

'I thought—' began Willie, then stopped.

'Well?'

'Oh, nothing.'

'As usual.'

'Oh well, Father, I was going to say that I thought you and
Uncle Dick weren't very friendly.'

'Oh, did you. What made you think that, may I ask?'

'Well, you never seem to see him.'

'That, I am afraid, is a subject that you need not concern
yourself about. Even so, it does not appear to be any reason
why your cousin should not come here. I merely thought you
would like it.'

'I do, Father,' Willie said. Why did Father always take
things the wrong way.

'Besides, you might have to live with your Uncle one day
soon.'

'But am I going to live in London?'

'Don't look so scared about it. Any one would think by the
look in your eyes you were so fond of us all that it would break
your heart to leave us,' his father replied, a faint bitterness in

his voice. 'As a matter of fact, I do not suppose that you will ever live with your Uncle, unless the idea of Australia appals you still further.'

'Oh, Father, but why must I go away?'

What had been found out? The blunderbuss? Cribbing? Mr. Rore was going to expel him, as he had threatened a dozen times. He must have discovered who put the carbide in Rattlethrough's ink-well the other evening; or who wrote on the tiny marrow in the summer in the school kitchen garden:

MR. RORE IS A BORE

which, when it was last seen, was a great big thing bearing the huge words:

MR. RORE IS A BORE

Or perhaps he had seen him hiding a cigar on the lavatory cistern cover in The Bog two days ago. Possibly even Taffy had found out who sneaked one of his little compasses and a coil of copper wire. He blinked quickly, not wishing his father to know that the idea of leaving the woods and forests and Jack and all the other things was so terrible.

'What have I done, Father?'

'Nothing, so far as I know. Not even any work at school. Guilty conscience, I suppose! But do you realise that you are growing up, and that very soon you will be a man, and that you will have to earn your own living? You've shown absolutely no bent for anything. What did Mr. Rore write last time in reference to your conduct: "His standard of honour is still too low." Heaven knows where you get it from. Well, you seem to like an out-of-door life. Your Uncle Richard wrote to me and suggested that you and Phillip should go to Australia together next year, and learn farming at the Sydney Agricultural College. I think it an attractive idea. What do you think?'

Willie looked at the ground, and swallowed; but the swelled feeling in his throat remained. He tried to speak, but could not.

'Of course,' went on Mr. Maddison, crossing one leg over another and resting his chin on his hand, 'I do not wish to force you into anything. My own father did his best to ruin my life, but I am not like him, and I do not think you are quite like I was. But still, that is nothing to do with the question. He died, as you know, a confirmed drunkard, leaving nothing but debts which your Uncle Richard and myself had to pay off. Now about the question of your career. As I said, you have shown no keenness in any direction whatever; as regards sensible hobbies even. Birds' nesting I do not consider important, as you apparently do. Usually one passes out of that stage at ten or eleven years of age. Now if the idea of going to Australia with your cousin Phillip appals you, as seemingly it does, there is one other thing open to you. As you know, we are almost on the verge of the workhouse.'

His son looked startled.

'Anyhow, I have not been able to afford to send you to my old school; nor will you be able to go to the University, unless you win a scholarship, which seems most improbable. You must do some sort of work to earn your own living. What would you like to do, do you think?'

'Do, Father?'

'Yes, *do*. Work. If you will try and scrape a hole in the arm of the chair with your nail, and not listen to me, I can't get any sort of idea from you.'

'I was only rubbing, Father.'

'Don't argue with me. I distinctly saw you trying to pick a hole in the covering. And that reminds me. Did you take one of the laces out of my boots the other day?'

'Yes, Father, I was afraid of being late for the motor, and I couldn't find any string.'

'Oh, were you? Well, I wish you wouldn't do it. It isn't as though you asked me first. You never do ask me. I suppose its in keeping with your creepy-crawly nature. Also there's another thing, my boy. I have missed three of my cigars. Do you know anything about it?'

'No, Father,' Willie lied, wondering if Big Will'um had told anyone.

'Well, I do not believe you. What have you to say to that? Nothing. You keep silent. Will you leave that armchair alone.'

'I'm sorry, Father.'

Willie sat quite still.

'Oh, it's all very well to say that you're sorry. You always exclaim that you are sorry, but it gets no further than exclamations. But being sorry is not enough. Then you did take the cigars?'

'No, Father.'

'Oh, very well, we will say no more about it. I suppose that Biddy has taken to smoking them among her other vices, which are numberless, and include the habit of considering herself my grandmother. But still, to resume the matter in hand. I am quite willing to discuss anything with you, only you never seem willing to confide in me. Anybody would think that I was a disagreeable, unpleasant bully! What did you say?'

'Nothing, Father. Only—'

'Well?'

'Only, well, I don't think you a bully, Father,' said the boy timidly, looking on the floor.

'That's very good of you,' his father assured him dryly. 'But about Australia. Your Uncle Richard has sent me a prospectus. The college takes students for two years, and then finds them billets on sheep stations, or fruit farms. There is a premium, of course, but I think I might manage that. How would you like it?'

Willie shuffled in the old horsehair arm-chair. Australia was many thousands of miles away; there were cactus trees, snakes, eternal deserts and no songbirds. So much he remembered from the distasteful maps—British possessions coloured pink—in Meiklejohn's *Geography*.

'The alternative,' remarked his father, looking sideways out of the window and scratching his beard, 'appears to be a city life. Now we get back to where we started—London. A job in an office somewhere. A bank, I suppose. One of your Courtenay cousins is a director of the Lombard Bank, I fancy.'

When Mr. Maddison said that the idea appalled Willie, he was not entirely serious; but, in fact, Willie was appalled. He had never thought of his career before, except vaguely, when he had dreamed of an existence in the woods and meadows, photographing birds' nests and writing in *The Field* an account of his observations. That had seemed an ideal existence. Sometimes at school a little group of intimates had discussed those dim and far-off days when they would grow up and be free and happy for ever. Macarthy was sure that if he were permitted an untrammelled choice he would be a great designer and even contribute to the *Model Engineer*. Beckelt would like to be a light-weight boxer in a booth; it was his ideal to see himself stripped and pink and fierce upon one side of a cigarette picture, upon the other a printed précis of his prowess. Rupert wanted to write poetry, Jack, of course, would have to be a farmer, Fitzaucher wanted to be a University Don, and Swann's ideal was to be Doctor of Divinity. ('Like Old Bullnote? Good Lord!'—but Swann only smiled.) Bony coveted a niche in the Ornithological Section of the Natural History Museum. And now, as Willie sat before the grave and gray-eyed scrutiny of his father, the ghost of these idle lunch-hour conversations came before him sadly. Suddenly he realised that he liked school. He did not want change; he wanted the same friends and the same fields, the same sun-painted yellow-hammers singing on the telegraph wires along the Colham road, the same brook with its sparkle and ripple and water song.

'Well, there is no immediate hurry for a decision, Willie.

In a month or so your cousin Phillip will be here, and you can talk it over with him. You're a funny boy, and I confess that I cannot understand you. But think it over, about the future, I mean. Come, let us discuss things as man to man! There's really no need to look so sullen—'

'I'm not sullen, Father!'

'You look it, anyway. My dear boy, there's no need to look on me as a jailer! It may appear unpleasant to you now, the idea of earning a living, but I should be a poor sort of parent if I did not try to help my own son. Why, if I allowed you to do as you want at present, where would you be at the age of five-and-twenty! A pubcrawler or a tout for a person like Isaacs, or one of those unfortunate scamps who stare into the windows of porkpie shops in London. Why, you would grow up to curse me, if I did not see that you were trained. Wouldn't you?'

'No, Father.'

'Yes, you would! Wouldn't you?'

'Yes, Father.'

'I'm glad you take a sensible view of the matter. You seem to like an open-air life; and England is played out—rotten to the core, with that fellow Lloyd George's tricks, and those confounded Socialists. Why if I had the chance of clearing out to Australia, I'd go in a moment.'

Willie felt easier towards his father, and said dejectedly, 'There are rabbits out there, I know, and I could have a gun and take my birds' eggs for a memory, couldn't I, Father?'

Mr. Maddison sighed.

'Even now, at your age, you can't get away from birds' eggs! What sort of a world would it be, peopled entirely by men who were insane over birds' eggs. Heavens, my boy, you are hopeless. Well, I can at least do my duty as a father.'

Willie turned away his face; the tears would not be held back. He muttered something about homework, and crept out of the room, and up the stairs to his retreat. Listlessly he glanced at his books, fingering the favourite ones. *Bevis: the Story of a Boy*, the most wonderful book in the world, with its companions, *Wild Life in a Southern County*, *Dick o' the Fens*, *Twice Lost*, *Our Bird Friends*, *Coral Island*, *Lorna Doone*, *She*, *Nada the Lily*, and a sad and beautiful story called, *A Tale of Two Cities*. They were old friends. He would take them with him, also his catapult. At evening he would wander over the ranch, potting at rabbits, while the eagles soared far up into the sunset. There was his fishing rod in the corner, with its loose top-joint; it would help to make Australia bearable.

In one drawer was a ragged and small bundle of letters, much cherished, from Elsie who was in Belgium and never wrote to him nowadays. Many times had he sought for hidden meanings in those rare letters, for something that he might nourish Hope upon. As he looked over them he discovered that a letter Mary Ogilvie had written to him had not been destroyed. It was a year old, and her writing was an awful scrawl, not neat and full of character like Elsie's. O Elsie, Elsie—

He looked at the Ogilvie girl's letter. It was more than a year old. He had kept it, he remembered, because it was about birds.

WILDERNESSE,

BRANTON,

NORTH DEVON,

14 August,

DEAR WILLIE,

I hope you are quite well. I am writing because I thought you might like to hear about the peregrine falcons of Bag Point. My friend Howard and I walked there yesterday, and we saw an oyster-catcher's skeleton picked clean on the cliff edge above the earye (can't spell it). Also cormorants on the rocks below. The young have flown (the falcons I mean). Howard wants one for to train to fly at ducks in our ponds. I told him how you climbed the rookery this spring. There is a heronry here near Penhill Point in the estuary. We see them in the fir trees by the quay when we sail up in our boat, near Dead Man's Pill. That isn't made up, its the proper name. The pill goes under the railway bridge. We land there sometimes, only the pill is very steep.

Have you found many good nests this year? We had a bittern in the duckpond, but my brother Michael shot it, and is having it stuffed and set up. I must stop now, as my little baby brother Ronnie, wants me to play 'ingins'. He's mad on trains. Were you ever mad on them? Or was it always birds? Goodbye.

Yours sincerely,

MARY.

P.S.—I like owls, too.

The wind outside the open casement stirred in the pear tree like a dirge for the dead days of that wonderful spring. Willie tore up the letter and threw the pieces into the darkness; the wind whirled a fragment back again. He picked it up and saw that it bore the tail end of the letter, 'I like owls, too.'

'I don't want her to write to me,' he thought, 'and who the devil is Howard?' He lingered over Elsie's letters to him, received far back in the dead past. After a while he tied them up again, and carefully put the bundle back under his best ties and handkerchiefs.

Homework. He emptied his satchel on the table, and flung it on the floor. The first lesson was Euclid—mouldy old Euclid: the first three Propositions in the Sixth Book. Soon he abandoned the incomprehensible tangle of straight and curved lines numbered AB, AC, AD, and HELL, for a glance into *Bevis: the Story of a Boy*. This made him wild with all longing, and he turned to his secret *Diary* and tried to write in it. Two sentences he wrote, then closed it with a sigh, and went down to supper in the kitchen with Biddy. But even a large slice of her special pasty did not dispel the hopelessness that loomed up in the future.

OPENING OF THE FLOWER

November dreared into December, a month of sombrous mornings and darkness at half-past four when the bell sounded the termination of the day's work at Colham School. Willie realised how near was the Senior Cambridge Local Examination, and began to work with an earnestness that puzzled his father. Every night he pored over his books, but the intricacies of Euclid, Algebra, Trigonometry, and Vergil, were beyond his following. So he abandoned his general study, and confined himself to the *Acts of the Apostles, Chapters I-XV*. During the final week he learned every speech, every context, read every note, and even went so far as to make an abstract of the most important speeches, a series of minute letters consisting of the initial letters of each verse, upon his bright new yellow ruler for a crib. He discussed with Jack the advisability of using this in the Divinity paper, but eventually decided to break it up. This he did, and experienced a virtuous glow, which was increased when he discovered that his labour had resulted in a perfect conning of the speeches.

The Saturday morning before Cambridge Week arrived. The senior forms, helped and hindered by the uprooted Specials, had the job of arranging the desks in Hall for the Examination that would begin on the Monday. Mr. Rore seemed to dispose of his horrisonous voice and serbonian glare, and to be a kindly, earnest human being. He called together the candidates for both the Junior and Senior Examinations, and exhorted them on no account to do any work during the week-end. He advised them to take strenuous exercise. 'Let Sport be your master this afternoon! Play hard! Forget that mental power!'—to go to bed early, and not to eat too heavy a dinner on Sunday. To popularise each of his points he called for a show of hands, either approving or dissenting, and seemed gently pleased when every boy ostentatiously agreed with his policy.

But that Saturday nearly every boy of 5b shut himself away in pursuit of mental power. Willie had tea with Jack, and afterwards both seemed restless; and Jack seemed positively pleased when Willie urged that he must return to swot up the *Acts of the Apostles, Chapters I-XV.* Willie explained to Mrs. Temperley that he was going to try to win the Bullnote Memorial Exhibition, a prize awarded to the boy who in the Senior Examination headed the Divinity List.

'Father, please don't muck me about,' implored Willie at half-past two on that Sunday morning, when Mr. Maddison came into his room clad in a shabby dressing-gown, decrepit slippers, and the white end of his nightshirt showing his thin legs.

'You should have worked before,' complained his father querulously, 'it's no good, this eleventh hour effort. Besides, you might set the house on fire, with that candle propped upon your pillow.'

'I'll be careful, Father,' replied his pallid son.

'I don't care what you say, for I at least have a little sense. Besides, I can't sleep with your hollow mutterings echoing down the passage. Come, put the light out like a good boy, and have your sleep.'

Willie sighed, and stared tragically through the dark window; then dropped the book on the chair. 'Good-night, Father,' he said despairfully.

'Good-night,' conceded Mr. Maddison, closing the door behind him. 'Now put that light out, and be sensible.'

Willie blew at the candle stump, and lay back on the cold pillow. Yellow sparks danced before his eyes. He felt himself to be a heroic figure, studying in the silent midnight. He touched his cheeks to discover any cavities or shrinking since his great labour. The wick fumed to slow extinction and yielded in its lone red smouldering a grayish smell that howsoever he waved the air clung to his nostrils. For hours it seemed he turned in his bed, phantasms passing before his mental gaze. Below in the hall the grandfather clock whirred in preparation for striking, then three decaying clangs filled the old house. Willie repeated parts of speeches in the intervals of praying for a revelation in his sleep of the Divinity questions. He must bring home the Bullnote Memorial Prize, which was valued at three guineas, and whose winner was allowed to choose any number of books, provided that the total value did not exceed sixty-three shillings. Why, he could have sixty-three of the Everyman Library, with the Presentation Plate in each one, and all signed by Mr. Rore. He must get the Bullnote Memorial Prize. Then the continent of Australia, coloured pink on the map and like a crushed crabshell, insisted its claim before that of the sixty-three volumes in the Everyman Library. The pink crabshell sank into the sea, and sheep began an enforced leaping over a hurdle. The fourth sheep could not jump, and all his will power could not prevent its front legs from banging into the top bar.

The pear tree tapped against the window sill, somewhere in the wall a mouse was gnawing. He wondered if it had a store of nuts, then turned over on his other side, wondered if a voice ever spoke to people as it had to Saul on his way to Damascus, then sleep fell upon him.

High was the weak silver sun in the eastern casement when he awoke feeling sore-eyed and unrefreshed. Biddy was coming with a cup of tea. She sat down on the bed, and held it out to him, but he neither spoke nor moved.

'Get out,' he grunted, at last.

'Come on midear,' she coaxed, 'it be hot and sweet enough for ee.'

'Don't want any tea, Biddy,' he grumbled, then sat up, remembering about his work. 'Yes, I think I will have the tea. I'm sorry I was so grumpy, only I was swotting rather late last night with the *Acts of the Apostles*, for the Bullnote Memorial, you know. Do you mind hearing some more of my speeches? Here's the book, and don't help me if I stumble. I'll remember all right.'

To Biddy's satisfaction and his own elation the various speeches came easily to him.

'I'll get the Bullnote Memorial, Biddy, you see if I don't! I'll beat Aunt Sally, Slater and Swann! By gosh, I will!'

Chapter 17

ALL that week 5c, 5b, 5a and the VIθ, sat at spaced desks in Hall while the great gas ring above burned its hundred jets, while the rain beat on the high roof, and the Visiting Examiners lolled at the green baize table on the platform, or wearying of this strolled slowly up and down the aisles, passing boys scratching out answers on unlimited paper. Sometimes the door of the Sixth Form room would open silently and the pink face of Mr. Rore, with its white moustache, gaze intently at the candidates. It was a time of tranquillity for him, after the anxieties of the first day. All the masters had an air of sympathetic calm. Even Rattlethrough's voice never penetrated the gloom made more abysmal by the flittering gaslight. Behind locked doors the junior forms gathered silent and undisturbed; upon the piano rested a light dust; the hot-air gratings, usually burnished by the passing of shuffling feet, lost their lustre and grew dim.

On Thursday morning at half-past eleven o'clock Willie sat with an anxious look at his desk, conscious that he had done badly so far. One of the Visiting Examiners for the Cambridge Local Examination, a tall thin man in a black gown, with the appearance and deliberate movements of a stag-beetle, handed out copy after copy of the pale blue question-papers. After an unbearable meander, it seemed, the beetle-eyed Visiting Examiner dropped a paper on his desk: with a trembling hand and sickening heart he clawed it: glanced quickly at the questions: found that they were practically unanswerable, consisting of unheard of queries and speeches: felt as though the base of his spine had become suddenly enrooted in the wooden seat.

He glanced hurriedly round Big Hall, and saw that most of the boys had taken up pens. Swann and Slater were writing eagerly. Effish had rolled his paper into the form of a tube, and was blowing a dying fly that crawled upon his desk. He winked at Willie, and shrugged his shoulders, then coughed wheezily.

Two hours were allowed for the Divinity Exam., and one quarter of the time had passed before the first question was answered. Repeatedly he turned to note the time, the enrooted feeling still holding him at the base of his spine. Other thoughts kept rising, clouding the narrative of the *Acts of the Apostles*. Whenever he glanced at Swann and Slater they were writing easily. Swann with head on one side, and tongue-tip wavering between sedate lips; Aunt Sally with red face held down and fat lips pursed.

'Oh, God help me,' prayed Willie, 'let me remember what Stephen said after—"Then fled Moses at this saying, and was a stranger in the land of Madian, where he begat two sons." ' But no inspiration arrived, only a repetition of a doggerel schoolboy rhyme that paralysed all memory as a spider with its poisoned fangs deadens the struggles of a fly. 'And the Lord said unto Moses, All ye shall wear long noses, all except Aaron, and he shall have a square 'n.' This rhyme obtruded itself so insistently that Willie found himself writing it upon the paper.

He put the paper aside: snatched another sheet; groaned, and flung his pen on the desk. The more he endeavoured to recall the speech of Stephen, the bigger grew the vision of Moses with an enormous nose examining that of Aaron which was square like a gigantic sugar box. The sixty-three volumes in the Everyman Library mockingly ranged themselves neatly before him. He thought of Biddy sitting by his bedside a few days before; he thought of his father with gaunt feet loosely within old worn leather slippers, of his white nightgown and straggling beard: it was at this part of the speech of Stephen that he had come in, and interfered. In despair Willie looked at the next question, an easy one, quickly answered, about the context of certain quotations.

Now he was writing speedily, unheeding the passage of time, and Swann with his tongue vibrating as he held his head on one side. To question after question he replied. As confidence returned so memory clarified.

With a sigh of satisfaction it was ended, just as the Senior Visiting Examiner, rising wearily from a rickety chair near the piano, droned that five more minutes would be allowed. Willie felt that except for the first question he had done well: but the Bullnote Memorial Prize he deemed to be lost.

Lunch that day was a jolly meal, for no master appeared at the head of the top table. One of the new Prefects took his chair, and said the Latin Grace, amid titters from the little group of Specials, who soon began to flick bread about.

Bread pills became obsolescent as the luncheon went on; and when the pudding came, crusts of bread were whizzing about surreptitiously. The Prefect tried not to notice them; he called for order, but his voice made little effect. When pieces of spotted-dog pudding, however, began to flop about the tables, he arose and handed a note to Willie who had just flipped some water in a spoon at Aunt Sally. The giving of a note was the limit of a Prefect's powers; the notes were supposed to be presented to the Headmaster at 2 p.m. Willie read, 'Maddison, Hoolyganism.' He screwed it up, and dropped it down the grating.

'Come on, chaps, don't let Mad Willie be alone!' said Jack, and flipped a tablespoon of water over the Prefect. 'We're all in this.' Bits of pudding converged towards the Sixth former, a tall and studious youth of nearly eighteen, named Latimer. In the general excitement, Effish gathered some knives and forks and poked them down the grating; but seeing that Soapy Sam was watching he took off his shoe, ostentatiously shook it, and put it on again. Beckelt ripped down a sheet of *The*

Illustrated London News. Suddenly the master appeared—it was Mr. Worley—and there was a stampede of the guilty towards the playground door. Laughing, they hid in The Bog until the scouts said it was clear.

All the boys of the Upper School who had had school luncheon were ordered to parade at 2 p.m. before the Headmaster. Mr. Worley, with the help of Latimer, aloof and obviously reluctant, and the porter in the background, pointed at the ring-leaders.

'A very disgraceful exhibition,' remarked Mr. Rore, lancing severity at them under his semi-circular glasses, 'very bad indeed. I understand, Burrell, that you hurled a segment of pudding at Dr. Bullnote's portrait, and also at the clock. Is that so, sir. And you, Effish, put the knives down the grating?'

'Yes, Sir,' replied Effish. 'I was afraid they might be used, Sir. Things looked threatening, Sir.'

'Do not lie to me, sir. Your excuse is palpably false! I shall give you that cane! As for you, Maddison, I shall consider your removal. You destroyed the note given you by a prefect. Well, sir?'

Willie looked on the ground.

'As usual, sir, you have nothing to say. I shall give you that cane! Bryers, I am sorry to see you here. And Swann too. And you, Manning! I thought I could trust you, and you, Lucas, and you Fitzaucher. Bad, bad. But it is the reaction, I suppose. Just so. Still, there should be moderation employed everywhere. I can quite understand your high spirits. You are boys who work, who throughout the year are hard-at-it! It must not occur again. Your promise, boys?'

They murmured that it would not occur again.

'Very well,' he cried sharply, turning to the lined boys. 'This must not occur again. The reaction must take place on the football field. What boys agree?'

Everyone agreed.

'Ah, yes. I am glad you concur. It is a period of strain, I

know. But control yourselves, boys, control yourselves! Learn control! To-night all boys must run five miles, and no sugar in tea for a week? What boys agree?'

Again the ready hands were displayed. Mr. Rore nodded.

Again Willie held up his hand with the others, eagerly hoping against hope that Mr. Rore did not mean what he had said. I will run five miles, he thought; anyhow, I was shortly going into training for the Harriers Race.

'Very well. You are satisfied, Mr. Worley?' The Head-master turned to the Junior Master. Willie felt a surge of joy in his heart—'Effish and Maddison of course, shall be caned, will you please dismiss the others, Mr. Worley?'

'Very good, Sir.'

The Headmaster floated away towards Little Hall.

'Effish and Maddison to remain behind when I give the word to fall out,' declared Mr. Worley, in his metallic voice. 'Now break up slowly when I give the word, and try and give a little better idea of behaviour to the Lower School when next a master happens to be absent for a few minutes. Effish and Maddison, go and wait in Little Hall. The remainder may now fall out. Quietly, now!'

Chapter 18

THE Cambridge Local Examinations ended on the next afternoon, and Mr. Rore announced that those candidates who were feeling the mental strain need not attend at school on Saturday morning. Everybody must have been strained mentally; no one appeared except the Goldings, who, helping to shift the desks into various classrooms, managed to secure between them, one hundred and seventeen unused nibs, nineteen pencils—four being the super-valuable Koh-i-noor—nineteen penholders, seven rulers; then these ablative youths went home.

On Monday 5b did even less work than usual. Only five more days, and then the Christmas holidays would begin! The school was to break up on the Saturday morning; and on the last whole day, the Friday, would be performed that rite of the Dark Age known as the Christmas Magic Lantern Lecture, performed by Sir Heland H. Donkin, the distinguished Old Boy who was said to be a Big Bug in Whitehall.

During the days preceding the Lantern Lecture, 5b ragged in the classroom of Useless, endured the thunders of Rattle-through and the wit of Taffy, enjoyed itself under genial Bunny and tranquil Old Scratch. Not always did Rattle-through break into thunder—indeed, towards the end of term-time, his face was frequently charming with smiles. On one occasion he actually passed forty minutes out of forty-five without once loosing off a thunderbolted epithet or even shouting. Nor did he show any desire to keep the nose of 5b down to the grindstone. He conversed pleasantly with various boys, his forget-me-not eyes twinkling delightfully as he fingered his moustache. Only twice did he vibrate his right leg. He astonished 5b on the Wednesday afternoon by giving, quite unofficially, a verbal examination in general knowledge, which 5b enjoyed keenly.

Rattlethrough, leaning back in his chair, gazed at the ceiling, two hands in his pockets, jingling a bunch of keys and some coins.

'Tell me—er—Watson,' his modulated voice inquired, 'tell me, or rather, inform all of us, since we are in quest of knowledge . . . er . . . ephemeral knowledge . . . tell us what you would do if you, if you had a pin stuck . . . er . . . in a bicycle tyre, of course, not . . . huh, huh-huh . . . in your head!'

5b ha-ha'd, and Bony, not daring to reply boldly that he would slosh the chap who did it, answered:

'I should take off the tyre, Sir, with the levers, or failing levers, I should use spoons, Sir.'

'Good, Watson, good.'

'Then, Sir, I should carefully remove the inner tube, Sir—'

'How, pray, Watson?'

'By taking it out, Sir.'

'Correct, Watson. *Continuez, s'il vous plaît!*'

'Yes, Sir. Then I should get a bowl of water, Sir, blow up the tube, Sir, and detect the puncture by a stream of air bubbles, Sir—'

'Excellent, Watson, excellent. Effish, what next?'

Effish distended his nostrils, slid his tongue round his cheeks, and stared at the floor.

'You have no such means of locomotion, perhaps, Effish?'

'No, Sir.'

'Ah, well. Perhaps it is a blessin' in disguise, Effish. You might, in a moment of abstraction, get run over, and that would be . . . er . . . and undisguised blessin', what? Huh-huh-huh-huh.'

5b re-echoed his mirth.

'*Dites-moi*, Effish, *s'il vous plaît, que voudriez vous* . . . er . . . what you would like to be on leavin' . . . er . . . Colham School. A dustman, an engine driver, or one of the other conventional professions that are so dear to the infantile . . . er . . . childhood?'

'No, Sir.'

'What then, Effish? Come, do not be shy.'

He waited, with twinkling blue eyes, that nevertheless held a hint of frost. Effish saw one drooping end of his moustache being licked by his tongue; at any moment it might be sucked into his mouth; and chewed; and then—Rattlethrough's right knee moved, up and down, twice.

'I should like to be a schoolmaster, Sir.'

'Don't be that Effish. You might have a class like 5b to deal with. Huh-huh-huh.'

The crisis was passed.

Willie put up his right hand.

'Well, my boy, well?' inquired the French master.

'If you please, Sir, may I ask *you* a question.'

The class gasped. Rattlethrough stared, then smiled.

'Certainly, *continuez*, *mon ami*, *continuez*, rash youth!'

Willie produced his satchel, and took from it a bunch of dried weeds.

'What—' began Rattlethrough, seizing one end of his moustache.

Willie went towards him, and held out the handful.

'I found this Sir, and can't identify it. That is one question.' He started to giggle with excitement, and Rattlethrough appeared to be enjoying himself immensely. 'The other Sir, is what does the flower smell of?'

'Good heavens, Maddison is cracked!' said Rattlethrough, and everyone yelled. 'However, let me smell. Er, yes, most peculiar. Let every boy smell it. Pass it round. Most extraordinary! Let every boy write his answer on a piece of paper.'

Which was done, after restrained noise. Every boy guessed

the smell correctly, but only Bryers wrote the name of the plant, which was Hound's-tongue, smelling of mice.

'Most interestin',' said Rattlethrough, 'but now let us continue. Er . . .'

'Er . . . Cerr-Nore. Ah, *oui*, Cerr-Nore. *Dites-moi*, Cerr-Nore, the author of "*Le roi des Montaignes*".'

'Dumas, Sir.'

'Quite right. Clemow, tell me, who was . . . er . . . Chaucer, and what is he distinguished for?'

'*Canterbury Tales*, Sir, and the *Tabberdin*.'

'*Tabard Inn*, Clemow. It has a heraldic derivation. Er . . . Macarthy, what notorious poet has died within the last few years?'

'Keats, Sir.'

'Recently, I said, Macarthy. Keats died in the sixteenth century. You ought to know more about our Great Elizabethans. Try again.'

Macarthy mused.

'Bryers?'

'Swinburne, Sir.'

'Splendid. And what did he write that was so beautiful and inspiring?'

'May I reply critically, Sir?'

'Certainly, *mon enfant, mais oui?*'

'Very little, Sir.'

'What Bryers? Do you think that his . . . er . . . outpourings were . . . er . . . unbeautiful?'

'All except one or two, Sir. He was just a jingle of words, Sir. A barrel-organ poet, Sir, mostly.'

'I see you have the critical faculty of using the carvin' knife! Hur-hur. However, nothing approaches Shakespeare. Let me see now, Fitzaucher, what is there so remarkable about salmon fishin'—the great salmon industries of Cana—of the world?'

Fitzaucher made an effort to think. Rattlethrough chuckled and explained.

'They eat what they can, and can what they can't.'

5b was silent.

'Huh-huh-huh,' laughed the French master, with Effish, whose mirth was a daring imitation of Rattlethrough's.

'Explain, Effish, explain to these thick pates!'

Effish, with an empty laugh, said that it was so silly.

'Why, Effish?'

'They cannot can what they cannot, Sir, even if they are cannibals, can they Sir, huh-huh-huh?'

'What, Effish?'

'They eat while they may, for to-morrow we die,' explained Effish quickly, fearing an outburst.

He was not mistaken. Rattlethrough glared rapidly.

'Are you trying to be impertinent, Effish?' he thundered.

'Stand out there, long-eared Ass! Bottle-eyed BABOON!! Face that wall. You are an ingrate, sir. Yes, an ingrate. Never before have I met such an unruly lot of hooligans. Maddison, I've told you before, I won't have this sniffin'! Coughin' and sniffin', mornin' and evenin'! Stand out there, snivellin' SNIPE! Very well then, as you all take advantage of a little freedom, we will resume. Page, page! *A qui est le tour!*'

'*C'est a moi, mersewer,*' squeaked an undersized boy with a pixie-like face and a faint voice, name Power, who was nicknamed the Musical Mosquito.

'CONTINUEZ, *s'il vous plaît.* Ah, there's the bell. Go away, 5b. Leave me, you ingrates. Yes, go away. Return to your muttons of idleness. Watson, you starin' fool, don't grin at me. Just look at our bony friend!'

5b, straggling out, shouted with glee at this unexpected remark, and Rattlethrough, as unexpectedly humoured, twinkled at them with his eyes of forget-me-not blue, as he hung his gown upon its accustomed hook.

At last Friday afternoon came, and the Christmas Magic Lantern Lecture was imminent. Soapy Sam, somewhere from his tunnelled recesses, brought forth a creased sheet with ropes and a dozen Specials managed to fix it almost diagonally against the wall behind the platform. While this was being done another dozen Specials, under the direction of a high-voiced, button-eyed Junior master, removed the dais; they dropped it as often as possible, trying to break it. Mr. Ellison cracked his fingers, and hopped nervously, while he shouted many confused directions. A swarm of other workers appeared to arrange the desks in Big Hall, while the lackadaisical Specials stood around and ate nuts, and held torn green copies of *Pitman's Shorthand*, and stuck fallow pens behind hair-fringed ears. Another gang, under the direction of Mr. Waugh of the Chemical Laboratory, dragged two heavy cylinders containing oxygen and hydrogen and some pipes into Hall. Importantly Mr. Croodrane unlocked one of the glass cases adjoining the Physics Room, and fifty or sixty boys endeavoured to be selected for the honour of carrying the Magic Lantern to its table just under the horizontal bar.

Meanwhile, in the sulphuretted atmosphere of 5a and the Sixth Form room, the pursuit of mental power was not relaxed. Clenching his fist, Mr. Rore moved it tensely across his brows. 'Hard at it! Hard at it! Every moment is valuable. Get that power, boys. There is still another five minutes. Don't let me see your eyes, Fortescue. Foxy, sir, foxy! Sport is not every-thing. Quite quiet boys, quite quiet!'

He stepped from the room and closed the door; with a mammoth sigh 5a and the Sixth abandoned their problems of Projectiles, until a warning step on the loose grating out-side—a boy of a past generation had effected this ingenuity one lunch hour—rebowed their heads over the desks.

When the bell sounded nearly every master yelled out that there was no need for such a noise. Doors opened and gobbed eager classes into Big Hall. The quiet and little boys of the Second and Third Forms sat meekly in the front rows, where during the illustrated lecture by Sir Heland, the distinguished Old Boy and Big Bug in Whitehall, they enjoyed the blurred pictures thoroughly. After much shuffling and confusion of shouted commands, in which it was thought by Willie that Mr. Worley—a very youthful master with a moustache that gave the impression that two small house-flies were stationary on his upper lip—and Rattlethrough were shouting against one another, the entire school was seated in Big Hall.

'Now portah,' commanded Mr. Rore, and while every one sucked in breath appreciatively, the yellow gas jets high overhead died to blue points in a circle: the oxy-hydrogen lamp hissed; a white glow radiated from the lantern: 'All right, Croodrane, I con manage by myself, thonk you,' came acropically from Mr. Waugh. The school tittered. A daring boy named Farthing, whistled suddenly; the school tittered again. Another boy catawauled softly. 'Quiet there,' warned Rattlethrough.

A-a-a-a-ah! followed by laughter, for a hand-tinted photograph appeared upside down on the sheet, and was hurriedly withdrawn. It appeared again; the right side up; and the gentle voice of Sir Heland began to explain the wonders of Tea Growing in Ceylon. The Lecture went on while the Specials, who all day long had been announcing their joy at leaving that evening, flicked chewed pieces of paper at boys and masters, and blew dried peas through a tin tube indiscriminately, which they handed surreptitiously from one to another, to disconcert any dark attempt at detection. Farthing managed to hit Mr. Rore in the ear; quietly the Headmaster summoned Crinkle, and ordered him at a given signal to turn the gas-cock full on. This was done, and Farthing was detected by Soapy Sam, who tried to drag him from his seat. Farthing shared the universal dislike of Soapy, and gave him a black eye. Mr. Rore sternly ordered him to go home, and with a miserable attempt at a swagger the red-faced Farthing got his overcoat and walked away, turning round to quaver, 'So long, you fellows,' but no one dared to answer. In an awed silence he clattered over the tiles of Little Hall, past the model steamship, and so out into the night unfriended.

In spite of the hot-water pipes, the packed boys, and the unventilated Big Hall, a chill seemed to have struck at the heart of the school. After a brief and almost undetectable tremulant in tone, the voice of the lecturer flowed on gently as before, and with an inadequate stick he pointed at various landmarks. The cylinders were not equal to their work, and towards the end of the lecture the limelight grew feeble, and every other slide, it seemed, was either cracked or chipped. A hum rose in Big Hall, and no voice was raised to check it. The Lecture came to a noisy conclusion when, through inadvertence, a family group was thrown on the sheet and as hurriedly obliterated by a flurried Mr. Waugh. Mr. Croodrane, rising to the crisis, thumped out the opening bars of the National Anthem, and the school rose to its feet and stood to attention, while singing and even bawling with all its might. After the singing, every junior master yelled, 'Sit still, you boys.' Mr. Rore mounted the platform and spoke briefly of the debt that every boy owed to Sir Heland and his set of coloured slides. That distinguished Old Boy was given three hearty cheers, and in reply he said that it was so great a pleasure for him to return to scenes of his boyhood that to say anything further was unnecessary. He hoped that all on leaving would join the Old Colhamean Club, five shillings per annum, and that was all that he had to say; he had always been a poor speaker, he feared. Then he wished them all a Merry Christmas; and to those who were leaving, God Speed! and a Happy New Year to all. He was so glad that his Lantern Lecture was liked; and, with the Headmaster's permission he hoped to show them another next year. Then Sir Heland, editor of *The Old Colhamean*, gentle bachelor, well-wisher of all men, got down amid a roar of cheers, which, gradually diminishing, gave place to various admonitions of, 'Don't move till you get the order, boys.'

Some one in the Specials requested, 'Three cheers for

Moneybags,' meaning the expelled Farthing—to which a few replied with faint-hearted bravado. 'Proceed,' called Mr. Rore, and the classes scampered, uncontrollable, to form-rooms, where amid unnecessary lid-slamming and unchecked noise, the boys routed for caps and gloves and satchels.

Then into Big Hall they rushed, to pause a moment to watch the important Specials who were showering their fare-wells upon big and small alike; but for some reason they did not look as happy as they should have done. Indeed, they looked almost forlorn behind their shy grins as they shook hands with an effusive Rattlethrough, a wan-smiling Useless, a gruff old genial Scratch, a benevolent Bunny, a big-brotherly Taffy, and an OLD BIRD magnificently courteous.

Chapter 19

WILLIE and Jack were waiting on Colham Station to meet the London cousin. Willie was wondering if Elsie would be coming on the same train. A soft rain fell from the grey sky. They walked up and down the platform, hands for warmth within mackintosh-coat pockets, speaking about Phillip.

'I hope you'll like him,' said Willie, trying not to think of Elsie. 'He's sleeping in my room, for Father said the other rooms were damp, and when we tried to light fires in first one, then another, we found that the jackdaws nests were wedged tight in the chimneys. Jack, I wish you were coming to sleep with me, instead. Still, we'll see each other every day, won't we?'

'Jack, isn't it lovely to think of being friends for ever?'

'Lovely. And we will be, won't us? I shall always be at the farm, and you'll always be at Fawley. Even if you do go to Australia, you're bound to come back!'

'I shan't go to Australia. Then I can see you in the holidays if I work in a London office, can't I? And I will always write my *Official Diary of Observations*, and send them to you to read. Hullo, here's old Rupert.'

Rupert was approaching them, smiling with pleasure.

'Hallo, Willie,' he said, his cheeks faintly rosy like those of a girl. 'Hallo, Jack. I've just had lunch with Rattlethrough. He is awfully decent really. Are you chaps going on the 2-21?'

'No,' replied Willie. 'We're just waiting for a cousin of mine from London who is staying at my house for the hols. How's Bony?'

'Fine, thank you, Willie. I say, I saw old Moneybags Farthing yesterday, and he isn't expelled after all. Afterwards he went back and said that he was sorry he hit the porter, but it was the last day, and he was feeling rather as though he would like to do something to be remembered by, like the Old Boy who had let out the rats in the Head's study long ago. Effish suggested that excuse. The Bird said; "Will you apologise to Portah, Farthing, for rendering blue the lower portion of Portah's eye socket?"

' "Yes, Sir," said Moneybags, "for your sake, Sir."

' "What do you mean, boy?" asked The Bird, and Moneybags said, "May I speak out, Sir?"

' "Yes Farthing, you may," said The Bird.

' "Well, Sir," said Moneybags, "when I was going down the hill I suddenly realised that you were right about lying down under a banana tree, and so I determined to come back and tell you I was a pauper spirit, even if I was expelled." Effish told him to say that too!

' "You are a senior boy," said The Bird, "and the junior boys must always have an ideal. *What should be, shall be*".

'It's a fact, Willie, so old Moneybags told me! "Yes, the responsibility of a senior is very great, Farthing. Also you should not strike an inferior. Also, my brother lost an eye through a pea, which, if it hits the pupil, which some people call the apple, is considerably destructive. A cricket ball, Farthing, is infinitely preferable!"

'Then Moneybags said that The Bird sent for Soapy Sam, and asked for a cricket ball. "I thought he was going to give me a wallop in the optic with it," said Moneybags, but when he returned The Bird placed it in Moneybags' eye and said, "You understand now, I hope. The socket saves the pupil. It will be a lesson to you, Farthing. Do you agree?"

'Moneybags held up his hand, and The Bird nodded. "Portah," he said, "Mr. Farthing will apologise." "I apologise

porter," said Moneybags. "Werry good, Farthing," grumbled
Sammy. "Ah, Portah," corrected The Bird, "ah, he is now
Mistah Farthing. And Mr. Farthing wishes to pay ten shillings
towards the Staff's Annual Outing Fund. Here is his donation,
Portah."

' "Thank you, Mr. Farthing, I'm sure," said Sammy, and
went out pleased as Punch, with the half quid in his hand.
The Bird had paid it himself!'

'Coo!' ejaculated Jack and Willie together.

'But that wasn't all! The Old Bird gave Moneybags a single
whack, and then told him that he was not expelled. "I hoped
that you would return to apologise," he said. "I am glad,
very. *What should be, shall be!* Remember that all your days,
Farthing. Influence your fellows!" Then he rang the bell, and
said, "Ah, Portah, bring biscuits and two cups of tea." When
they came, he offered Moneybags a fag, and Moneybags said
he was so nervous that he spilled all his tea over the carpet,
and down his waistcoat, and couldn't light the fag. He half
expected it to go off bang, but it didn't, and as soon as he could
he hopped it, having swallowed half the fag. He was sick
outside, but puts it down to some jollop he swears Sammy put
in his cup for revenge!'

To this account Willie and Jack listened with laughter
and amazement. Such behaviour from Mr. Rore was stag-
gering.

'I reckon The Bird isn't so dusty after all,' said Jack.

'Not half dusty!' they agreed.

Rupert told them that his partner Bony was building a
museum for objects of natural history, geology, and curios. In
fact, he said, he must be away immediately, as he had promised
to help that afternoon in digging the large hole in the garden
from which the museum, with sides and bottom duly cemented,
and covered with glass, would as years went on expand till
Colham Town Council adopted it as its own and made Bony
its curator.

'Good-bye, you chaps,' smiled Rupert. 'Merry Christmas,' and having thanked them for their returned wishes, he went away.

'Let's get a paper and see if my letter protesting against compulsory education has been printed,' said Willie suddenly.

'I'd forgotten all about it,' replied Jack. 'Come on.'

They hastened to the bookstall farther along the platform.

Willie bought the *Colham and District Times and Advertiser with which is Incorporated Smellies' Weekly Argus*, but could not find his letter in print. He felt disappointed, because he had told all 5b to look out for it; he had signed the letter 'One who rattles through life with fifteen children.' A great joke, since Rattlethrough was rumoured to have fifteen offspring.

'They're closing the gates,' remarked Jack, and Willie's heart beat faster.

A red-faced porter was swinging the white barriers athwart the level-crossing. Far away against the grey clouds steam was straggled by the wind. Larger and larger grew the Great Western engine: it rose up black, and glided upon them with a mild roar. From the Paddington corridor coach a white face under a bowler hat peered out, and on seeing them was withdrawn.

'That's him,' said Willie; and leisurely he walked up the platform, followed by Jack wiping his hand on his handkerchief.

The two came to the carriage as a tall youth opened the door, with a much-botched bag of black leather and a fishing rod in one hand. Seeing them he smiled quickly and disregarding the awkward step jumped to the platform, which was two feet below the step. The fishing rod caught in the vertical handrail as he leapt, shooting the black bag from his hand and casting him in a heap upon the wet platform. His bowler hat rolled over and over, and the black bag, yawning suddenly, debouched collars, handkerchiefs, and half its other contents.

Willie and Jack picked Phillip up, but he clutched his right knee.

'Are you hurt?' inquired Willie anxiously.

'It'll be all right in half a sec,' moaned the other in a soft voice. 'It's these beastly boots.'

His eyes looked very blue against his black hair and pale face. He pressed his lips together, as though in pain.

'Blast,' he muttered. 'Don't trouble, I say, thanks very much,' he cried to a small boy who was picking up the collars on the platform. 'I'll do it in half a sec. Only my knee hurt a bit. Yes, blast these damn boots,' he mumbled fiercely.

Willie looked at them, and wondered if everyone in London wore such extraordinary boots. They were long, and fastened with loose buttons, with patent-leather toecaps cracked and split, and around his cousin's ankle was a space of at least half an inch, so that it appeared as though the smallest shake would cause the boots to drop off in walking. Phillip saw him looking, and his face went pink.

The stationmaster, forgetting his hat, came out of OFFICE— PRIVATE and asked if he could be of service. Every one on the platform stood round, staring. Another small boy had retrieved the dinted bowler hat, for which Phillip gave him a shilling. Soon he announced that his knee was better, and stood upright.

'Oh, this is my friend Jack, Phillip.'

Phillip smiled and shook Jack's hand, although the small boy was endeavouring to thrust the bag into it.

'Bad luck about your fall,' said Willie, while Jack frowned heavily at the silent onlookers.

'It's all right now, thanks very much,' Phillip announced, but no one moved.

'Would you like a cab?' suggested Willie, hoping that his cousin would refuse, since he had but a halfpenny in his pocket.

'Oh, no, thanks very much,' said Phillip, knuckling the

dents from his bowler hat. Three barefooted boys immediately rushed away to secure one.

'Your hat has left a ring of mud round your forehead,' Willie pointed out, after his cousin had carefully put the hat on his head. 'But that's a detail. Well, let's come on. You take Jack's arm, and I'll carry the rod and bag.'

Sympathetically the little gathering moved with them; a fat old woman in her excitement getting wedged in the pass-gate. The stationmaster retired for his braided hat and returned. Waving aside unofficial endeavour, he began to push her, but she waved him away. 'I'll get me breath in a minute, Mr. Slee, thank you all the same,' she puffed. At last the pass-gate was free, and the stationmaster returned to OFFICE—PRIVATE.

'No, we don't want a cab, Jim Perryman,' said Willie to a battered individual who was waving a scaley whip in their direction.

'I'm sorry the young gentleman hurt 'isself, sir,' said the cabman, speaking through the wet brown fag-end of a cigarette between his lips. 'Thanks,' said Phillip, and began to look happier. Willie looked happier, too. Elsie had not been on the train.

'I say, it is fine to be in the country,' said an enthusiastic Phillip, when they had left the streets and were walking across the fields. He gazed at the line of downs over which a low cloud was dragging. 'By Jove, that's a hoody crow. You don't see them about where I live. Mostly bricks and mortar.'

In the silence Phillip frowned at his boots as though he would like to kick them into the hedge. 'The beastly things got split somehow,' he said in an apologetic voice.

'How's Auntie and Uncle?' asked Willie, suddenly remembering that he ought to have inquired before.

'Oh, all right, thanks very much. Mother—Mater—sent her love to you. She said you must come up and stay with us sometime. Only, of course'—hesitatingly—'it isn't quite so decent as this. It's only a suburb.' He laughed apologetically.

They passed the hamlet of Snedlebarum, before the cottages of which children played around the puddles, floating matchsticks for boats, and all pausing to stare as the three trudged past. A watery sun washed the broken clouds with wan silver, and raindrops shaken from the bare branches of the elms splashed upon their heads and shoulders. Willie looked at Phillip from time to time, and thought how drawn were his cheeks, how deeply blue were his serious eyes, how palely delicate was his profile. Now and again Phillip glanced with uncertain timidity at his cousin, the knowledge of which gave to Willie a sense of easy superiority and therefore kindliness. Suddenly he said:

'Father wants me to go to Australia next year. He said that you were going. If you go, I shall have to!'

'Oh, but I'm not going,' replied Phillip. 'I'm going into the Moon Fire Office after my holiday. Do you think we shall be able to do any shooting?' he asked, looking round at the fields with eager eyes.

'Oh, yes, rather,' said Jack.

'How spiffing, man! And is there any fishing, do you think?'

'There's some pike in the lake, and perch—'

'Perch?'

'Hundreds, and roach. We want a little frost, and they'll bite like fun.'

'Oh, how lovely. Oh, Willie, I am so glad I came. I say, you chaps, you don't mind me butting in, do you? I mean to say, I've got a friend at home, and understand, you know.'

'You must join the Owl Club, Phillip. It's very select. There's no subscription'—Phillip looked relieved—'but it's only for special chaps like Bony—he's a chap at school—Rupert Bryers—he's another, good poet, too—and, in fact, all decent chaps, you know. We are going to meet once every year in a linhay and pour out a libation to the gods, as The Bird would say. Will you join?'

'Rather—I mean, thanks very much, Willie. You are jolly decent to me.'

'Oh, rot.'

'Oh, but you are,' said Phillip. 'After all, I am an outsider.'

'Idiot! Jack and you and I are going to have a spiffing time. It's the last holidays we shall all three have together!'

Jack said good-bye to them at a fork in the road. 'You chaps will come over s'evening won't you?' he urged quickly, lest in his voice should appear anxiety about Willie's need of his company now that Phillip had turned out to be such a decent fellow.

'Of course we will. After tea. Shan't we Phillip?'

'Not half!'

'Good-bye, then,' and he turned away.

'Good-bye, old man,' they answered.

Biddy opened the door to them graciously. She was over-joyed at the thought of company for Willie.

'Hallo,' said Mr. Maddison, dropping *The Morning Post* and jumping up when they went in to him. 'How do you do, Phillip? Tired after your long journey? Well, the next thing is food. And how are your father and mother?'

'Very well, thanks very much,' stammered Phillip, nervously trying to conceal his boots. 'Father sent the goo-goo-good wishes of the season to you, and thanks you so much for having me, Sir.'

'I'm glad to have you, my boy,' heartily replied his Uncle John. Willie felt embarrassed and almost wished that his father were not so genial. 'Now Willie, take Phillip upstairs. Tea will be ready when you come down.'

Upstairs Phillip sat down on his bed and removed his boots, thrusting them far out of sight. He wore a black coat and waistcoat, with striped trousers. From his bag he pulled a tweed coat, shook it, and hung it behind the door. Then he slipped on a pair of old black dancing pumps, obviously too big for him.

'Do you think Uncle Jack would mind me having sup-lun-er dinner in this coat?'

'No, of course not,' replied Willie. 'I say, you're pretty swagger. I wear this old coat when I can. Look, it's got a poacher's pocket.'

'Then I can wear mine!'

'Of course. Why ever not?'

With a smile of relief Phillip cast the black coat on the bed and put on the tweed one.

'Do you think your Pater would mind me calling him Uncle?' he asked.

'No, of course not!'

'He's awfully decent, isn't he?'

'Oh, not half bad.'

'I think he's fine. I wish my father and yours would see each other a bit. Father doesn't know anybody in London. This is a lovely place, Willie. Isn't it big. I wish I lived here, instead of having to go into the Moon Fire Office after the holidays. I say it will be fine if we both get into the same office, won't it?'

Willie nodded, but said nothing. Elsie, Elsie—

It was quite a jolly tea. Willie noticed how his father seemed to like Phillip, and how Phillip, who had appeared very nervous at first, soon became confident, and made his father laugh with his funny way of describing the train journey. Biddy almost bounced into the room with the plate of hot toast.

'Don't be late if you can help it,' said Mr. Maddison after tea, when, with coats donned and caps held in hands, the two boys were standing in the soft shine of the hall lamp.

'Be back about half past ten; I'll be waiting up.'

Half past ten! Never had he been allowed out after ten before, Willie told Phillip, as with linked arms they trudged down the road. Phillip frequently exclaimed that it was ripping, and every time Willie surged with happiness at the other's joy. On either side of them a black hedge loomed, and sometimes a star glimmered through vaporous space above.

At Skirr Farm they were welcomed gladly. Peggy, a golden-haired girl of fifteen, became shy-eyed when she saw Phillip, and for the rest of the evening her gaze was covertly for him whenever she imagined herself to be unregarded. Doris, a serious little maid of thirteen, crouched by her mother's side, listening eagerly to the talk of the great Willie and this grown-up stranger.

A fire of split beech-logs burned in the open hearth, throwing its gleams upon their faces as they sat on the oaken benches inside the hearth, after supper. Phillip told them of the trams that were spoiling the country at his home, and how the elms had been thrown along the road to a Kentish town called Bromley; of the field behind his house where once he had actually seen a pair of kestrel hawks soaring. He told them, in a hushed voice, of a certain place called Piccadilly, all glittering with lights at night, where he had been on two occasions; of the wonderful play his father had taken them to last Christmas. But, he affirmed, it was not a quarter so good as Rookhurst.

After a while their voices were silent, and they stared into the fire-splitten logs, tranced with the flutter of gold and red, the hovering and dying of blue and green flames. To-morrow would be Christmas Eve; the crickets jingled in the hearth about them; the fire was warm; the long shadows held mystery. Phillip realised that for a little while his dream of such a life had come true, then a pain came into his heart as he thought of his mother at home, of his rudeness to her just before he had left. Mother, mother— He saw her sad, sweet face and heard her say, as sometimes she did when he or father had been beastly. 'Ah, never give up everything for other people.' She was like a little child in most things. He and mother had gone down to a second-hand shop to buy the boots, because he had insisted that they were the right thing to wear coming from 'Town'; and here he was, after a wonderful dinner of jugged hare and roast mutton and coffee, not a scrambled supper in the kitchen; and mother at that moment was probably sitting in her chair while father read bits out of the paper aloud to her. Here he was, and to-morrow he was going shooting!

Phillip turned his head, enthralled with this wonderful farm-house, with its diamonded windows, and ovens let into the thick wall on each side of the hearth, and grandfather-clock reflecting dully the flamelight on its face. Perhaps highwaymen had used that blunderbuss, with the gleam of fire on its barrel. He sighed, and saw the face of Peggy, regarding him with eyes large and wondering in the shadow.

The little servant-wench came in with a tray of cake and cocoa. Quickly it seemed the scalding cups were cooled and it was time to leave; the first evening was ended. Bright were the stars as they walked to the roadway arm in arm. The broad constellation of Orion with its studded belt and trailing sword lay in the south, and there too was flashing Sirius the Dogstar; a half-moon was golden above them. They both declared that they glimpsed the sweeping wings of a heron that krarked across the wintry sky, flying for the Longpond. Willie told Phillip of Heron's Island and their hut, and of the races Jack and he had in the catamaran and the canoe.

'Spiffing. I say, Willie, do you hunt? Grandfather used to be a Master of Otter Hounds, wasn't he?'

'I don't hunt, but I've been out on one of Jack's father's ponies sometimes in the Christmas hols. I've taken one or two tosses. Why? Would you like to go out with the hounds? The d'Essantville meet at the *Moon in the Mere* every Boxing Day.'

'I can't ride,' confessed Phillip. 'But I'd love it if I could.'

'Right, we'll go on foot, and run.'

'Glorious!'

Mysterious was the night as they lay in bed, talking softly, seeing each other dimly.

'Oh Phil, can you see the moon?'

'Yes, isn't it beautiful. Do you like music, Willie?'

'Yes, only I seldom hear any.'

'Father's just bought a wonderful gramophone. It's glorious —it's—it's like the trees outside now; and the wind, and the lovely moonlit clouds.'

'Phillip, can you see the moon? I often think its like a—oh, you'll think me soppy—'

'No I shan't, honestly Willie. Go on.'

'Its like a maiden walking in heaven, isn't it?'

'Yes, I understand. I love the moon, too.'

Across the window crept the white moon-maiden, and the shadow of the pear tree moved towards the eastern window with her. Listening in the intervals of their whispered confidences Phillip could hear the whistle of curlews passing to the moors. Willie told him of Jim Holloman, and he shivered with excitement, asking to be shown the spinney where actually the romantic figure had lived, and where mice were searching among the leaves, and perhaps wild-fowl flighting overhead.

The white moon-maiden entangled in the thicket of shadows stole nearer the casement through which the dawn, seeking to dispel her sadness with his fervours, would peer too late. More drowsy grew the talk of the boys, more infrequent their exchange of loved recollections: and to the rue of the wind in the chimney they sank into slumber.

The next morning all three tramped up to the spinney, and found Bill Nye carving a piece of wood with an old knife. Sheepishly he hid it when they appeared, and then stared at Phillip, who regarded him as though he could not understand how a boy of his age managed to live all alone and feed himself. Bill Nye was so undersized, indeed, that to Phillip he appeared no older than eleven or twelve years old. His bare feet were muddy and his head like a malkin—the bundle of wetted rags on a stick with which the cottagers used to clear dust and ashes from their clome baking ovens. Willie gave him an old pair of trousers for a Christmas present, which the boy, grinning with delight, at once pulled over those he was wearing.

'Thank ee, Ms'r Will'um. Proper trousers they be, thank ee!'

On the following day Mr. Maddison went into Colham, after telling Willie at breakfast that on Christmas afternoon all at Skirr Farm were coming to tea. His son was astounded. Again Phillip confided to Willie that he thought his uncle was a ripping chap. Willie, immediately assuming the mantle of responsibility, invited Jack to lunch, and the trio solemnly sat down in the dining-room at one o'clock.

'You'll have a sherry and bitters of course?' asked Willie of Phillip.

'I—I don't think I will, thank you!' replied Phillip, slowly. He was sitting on his hands, a habit of his when ill-at-ease.

'Good, for I don't believe we've had any in the house since grandfather drank himself to death. But in the paper novels that Biddy reads, the villain, Sir Robert Ffoulkes, always asks his guest to have a sherry and bitters, and then with a saturnine smile he extracts poison from his ring and does the bloke in.'

Phillip laughed, and then replied enthusiastically that he liked ginger wine, and raisin wine, but best of all, cider. He ceased to sit on his hands.

The meal went merrily. Afterwards they raced upstairs to Willie's bedroom. Phillip was shown once more the collection of birds' eggs. Among the rarer eggs Willie and Jack had collected were those of the Big Buzzard, or Coney-clitch, found in an enormous eyrie up a fir tree in Northside Wood: the Kingfisher, or Rainbow Bird, whose white shiny eggs were pink when unblown: the Heron or Mollern, a wading bird that nested in tree-top colonies like the rooks: the Merlin Falcon: the Greater Spotted Woodpecker or Tom-tap-all-the-afternoon: the Golden Crowned Knight, or Golden Crackey, the smallest British bird: the Long-eared Owl or Devil-horned

Jinny Oolert: the Evejar or Skep-swallow, so called by the countrymen on account of its fondness for bees: and the Red-backed Shrike or Hedge-Grawbey, which name Willie had invented, awarded for its habit of stealing fledgling birds from their nests and impaling them upon a long thorn, for a larder. These treasures were gazed at fondly until a new attraction was offered by the host, on his hands and knees peeling back the carpet.

'Why, I made a trap-door like that,' exclaimed Phillip, 'when I was a kid. I wanted to make a tunnel from my room, into the cellar, and under the garden into the Backfield, only I knocked a lot of plaster down into the sitting-room. I tried to fill the hole up with plaster of Paris. I don't think that Father's seen it yet, or there would have been a row. Father's got a fine air-gun, and used to hide it in a cupboard, but I found it and once broke two hundred wine bottles in Grand-father's garden which is next to ours. His housekeepr sneaked, and I was taken to the police-station, and warned!'

'What a mouldy thing for your father to do!' remarked Willie, immediately feeling uncomfortable when Phillip's cheeks grew pink and he said:

'Well I broke my promise in using the gun.'

Willie pondered on the change in his own parent when on Christmas morning he and Phillip were each presented with a saloon gun, and a box of No. 2 bulleted breech-cap cartridges. Phillip's joy was great, and his gratitude hesitant with emotion. Anxiously he confessed to his cousin that he had no present to offer his uncle, or indeed to any one, as he had only brought a shilling with him; but he was reassured when Willie explained that his father would only have been angry, as he refused all birthday and Christmas gifts.

'I'm so glad that I gave Bill Nye those trousers,' said Willie, 'for he has given me a carved wooden rabbit. Do look at it, just like a savage totem! Let's hop over and see him this after-noon before the others come, and also old Bob Lewis, shall we?'

OPENING OF THE FLOWER

They went to the cottage in the pine wood first, and knocked at the back door. It was opened by Dolly; her face lightened when she saw them. Willie introduced Phillip, who wondered whether to shake hands or not, the same embarrassment being felt by the woman. He made several false starts, finally letting his arm fall by his side and bowing stiffly, blushing.

'How is Bob, Dolly?' asked Willie.

'They've both eaten too much, and be asleep in their chairs.' She pointed to the closed door of the parlour.

'Aren't you cold all by yourself out here in the scullery?'

'Not much. The old people want to rest awhile. Hark now, what do you hear?'

They listened. Dolly looked at the blue eyes of Phillip, for something in the dreaminess of the boy's gaze was curiously akin to the look of one she frequently imagined; a spirit too sensitive, ever shrinking as though conscious of its own imperfection, called forth protective tenderness from her loving heart. Phillip looked on the stone floor, nervously tapping the toe of his left shoe with his right foot. Dolly smiled, and his timidity passed with the instinctive knowing of kindliness. In a soft voice, she whispered,

'Can ee hear anything?'

'What is it?' asked Willie.

She beckoned them forward, pausing beside a heap of potato sacks in the small shed called the backhouse, connected by an open door with the scullery.

'Why, it's Bill Nye,' exclaimed Phillip.

Willie said eagerly,

'Has he had dinner here, Dolly?'

Dolly nodded, and pointed to a litter of goose bones on the stone floor, surrounding a white plate licked clean.

'Young limb, what do ee think he did now?'

They looked puzzled.

'He took a bottle of Gramma's turnip wine, and now he'm mazed drunk!'

A faint snore came from the curled bundle on the potato sacks. Willie shook his shoulder, but he did not wake. Hair hid his pointed ears. His attitude was so comical that Phillip started to laugh.

'Well, if Bob's asleep, I won't wake him,' decided Willie, eager already to get back to Jack. 'What are you doing s'after-noon, Dolly?'

She did not answer immediately, then told him that Tom Sorrell might be strolling round for a cup of tea.

'Old Bob thinks Tom Sorrell a nice chap. What do ee think, Li'l Willum?'

She laughed, and on impulse touched his cheek with her hand.

Chapter 20

PLOUGH MONDAY was celebrated in the village in the third week of the new year, and Phillip on his last afternoon was able to see the strange procession. This rite had been held in Rookhurst ever since the walls of the first cottage had been raised from a mixture of straw, cowdung, mud and stones.

The Ploughing Matches were held in the morning. At the far end of the field away from the spectators, behind the teams with their straw braided manes and tails bound with coloured ribbons, many birds screamed and wheeled; the gulls graceful and soaring, alighting with grey pinions upheld on a glistening furrow suddenly to seize a worm or a bettle-case; the rooks jostling and flapping sable wings, the starlings chittering and running with eagerness. Sweet chirrupings in the wake of the turmoil were made by the dishwashers, some of them winter visitants with slender breasts of daffodil, and all joying in the food turned up in the gleaming furrows.

Bill Nye the crowstarver, and Samuel Caw his mate, a still smaller boy, were enjoying themselves during the Ploughing Matches, for repeatedly from the spinney in the Big Wheatfield, where with other boys they had a roaring fire, the clappers sounded with the clang of the rail, and the beating of tins and sometimes the hollow voices floating in the air.

Rookhurst rejoiced in the afternoon. It was a half holiday, and all made merry. The crowstarvers left their fire and turfed hut and clappers, and joined the revellers. Dressed in the skins of donkeys, and harnessed to an old plough with an applewood-share, they started off for the annual round of the cottage thresholds. Big Will'um, the bailiff, tall and gaunt and heavy-booted, guided the barefooted pair. He himself took long loose strides; a boyhood in the heavy winter fields, dragging feet from the sticky clods, had given him a slouch. Every aged cottager, clad in best clothes, hobbled to his doorway. 'Whoa, now,' growled Big Will'um. The pair pattered to a standstill, then wheeled several times before the cottage, drawing the plough after them. The old people beamed, and nodded, and their gratitude when the corn-spirit had given its blessing. Now the garden would be in good heart for the year's potatoes, beans, onions, cabbages, lettuces, the roots of rhubarb in the sun-warmed corner. The long black pig not get fever, but fatten well and perhaps reach a weight of twenty score.

From cottage to cottage they passed, making as to furrow the ground before each one. George Davidson carried a blown-up pig's bladder on the end of a stick, with which he belaboured grinning labourers and the padding donkeys alike. Ribbons were wound round his body, and a red paper cap was on his head. About a hundred children, men and women, many with cameras, followed the procession, accompanied by dogs of all sizes and breeds. Everyone was happy. Bill Nye had never grinned so much before, enwrapped as he was in the ass's skin. He knew that a big good meal was at the end of it, and, with luck, a packet of fags and a pair of boots.

Willie felt proud that this was his village, so impressed was Phillip, who declared that he had never heard of such a glorious idea before. Neither Jack nor his cousin was able to tell him why the asses' skins were always used by the boys who drew the plough. 'It's only done in this village, having died out elsewhere,' said Jack.

'It's a jolly old custom too,' remarked Willie. 'At least as old as Doomsday Book.'

It was a survival of the rites of the corn-spirit practised since the first thought of man was to put the idea of a god into stone and food. Likewise at the harvest—to eat the first-fruits was to have within the body the power of the corn; a survival, possibly, of instinct combined with early human reasoning; the practice of eating the conquered and, therefore, possessing his strength and cunning.

Everywhere they visited, even the hollowed chalk quarry leading off the roadway and screened by bushes, where Tom Sorrell was raking out lime from the base of one of the two cold kilns. From the circular rim of the far kiln a misty vapour arose. He threw down his long shovel as they came in through the gate, and wiped his white hands on his corduroy trousers. Eyebrows, cap, hair, nostrils, ears, clothes, boots—all were dusty white with the lime.

The donkey-boys drew the wooden plough across his threshhold, while several of the people glanced at Dolly, standing near. Tom Sorrell nodded to Big Will'um, who tossed his nose in recognition.

'Could do wi' a quart,' he said.

'When's price o' lime coming down, Tom?' asked George Davidson, the mason.

Tom shook his head. 'Ask maister. Nobbut do with me, midear.'

'This is the place,' Willie told his cousin, 'where Jim and I came that night. See those blocks of chalk above the edge of the kiln? We lay next to those, on the leeward side, so that no poisonous gas came across.'

'I say, it's a wonder you weren't choked in your sleep.'

'The chalk in the kiln sunk right down in the night, but I dared not look over. Yes, that's the kiln, and from that day Jim has not been heard of or seen.'

Phillip stared at the circular stone rim.

'Look,' he cried, pointing.

Over the burning kiln hovered a lonely flame, a flame of pale fire, rising high above the fumes enfretted by the chilly wind of the oncoming dusk. Wanly it shone and wavered, and like a dream it faded in the vain and empty air.

THE SEED LOOSENING

'In the sunshine, by the shady verge of woods,
by the sweet waters where the wild dove sips,
there alone will thought be found.'

RICHARD JEFFERIES, in *Pigeons at The British Museum*.

Chapter 21

COUSIN PHILLIP went home having made himself most popular at all the houses where he went with Willie—the Cerr-Nores, the Margents, the Temperleys, Dr. Priddle's, and the Normans. Indeed, so much did Mrs. Norman like Phillip that she hinted to Willie afterwards—to his secret mortification—that he ought to try and be more like his cousin.

The new term began; Willie went along to the Halt every morning, to await the motor. On the first morning Jack went with him; on the second he came half-way; on the third morning he was busy with the lambs. Every evening for the first week Willie called in to see Jack, to tell him about 5b, and what changes had taken place. Willie was now nearly six feet tall, having grown amazingly during the past six months; the change to 'puberty,' once so much desired, had come almost unnoticed.

One evening Mrs. Temperley said that Jack was going to be confirmed by the Bishop in March, and wouldn't he like to join the class with him? Yes, it would be nice to go together; and so, twice a week, he was excused homework in order to attend the Vicar's classes in the Vicarage—at which some of the boys, led by Charlie Cerr-Nore, the Vicar's son, told funny stories when the Vicar was out of the room. This led to a bi-weekly exchange of smutty yarns, some of which Willie thought funny; but, although he laughed, he secretly flinched from those which might have applied—but he did not realise this—to Elsie or his father. He smiled even at those which were just horribly filthy, lest the teller should feel hurt.

On his way to the Halt one day in late February, Willie met

Bill Nye and his friend Samuel Caw, a black-eyed boy with jet hair sticking straight up on a head that, with its long solemn brown face, resembled a parsnip. These two had with them a bitch-puppy of unusual appearance. One of the puppy's parents had been a whippet, and the other the spider-faced prick-eared Dutch shipperke owned by Mrs. Cerr-Nore. One night this creature had bitten a hole in the rotten wood of the door of the shed where the whippet had been tied up, howling. The resultant litter was a surprise to George David-son, and so obviously a disaster that he had drowned all except the one necessary to keep the mother in health. The miserable puppy, with its thin narrow head and large hazel eyes, long body, thick legs and fox-like tail, having been discarded during its third month of life, had wandered across the wheatfield in a semi-instinctive search for someone who would give it warmth.

Hearing Bill Nye's voice, it had crept through the trees of the spinney with downcast head and trailing tail. The crow-starver thought to heave a flint at it, but nothing heavy enough was at hand. Meanwhile the puppy, its belly almost dragging on the earth, approached near, swishing its tail. Bill Nye sat still, and it came closer, finally coming to him and licking his ankle. Thus assured of its utter humility, Bill Nye thwacked it with a stick, while the puppy squealed. He told it to stop its hollering, which it did, at the same time lying on its back and holding erect its thick legs. Bill Nye tossed it a rabbit's head, the puppy bared its teeth in a happy leer; and so the friendship had begun.

At night the creature crept into the shelter and slept happily against the skinny ribs of its master. Never before had Bill Nye had anything to love him. He had been an unwanted baby, pale of smirched face and little of body. The child-mother who had borne him had turned common market troll and died young in Colham. She had asked to see the boy just before her death in the dreaded Grubber—as they called the Union, or Workhouse in the town—but her grandmother, Aholibah Nye,

had refused to allow the child of sin to see her lest he might be
tainted even more. Bill Nye grew up with a sealed heart. The
bigger boys had jeered at him and kicked him on all occasions.
But Bill Nye did not care. He had plenty of things to interest
him. There were little birds in spring to be caught and teased,
their feathers to be pulled out. There were dozens of eggs to
be taken, and naked baby birds to be strung on a thorn, little
rabbits to be stoned to death; in autumn apples to be stolen
and always lies to be told to everyone. Granmer, to be sure,
whipped him and put soap in his mouth, and locked him up
every Sunday morning in a shed with the Bible open before
him, but that was nothing; in the shed were flies to be caught
and stuck on a pin, and regularly he spat into her milk-jugs
and put dirt into the lardy puddings she made. 'Her wouldn't
best he, noomye!'

Dolly was good to him, but nothing in him cared for her
except his stomach. Jim Holloman had sometimes allowed
him to sit by his fire, but of him he had been scared, because
he was mazed, and a witch. Willie he admired in his distorted
way, but Jack he feared and avoided. No one cared for Bill
Nye—the King of Oddmedodds, they called him in Rookhurst.
His affections were writhen like one of the pollard beeches in
the spinney that the winds and frosts of early spring upsweep-
ing and drear had blasted immaturely. But since the puppy,
who answered to the name of Tiger, had attached itself, the
sap of kindness had been rising in his hoof-marked spirit.

Bill Nye and Samuel Caw touched forelocks to Willie, and
the dog, Tiger, wriggled its belly in the grass in gratitude for
the pats on its head.

Samuel Caw had no dog, he told Willie, solemnly. His
father was a swineherd, employed on the pig farms of Sir John
Shapcote. In the autumn he would lead his drove into the
beechwoods for the brown mast that crunched under the foot.
He wore a pair of greenish boots too big for his feet by six
inches, and the sole of the left one had fallen away and flapped

as he walked, or rather shuffled. The boys were going to set springes of horsehair for moorhens that ran about in the water-meadows.

Willie walked on down the road. He would be in ample time for the motor, so he crossed a field to walk in the withy beds by the brook, to see the wildfowl. It would be but a slightly longer way to the Halt.

The wands were ruddy and yellow, and the ground squelched under his feet. Snipe and the smaller winter migrant, the Jack snipe, which to himself he called the mothflisie, jerked up from their feeding almost at their feet, and sped away in zig-zag flight. With bright eyes he watched a large marsh owl, with pensile and feathery talons, wafting itself from its roost beside a patch of flowering-rush, on wings yellow as the sedges. He looked for a nest, although he knew nothing would be there save perhaps a dead mouse or a cast pellet of bones and fur.

A family of longtailed titmice flitted among the wands, wheezing to themselves as they hung downwards in their restless search for insects. As they went from tree to tree the grey wings made a tiny drumming, and their long tails rustled on the moist still air of winter. The leaves of the early celandine were among the grasses, shaped on their curved stems like hafted delving spades. Seeing them, he felt a rush of joy in his breast. It was almost spring! Then in a hedgerow he found a dandelion, bedraggled and small, but it received a loving thought—dandelions wanted the spring just as he did.

Leaving the withy fields and the wimpling brook, he had to pass through a patch of waste land in order to return to the roadway. Scattered ashpoles reared starkly from the trodden wilderness of bramble undergrowth. Black circular patches and charred stick-ends showed where gipsies and tramps had made their fires during past wanderings. The waste land bordered the roadway for about a hundred yards. In front he saw a man crouching behind a chestnut-stole, holding something in his hand, and unmoving. With a start he recognised John Fry.

Warily Willie crept forward, trying to avoid stepping upon any twigs that would give warning of his stealthy approach.

Innumerable thistle heads of autumn bleached and downy pricked through his socks. Finches perching on the ashpoles called one to another, and sweet notes came from a clearing in front of the watching man. More flocks joined the twittering specks above, with them about a dozen red and black bullfinches, piping their call-notes. Willie wondered that John Fry should take any notice of birds. Or perhaps he was watching some one invisible to himself.

John Fry pulled something, leapt up, and ran forward. He carried a small square box in his hand.

'He's catching birds,' whispered Willie to himself.

John Fry knelt awhile, then returned, holding the cage under his arm. Willie watched him put down the cage, then sit on a log and fumble at the hem of his coat. John Fry bent slightly forward.

Willie watched, mystified. He heard a little cry, a little scream pitiful and despairing. Another and another, each feebler than the last. John Fry took up another cage and thrust a bird through the wire doorway.

Willie tried to shout, but his voice would not come. He ran forward, managing to gasp, 'What-what-are you doing, Mr. Fry?'

John Fry looked over his shoulder, and then back again at what he was doing.

'Wh-what are you doing with them?' cried Willie again, swallowing to free a constricted throat.

'What be that to do with you?'

'You are torturing them, do you know that?'

John Fry scowled. His nostrils were open wide.

'Be off before I trim you up!' he growled. 'D'ye hear?'

The finches in the treetops were still talking among themselves, and answering the decoy birds tied to string below. A flutter sounded from the cages on the ground, a ceaseless, beating of wings as the finches tried to escape. Peering nearer Willie saw that the crimson feathers around the beaks of the goldfinches were ragged, where the blood had stuck them together as they pushed their beaks between the iron bars. Small brown linnets hung to the wires and again and again strove with beating wings to be free.

In his right hand John Fry held a large pin. Willie went forward and looked over his shoulder, then stared at John Fry; for in the fearful glance he had seen that the chaffinches in the cage were dishevelled and clawing one another, and in their empty sockets the bright red blood was smeared.

At the river pothouses of Colham they matched the cock birds in song, each trying to outsing the other. The owners made bets on the endurance of their birds, which sang longer in the dark; so they blinded them.

'Y-y-you oughtn't to do that, Mr. Fry!' said Willie, stuttering. 'You must let the goldfinches go, please. I-i-it's too late for the blind chaffinches. I'm g-g-going to open—the—cages.'

John Fry had been sitting still, held by the boy's eyes; but when Willie knelt down and opened one door, releasing a tumbling, twittering, wry-winged flutter of goldfinches, he sprang forward and snatched the cage from him. Letting out a shrill scream Willie flung himself at John Fry, clutching his throat. The man gripped him round the waist and flung him against an ash-stump surrounded with brambles. Willie scrambled to his feet, and saw the birds fluttering in the cages. He ran towards them, but John Fry made for him.

'If you titch they bliddy cages, I won't answer what'll happen to you,' cried John Fry, his face and lips tightening.

'Hurray!' shouted Willie, half hysterically. 'Where's your Bible?'

John Fry started leaping over the brambles towards him, but Willie ran away, shouting out that he would get Big

Will'm to tear his head from his shoulders. Yes—backing away—Big Will'um would twist it and draw it out of his body with his bloody windpipe stretched like a bicycle tube. His father would hound him out of Rookhurst. They would go straight to the policeman's cottage about it. It was against the law—moving rather fast as John Fry started to crash after him—and he was a white sepulchre. Preacher, bah! God would send him to hell, the great hulking pig-stinker-horse-cheating bully. Wanted to marry Dolly, did he, and bullied Granmer Nye—

At this he hared away in alarm, for John Fry made a rush for him. But he was fleet, and fear gave him an added speed. He was chased as far as the roadway, where, to his relief and gladness, he saw the Cerr-Nores.

'John Fry netting birds! And blinding chaffbobs with a pin!' he gasped. 'The swine!'

'You do a bit of trapping yourself, sometimes, don't you?' replied Charlie Cerr-Nore, continuing to walk on. 'My dear fellow, why interfere with the man getting his living?'

'I haven't trapped for a long time,' stammered Willie, glancing round to see John Fry watching him from behind a willow tree.

'Write another letter to the papers about it,' suggested Cerr-Nore, walking on with his young brother.

Willie followed them to the Halt, hating the supercilious Charlie, and almost crying with impotence as he thought of a tiny chaffinch struggling in a great big hand, struggling as the pin was pushed——

He rode in the back of the motor, avoiding the others, formulating wild schemes against John Fry in his head.

In Colham High Street he met Bony and Rupert, and before nine o'clock every one in 5b knew that Mad Willie had been fighting a man trapping birds; and had even marked him, some declared.

Certainly Willie's scratched face, and bruise on the cheek

gave some sort of substantiality to all the tales that were told.

Just before break 5b seemed to become, in spite of the nidorous atmosphere in the classroom, a vitalised and eager band of boys, where before it had been a soporific mass. For Mr. Rore suddenly entered the room where Mr. Croodrane at the blackboard was talking about quadratic equations. Three smiling boys followed, bearing between them packages of white booklets. A sibilance ran round the room.

'Now you shall know your fates,' murmured the Headmaster with grim cheerfulness, 'Pass them round. One to each boy.'

'The Cambridge, the Cambridge,' hissed the boys, with trembling voices. They turned the pages, which seemed so flimsy and to stick together. Some one found the list of First Class Honours. With a dry throat and feeling as though he had swallowed some pepper, Willie turned over the pages. Everyone seemed to be speaking.

'Good Heavens, both the Goldings have got a First!'

'Effish, you've a Third. Coo, old Bryers 'z got four distinctions!'

'Fitzaucher's got distinction in Maths, Trig, Stinks, German, French, Geometry, and English.'

'Dove and Beckelt aren't in the list—they've failed. Lummy!'

'Where am I?' asked Willie.

'Here you are. Pass. With Bony, Macarthy, and about twenty more. Your pal Temperley's failed. By Jove, Swann and Slater have got a 'D' in divinity. They'll probably share the Bullnote Memorial.'

Mr. Rore was gazing intently at the various boys who seemed to him to typify humanity. There was Swann, tall and scholarly, with a curious manner of writing with his head first on one side then on the other, and with mobile tongue. Symons, a clever boy, with great natural abilities—Fitzaucher —the lad would go far. Bryers, a distinctly charming fellow, of good stock. Slater, inclined to be easy-going, but earnest, earnest. Walton, a clever boy, but his nose should be kept to the grindstone. Beckelt—foxy, like Effish. Watson, a curious mixture, his mentality was too loose-fibred to permit of any intense concentration. Dove, a wild impulsive but generous idiot. Macarthy a dull boy, representative of mediocrity. Maddison—

'Ah, Maddison.'

'Sir!' replied an uncertain voice.

'Come with me to my study, will you, when I leave? I have something of import to impart.'

Oh, what has he found out about me this time, wondered Willie. Ah, I know—John Fry! He would be expelled. His sight blackened momentarily with his bumping heart; with a feeling of unreality he went to the front of the class and stood before Mr. Rore. Jack, Phillip, he thought. I'll always have Jack and Phillip, whatever happens.

'Now boys, the results are distinctly good—and distinctly bad. Swann, Golding major and minor, Lonsdale, Moffat, Manning, Lucas, good. Distinctly good. Some, however, are distinctly disappointing. Beckelt, for instance. Pauper spirit, sir. You are paying the price of your folly. Papescent mentality, sir. Be sure your sins will find you out! In life you will go to the wall. Nature never forgives and never forgets. But trials are sent us to test our strength. *Ad astra per aspera!*'

Willie's heart was easier now, settling to resignation. He watched The Bird's face, the keen eyes under the semi-circular glasses.

'The great thing, boys, is this. Make the most of *now*. No failure is entirely wasted if its significance is apprehended! What boys agree? All of you. Good. I am glad that you are wise, even after the event! Let bygones be bygones. To the failures I say: Don't let it happen again. The only thing of value in this world is work. Hard at it, hard at it! *What should be, shall be!!* As you are now, so you will be out in the world. Take the example of the savage. The savage cannot benefit by experience. He is content—smug. He has not advanced because he is content to lie on his back in the sun all day and let ripe bananas drop into his mouth. Overcome that banana inclination! Maddison, follow!'

While he had been speaking the boys were still. Mr. Croodrane stood by his visible labours of chalk, square roots. and quadratic equations, like one who was waiting for the Headmaster to leave the room before he could resume his complete personality.

Willie followed the Headmaster, walking swiftly with his pink shiny head held so high that he gave the follower the impression of floating over the wooden floor, past the brown desks where the Specials frowned over deep problems arising from debtor and creditor balances. Under the clock and the portrait in oils of the late Dr. Bullnote, D.D., Mr. Rore floated, his heels echoing on the tessellated floor of Little Hall. By the shiny glass of the model steamship, and so into the dread study with its little square of worn carpet, yellow wooden chairs, and window view of evergreens with the asphalted entrance beyond.

Mr. Rore sat down, and took up a large sheet of paper. His modulated voice urged itself impersonally towards the boy standing motionless, scarcely breathing, before him:

'Ah, Maddison. Yes. The Divinity Exam. The Visiting Examiners have appended a note about your papers. Were you ill?'

His gem-hard eyes were fixed on the boy before him, regarding his fixed stare on the ground, his inability to meet his own eyes.

'Is the boy mad?' his voice incised, like a diamond cutting into glass.

A tear rolled down the boy's face. For some extraordinary reason a phrase passed through the Headmaster's head. 'In vain he breasts the bars of brass.' In vain himself tried to stimulate the finest in the natures of his boys. The boy before him, a senior boy, was weeping. He had no moral backbone!

Mr. Rore went on, evenly and swiftly:

'I have been sent your Divinity Papers. The Examiners state that on the whole the paper is good—very good. However in the first question there is a deliberate impertinence. Read that, sir! Do you recognise your own handwriting?'

He handed the boy a sheet of paper. How strange it all looked, how long ago it was written. Then, underlined in red ink, he saw the awful rhyme:

'And the Lord said unto Moses, All ye shall wear long noses: All except Aaron, and he shall have a square 'n.'

Willie stared at the paper, unable to think or speak, waiting.

'Well, can you explain it, Maddison?' asked Mr. Rore softly.

Willie waited.

'Come, come. Answer my question.'

'No, Sir.'

'I shall have to consider seriously your removal. The other questions are answered with brilliance. That is so curious. Your total marks, were it not for a distorted comic spirit, would entitle you to the award of the Bullnote Memorial Exhibition. Come sir, come, there must be some reason. Were you overworked?'

'I worked very hard, Sir,' pleaded Willie, simulating pathos and looking up at the master.

'Did you work on Saturday and Sunday?'

Willie hesitated.

'Come, sir, I will not eat you.' Mr. Rore was nearly smiling.

'Yes, Sir,' smiled Willie.

'Ah! Therein may be the solution. But you will not take my advice. I am older than you, sir. I can see with clarity. An eleventh hour pressure, sir! Why, just think of it! You have done brilliantly, brilliantly! Ah, foolish boy, why do you waste your talents? That pauper spirit, sir, showing its hand in all our works! Then you were unaware of this blemish?'

'Yes, Sir.'

'Ah, yes. Is it your own poetical effort?'

'No, Sir.'

'Where did you learn it?'

'Here at school, Sir.'

'Oh!' Mr. Rore smiled. Willie smiled. 'And I dare say it was a rime in Shakespeare's time, my dear sir! Or should we say Lord Bacon? Recently I have read a pamphlet that proves the authorship of the plays. All boys should read it. That reminds me, I will give the Sixth the benefit of my good fortune.' Mr. Rore made a minute note in his pocket book. 'They will appreciate it. A tailor's dummy, sir, your William Shakespeare! The woodcut proves it. By the sleeves. How illusion exists in the human race! Well, Maddison, your paper will stand. The examiners left the final award of a distinction to me. Now, do better next time, Maddison. Our trials are sent to test us. You have won the Bullnote Memorial Exhibition. A brilliant paper, Maddison. Let me see you in future, among the workers! You are too fond of bananas, you know!'

Mr. Rore smiled again, and Willie smiled again. 'Come Maddison, you have the power in you to do good work! Overcome the banana habit! Now return. Double! Make up for lost time!'

Which Willie did, meeting a tongue-curling Taffy with happy face. Mr. Croodrane smiled lazily.

'Ah, the wanderer returned, wha'?'

'Yar,' said Willie, but instantly coughing to conceal his impertinence.

'Ahha. Wonderful. You have not been showing to the Headmaster your stuffed elephants, have you? Ah, ah, um, Oh, wha'?'

Loose laughter from 5b.

'For one who has recently been—um—interviewed in secluded—um—incarceration, your expression is one of intense optimism, bor. Doubtless you are pleased with the result of your studies!' Mr. Croodrane's voice became niminipiminy with sarcasm. 'I observe that your name graces a most distinguished place in the list of—um—shall we say, honorary honours. What a pity that there was no paper upon "How to Stuff Birds," was it not?'

'I really cannot say, Sir.'

'Oh, perhaps our humour does not interest you now you are among the superior Passes?'

'The humour interested me the first few times I encountered it, Sir,' replied Willie, and one boy said, 'Ha, ha! Mad Willie's idea of a joke.'

'Stop that!' said Mr. Croodrane, looking round.

Willie at his seat could afford to look disdainfully at the ceiling, and to raise supercilious eyebrows. He had won the Bullnote—sixty-three volumes of the Everyman Library. He would try for the works of Richard Jefferies, Isaak Walton, and books upon Shooting and Fishing. He would not tell father. Father should see him appear upon the platform again and again, flushed of face, and stagger off with an armful of books, while Big Hall would be filled with a storm of cheering, and the kids in the Lower School would point him out afterwards to their parents and sisters. He would probably have to make a speech, in which case he would tell them how much was due to the Dear Old School. He would send a copy of the paper anonymously to Elsie in Belgium.

He sat, simmering with happiness, and heedless of the stink of the classroom; for no windows were open, the hot-water pipes were full on, and Willie was never happy in any room where the windows were closed. He had won the Bullnote! He, Maddison. Ha, ha! Sixty-three volumes of the Everyman Library. He would send them all to Elsie, as a birthday present!

During the break Golding major offered to bet any one about the results of the Bullnote. As every one favoured Swann he said he would give three to two in pennies on Swann. The brothers had a preliminary argument about this, and apparently disagreed, so Golding minor retired to another part of the playground and offered three to two in pennies on Slater. In little notebooks they wrote down the names of their clients. Willie called Bony, Rupert and Mac apart, and hidden behind one of the buttresses in the upper playground he advised them to bet that the winner would be neither Slater nor Swann. They scoffed at first, but he was so in earnest that they pressed for more information. Willie shook his head and smiled. Bony said that it was absurd, since only those two had got distinctions.

'You won't regret,' affirmed Willie. 'I've got some inside information. Honest, I have. I swear I have, Bony, you needn't scoff. Have you ever known me tell a lie?'

'Thousands of times.'

'Well, perhaps hundreds. But this is on the sacred honour of the Owl Club. Do it quickly! The bell will go in a tick.'

But they would not.

When 5b filed through Hall a minute later the line, straggling by the Senior Notice Board, joined the surge round its green oasis upon which was pinned a small piece of paper with Mr. Rore's tiny writing upon it

Sn. Lcl. Camb. Exn.
Bullnote Mml. Exhb.
Winner, ex 5c, 5b, 5a, and VIθ Fms.
W. B. Maddison.
Hdmstr. offers congrtlns.

Various effects were made by this announcement.

Bony, peering like a lean and featherless bird over the heads of the crowd, cracked his fingers and from his throat came a crow-like ejaculation, ' Cor!'

Aunt Sally seemed visibly to swell, and his red hair to lose its blood-orange sheen: he grinned with disappointment. His fat legs, in black breeches, became gradually elliptical under the disappointment, for his insteps were weak, and when meditating he always stood on the outer welts of his boots.

Golding major glanced at Golding minor; their eyes were round as pennies.

Swann turned his mild bespectacled face to Willie, smiled whimsically, then sought his hand, murmuring, 'I say, I'm awfully glad, Willie.' Ever afterwards Willie had a warm affection for Swann.

Effish for once said nothing, but simply stared, while his chum Beckelt shot a blot of ink from his fountain pen upon the paper. Effish then crept up behind, and emptied Fitzaucher's satchel on the floor. Several boys immediately commenced to kick the fallen books as far away from Fitzaucher as possible.

Cerr-Nore said, 'Poo, any fool could have won it. Frankly who wants a beastly scripture prize? I don't.'

Willie wondered why at the moment of his triumph he felt so uncaring and languid. Nor did this mood change when he got home. He hoped that father would speak to him again about his homework, and tell him that he was a slacker. He would reply nothing, but let father declare many things for which afterwards he would be sorry. Somewhat disappointingly father appeared to be in a good temper when after tea he came into the kitchen; and Willie managed to slip into a prepared hiding-place a volume of ghastly murder tales lent him by Macarthy.

Mr. Maddison sat on the edge of the table. Suddenly his son told him that he had 'passed his exam. all right, and had won the certificate.'

'That's good news,' commented the father, 'it will be an advantage to you. This will be your penultimate term at school.'

Willie waited.

'I've heard from your Uncle Richard. He is prepared to mention about you to the Secretary of the Moon Fire Office, where Phillip is going to work, apparently. Well?'

Willie replied nothing.

'Aren't you grateful for any one taking a little interest in you?'

'Yes, Father.'

'Your gratitude is admirably concealed, my boy. The Moon Fire Office is a good office, I believe. Mr. Rore told me last term that you had plenty of ability, only you were lazy and slipshod. If you are lazy and slipshod in London you won't last very long. The competition there is tremendous, and the weaklings go to the wall.'

'That was a grey lag goose honking,' suddenly cried Willie, listening to the night outside. Immediately he felt foolish and confused. Mr. Maddison seized upon his involuntary remark.

'Even at a serious moment like this your attention is absorbed by trivial things. I am afraid it's no use my talking to you. Your wretched hobby, or rather obsession, will be your undoing. Well, I shall say no more. Don't blame me, however, when you realise your foolishness too late. Don't come to me and say, "Why didn't you *make* me work, Father?" You will get no sympathy then. No. I shall have no loafers round me. Well, I've done my part, any way,' and he went out of the kitchen, his slippers dragging on the floor.

Willie tried to read the tale of a young and beautiful woman found in an open boat on the Thames, 'with a brown stain on her blouse, ringed and burnt by three pistol-shots at close quarters.' But it had no interest for him. 'It was immediately obvious at the post-mortem that she had been pregnant.' The tale lost its sinister fascination for him as he thought of having to go away, far away to London.

When Biddy came in half an hour later, she found him sitting staring before him, lolling on an elbow. An unattended fire was low in the grate. She spoke to him; but he frowned, and did not answer.

'Homework be hard to-night?' she enquired, coming in with some kindling sticks.

'Homework! Jack and I never do any. Didn't you know that?'

' 'Tis a lot of old nonsense, anyhow. I don't see that anyone be any better for having all that stuff inside 'em.'

'You're a pauper spirit, Biddy, that's what you are. Like the black man, who is content to let ripe bananas drop into his mouth, and lie down all day!'

'A black man, be I?' Well, I'd sooner be black than scarlet!' replied the old woman, significantly.

'Oh shut up, you old fool!' he cried, jumping up, and slinging his books into the satchel, he went upstairs to his bedroom. Why must all things change and die, he cried to himself, flinging wide the window and leaning out into the night. There was no answer in the starry darkness, no reply from the moon peering like the head of a luminous owl over the beech wood.

Chapter 22

YELLOW celandines starred the hedgerows and the meadows, rooks clamoured in the massy beech trees, every day the bird-song grew happier. In March the chiffchaff came to the lake-side, and the sand-martins flitted about the quarry. Easter brought bloom to the sallows, and the happy humble bees yellow with pollen. The Bishop stayed a night with the Rev. Odo Cerr-Nore; and Willie and Jack in their best dark suits knelt on the Chancel steps before him, feeling very good as they were blessed. After this came the annual cross-country Inter-House Harriers Race, when Willie, who had not been selected as captain, much to his disappointment, came in third, but first in his House. Then came the Easter holidays, when Jack came nesting with Willie once, and then no more; he was busy on the farm. Macarthy went out with him, but after he had failed to climb the beech tree that Willie climbed—the same tree as in the previous years—he too came no more; and Willie went alone.

More change after the holidays. New prefects; and more than one half of 5b, including Maddison, became 5a, and in the slang of Upper School, entered the Roaring Oven. Macarthy and Bony, members of the Owl Club, drifted into the Special Class, and as Effish said, arrived *per aspera ad astra**.

In the classroom adjoining the Headmaster's study, Mr. Rore instructed 5a in nearly every subject. The last Cambridge results were good; the next year should be better. Among what were known officially as Secondary Public Schools, Mr. Rore hoped to raise Colham School—Colham Grammar School was

* Through difficulties to the stars.

212

going out of use; Colham School, or simply Colham, was the new style—to be among the leading schools, as judged by the results of the Cambridge Local Examinations. Therefore, for 5a, there was slight relief from the enforced swotting in the Roaring Oven, except during the weekly half-hour gym, the visits to the Physics and Chemical Labs., and the bi-weekly occasions when the class sat round Big Hall in a great oval of end-to-end forms, and copied Mr. Worth's artistically arranged jumble of spheres, pyramids, cylinders and cubes.

During the Drawing Lesson, Mr. Worth himself would perambulate outside the oval, examining the work over the artist's shoulders, praising this one, remarking to the next that the use of rulers or compasses was forbidden, sketching a less wrong perspective here, passing in silence a hopeless case there. Nowadays the drawing classes were kept in the strictest order; no boy, even Effish, dared to rag Mr. Worth. Literally and metaphorically Mr. Worth showed his teeth at the least irregularity.

A remarkable transformation had taken place in the drawing master's appearance since the Easter holidays. He walked vigorously up Colham Hill to school in the morning; his eyes were bright; he ate school luncheon with vigour, always leaving a clean plate, when on luncheon duty. The reason of these changes had been quickly made known to the Upper School by a boy called Crimp, whose father was a dentist in Colham. During the holidays Mr. Worth had had all his teeth drawn. For years he had suffered from slow self-poisoning, and therefore Willie's former description of Mr. Worth looking as though he were being embalmed against his will was less fantastically exaggerated than might have been thought. Mr. Worth was now a popular master—when before he had been scarcely considered—but it was dangerous to attempt to rag him.

However, whenever the back of Useless was turned, boys still talked and laughed quietly; but this manifestation of the social instinct was sought to be repressed like every other one.

Mr. Rore was liable to peer round the doorway of 5a—which was the Roaring Oven also for the Sixth—and cry, 'I saw your eyes, sir. Come along, Sir, come along,' and take him for 'that cane' like a hawk seizing a sparrow in the stubble, or rather, like one of the unrealisable names which, in History lessons, were described by him as tyrants, against which their forefathers had ever striven for justice, so the uninterested classes were always taught.

Only those boys possessing more nervous vitality than the sedate majority were caned. Irregularities among what Mr. Rore considered the better boys, comprising that sedate majority, were usually dealt with by contributions demanded for the Fresh Air Fund. This minor punishment was in use only among the Fifth Form classes, all contributions to it (usually by way of maternal pockets), being, declared Mr. Rore, voluntary. Also voluntary, declared Mr. Rore, were the trusting-to-honour penalties of 'No sugar in your tea for a week?' or 'No jam for two days—is it agreed? Very well. Don't let it occur again! Hard at it, hard at it! Quite quiet boys, quite quiet!'

The boys of 5a used their natural faculties to avoid unnatural mental and nervous stress. Lightly and easily they knew that they were liable, if detected, to be caned as cheats and hypocrites, never realising how their minds were being served by the protective instincts deeply rooted within their very beings.

Since Mr. Rore set nearly three hours homework every night during the spring and summer terms, some method had to be invented to give the appearance of this amount having been prepared. Among the section habitually accused of mental pauperism—Willie would never have been admitted to 5a had he not won the Bullnote Memorial—were a few bold boys who rubbed out the blue-pencilled tick passing a Mathematical homework exercise of a previous night, and showed up the same Mathematics again and again, trusting to the Headmaster's speed as he passed down the rows of desks to avoid detection. And when correcting papers, the two boys in each desk were supposed to exchange papers; four-fifths of 5a retained its own papers, and behind piled books jotted down the answers as Mr. Rore read them out. By this means the extraordinary efficiency of the Headmaster's method, was, he told members of his staff, being proven continually to himself. Few boys failed to obtain at least seventy-five per cent. of the possible marks.

5a was expected to prepare four or five pages of Latin in the space of forty minutes allotted in the three hours of homework. Livy and Ovid were indecipherable to most of 5a, but in response to the query of 'How much prepared', no boy dared to show a hand for an amount under four pages. This communal euphemism had to be upheld in practice; so 5a devised a system by which it was possible to ascertain the approximate passage to be translated by each individual. Mr. Rore always began at the lowest boy (word-perfect was his rendition), and allowed the next boy to continue, as he wished. The turns were passed up from the bottom of the class to the top. Sometimes the minor disaster known as 'mucking the turn' occurred when it was not unusual for two rows of boys being unable to proceed. Intense agitation greeted a mucked turn. Each boy, crouching behing his parapet of books, waited ready to search dictionary or notes as the prairie-fire of 'Next boy—Next boy —Next—Next' swept nearer. 'Turn, turn,' was whispered, 'Pass up the turn!' After each of a series of disasters a phantom turn would float up the class, followed by another, and still another. Those who had been passed crouched stilly over their books, waiting, waiting, waiting, for the end of tension.

Mr. Rore had invented his own methods of teaching History, Geography and Latin Grammar, based on the requirements of examinations; the cramming of a vast amount of dates, names and facts which must be committed to memory for the purpose of reproduction in sets of dates, names, and facts on paper at the end of the Christmas term. Names, dates, places, speeches, products, imports, exports, irregular verbs, genders, declensions, were printed in his own special shorthand and word-essences, in strings and series of strings of letters, punctuation marks, and figures, in thin booklets which were distributed to the class. There were by-products of fun even in these booklets, which were certainly helpful to memory; such as the line, 'The poppy teat of the bony mouth corpse,' made up of words whose Latin equivalents had something tricky about them. What the trickiness was Willie never realised.

The Headmaster's method was similar to the method secretly evolved by Willie by which to learn-by-heart—as the educational process was called. Such as the secret ruler crib he had prepared, but never used, for the Bullnote Memorial Prize. He remembered most of the map of Europe by the faces he saw in the outlines of countries. Wales was a pig's face, with cocked ear, snout, jowl, and chinlap; France was a chinless *chef* with nibbled features in profile, his cap crumpled and pushed back on his head; Italy was a riding boot with decayed toes; Greece was the roots of a parsnip-cluster which the gardener had not thinned properly after sowing the seeds in a dibber-hole; Spain was a square-faced moor, with nose flattened like one of the boxers in the booth at the Colham September Fair.

Shakespeare was hopeless; a mass of queer words giving few pictures, and long speeches unlike real talk. Boys had to underline passages of *King Henry the Fifth*, and the notes at the end, at Mr. Rore's dictation, for the purpose of making easier their memorising, so that extra time could be devoted to the more important Mathematics. Shakespeare was hopeless; unlistening Willie dreamed of Rookhurst forest and the sky, and drew herons, trees, owls, eggs and fish on the borders of the pages, not bothering to underline.

Mr. Rore sometimes suffered from neuralgia. The pains of this human ailment had prompted consideration for all possible sufferers. Therefore he excluded draughts, and with them, fresh air. The windows were often closed, even in sunny weather. Through the glass rendered opaque by moisture the morning sun glowed like an immense shine-bedraggled dandelion, soon, too soon, to move away from Willie's desk and leave him in shadow. He dreamed back into the ancient sunlight of his past happiness. In the gloomed school arose the carking hum of learning. So for hundreds of years, hid from summery beauty, the hum of learning had filled the school; centuries of wasted sunshine, while under the northern eaves the martins built their nests, and flew at will in the blue air of heaven, heedless of the everlasting drone within the shut and shaded rooms. Sometimes their happy twitter came through the window, heard by Willie as he endured the days.

Everlastingly Mr. Rore spurred himself to an unflagging zeal, girding himself to maximum effort. By the power so acquired and with it a righteous confidence did he urge his boys to do likewise. Continually he sought to drive home his ideals. Thus one day, during a passage of the Æneid, he broke in upon the changing murmur of voices:

'Boys, do you fully appreciate your great good fortune, having the fruit of Vergil's genius before you! What boys are enjoying this lesson? Ten? Nine? Eight? Six? five, four, three, two, one, nought? Minus ten? Only Maddison! I can't hear, sir? Oh he enjoyed it ten! I wonder, sir, are you lying again? Your mind cannot soar. You are of the earth earthy. Continue, next boy!'

Ten minutes later Willie lifted his head again, and gazed towards the window. 'Ponder, Maddison, ponder! Your mind wanders too often, sir! Well, Maddison, what is it! A window open? Very well, two inches, no more. Neuralgia—what boys have suffered? All except Maddison! Lo! he asks for a window!'

Mr. Rore smiled round the classroom, and continued:

'Work is the greatest good. Nevertheless, all our human works are webbed with imperfections. We can but do useful work, and take what light it brings. Work, for its own sake!

Work should not be sought for making money solely. Money is a false god. An entirely erroneous value is placed upon money by a short-sighted civilisation. What boys agree? All except Maddison! He sulks about his window?'

'Headache, Sir,' mumbled Willie, in a panic at Mr. Rore's attention to himself.

'I'm sorry,' murmured the voice of the Headmaster, suddenly gentle, and the tortuous lesson went on.

School hours terminated, according to the prospectus, at a quarter-past twelve in the morning and at half-past four in the afternoon. One day Mr. Rore made a suggestion, about extra work. 5a, he said, might accept or reject it at will. His proposal was that in the morning 5a should agree to stay till twenty-three minutes after twelve, and until a quarter to five in the afternoon. What boys agreed? A show of hands was requested. Every boy agreed. The Headmaster determined that these times should be adhered to; so he ordered the boy in the desk nearest the door to remind him of those times when they were reached by the hands of the school clock. This boy was usually Willie, and he performed his duty conscientiously. But occasionally Mr. Rore might be tremendously interested in a problem of Differential Calculus or the Binomial Theorem, and would suggest an extension. 'What boys agreed?' All boys showed hands and expressionless faces—until Mr. Rore turned back to the blackboard. On many occasions after five o'clock a mutinous 5a left the inspissated atmosphere of its classroom, weary and grumbling. The oats were in jag in the fields by which Willie cycled; the wind swayed the barley graceful and topped with hail; it rippled silky currents on the wheat and fluttered the green pennons. Dreamily the spreading colour recharged him, and the effect of the day was shed.

Mr. Rore had further suggestions. The 11 o'clock break was reduced, after a show of assenting hands, from five minutes to two minutes—'In and out again immediately, boys! Then hard at it, hard at it! Make the most of your opportunities!'

THE SEED LOOSENING

The clenched fist of Mr. Rore, moved dynamically against his forehead, illustrated the store of his mental power. 'In and out again immediately!' There was no time for a drink out of the cast-iron mug chained to the iron basin, into which the water trickled so slowly. Coming in again even from The Bog the stench of the classroom, with its windows closed or nearly closed since 9 o'clock, often made Willie protest. 'Poo, what a f—ing stink, chaps! Algebra, what boys have suffered? All except the Old Bird. Lo! he asks for more power. Lonsdale, Lonsdale, you're under the window, open it, for God's sake. Quick, for the love of God, before The Bird comes in!'

But Lonsdale, first-class honours in the Senior Cambridge, with four distinctions, never did anything without instruction and, owing to the design of the room, it was cold under the window near the top of the class, owing to down-draught.

'I'll knock your blinking eye out, if you don't open that blasted window, young Lonsdale!'

'Shut-up, Maddison,' demanded Manning, curtly. Manning was nearly eighteen years old, and a Prefect—one with the power to give notes, or reports to the Headmaster. He was a great hefty fellow, captain of Willie's House, and strong as an ox.

A sudden, paralysing voice from behind: 'I saw your eyes, sir! Be careful, sir! Put Maddison's name down for twopence for the Fresh Air Fund, will you? Agreed Maddison?'

'Yes, Sir.'

'Quite quiet, boys! quite quiet!'

The door of the study shut as silently as it was opened.

'I have to pay for Fresh Air, and yet I can't get it,' said Willie out loud, dashing down his pen and flinging his head on his elbowed hand with a loud jolt on the desk-lid. 'One day, I tell you, chaps, I shall—'

'Pay another twopence to the Fresh Air Fund. Is it agreed, Maddison?'

'Yes, Sir.'

'I shan't tell you again. Be careful, sir, or you will have to leave this school, sir!'

It was not safe to shift about on the wooden seat too much; to laugh or smile with a neighbour was to risk the talon-stroke of the hawk, and the demand, varying from soft to gem-hard, 'Come along, Maddison! Come along!'

Sometimes, when 5a was with Useless, Zimmy, or in either of the laboratories, and Mr. Rore was engaged with the flower of the school, the Sixth, the door would very quietly, almost stealthily open, and a figure creep in, close the door, and glide like a long shadow into the corner. Sooner or later would sound the blast, 'Who sent you in? Can't hear! Use your lips and teeth, sir!'

A dejected voice would murmur that Mr. Worley—a regular injector—had sent him in, please Sir.

'Pauper spirit, sir! Wasting my time again! Do you think I have nothing to do that you should come here bothering me? Face the wall!' the voice would storm, out of the consciousness torn from its blackboard problem.

His eyes eight to ten inches from the cream-coloured wall, the pauper spirit would stand there in suspense during a period varying from a minute to eighty minutes—a double hour— finding wan interest in counting the specks, or the brush marks in the area opposite his face; and in seeking, in the slight contours in the plaster, the outlines and shapes of objects living in his memory—fish, stamps, locomotives, fields, lanes, build-ings, birds, trees, a girl's face or shining hair—while listening remotely to the jumble of words and answers over his left shoulder; words and answers of a familiar but unrealisable lesson about the pre-arranged crucifixion of Jesus of Nazareth; the dim-visioned descent of Aeneas into Hades; the mechanics of Projectiles; or philosophical asides incomprehensible to the consciousness, deracinated and enslaved, awaiting the strokes of pain—the murmured and incisive wisdom of Mr. Rore:

'Humour and Paradox, boys, are well worth a little analysis.

"He that hath most, hath least"—for what befell the cup of Diogenes? "The wise man is the fool" merely a paraphrase of Socratic "Knowledge is the consciousness of ignorance." Are there not Fools—and Greater Fools? This leads to a little fooling with

> "Man wants but little here below,
> Nor wants that little long,"

for I remember I must to the barber after half-past five this evening! So strangely do our thoughts leap from crag to plain in the ranges of the mind! And behold, an extraordinary sight. Lonsdale's tongue darting in and out of his lips like the tongue of a little bird! There, Lonsdale, I did not mean to embarrass you; but it was so comic a sight while I was speaking.'

Modulated smiles from the privileged Sixth Form around the blackboard, brought in from private study for Higher Mathematics—the trusted and magnificent Prefects; and a simulated smile from the corner culprit, hoping to escape the whack by an obvious appreciation of The Bird's wit. On one such occasion the smile succeeded; and Willie left swiftly, thinking in bright gratitude that he would try never to be sent in again. Indeed, it was chiefly owing to a desire not to displease Mr. Rore that during his last term at Colham School he spent several hours in The Bog, writing various idle thoughts and opinions on the wall, and listening with melancholy to the dripping of water in the tanks overhead.

Out of school, the air and grass and corn and sun-flashing water came slowly to full summer. Among the hardening stalks of the wheat the partridge led her chicks, while the mouse-hawk soared in the wind over the meadows. The wind came over the heated fields, changing the green hues of the corn as it passed sighing, as though in regret that all must change.

Willie prepared himself for the end. He got permission from

Mr. Rore to go to the dentist twice in one week; and in the afternoons he walked far and alone on the thyme-grown downs, passing swallow-haunted dewponds, hazel thickets and thorn brakes in the combes and hollows by lonely farm houses, with the high clouds for his serene companions. Every Wednesday and Saturday afternoon he missed cricket, and church on Sunday, and set out alone. He sought to tire himself in these walks, but drew strength from the firm sheep-cropped sward, mile after mile on the top of the green world. His voice became softer; he shrunk into himself in 5a classroom—in his mind he was walking under the sky, revisiting old twisted thorns, the Roman encampment, the dewponds, the beech-clumps where the wind was ever wandering.

One evening he strolled down to the dipping pool, and watched with quiet melancholy the boys splashing and shouting. Returning along the water's edge he met Dolly, and sat down under an oak tree with her, among the poppies and the reddening sorrel spires rising by the bushes overgrowing the bank. Shining flies danced in the gold-westering light of the sun, and the ghost moths spun and hovered among the grass-heads. They spoke of Jim—he would never come back now, said Dolly. It was no good ever trying to love anybody— 'Don't you ever think of anyone more than yourself, Will'um.' Willie chewed his stalk of sweet grass and stared at the water in sympathy. Voices and the rustling of feet came near; and Charlie Cerr-Nore walked past with a friend, giving him a sidelong glance that made Willie, when they had gone by, rise and say goodbye.

That next evening Mr. Maddison said to him, while he was sitting at the kitchen table with a heap of books beside him, and a pen in his hand. 'I'd like a word with you a moment, please.'

Willie got up and followed his father into the library.

'Shut the door, please.'

Willie stood still, with an expressionless face.

THE SEED LOOSENING

'Apparently you have been seen lately in the company of that woman from the keeper's cottage in Tetley's plantations. You're almost a man now, and must think of what other people might say. I'm not accusing you of anything, please bear in mind. Just a friendly tip, old chap.'

'Thank you, Father.'

Mr. Maddison waited, as though half-expecting his son to say something; but when Willie said nothing, he added, 'Well, that's all, I think.'

Willie went out of the room, and returned to the kitchen. Biddy would not meet his direct gaze. He sat down at the table and resumed his homework. After making a few minute notes in pencil between three lines of Ovid's *Metamorphoses*, he closed the book, packed his satchel, and got up.

'I've made ee a lovely cherry tart for supper, Master Willie,' said Biddy, not looking round.

'Thank you; but I shall not be in to supper,' he replied, going out of the door. The wind and the evening star were everlasting on the hills.

Chapter 23

THREE weeks before Speech Day the music master, known as Beerface, reappeared at Colham School in his wide black hat and black cloak, which partly covered his ginger hair, ruddy face, and five feet nought of stature. Every boy exulted at his appearance, on account of the promised choir-practices and their attendant easy times, and because Beerface was popular. All the first morning pairs of boys were summoned to the piano in Big Hall, and those who were not immediately rejected were put among the trebles, altos, tenors or basses. Willie was placed among the tenors, for which he was sorry, since Bony, Macarthy, Clemow, Hoys, and all his other friends were selected as basses.

The practices were looked forward to eagerly. *The Wreck of the Hesperus* was the cantata chosen for that year. Three mornings a week Big Hall was filled with the sounds and noises of practice. Shrill trebles piped their parts, combining sometimes with a band of altos cooing most harmoniously. Again and again the deep basses growled, *It was the schooner Hesperus that sailed the wintry sea*, then the mellow altos took up the story, *And the skipper had taken his little daughter to bear him company*. Now was the chance of the soaring trebles, *Blue were her eyes as the fairy-flax Her cheeks like the dawn of day And her bosom white as the hawthorn buds That ope in the month of May*. Thus in portions would the tale be told. Sometimes Beerface sang parts himself. Willie thought he was wonderfully clever, since he was able to sing a high treble, a plaintive alto, a ringing tenor, and a basso profundo, by turns.

Sitting on the form among the tenors, Willie soon learned

the melodies, and did his best to swamp the numerous basses who bellowed thunderously just behind them. He urged the score or so singers of his own section to sing with such effect that the basses would be inaudible on Speech Day. He strained his voice and grew so red in the face that the music master interrupted the practice, and said gently, 'Go easy, boy! You are supposed to be singing, not emulating one of your screech owls!'

There was mixed laughter, since the Owl Club was held in derision. It had developed into an Anti-Prefect Society, and conducted a wary guerilla warfare against the Sixth Form. Mad Willie was considered by the Sixth to be a rotten little tike, as he sided with boys of the lower forms, when, for instance, senior boys wanted to break up a game in the fives court by the traditional method of rooting their pill out of the playground. He had been called several times before the prefects, and once had been given the whack by The Bird. The Lower School said, 'We votes Mad Willie is a decent chap.'

During the last week Mr. Croodrane joined the basses. He sat just behind Willie, and blast-like noises came sonorously from him. Even the addition of Mr. Worley and Mr. Ellison to the tenors could not swamp Taffy's terrific notes. Rattle-through, fingering nervously his oakum moustache and wearing his torn gown, also joined the tenors, but he was tone-deaf, and by his earnest cacophony threw the two rows into mingled despair and mutiny. He appeared oblivious of his defects, and continued earnestly to sing wrong notes and at wrong moments. He came but once, but was heard frequently in class to be humming his part, to the accompaniment of absent-minded fingernail-nibbling and knee vibration.

Speech Day loomed very near. A restless excitement drifted about the school. Horizontal and parallel bars, the vaulting horse, ropes and rings were removed. The face of the clock was cleaned, and it promptly stopped. Strings of flags were arranged overhead, all the friends of Great Britain—France, Russia, Belgium, Japan; together with an assortment of maritime signals—which, accordingly to Effish, indicated Cholera, Distress, Any Port in a Storm, Shivered Timbers, etc. The gay coloured string radiated from the gas ring. The display of the obsolescent illustrated weeklies was removed from the walls, and the dust from various ledges flicked to the floor. The portrait-frame of the late Dr. Bullnote, D.D., had a wreath of spotted laurel-leaves pinned to its top. Gangs of boys were set to work. The miniature platforms supporting the desks of some masters were commandeered, lugged by shuffle-footed boys to Big Hall, and laid against the main platform. The Specials seized every opportunity to rag the workers. Thus one alarmed small boy arrived in Rattlethrough's room with a wooden cube, with Mr. Worth's compliments, only to make a terrified return with his burden.

The morning before Speech Day came, spent in a noise-scatter of work and petty ragging. Partitions were rolled back, disclosing hollow and unfamiliar classrooms. The Specials enjoyed themselves hugely. Some were leaving at the half-term. Wastepaper baskets were emptied over the heads of smaller boys. Mr. Worth's models suffered an unnecessary violence; his sphere was found in two halves, much to his consternation. Inkwells were emptied into desks, books intermingled, nibs shattered, puncture solution stuck on some seats. The French master's gown was found in his waste-paper basket; the words I DON'T THINK were chalked across one of Mr. Kenneth's brown-paper geneological trees of English kings and queens. GET THAT POWER, QUITE QUIET BOYS, and HARD AT IT appeared in chalk in various lobbies. One of Mr. Croodrane's cat-skins was found inside the hired grand piano, muffling several hammers.

Mr. Rore, never flurried, but always working at the highest speed, announced that a rehearsal would take place that afternoon. Willie knew what a rehearsal meant; he had taken part in the previous seven. It meant hauling gymnastic apparatus upon the conglomerated platform: it meant coming out of the open space behind the platform, composed of the combined classrooms of 3a, 4c, and 4b, a dozen times like a swarm of ants: it meant sitting still on narrow crowded forms while master argued, pointed, directed, and wilted before Mr. Rore: it meant having one's knees cracked against the form in front, and doing it all again and again and again and again. So he decided to be absent for afternoon rehearsal, and went to Rookhurst instead by the fields.

He wandered about in the beech wood all the afternoon. In the tree-tops the young rooks made a vast commotion and flapping.

Elsie will be home next month, he thought, as he stared at the bright green shuffle of leaves over his head. He lay on the moss by the roots of a beech tree. The dancing shadow of summer played over his half-closed eyes; he yielded himself to the dreamy beauty of the afternoon. A green woodpecker, called gallypot, came round the trunk above, and peered down, lowering its red head. He heard its claws scratching on the bark as it pushed itself up with the spread and pointed feathers of its tail. *Knack, knack, knack!* the strokes of its beak rang through the forest. Then a brown squirrel ran across a branch, and the gallypot flew away. The green leaves above glittered in air-play.

> At daybreak on the bleak sea-beach
> A fisherman stood aghast
> To see the form of a maiden fair
> Lashed close to a drifting mast.

Elsie was that maiden fair. He was the fisherman. Somewhere on the lonely coast of Devon he had been living alone, broken-hearted. The sands were yellow, and great rocks towered above. Attracted by the drifting wreckage, he had come out of his driftwood hut, eyes shaded by his hand. He was standing by the sea now, aghast.

> The salt sea was frozen on her breast
> The salt tears in her eyes
> And he saw her hair like the brown seaweed
> On the billows fall and rise.

The leaves, so light and fluttering, were now dim as the under-sea.

And he saw her hair, like the brown seaweed

O sea, O sorrow-drowning sea—', he said aloud.

like the brown seaweed—the brown seaweed.

A hand was laid on his knee. He started and looked up. Jack's voice said, gently,

'Why Willie, what's up?'

Willie rolled over, and hid his wet face across his arm.

'Is it anything I've said or done? You haven't been near me lately. I saw you come on here, and I've been tracking you, like old times.'

Willie lay still, and made no answer.

'Don't Willie, I can't stand it. What have I done?'

Willie rolled over, and smiled into those eyes of friendship puzzled and hurt above him.

'Hullo, Jack. I'm a soppy fool, that's all.'

'What had you been thinking of, Willie?'

'Oh, nothing.'

'Is it anything I've done?'

Willie shook his head.

'We're friends for ever, aren't we?'

Willie nodded.

'You're everything to me, Willie. Honest, you are.'

'You are my best friend, Jack.'

'Yes, but yet I don't seem able to help you. Why have you chucked me lately? I've seen you going off alone.'

Jack sat down beside his friend.

At length Willie said,

'Oh, Jack, everything is so different.'

'Even me?'

'No, not you Jack! Only I've been thinking a lot, and getting ready, if you understand. For what, I don't know exactly. But it all seems so strange, somehow. I can't imagine the future: I feel that something——'

They sat and talked under the tree. The sun shone down through the tree-tops, the shadow-dance of summer leaves moved silently on the ground.

They made a fire. It was like old days—old Jack would always be there; dear old Jack. Even in London, he would have Jack to think of, and write to—. Suddenly he clasped Jack's hand, and bent his head to hide his tears. Jack clasped him and kissed his cheek shyly, for the first and last time in their friendship. O, beautiful was the summer in the forest.

Chapter 24

THAT evening, before the kitchen table, Willie spent much
time ironing his best trousers, which he had worn last during
the Confirmation by the Bishop. He must get a crease like
a knife-edge. Mr. Maddison turned out his old frock coat and
silk hat, and hung them out in the sun next morning to air.
At one o'clock father and son, one in his antiquated silk hat
and the other in a four-and-sixpenny 'Pride of the West'
bowler, started to drive into Colham in the Rookhurst Halt
cab. Willie wished that it had been a motor car, like some of
the chaps' fathers owned. At the Masters' Entrance they
parted, Willie raising his hat and bowing. Soapy Sam the
porter touched his cockaded hat to his Father, Willie
noticed with approval.

At half-past two Willie was jammed with nearly four hundred other boys in what Mr. Rore called, for the sake of
terseness and clarity, *Behind*. Mr. Rore had invented a special
short word-code during the rehearsal.

Speech Day began rather tamely. Upon the augmented
platform in their robes of office the Governors of Colham
School—the Worshipful Company of Tanners—leaned back
in their chairs, and Behind was more or less able
to get during the monotonous addresses and reports
its annual view of the back of their heads and of the specially-
hired chairs. The addresses and the Headmaster's Report for
the Year having terminated in a ghostly clapping, from far
away under the strings of flags—where parents and relatives
occupying Before were crammed nearly as tightly as Behind
—Mr. Rapson appeared at a side entrance of the platform.

THE SEED LOOSENING

Rattlethrough wore his best gown. His hair was smooth and shining. One end of his moustache was waxed to a point; the other, from constant nervous nibbling, was wet and unstuck. Rattlethrough beckoned imperatively, earnestly, with profound importance, a weighty anxiety pressing on his brow and emerging from his blue eyes.

'Come along, tho-ose boys,' he hissingly whispered, refixing the masticated end of his moustache with his fingers. 'Come along there, what are you waiting for? Hush, er, hush that boy.' He glanced fearfully at the line of Governors' profiles. 'Hurry, hurry, tho-ose boys!'

One of Rattlethrough's duties was to superintend the collection of prize takers. He moved about, gnawing and fingering his moustache, and feeling that failure was inevitable. For some of the prize-takers were among the choir, others were changing into gymnastic kit for the *tableaux* superintended by the gymnastic instructor. Others, having been detailed for refreshment waiters after the Ceremonies, had disappeared. Where were they, oh, where were they?

'Are you ready, Mr. Rapson?' inquired Mr. Rore suddenly appearing, magnificent in a new gown, hood, frock coat, trousers and boots.

'Er . . . yes . . . Sir, er . . . yes,' sibilated the French master, 'er . . . yes, I think so. Of course . . . Headmaster . . . er . . . that is to say, a . . . er . . . a little confusion exists on account of . . . er . . . the gymnastic—'

'Quite quiet,' murmured the Headmaster, absently.

Willie was standing near, silent in the presence of mightiness, dressed in a black coat, an undersized butterfly collar that pinched his neck, and striped trousers.

'But surely that was rehearsed correctly? Come, Mr. Rapson. The Governors await. The award of prizes must commence.'

'Yes, yes . . . er . . . Head Master . . . yes, yes.'

But Rattlethrough, his face screwed with pain, continued

231

to twist one side of his moustache. The Headmaster said tersely,

'Postponed another quarter of an hour!' And in the same breath he ejaculated, 'Anthony!'

A Sixth Form prefect, who in a tail coat was standing near, muttering to himself and rubbing the palms of his hands with a handkerchief, jerked himself to startled attention.

'*Morte d'Arthur!*'

Anthony looked flabbergasted. 'Now, Sir?'

'Immediately! Follow!'

Mr. Rore turned about, and Anthony, with a grin at Willie, but with a glazed eye, moved after the tall, broad figure of the Headmaster.

By the lobby door he assumed a feeble swagger attended by a repeated shootings of his cuffs. Coughing discreetly, Anthony mounted the platform. All the Governors with one exception, who was lolling back, looked up with benevolent interest. The exception was a very old man with glossy white hair named Major-General Craugh-Cliftonhaugh, who was asleep and snoring faintly. He had eaten too much at luncheon and drunk more champagne than anyone else. Every year he gave the same address, telling them to shoot straight and to remember the honour of the Old School. He was an Old Boy. Every year he ate too much Speech Day luncheon, and drank too much champagne, so his speech invariably came last. Till then a vague droning came from his chair.

Mr. Rore whispered to the Most Worshipful Master, who, after an attempt to catch, hand to ear set in much white hair, what was said, rose to his feet, removed his spectacles, cleared his throat, and announced in a sweet voice that Camworthy would sing a patriotic ballad. More whisperings and hand to ear. The Most Worshipful Master again cleared his throat, and sweetly corrected himself; the lad's name was Anthony, and he would recite.

During this preliminary, Anthony was standing, with a

fixed easy smile, against the doorway. Faint clappings rippled under the flags as he moved forward, coughing discreetly and verifying the horizontal setting of his tie. Then he had a conviction that he needed to blow his nose. He flicked out his silk handkerchief; then put it back again in his pocket. He braced himself, facing the vast receding area of white frocks, large decorated hats, and watching faces.

He continued to face them for half a minute.

The Governors waited, the Visitors waited, the black squirming nonentities Behind waited. Anthony stared at the specially hired carpet, but no inspiration came from its damasked pattern. He seemed to be bracing himself against a thunderbolt; quite pale of face, white kid gloves in his left hand, starched collar and immaculate bow-tie, exquisite cuffs and patent leather shoes—all for nothing. No pennant moved on its string, only the soft droning of the old Governor who slept with fat hands round a chain-hung paunch. Suddenly Anthony said, 'Er,' and looked up, clenching his kid gloves. He cried,

> 'Then from out the lake rose a white arm
> Clothed in white samite!
> Wistic!!
> Monderful!
> And seized Excalibur!'

His voice ceased; his face took on an expression of pain; and he retired amid sympathetic clappings from parents and relatives, and ironical applause from the Specials and their admirers.

After this the Most Worshipful Master distributed the Prizes. The first senior boys were loudly clapped, but after awhile the sultry air in Big Hall rendered this a mechanical exertion. The Golding brothers, who were Prefects, had a fine reception; their little band of relatives, who had secured the best seats, applauded quite noticeably. Both had a long armful of books, all with gilt edges; like most of the prizes, they looked very costly, but actually they were bankrupt stock and publishers' remainders. One after another the prize-takers, each feeling that the gaze of every Visitor was for himself alone, trooped across the carpet, shook hands with the Most Worshipful Master, was handed a volume or volumes, and disappeared in a doorway beyond.

Willie's triumphal passing with sixty-three volumes of the Everyman Library did not take place, his expectations having been shattered when Mr. Rore, a month before, had informed him that three volumes of *The Bible in Art* would be his reward. However, these three volumes were of immense size and thickness, which perhaps compensated, he thought ruefully, for the subject.

When all the books had been presented, the smiling athletes, clad in white flannels, silk neckerchiefs, and school blazers, trooped across to receive their trophies. The black and sweltering mass Behind rose on the forms and cheered frenziedly as Fortescue, his red face smiling, took a mighty silver cup from the Most Worshipful Master. The Most Worshipful Master congratulated the Champion of the School on his magnificent prowess in the field. (*Cheers*) He hoped that equal prowess would be displayed in the conflict of a mature life, when perhaps the Champion of the School (*renewed cheering*) would bring home the Challenge Cup of Life (*loud cheering*) for the honour of the Old Country (*frenzied cheering*) and the Old School (*Loud and prolonged frenzied cheering*). He made a few more popular remarks, each of which called forth applause from Before and a roar from Behind. Boys stood on the forms while the Most Worshipful Master, smiling with white-haired patriarchal sweetness, shook Nosey Fortescue's hand, many times. Nosey stood there, smiling, and very modestly self-satisfied; his father, mother, sisters, brothers, and at least three of his girls from the Colham High School for Young Ladies, were seeing and admiring him.

THE SEED LOOSENING

The Champion retired, and the cheering subsided; to break out again and again as Nosey Fortescue returned for a silver clock, a set of fish knives and forks, an alarm clock, a tennis racquet, a silver butter-dish, a silver-plated jam-jar, a gold-mounted fountain pen and a silver inkpot, a silver-plated teapot and a pair of nut-crackers. Once more he returned, for a shilling pair of round-headed scissors that was the reward of tug-o'war. Excitement in Hall among the white-clad girls and maidens died down, and the frenzy Behind subsided, and with it two whole rows of boys who had been standing on the forms. Effish and Beckelt had arranged that small piece of fun, which caused Rattlethrough the most poignant anxiety.

'Quiet there, quiet, quiet!' he pleaded.

The prizes upon the table having disappeared, the Most Worshipful Master repeated the address that he had given for many years.

Waving his gold spectacles to emphasise his smiling statements, which delighted all the parents in Big Hall, he declared that the Headmaster, during the fifteen years he had been Headmaster, had been an overwhelming success in that proud and responsible position. (*Hear, hear*). He had furthered the interests of the School and of the boys on all occasions, in a most selfless and noble manner (*Applause*). He had furthered those interests on all occasions and in all matters to the best of his great ability, carrying it to such heights that it could claim to be one of the best day public schools in the West of England (*Loud applause*). They were all extremely proud of the School and their gratitude was due to Mr. Rore, who undoubtedly was in the tradition of Great English Headmasters (*Applause*). Nay, he would go further and declare, with all sobriety of judgment, that Mr. Rore was the greatest headmaster Colham School had seen in the three hundred and fifty-two years since its foundation in the glorious golden age of the Elizabethans!

Willie felt so proud of his School that, with all Behind, he stood up and yelled for nearly half a minute, screeching into

the thunderous din. When it had subsided, the pleased mur-
murs of parents Before were audible; and the white-haired
Master continued, now addressing his remarks, he said, chiefly
to the boys, although perhaps some of the older boys he saw
before him, were not too old to give ear to an Old Fogey (*No,
No, Sir*). Had anybody received as a prize a copy of that
wonderful book, Smiles' *Self Help?* That was a fine book, and
one that should be in every home. It was that spirit, he ven-
tured to say, that had made the Old Country what it was.
Smiles' *Self Help* won the Battle of Waterloo—it was that spirit
that had won for England the priceless heritage of the British
Empire—it was that spirit that had made the Great Man,
whose portrait was above the platform at that moment, of
whom Colham School was so very proud, win for The Great
White Queen, and for Christianity, the vast continental spaces
of Dark Africa. It was—

After the charming white-haired figure had sat down, having
roused his adult audience to that amiable freedom of mind
known as benevolence, Mr. Rore arose, and replied in his
incisive clear tones. He thanked, on behalf of the School, the
Most Worshipful Master for his encouraging words. He realised
with all humility that he was, even as the smallest boy, but a
part in the living organism of Colham School; that the School
was a coherent whole, every part of which had its selfless
obligations and clear-eyed responsibilities. Therefore any
praise that had been spoken was due to Colham School!
(*Applause*).

Every endeavour was made to maintain the traditional tone
of the school. Every boy was encouraged to reason for himself.
Every pupil was made to realise the value of work. *To the stars
through difficulties!* That was the translated motto of the School.
Mankind by continual research and thought could achieve
immensities. By constant striving mankind could eliminate
the ills of which the flesh hitherto had been considered the
heir. After the ills, real progress could be made. By constant

work one might eliminate even Chance, that ironic factor, wind-like, blowing where it listeth over the human race!

The Year's Work was satisfactory. The efforts of his colleagues were rewarded. The scholars, especially the senior boys, had done well. The results of the Senior Cambridge Local Examination were an advance on the previous year. Himself was fortunate in having such a brilliant staff.

Every one applauded, Rattlethrough giving a solo when the others had stopped.

'And now,' concluded Mr. Rore, 'our Aesthetes have been rewarded, we are to be entertained by our Athletes, under our doughty Sergeant-Major Featherstonehaugh.'

Immediately three boys ran on to the platform to move the table, but their premature enthusiasm, undiminished by a dozen rehearsals, was checked by the authoritative voices of several young and sprightly masters. The three boys effaced themselves; the old General was awakened tactfully by a prod in the paunch, and he made a grab at his chain, as though fearing larceny. Led by the Most Worshipful Master, the Governors walked from the platform and occupied reserved seats in front.

The Wheelbarrow, who in his younger days had been an army gymnastic instructor, had led such a sloppy life at the school that every part of him seemed to sag. His ears sagged, his cheeks sagged, giving to his face the likeness of an octopus or sea-parrot. His arms and chest and thighs were immense, with muscle run to fat. He wore a white singlet and flannel trousers, and the boards sagged and creaked he walked over in his immense rubber shoes. Willie thought that it was fortunate that a skinny kid of 2c had been chosen to wave the Union Jack at the top of the human pyramid, and not the Wheelbarrow.

The various items of the Gymnastic Display being over, the vaulting horse and parallel bars were removed, and a horde of black-coated, white-collared boys appeared with the grand piano. This was placed in the middle of the platform, and Mr. Ellison, who with importance was directing the emplacement, managed to get his toe under one of the legs, but he said nothing audibly. Then the music master, gowned and with a hood of white fur and pink silk, stepped upon the platform, and gave the signal. Immediately ant-like blackness surged out from Behind, and ranged itself into crescentic formation. Before waited. Choir-boys cleared their throats. The mæstro went to the piano. Scores were fluttered, more throats cleared.

The music began.

> *It was the schooner Hesperus*

Never had there been such lovely melody, thought Willie in the back row. How sweetly the trebles were singing

> *Blue were her eyes as the fairy-flax*

Then surely his own voice was floating above the voices of the others when the tenors were singing

> *Last night, the moon had a golden ring,*
> *But to-night no moon we see*

answered thunderously by the basses

> *The skipper he blew a whiff from his pipe*
> *And a scornful laugh laughed he!*

The ardour of every one increased as the storm came on, and from the grand piano, with its raised lid, crashed the chords of terror. Now the blue-eyed maiden—Elsie—was crying

> *Oh, Father! I hear the sound of bells;*
> *Oh, say, oh, say, what can it be?*

Mr. Norman, the skipper, was lashing her to a mast. Great barbarous waves were slapping against the side of the barque, and pouring in cold green masses over the deck. Through the mist was heard the warning bell on the reef.

How could the parents in Big Hall keep silent, why were they not weeping, when the music died and the sweet altos were telling of the drowned maid

> *At daybreak on the bleak sea-beach*
> *A fisherman stood aghast*
> *To see the form of a maiden fair*
> *Lashed close to a drifting mast*

More slowly and sadly they sang. Now was the great part, the loveliest moment, the most haunting melody. If only his voice could fill Big Hall and persuade the Visitors, fanning with their programmes, and the Governors, looking so ordinary, of the exquisite tragedy.

> *The salt sea was frozen on her breast*
> *The salt tears in her eyes,*
> *And he saw her hair, like the brown seaweed,*

Deeper and sadder flowed the music

> *And he saw her hair, like the brown seaweed,*
> *On the billows fall—and rise.*

The choir paused, the music master repeated the refrain. Several people were coughing and many talking. 'O, be quiet!' cried Willie in his mind. The grand ending commenced, every singer opening full his throat

> *Such was the wreck of the Hesperus,*
> *In the midnight and the snow!*
> *God save us all from a death like this*
> *On the reef of Norman's Woe!*

Now they were clapping, and it was over.

Then Mr. Croodrane sang the song they had heard him rehearsing in the masters' room, through Little Hall, several times during the past week. *Ruddier than the Cherry*, it was called, by Handel. Behind enjoyed it immensely; it went on and on, up and down and round about and on and on again, until half the boys were writhing in laughter. Even Rattle-through had to go away round the corner to hide his face. *Oh ruddier than the cherry, Oh ruddier than the Cherr-y, Oh ruddier than the Cher-he-he-he-he-he-he-he-ry, Oh brighter than the berry, Oh rud-dier, Oh—*The song ended at last, in terrific applause hiding much laughter.

The School song followed, words and music by Sir Heland Donkin, the Big Bug in Whitehall, who was sitting in front with the Governors. Willie sang it with fervour now that he was seeing his schooldays in ancient sunshine.

> *Come, sons of Colham,*
> *Come one, come all!*
> *Tell out in joyful song*
> *The stirring deeds on heath and field*
> *To which we all belong.*
> *Or lost or won*
> *The games we play*
> *Will stir our hearts*
> *For many a day*

Sir Heland, with gentle eyes, smiling but moist, joined in the chorus; and the lips of some of the Governors moved to the unheard words.

> *Then, gather, ye Sons of Colham around*
> *Your voices lend with a will*
> *Here's a jolly good luck*
> *To every man!*
> *And a cheer, Hurrah!!*
> *A cheer HURRAR!!!*
> *For the School on the Hill!!!!*

The choir and all Behind let itself go during the last chorus, and the faces in Big Hall smiled at the massed vitality of the boys.

THE SEED LOOSENING

After Major-General Craugh-Cliftonhaugh had delivered his address, Honour of the Old School, Shooting straight, Best School in Best County in Best Country in the Best of All Possible Worlds, etc., the Most Worshipful Master announced that the morrow would be·a whole holiday. Behind cheered wildly; Before smiled tolerantly.

Some of the Specials had planned a raid upon the Refreshments, under the pretence of serving the Visitors—a duty allocated to the Sixth and senior boys of 5a. They slipped through 3a classroom lobby, and so in the shell of 2c, where the Matron, the Porter, and various maids were standing very smart and clean behind the loaded tables. Willie and Bony joined them, the former with his three immense prizes under his arm, and Bony with a pair of scissors—the reward for tug-o'-war. After a hasty guzzle they moved among the Visitors, Willie intending to seek out the prettiest of the chaps' sisters; but once in Big Hall he handed his tray of cups and plates to the nearest ladies, who smiled and thanked him so nicely, that he became the more anxious to behave his very best.

'There's your father,' said Bony. 'Shall we go and see him?'

'No,' replied Willie, in a panic. 'He may ask The Bird questions about me! I say, look at old Taffy over there, grinning at Effish's guv'nor! I bet he don't guess how Taffy clumps his son's nut! And look at Bunny!'

Mr. Kenneth wore a brainstarver collar, so tall that it appeared to conceal that portion of his face below the tips of his ears.

'We'd better scoot!' whispered Willie, nervously, to Bony. He had seen Mr. Rore looking in his direction. And giggling, they scooted.

Chapter 25

AN incident occurred only a few days after Speech Day that, disastrous as it appeared at the time, led to happiness for Willie. It was during a visit of one-half of 5a to Mr. Waugh, the Chemistry master. Mr. Waugh was not unpopular, nor was he liked. He had a habit of creeping up behind boys and listening to their conversation, and then staring at them for perhaps half a minute at a time while the whole class looked on and tittered. Mr. Waugh's head and body were lean, and over his face a reddish-yellow skin was stretched tightly, intensifying the thinness of the lips and giving his cheeks the suggestion of having been chemically glazed; while his dark eyes, in yellowish whites, were expressionless.

Effish, whose knowledge had been augmented by experiments conducted at home with a Magician set of chemicals, came to Willie during an analysis of a mixture and suggested a joke. If Mad Willie crept into the store-room and took some lumps of potassium chlorate Effish would tell him what to do.

Willie came back with a beaker full of the compound, and Effish, sniggering to himself, advised him to put it in a flask with some concentrated sulphuric acid and to heat the contents.

'What'll happen?'

'Fireworks.'

'Will it blow us up?'

'No. But it makes a noise like miniature rifles on the range. Tell Hoxy, if he says anything, that you don't know what happened. He can't prove anything.'

Willie heated up his flask over a bunsen burner. A brownish

vapour arose off the mixture, with a series of crackling explosions. Boys crowded round, and Effish, who was going to be a chemist, pretended to fall into a fit, accompanied by groans. As the mixture began to boil the detonations increased.

'Get back,' cried the Chemistry master.

The boys rushed away, managing to upset a long desk and to jerk a dozen inkwells from their holes. In the confusion Effish slipped into the store-room and began to mingle the contents of several jars of chemicals. Then he pushed a jar of nitric acid through the window, which happened to fall on Colham Charlie, the school cat, who in a warm corner was sleeping off the effects of school luncheon. A few drops of acid spilled on his coat, and Colham Charlie rushed away yowling wildly.

Meanwhile the flask, with a spluttering of boiling acid, had cracked and brownish choking fumes were causing irritation to various throats. Thus encouraged, 5a started to cough and groan and even catawaul. Mr. Waugh yelled to them to go into the playground. He advanced towards the smoking bench just as Willie, endeavouring to make amends, managed to empty a pail of water over his legs. Mr. Waugh yelled and called him a blighter.

Five minutes later the porter Crinkle, who had been scratched by the poor cat, was fanning three boys hanging head downwards from a pair of parallel bars. They were Effish, Beckelt, and Sheppard. They had complained of a choking feeling in the lungs, so Mr. Rore, arguing that the gas was heavier than air, ordered the posture. The foresight of the three was rewarded, for as soon as they said they felt better, Mr. Rore told them to go home and on no account to do any preparation that evening.

Afterwards Mr. Waugh returned with Willie to 5a classroom. The Headmaster, sitting at his high desk, was displeased with the second interruption, and pierced the boy with his keen blue eyes. The downs will remain under the sky, thought Willie, trying to force himself—a habit started that year—to get away from what was happening. Think of the green downs, and the everlasting wind. It helped him a little.

'I will deal with him, Mr. Waugh. Stand there, sir! Face the wall—and think!'

The downs will remain, and the larks, and when I die I will return with the wind, I will be as the sun, which alone has no shadow. He felt happy in his corner; but the lesson ended, and he fortified himself; and another lesson began, and still Mr. Rore did nothing. I will be as the sun, and as the grass—O, why, why were his eyes brimming with tears. Quick, blink them away; and pretend to blow his nose. No handkerchief —Use the back of the hand, no one will see, and pretend to scratch the hand afterwards.

After seventy-eight minutes, Mr. Rore said,

'I will now leave you on your honour to work. Maddison, come with me!'

He led the way to his study, by a gangway through the desks. A boy with head bent over a book glanced sideways and clasped Willie's finger as he passed, and gave it a brief friendly shake. Willie never knew who he was. The door closed behind him.

'Wasting my time, sir! You are a confirmed pauper spirit. You are no use here, sir. Were you not leaving at the end of the term, I should ask your father to remove you. As it is, you will leave 5a. There are better boys waiting for your place. And if this occurs again, I shall expel you! You are a disgrace to the traditions of the School, sir!'

He opened the cupboard and took out a cane.

He put the yellow chair in position.

'Down on your knees, sir. Over, over. No, hands right over. Touch the carpet. Think! Eyes shut! "I must do what I am told to do, lest I be expelled." Think three times. Keep your arms stretched. Now—think!'

One.

'Think, "I must behave!".'

O sun, make me steadfast as thou art, O downs—

Two.

'Still, sir, still! More if you wriggle!'

Three.

'Think! "I must get that power".'

O sun, make me—

Four.

'Now, quite still. Think!'

O sun—

Five.

'One more for wriggling! Now quite still!'

Six.

'I told you to close your eyes. One more. Very still. "I must do as I am told".'

O sun, O sun, O—

Seven.

'Now report to Mr. Worley with my compliments, that you are to join the Specials.'

Willie left The Bog five minutes later, and reported to Mr. Worley in 3a classroom. Thenceforward he sat in Big Hall with the Specials engaged in killing time by various methods. He felt happy that he was with Bony again. Long hours in Hall drifted by in a luxurious indolence. They played football with a piece of paper; they flung tennis balls at the wall; they interchanged the notices on the various boards; they fought for the bell with the boy from 5c who announced the hours, depriving him of the satisfaction of shaking it vigorously; they scattered caps for toy pistols on the floor for the classes interweaving through Hall to detonate; they flung paper darts at the ceiling, and orange peel at Dr. Bullnote, D.D. Once Dove took down an obsolescent number of *The Illustrated London News* and substituted for it the spread pages of *La Vie Parisiene* that a sailor-brother had brought home with him; and Willie gave a bizarre touch to the feminine illustrations by the addition of inky beards and moustaches. Mr. Ellison, emerging suddenly from 2b to see the time, saw the drawings, and tore them down. Ever afterwards the Specials respected him, for his remarks upon that occasion were:

'There would be hell and the devil to pay if the Old Man saw. Advise you not to do it again. Very humorous though.'

With this he popped back in to 2b classroom and through the partition they heard him yell in his high-pitched jerky voice:

'Peacock minimus, come out here. I don't care if Dingleberry did take your pencil. That's no excuse for eating sweets. Dingleberry, return the pencil to Peacock minimus. I don't believe your sister gave it to you. Bottomley don't kick the grating. Winkle minor, you are cheating off Winkle major's paper. Oh, you naughty boy! Stand on the form, Winkle minor!'

Then followed the sounds of faint sobbing, probably from the woebegone Winkle minor standing on the form.

The weeks spent with the Special Class were the happiest in Willie's school-life. Owing to the smallness of the class it was possible to know intimately every boy, and in those boys whom he had disliked before Willie found much that was lovable. One day the Specials had a debate about Friendship that warmed his heart.

'You know,' suggested the dreamy Yeates, swallowing an American gum, 'You know, Mad Willie, you're a funny bloke. You take such violent dislikes to a fellow, then you are suddenly decent to him. You're quite mad.'

The chaps agreed. Dove said:

'I vote that Mad Willie should be our Chief against the Prefects.'

'Don't get cocky, young Dove!' replied Mad Willie, embarrassed. But Dove did not hear him, for having just completed a dart made from a pen belonging to some one else, he was standing up and about to hurl it into the rafters.

THE SEED LOOSENING

The astral happiness of the Specials in Big Hall was sometimes interrupted by visitations from Mr. Worley, who had
abandoned his futile attempts at moustache-growing, and
assumed with the responsibilities of matrimony the bare face
of his boyhood. Mr. Worley had lately developed a habit of
dictatorial interference regarding their work in Hall, and
frequently his door opened and in a tinny voice he required
each boy to show up his efforts of the past hour.

'Damn Worley,' remarked Burrell one day; 'Hasn't he
enough to do to manage those kids in 3a without sticking his
twisted snout into our business. Let's rag him!'

The opportunity came the next day, when Mr. Worley
came to the Specials at their desks in 3a classroom—two rows
of which they sometimes occupied—and gave to each boy a
piece of notepaper and an envelope. The weekly letter,
apparently considered an important part of their business
training, was an innovation of his own which, on being suggested, was approved immediately by an uncaring Headmaster
who, like Nature, had but little regard for the inferior indivi-
duals of a species.

'Now then,' the tinny voice insisted, 'just you in the Special
Class listen to me now. Every one pay attention to me. For
to-night's letter I want you to write a letter to the newspapers.
Each boy may choose his own subject. Now then, is that quite
clear to every boy? A letter to the newspapers. Stop talking
there! Maddison, you haven't paid the slightest heed to my
words. I distinctly heard you use a foul and obscene swear-
word! Go into Mr. Rore! Continue with the book-keeping,
and prepare shorthand for an hour. Now is that quite clear
to every boy?'

After school the Specials found Willie lounging in The Bog
waiting for them. He suggested that they all should write a
letter about the cuckoo, and it was agreed. When Mr. Worley
ordered Burrell 'to read his effort', the next afternoon, Burrell
began,

'To the Editor of *The Daily Mail*.

Dear Sir—'

'I should say "Sir",' corrected Mr. Worley pleasantly, 'dispense with unnecessary affection, especially where the *Daily Mail* is concerned.'

'Haha,' said Burrell.

'Don't be impertinent, Burrell! Go on, Burrell!'

' "SIR—Yesterday afternoon while walking in the woods I heard a cuckoo calling—" '

' "Singing" would be better,' advised the master.

' "Surely this is early to hear its song?" '

' "To hear its call", I would suggest. A cuckoo, strictly speaking, has no song, Burrell.'

'Yes, Sir. "Yours faithfully, Horace Burrell." '

'A short letter, Burrell, for three-quarters of an hour's work.'

'I did not want to pad it, Sir. *The Daily Mail* specially asks for letters to be brief, Sir.'

'Don't argue. Now Yeates, read yours.'

Yeates began,

' "DEAR AUNTIE BELLE—" '

'Now then, no nonsense, Yeates!' warned Mr. Worley.

'I am writing to *Home Notes*, Sir!'

'Go on.'

' "DEAR AUNTIE BELLE—I have something of import to impart. Can you guess what it is? No. Then I'll impart. Yesterday, while perambulating in a bosky dell I heard a mocking call. It called again and again, so cheerfully, so I thought I would write to you about it. The little birds chirped, and the leaves danced, because it was the cuckoo back again. I was so happy that I recalled that old poem beginning, 'What should be shall be,' or 'Why are we all pauper spirits, with the exception of the Roaring Warbler?" '

Several boys shouted with laughter, and Mr. Worley went red in the face. 'Take that trash in to Mr. Rore,' he yelled through his nose.

With an injured air, and his pale face amazed, Yeates walked out of the room, watched by the silent little chaps of 3a.

'Go on, Effish,' ordered Mr. Worley.

Effish smirked, rolled his eyes, gazed around him, and then gabbled:

' "To the Editor of *What* " '

        "Sir—"

'To the Editor of what?'

'Yes, Sir. To the Editor of *What*.'

'What do you mean? Don't be impertinent. Now then! To what paper are you writing?'

'To *What*, Sir.'

'Well, it's wrong. You should have addressed it to one.'

'Which one, Sir?' asked Effish respectfully.

'Oh, don't be foolish. If you don't put any address, how can you expect it to reach its destination.'

'But I wasn't going to post it, Sir, to any. I thought it was just a lesson. I invented *What*, Sir. *What* should be the proper address, Sir.'

'I've already explained!' cried Mr. Worley.

'What should be, shall be,' said Bony.

'Watson, go into Mr. Rore!'

'The Headmaster,' muttered Bony.

'May I continue, Sir?' asked Effish, when the door had closed behind Bony.

'Yes, go on.'

'To the Editor of *What*' began Effish.

'Sit down,' cried Mr. Worley. 'You are merely an idiot, Effish. Go on, Beckelt.'

Beckelt stood up, and began,

' "Dear Sir—I think that Mr. Balfour should see about it—" ' then he stopped. He could not improvise further; he had not read his letter about the cuckoo because he feared to be sent in to the Headmaster.

'Go on, Beckelt,' cried an exasperated Mr. Worley.

Beckelt squirmed, and the master asked to see his letter.

'Have you all written about the same subject? I thought so! You are a lot of fools. All will be kept in till five o'clock this evening.'

But when half-past four came, all the Specials went home, including Yeates and Bony, who had been skulking in The Bog; and the next morning Mr. Worley made no mention of the matter.

Chapter 26

PLEASANTLY the end of term drew near, and the boys spoke eagerly of the time when they would be free of the tyrannies of school. Burrell was going to an Agricultural College, Bony was going into the works of the Colham and District Gasworks Company, Effish was going to learn the chemistry of brewing, while Beckelt's occupation was not yet decided. Clemow, Hoys, Yeates, Macarthy, and three others would not leave till Christmas.

The little band of friends received a mild jolt one day, in early July, when Bony came to school with a cheerful grin on his face, and did not join the others in Big Hall after prayers, but went instead into Mr. Rore's study. Later he emerged, and a dozen curious boys demanded if he had left. The lank naturalist replied that they had guessed his secret. One and all agreed that he was a lucky dog. Bony assured them that he was a lucky dog, but, he said, he was having a week's holiday before going into the Gasworks.

Although he had left and had declared his joy, he did not appear anxious to begin his week's holiday, but sat all that morning in Hall with them, talking about old times.

'I'll keep my *Nature Diary* as usual, Willie,' he said, 'and you'll keep yours, won't you? Then when we see each other, we can exchange, just like old times, can't we? And don't forget the meeting of the Owl Club this year, will you? Rupert and Jack and me and you, and all the chaps. Rather!'

Willie assured him that he would not forget. They were having a general conversation when Mr. Rore peered from the 5a classroom, and his voice reverberated through Big Hall.

Every head bent over ephemeral work. Mr. Rore inquired the meaning of Bony's presence, and told him to go home. With the dread eyes upon him Bony rose, collected his pens and books, and shuffled away into 3a classroom to gather the remnant.

'What are you doing, sir?' the stentorian voice asked as Dove jumped up and shook Bony's hand. The other Specials looked up, covertly, admiring the bold Dove.

'I was saying "Good-bye," Sir,' replied the Irish boy, as Mr. Rore floated swiftly to them.

'I beg your pardon,' replied the Headmaster, inclining his head courteously. 'It is most natural. Watson is going to face life. Remember, Watson, that there are sharks and tigers in the world. Watson, I wish you all success. It will come only through work. Hard, unceasing work!'

'Crawling up the gaspipes,' whispered Effish, out of the side of his mouth, to Willie.

He shook hands, for the second time, with Watson, and awkwardly the others rose and bade him good-bye.

'Was it not Catallus who expressed the emotion of farewell in immortal verse?' exclaimed Mr. Rore. 'You will recall—

> Accipe fraterno multum manatia fletu
> Atque in perpetuum, frater, ave atque vale.

'Now then boys, you have a week or two left. Make the most of it. No preparation can be too thorough for the life that awaits you; relentless; the weakest to the wall. All the world's great deeds were wrought by constant effort. Even genius is nothing—a shooting star—without constant labour to keep the mind taut and healthy. Remember the parable of the buried talents. 'By the sweat of thy face shalt thou eat bread!' That is an ancient allegorical embodiment of a great Truth. Now on with your work, master your difficulties—through work shall ye find happiness!'

He turned and floated away under the horizontal bar, and

so into his classroom, the loose grating giving all within a second's grace to bow their heads in silence.

Bony appeared a disconsolate figure at the main gate after morning school, explaining carelessly that he happened to be passing. He said that it was fine to have left school. He was there, a lonely figure, again at half-past four, and this time he had discarded his black cap and silver badge, and wore instead an enormous check cap, under which he appeared lost. When Willie, emerging from the playground door, saw him standing outside the gate, he did not recognise him at first. A few minutes later the Specials had gathered round him, now smoking a cigarette. The appearance of Mr. Kenneth in the playground, however, caused the cap to be hidden and the cigarette to be thrown away. Bony looked quite nervous.

The end of the summer term came inexorably upon the Special Class. Every boy in the school knew the breaking-up date, for it had appeared in both the Upper and Lower School Notice Boards, in Mr. Rore's handwriting, black and thick, but minute with the strokes of a relief-nib.

C. G. S.
Summer Term ends 26th July.
Winter Term begins 12th September.

The second line had been scratched out by the pencils of various Specials.

'We must do something to celebrate our leaving,' said Willie. 'Only one more week left.'

'How about if the Special Class disappeared *en bloc* one afternoon?' asked Macarthy. 'I bet no one would miss us!'

It was arranged that they should meet by the bridge over the river at 2 o'clock on the Monday afternoon, on their bicycles; those with steps on the back wheels should take the bikeless boys.

While waiting for the late ones to turn up on the Monday, the little band awheel by the bridge was entertained by the sight of a drunk man coming out of *The Rising Sun*, a woman with bedraggled hair, and hat askew, hanging to his arm. Willie recognised John Fry.

'Jolly good job if he were to fall in the river. I hope the policeman gets him,' said Willie.

'He'll never be able to drive his pony and cart,' said Yeates, 'Look at him—he's absolutely incapable.'

They waited hoping to see some fun; but the man sat down on a seat under a tree, and rested his head on his hands.

'Here's Mac. And Old Bony!'

'Sorry I'm late,' said Mac. 'But I've been digging Bony out of the Gasworks.'

'My boss gave me leave,' said Bony, puffing at an enormous meershaum pipe. 'He's an awfully decent chap. He's got a beautifully coloured meershaum. You ought to see it.'

They rode away over the bridge, and along the Colham Road. By the time they had reached Rookhurst Forest their pockets were bulging with scrumped apples. After a swim in the Longpond,—Willie carefully kept them away from the catamaran and canoe, hidden in the rushes—they split up into two parties, one under Willie and the other under Hoys, and all the afternoon their shouts and cries were heard about the wood.

The sun was looking through the trunks of the beeches when they decided to stop. Most of the chaps had gone home, or lost interest, and strayed away; it had been so lovely, and now was almost over, thought Willie by the fire he had lighted. Bony, Yeates, Macarthy, Burrell and Cerr-Nore—who had come upon them in the wood—were left. They were pleasantly tired, after much running and wrestling. They talked about the drunken man.

'*I* shall never take to drink and women,' affirmed Willie. 'I think they must both be beastly. I mean the sort of woman like Lizzie Boon.'

'Girls are all right,' suggested Charlie Cerr-Nore with a

smirk, 'they like a chap to cuddle 'em up sometimes. Don't they Willie? But you like 'em full-grown, what?'

'I dunno,' mumbled Willie, hating Charlie, and mentally flinching lest he should mention the name of Dolly. He lit a cigarette hastily, and puffed out a mouthful of smoke, 'Jolly fine aroma, these cigarettes.'

'Ah, you wait till you've tried a meerschaum!' said Bony, slowly filling his yellow pipe, and turning it sideways to approve the minute brown stain that, after much anxiety, had begun to appear at the bottom of the bowl.

'It's not such a dusty pipe,' he told them, 'and I like a big bowl because it's a cooler smoke. We all smoke this kind at the Gasworks.'

He wasted half a box of matches in vain efforts to light it, and then, announcing that the tobacco was packed too tightly, he tapped it out and repacked it. Still it would not light, and Cerr-Nore said that it was no wonder that they all smoked that kind of pipe at the Gasworks.

'There wouldn't be much danger of an explosion, would there?'

Bony ignored the comment, and Charlie went on:

'Or perhaps it's the sort of pipe they make the coke in, is it? I've heard Cook say she can never get it to burn.'

'We make the best coke round about here, and don't you forget it, Cerr-Nore!' rejoined Bony.

'And what you make on the swings you lose on the roundabouts, what? Have I guessed your secret? The gas is pretty poor muck, ain't it? It stinks like Sulphuretted Hydrogen!'

'Well, if you knew anything about it, you'd know that all coal gas contains an unstable amount of H_2S.'

'Your beastly gasworks stink as bad as a stable.'

'Oh, shut up,' the others groaned, 'stop that gassing. You're like Taffy.'

Cerr-Nore started playing with a stick, and Bony at last managed to induce a red glow in the pipe. He coughed a lot:

because it was a new pipe, he stated. Yeates said that it stank like a school luncheon, probably because it was half putty. It required such a lot of blowing instead of sucking to keep it alight, that finally Bony, eulogising the brand of tobacco, tapped it out on his boot and in doing so accidentally snapped the bowl from the imitation vulcanite mouthpiece. He threw it in the fire, and dolefully watched it burning.

They talked till the evening sun was standing on its golden stilts over the fields, and then went slowly down to the gate against which leant their bicycles. There they talked awhile about past days, agreeing to write to one another; and of course, all would join the Old Boys' Club.

'But term isn't over yet, is it?' said Willie.

'We'll see each other to-morrow and the next day, won't we?' said Mac.

'Oh, rather,' they agreed.

Bony looked rather glum, and in the evening stillness the others rode away, leaving Willie standing in the lane. When they had gone he looked back at the beech trees, and at the high summer cloudlets, at the wheel-marks in the dust, at the empty lane. O, sun—

As he lifted his bicycle out of the hedge he heard a scamper of feet, and something licked the bare back of his knee, between knickers and stocking. Looking round, he saw the mongrel called Tiger sweeping the dust with its tail. It bared its teeth, swayed its head, glanced out of the corner of its eyes, which appeared to fix their sight on some dream. It whined, and looked at Willie, with such a beseeching look that he let his bicycle drop back into the hedge, and knelt to Tiger. The dog lifted up its nose and howled. Then it grovelled, sweeping its tail; it pranced and barked as he went forward, and ran before him.

'I'm not going to take you for a walk,' said Willie. 'Where's

Bill Nye, your master? Turned you loose because he's tired of you?'

The dog stood still in the road, trying to draw him on with its eyes; its ears sank, its tail swept; it stood prick-eared and alert again, and whined. As Willie continued to stare at it, it threw up its head and dropped its tail and howled again.

'Lost Bill Nye? Bill Nye. Where's Bill?'

Tiger ran to him, and nuzzled his hand; then spread its legs and waited expectantly.

Knowing that the dog was asking him to go with it, Willie lifted his bicycle out of the hedge, and wheeled it round in the direction Tiger wanted him to follow. It bounded along ahead of the wheel, turning round every few paces to assure itself that he was following. Willie followed it down the road and into the lane bordering the eastern side of the Big Wheatfield. Tiger pushed through a dog-gap in the thorn hedge, and waited on the other side, with flacking tongue.

'You want me to come to the spinney, I believe!' said Willie, leaving his bicycle in the ditch, and scrambling through.

It was exciting, running along the right-of-way. Like a fox before hounds Tiger was running straight for the spinney, silently, tail out behind him. A covey of partridges whirred up before the dog, and on down-curved wings glided across the field. Tiger disappeared into the spinney. Willie was breathing fast when he reached the trees. He heard the whining of Tiger in the dug-out, and went to the hole in the southern side.

'Who's there?'

Tiger whined, sprang out of the dark hole and licked his face. Willie crept on hands and knees into the hole and listened. He struck a match, and lit the candle stump he always carried in his pocket. The flame sank, and he waited for the grease to creep up the wick. The dog Tiger was beside him, making noises in its throat, and its long tail was thumping against a root.

Someone's restless breathing was near him. The candle flickered, a sighing seemed to fill the hollowed cavern. Beside him he heard a wheezy rasping, as though something had been caught a long time in a trap. In the candlelight he saw that Bill Nye was lying almost before him, with the dog Tiger pawing frantically at his ragged coat, and caressing the thin peaky face with its tongue. Bill Nye wheezed again, and rolled on his side. His dark eyes stared at Willie, not seeing him; his right hand clawed the air, coming to rest, hot and dry, on Willie's cheek.

'What's the matter, Bill Nye, what's the matter?' whispered Willie, 'Are you ill, poor Bill Nye. All right, Bill, you keep still. Don't worry. Can you hear me?'

The wasted face was blank and wheezing before him.

'My Lord, you're delirious. I wonder if it's catching? I don't care if it is. Bill Nye, can't you answer me? It's me, Willie Maddison. Lie down Tiger, you silly dog. I won't hurt Bill Nye. You've got fever. I'll go and tell Dolly, and we'll fetch you into the cottage in a warm blanket. Can't you answer, Bill Nye? Your dog is a skeleton, too. How long have you two been here like this?'

Having taken off his coat, and wrapped round the sick boy, Willie shuffled backwards from the cave. Outside the light was too bright for a moment, but swiftly he ran towards the cottage. It was a mile away, but he got there in seven minutes, to learn from Old Bob, as he leaned his hands and head on the gate-post to ease his breathing, that Dolly had taken Tom Sorrell's washing down to the Quarry Cottage. After a minute's rest, and a gulp of water, he ran off again, towards the quarry.

Chapter 27

DOLLY would have ceased work for Mrs. Nye long before, were it not for Old Bob, the grandfather of Jim Holloman—for now she knew that Jim's father had been Harry Lewis, and his mother the wife of Colonel Tetley. It was the Colonel's wife who had brought the little boy back from London after the death of his father, and had left him early one morning in the village street, wearing a label in his button-hole, 'Jimmy, c/o Mr. Robert Lewis, Gamekeeper, Rookhurst.' Dolly often had a glimpse of Jim in the face of Old Bob.

Dolly had no relatives who cared about her. Her father was dead, and buried in a pauper's grave in the cemetery attached to the Grubber. Dolly hated Grandmother Nye as a nasty, cruel old woman, who would not die, but was always grumbling. To her accusations and complaints she was by now indifferent, but the cumulative effect wore her. Granmer Nye habitually accused Dolly of wearing her boots—large misshapen things that resembled crushed cockroaches. She screamed at her for washing Bob Lewis's sheets and pillow-slip once a week instead of once or twice in a year, as her own were, saying that soon they would be scrubbed threadbare. She screamed if a window were opened, or when Bob went and stood by the door. 'Ye girt dawbake, ye be stealing granmer's tarnip wine, you. Stealing from poor old 'ooman whose teeth wor brukken dwenty vor year agone, you. Master grawbey! The Lard'll take ee into fire and darkness everlastin' you. Now then, Barb Loos, closen that door, wull ee. Lattin' in they windiblores, thou girt loobey.'

The tirade of this ancient scold included obscene words

259

that had been learnt in childhood from her father and mother. Nevertheless, the last interview with the local representative of *The Colham and District Times and Advertiser, with which is Incorporated Smellie's Weekly Argus* had resulted in the headline

> OLD LADY'S WONDERFUL LIFE.
> Hale and hearty at 102 years.
> 'I'm all right, but I confess I miss my teeth.'

Even of Old Bob Dolly was getting impatient, for he sat in his chair all day, or pottered about the garden, muttering to himself. The calm of his former life was seldom with him now. When Mrs. Nye scolded him he never answered; but he would argue when alone under the apple trees, for an hour or two on end.

Perhaps in another place Dolly would have shaken off her brooding long before. She too held conversations with herself, and was troubled with dreams that left her heavy-hearted. In these dreams Jim always came to her, and told her that he loved her; and she would clasp him to her heart, and the dream would break, and she be lying in bed heavy-hearted in the greyness of the dawn. Ah! long ago it had been sweet like the dream. She remembered how Jim had loved the nightingales; even as she had since learned to love them, strangely sorrowful in the moonlit nights, almost as if Jim were in their song. How many springtimes had come and gone since she had been at Skirr Farm, in the room over whose ceiling at night the white owlets had worried their food, and the old birds had screaked as they sailed past her lattice. On the sill she used to lean her elbows, watching the far spinney dark against the sky, yearning to be where a twinkling speckle of red in the dusk was Jim's fire. If only the night would bring again the well-remembered whistle, if only he were there so that she could embrace him; before, she had been young and half-afraid: now she would love him and bind him to her for ever.

The weekly walk to Tom Sorrell's cottage with his washing

was something she looked forward to. Sometimes she set out almost joyfully, but on seeing him the feeling had gone. In absence Tom Sorrell was often in her thoughts; when present she had no feeling for him beyond gladness that she had someone to talk to. Tom did not say very much to her, but she knew that he loved her.

As she walked along the forest path with the wicker-basket, its top covered by a white cloth, under her arm, she saw some school-boys round a fire in a hollow. One of them was standing up, whirling a stick with a glowing end round his head. She recognised young Will'um Maddison, who soon would be leaving now to go to London. He was smoking a cigarette, the young monkey. She walked on, unobserved, and the voices dropped behind.

Soon the sound of Will'um banging his stick against a tree-trunk ceased, and she was alone with shadows and the shifting sunlight on the leaf-drifts and mossy banks and fallen trunks beside the path.

At the lower edge of the forest slope ran the brook, fringed with tall green plants. Beyond was the white way of the Colham Road, and the break in the cornfield, fringed with bushes, that was the quarry of her destination.

She sat down on the bank, and took off her shoes and stockings and paddled. When her feet were clean she rested on the bank again, thinking of Tom Sorrell. If only he were not so quiet; lime-burning seemed to content him. While she rested there she watched the red and green dragonflies darting over the water; she could hear the snap and rustle of their wings. A vole came out of a hole on the farther bank and started nibbling a grass; and seeing her, it dived into the current, with hardly a splash. She thought how lovely was the summer day, how simple the lives of the flowers and the water-folk. Years ago Jim had told her of them, but she had not heeded much. She had liked only to hear his voice; that had been sufficient. He had never understood that. It was no

good thinking about that any more. Jim was probably wed
to someone else by now. Well, it served her right. She picked
up her basket of washing, and went on down to the quarry.

Tom Sorrell was standing by his tin-roofed cottage as she
walked down the chalky cart-track. He looked on the
ground; she knew how he was feeling. Poor Tom! She did
not want to hurt him, but—

The nearest of the three kilns had been banked the night
before with blocks of chalk, and now the circular rim was
unencumbered. The second kiln was cooling; the chalk, freed
of its carbonic acid gas, had become lime. From the pile at the
top of the third kiln strayed a vapour, for the faggots and dry
tree-limbs below had not long been kindled.

All three were built into a bank, so that one half of a kiln
was embedded and flush with the higher ground. The other
side was bare, built of stone and mortar. At the base were the
flues and iron doors. A heap of flints and a long iron shovel
lay at the door of the near kiln.

When she came to him, Tom Sorrell wiped his mouth with
the back of his hand.

'Fine weather,' he said.

'Ais, Tom, it be!' she replied, in the broad tones of the older
men. 'Ye bain't working, tho' (then)?'

Tom scratched his head, and tilted his rusty straw-hat over
his blue eyes. Then he coughed and spat.

'Turrible thirsty work it be, drawing the lime.'

'Sorry I haven't brought any beer, Tom!'

'I were just going to have my tea. Will 'ee take a dish along
of me?'

'Doan't 'ee trouble, Tom Sorrell.'

'Aw, bant no trouble,' he smiled.

She liked his smile.

'Shall I make it for 'ee?'

'Thank 'ee, Dolly. But my place bant very tidy, if you'll
excuse it.'

Dolly checked the reply, which arose thoughtlessly, the almost invariable village-retort, 'You want a woman to look after 'ee, midear.'

She went into the house. It had but one floor, and consisted of two rooms, and a scullery with a hand-pump and sink. It was certainly untidy. The iron of Tom's boots rang on the floor behind her.

A fire was burning in the grate. On the table was a used plate, a knife and fork, and a cut loaf of bread.

'Just going to have tea, were you, Tom? And no kettle on the hob?'

Tom grinned, while she filled the black iron kettle from the pump that clattered and spouted its water unevenly.

She placed the kettle on the fire, and sat down. Tom still lounged about, moving things with his hand. The wallpaper was greasy and worn in patches, showing the chipped plaster. In one corner a damp stain was spread. Dolly went to the window and stared out, seeing the white quarry and the thorns on its lip, and tangled rootlets hanging down. Some large sunflowers grew outside, and hollyhocks.

'You'm very quiet here, Tom.'

'Aiy, 'tis quiet.'

After awhile Dolly said,

'In the wood I saw some skuleboys. Young Will'um was there. I don't reckon he likes the idea of leaving his mate, Jack.'

'And Miss Elsie,' added Tom, significantly. 'He'll feel lonely up to Lunnon, I reckon. Still, you can feel lonely anywhere, if so you'm placed.'

'Yes,' she said.

'I be turrible lonely, at times, Dolly.'

She did not answer.

Somewhere in the thorns at the quarry's lip above the cottage a wild dove was cooing, and its moan came softly down the chimney. Tom, leaning against the wall, said reflectively,

'I should like a lad like young Will'um Madd'zun. Plenty of spirit, but not rough with it. That's my idea of a man.'

'I mind he as a baby. A pretty baby, he were.'

'Your baby'd be pretty, Dolly,' he said slowly.

This was a strange Tom Sorrell talking. She wanted to look at him, but she dared not. Her heart started to beat faster. She felt his eyes drawing her, but she could not look up.

'Dolly,' said Tom Sorrell, huskily, still staring at her.

'Ais, Tom?'

'Won't ee wed wi' me, Dolly? Don't ee know that I love ee, and only ee? Won't ee? Won't ee love me, my maid? I've got nigh dree hundred pounds saved up, all for ee when ee likes. I've been putting the money by for years, Dolly.'

' 'Tisn't money, Tom Sorrell,' she whispered.

'Do ee love someone else, Dolly?'

She hid her face and began to cry.

'Be ee waiting for Jim 'Olloman, then?' his voice demanded, but she did not reply.

Coo-coo-roo, roo, from the dove among the leafy spines. The cottage was built under a steep face of the cliff, at the top of which lay the road between Colham and Rookhurst. The dull stamp of a horse's hoofs sounded in the walls of the cottage.

'Because if you'm waiting for Jim,' went on Tom slowly, speaking with difficulty. 'I don't fancy he will ever be coming back again. I'll tell ee for why—'

His hoarse voice broke. It stopped under a breathless emotion. The stamp of hoofs died away. Dolly looked piteously at Tom, who was leaning forward.

'I do love ee turrible,' his hoarse voice went on. 'Do ee come here now. Let me show ee something.'

He stared at her, and pointed vaguely behind him at the limekilns.

'Do ee rec'llect th' time when young Will'um rinned away wi' Jim?'

She nodded.

'Do ee rec'llect hearing how he couldn't find Jim in the morning?'

Tom was breathing very heavily.

'Ah'll tull ee,' he gasped, 'ah'll tull us fur why Jim 'Ollomum —' He gulped. 'Ah'll tull ee fur why Jim 'Ollomum won't come back no more. Ah looked over thiccy top'—he pointed to the kilns—'in the morning, and there I zeed—I zeed—'

He glanced round. Somebody was outside the window. Dolly cried out, and put her hand over her mouth. The blackness of the fainting fits she had had as a girl came upon her. She closed her eyes, waiting for her heart to grow small again.

A face looked in at the window; a face with bloodshot eyes, hanging mouth, and distended nostrils. The mouth shifted about, as though unable to find words.

'Who be you wanting, John Fry?' called Tom Sorrell sharply.

'Ha!' exclaimed John Fry, swaying upright and closing his mouth. His hand felt at his throat. 'Ha!' he exclaimed again, and leaning forward peered in at the open window. 'May I— come in?'

'He's drunk,' said Tom to Dolly, whose face was haggard.

'Eh?' exclaimed John Fry. 'Drunk? Who be drunk, midear? Eh? Now I'll ask ee a question. Who be whorin'?'

'That's enough of that!' exclaimed Sorrell. 'Just you take yourself off! I've just about had my bellyful of you, midear!'

'You haven't,' said John Fry, shaking his head and swaying. 'No you haven't. You mustn't say that, Tom Sorrell. If anyone's had a bellyful of anyone else I expect its—'

He did not finish his sentence, for Tom Sorrell, lifting the hasp, pulled the casement window shut.

Outside John Fry, working his mouth and glaring, was assuming his older religious personality.

' "Scarlet sinful woman, inhabitant of Gomorrah! Ye shall conceive chaff, ye shall bring forth stubble; your breath as fire, shall devour you!" '

'Be off!' cried Tom, jerking his thumb towards the Colham road.

For answer John Fry lashed his fist through the window, shattering part of the wooden frame and the glass, which fell on the inside sill with drops of his blood.

'You fool!' shouted Tom Sorrell, and then stopped, for a second face had appeared over Fry's shoulder; the face of a hatless, dark-haired boy whom he recognised. Tom saw that Young Will'um was panting, his hair wet on his forehead, as though he had run a long way. Before he could shout out to warn him, the boy had come up behind and laid his hand on Fry's shoulder, his head drooping in exhaustion. John Fry turned round, and seeing who it was, gripped him by the throat, and shouting, began to shake him. Tom saw the boy's head being jerked backwards and forwards as he vainly tried to tear the hands away.

'All right, I be coming,' he cried, and made for the door. His iron-shod boots slipped on the smooth lime-ash floor; a chair fell over, he swore in his rage. It seemed a long time before he got to the door, pulled it open, and was out on the white-worn patch of grass, between his threshold and the triple open rims of the kilns. 'Don't!—Don't!' the boy was gasping, doubled up and arms before his face against the kicks and blows of Fry.

'You bliddy great heller!' shouted Sorrell, catching hold of Fry's collar and tearing backwards so violently that he broke three of his finger nails. 'I'll knock the guts out of you!'

He hit him on the cheek, sending him reeling.

John Fry recovered, and lurched towards the lime-burner, showing his teeth between his lips drawn back. Suddenly he ran forward, whirling his arms and growling. The two men met and grunted with the shock.

'You—bliddy—heller!' grunted Tom Sorrell between his efforts of straining to break the clasp of John Fry. Fry was trying to throw him, and was butting him between the legs with his right knee.

'Oh!' groaned Tom in pain, and was compelled to turn sideways. He clutched Fry's hair, trying to force his head over his left shoulder.

Raising what felt like a shapeless, curiously lop-sided face, Willie saw them rolling near the top of the kiln. Dolly with her hands over her eyes stood near the cottage.

Willie felt a thrill in his backbone that made him shudder. He tried to make himself move, and go to the help of Tom, but he could not. He tried to shout, but only his mouth opened. The fighters rolled over and over, nearer and nearer the smoking rim of the middle kiln. Then Willie understood that John Fry was dragging Tom, trying to throw him in.

He leapt up and rushed about for help. Incoherent noises came from his throat. He ran to the kiln, ran away again, looking for a stick, while Dolly screamed.

Near the cottage he picked up a great flint, dark on its split side.

The faces of the men were blotched. The long bare scar on the head of John Fry was livid. Willie poised the flint to drop it on his head, just as John Fry flung off the quarryman, who lay for a moment as though his back were broken.

Willie ran away, but stopped, for John Fry was going towards Dolly. She screeched, and tried to crouch up into the wall. He put his arms round her, to uncover her face, but she bent her head and bit through the skin on the back of his hand. Willie came nearer, the flint poised. Dolly was kicking furiously, and with his flint Willie got within three yards of them. Holding it in both hands he heaved it at the back of John Fry, who with a snarl turned round and came after him. Willie ran away, terribly afraid.

But Tom had recovered, and as he passed flung himself at the other's legs. With a thump John Fry went over, and the heaving struggle continued on the grass.

Tom wrapped his arms round the other's chest and hung on. Constantly John Fry by nervous energy heaved himself up, as though trying to bite into the other's neck. Nearer the kiln they approached, while now and again a flame pale in the sunshine quivered upwards in wavy liquid heat and disappeared.

Willie recovered the stone, and feeling bolder with Dolly near, advanced with the sharp edge downwards. Their faces were bruised and bloody. Willie slung the flint at John Fry; it dropped on his ankle. Immediately the fight stopped, while John Fry writhed and groaned on the ground. Tom got up and rested his hands on his knees, panting.

'Oh, I'm sorry if I hurt you,' cried Willie, looking anxiously at the back of Fry's head.

John Fry was sick, after which he lay with his face in the grass, hidden by his arm, one leg drawn up.

'That's settled your game,' gasped Tom Sorrell, threateningly standing over the prostrate man. 'Do ee want any more, John Fry?'

'D-don't hurt him!' cried Willie, as he stared down at the shaking back. His own lip was fat and smarting, and his head ached.

'He didn't ought to be at large,' declared Tom Sorrell. 'The bliddy madman.'

'What shall we do?' asked Willie, a minute later, as John Fry continued to lie in the same position, on the grass.

'A lethal chamber's the place for his sort,' said Tom, contemptuously.

Willie followed him back to the cottage. He watched Dolly listlessly shaking her hair free, and felt very strange and hollow. Tom Sorrell watched her also, and Willie felt that he ought to go away.

John Fry looked so harmless now that he dared to go near again. He looked at him sprawling there for a minute.

'Mr. Fry, I've come to say I'm sorry if I hurt your foot.'

John Fry looked up at him, muttered something, then hid his face again.

'I know how it hurts,' said Willie, presently, 'when you get hacked at football, and that flint must have been ever so much worse.'

John Fry did not move.

'I say, please forgive me. I didn't mean to hurt you.'

John Fry still made no reply, and unhappily Willie turned away. As he walked to the cottage he remembered Bill Nye; and ran to Dolly. Hastily he told her about the crowstarver in the spinney.

'If only I'd come on my bike I would have come much quicker! And then you'd have gone before John Fry came along!' he cried. 'Oh, why didn't I come on my bike?'

'Don't you worry, midear. You're a brave boy if ever there was one. We'll come along now,' said Dolly. 'Oh, Master Willie, you're lip be hurt, midear.'

'That's nothing,' said Willie, trying to smile with his very fat lip. Wouldn't he tell the Specials to-morrow! He began to feel pleased with himself.

Before they left, Tom Sorrell went to John Fry, who was now sitting up, and told him to clear off.

'If I catch ee round here when I return, I'll give ee in charge,' Tom warned him, as he limped past.

When John Fry was hidden by the bushes near the gate, Willie said, 'I'll be back in a minute,' and ran after him.

'Mr. Fry, please will you shake hands?'

He winced at the leering contempt in the other's reply, as John Fry pulled himself up in his dog-cart.

Although Willie had heard the expression many times, both at school and in the village, the humiliation given by the retort remained even when Bill Nye had been safely taken away to Colham Infirmary. And when everyone whom he saw, having heard about the fight in the way of swift village gossip—the Normans—the Vicar and Mrs. Cerr-Nore—the

Temperleys—declared that he had been silly to have wasted sympathy on such a drunken hypocrite, the feeling of humiliation deepened into a sense of complete inferiority. Even towards Jack, to whom alone he repeated the words, he began to feel estranged, for Jack said, 'You were slow, Willie. You ought to have told him to kiss yours.'

OVER THE HILLS AND FAR AWAY

'Thus men's minds . . . are unlearning, the first step to learn. As yet we are in the fact stage; by-and-by we shall come to the alchemy, and get the honey for the inner mind and soul. I found therefore, from the dandelion, there were no books, and it came upon me, believe me, as a very great surprise . . . It is nothing but unlearning, I find now.'

RICHARD JEFFERIES, in *Nature and Books*.

Chapter 28

AFTER slow toiling in the sun, never once resting or looking backwards, he reached the summit of the downs, and seeing a solitary harebell, sat down on the sward beside it. Far below were the fields of corn, motionless and unwaved in the heat of the summer morning, the dark green hedges, the white-grey wandering lines of the roads and lanes. The barley was whiter than the yellowing wheat; and the oats were greyer when the shadows of clouds moved, so slowly, across the fields. Far away the smoke of Colham was grey in the lower sky. The shadow of a hawk glided over the grass before him.

The wind stirred the harebell by his side. He touched it with his finger. Soon it would die, and where would be its blue bell-flower then? We know each other under the sky, he thought, and smiled as he looked down to the plain once more. There was the low farmhouse of Skirr, the barns, the old ricks, and a glittering speck that was the sun shining in the horse-pond. The tame pigeons were circling over it—there had been pigeons in the cots ever since he could remember. Beyond was the village, a cluster of slate and thatched roofs under the summer haze.

The ancient forest rose dark along the ridge above the Big Wheatfield, hiding the Longpond. Here up by the sky, in the cool wind of the downs, he need not to think or remember. All of him felt in the sky. By the Longpond he remembered other days; the beechwood was empty; the rooks silent and gone; no purpose in walking over the meadows or to the spinney. They did not care that he was going away; but up by the sky he was himself.

The harebell grew beside a tumulus, on which was thyme, and yellow flowers of birds'-foot trefoil. Every day since her return, which had brought only anguish, he had climbed to the down and lain in the sun, and ceased to be Willie Maddison. Here on the highest hill with a view of many miles of plain, and the unseen sea beyond, the longings would be taken away by the wind. Here he might lie, and think himself away into the sunlight, like the spirit of the ancient Briton whose bones for centuries had lain under the mound. Here the singing lark, the gliding kestrel, and the wandering honey-bee were free in the sunshine, and he was free with them.

A blue butterfly flickered over the grasses, and rested on a flower of hawkbit. The colours suddenly made him happy; he would remember them, and be able to smile to himself, whatever happened. Blue butterfly on yellow dandelion—the sky and the sun. Always the sky and the sun wherever he went. He lay back on the grass, spreading his arms and closing his eyes, and smiling into the sky; the sun had always been, and he had always been. Before and after death the sky and the sun were the same, and all things with them. Lying there with outspread arms he felt himself merge into the sun-wandering air, until he was gone, dissolved and drifting in the bright air. So sharply strange was the feeling that he rose up on an elbow, and shivering, looked round to discover himself. How disappointing to be himself again! He was alone on the hill, alone with the sun, the wild bees burring about the thyme flowers, and the green mound whose grasses moved in the breeze.

He lay down again, trying to dissolve himself once more, but it was no use. What was that? A sound of feet swishing in the grass! Startled, he sat up, to see a girl standing half way down the mound looking at him. Her loose dark hair lay on her shoulders, and she was smiling.

'Hullo, Willie,' she said, and the smile remained, but her eyes looked on the grass.

'Hullo Mary,' he replied and stared over the plain, frowning.

'Would you rather be alone?' she asked, coming nearer and standing beside him.

'Oh no,' he said.

Her hands moved nervously; her eyes seemed to grow larger and softer as her cheeks glowed with colour. She wore a plain white blouse with a high collar and an old blue skirt. Her legs and feet were bare to the knee. She was slender and bright-eyed, her shape budding in the wind.

'I've brought a message for you,' she said.

At his glance she said at once, 'From Elsie.'

'Oh.'

'She says she is sorry she cannot come to-night.'

He forced himself not to move. 'I thought so,' he said and laughed.

'But will you come instead to tennis this afternoon?'

'No,' said Willie, promptly, looking away.

'Do come,' said Mary. 'You will make the eight. You were going to be asked anyhow, really, Willie.'

He shook his head. 'I don't want to play tennis. I can't play.'

'You're very good sometimes—your cannon ball service! Won't you come? Elsie will be disappointed.'

She sat down in the grass six feet away from him. She leaned forward to touch a bee, and her hair hid all her face except one pink ear.

'Yes, I think I will come,' he said, hope easing the frost in his breast. He imagined Elsie as he had seen her at the station; taller and bigger, her black uniform skirt half-way between her knees and ankles; her face with the large blue eyes, so beautiful, and her radiant cheeks. In her gaze had been no timidity, no shyness, but just happiness and friendliness. But she had been glad to see him. Surely that was a sign?

He plucked a grass and chewed it.

'Do come,' said Mary.

'Who else is coming?'

'Just the Cerr-Nores, and the—Margents, are they called?'
Charlie Cerr-Nore!

'I don't think I'll come,' he said. 'My tennis racket is warped, and all the strings are broken.'

'You served very well with it last year, anyhow!'

'How did you get here?'

Mary came nearer. 'I stalked you all the way. Did you see me? I thought you had, once or twice, because you didn't look back *obviously*.'

She sat near him, her face half-hidden by her hair; sitting cross-legged, her knees brown in the sun, her hands in the lap of her blue skirt.

'No, I didn't see you, Mary.'

Mary seemed to take a frank delight in regarding him. Then her lips closed, and the smile went from her face. 'Oh, your poor mouth. I'd forgotten it. Does it hurt much?'

'Not at all. I'd forgotten it,' he replied casually. 'Why would Elsie be disappointed if I didn't come?'

'It's your last day.'

'I don't suppose she cares,' he replied; and waited for the answer.

There was no answer.

'How did you get that socking great scar on your knee?' he inquired, quickly, not interested in the scar.

'Oh, that?' she answered, plucking at the hem of her skirt and exposing the entire knee, 'Oh, that's nothing. I fell out of a tree when Howard and I went after a heron's nest.'

'Oh yes, you wrote to me once about herons,' he replied. 'Have you got a heron's egg?'

'Yes, several.'

'Get 'em yourself?'

She nodded.

'What were they, elm trees?'

'No, fir trees.'

'High ones?'

'Fairly. But I fell from a low branch.'

'You must be plucky to climb a high fir tree.'

'I love climbing,' said Mary. 'I wanted to climb with you when you and Jack climbed the rookery. Do you remember? Two years ago?'

The hawk glided along the hillside below them, and they both watched it.

'You must be a plucky kid,' he said.

'I think you're plucky,' said Mary, looking at his broken lip, which she noticed he kept touching with his tongue.

'I did nothing,' he said. If only Elsie would say things like that! But Elsie never said anything.

'I like Bill Nye,' said Mary. 'I'm glad he's going on all right. I had double pneumonia once.'

'Bill Nye's all right.'

'I like Dolly, too. In fact, all your friends are decent.'

'She's pretty decent. I'm glad she's going to leave Rookhurst. They are a miserable lot of talkers there. They talked about her and Jim, and now they talk about her and Tom Sorrell. As though people can't be friends!'

Mary was clasping her skirt round her ankles, and resting her chin on her knees. Quite unconsciously the girl had copied the meditative attitude of the boy. 'May I be your friend, Willie?' she asked.

'I'm going away to-morrow.'

'Shall I write to you? But I expect you'll make lots of friends.'

'Have you any brothers or sisters?' he said after a pause.

Mary nodded, peering sideways through her hair. 'Two brothers and two sisters.'

'Who's Howard then?'

'A friend. He lives across the estuary, in Appledore. We go sailing together.'

'Has he got some decent eggs?'

She nodded. 'He keeps hawks for falconry. Peregrines.'

'How ripping. I want to keep hawks.'

He stopped, remembering London.

'Don't worry,' said Mary. 'You'll come back.'

'I shall be jolly glad to go away,' exclaimed Willie vehemently.

Mary seemed to absorb his mood, for she brooded. A grasshopper that with risping chirrup had been praying to the sun flipped to her bare foot and straddled its bright greenness across her toes.

'Here I am on someone's foot, but I'm not going to stay long. A-way I go!' said Mary softly touching it with her finger. The grasshopper flipped away, and joined the sun worshippers in the grass. She sighed, very softly, and touched with her finger the solitary harebell.

'Mary.'

'Yes, Willie?'

'Promise you won't tell anyone?'

'Yes Willie.'

'Well then, do you think Elsie—likes—er—anyone?'

'You mean you?'

He nodded, with averted head.

'Yes, I think she does, Willie. But not perhaps in the way you like her.'

O, why hadn't John Fry held his throat until everthing had remained black for ever? He turned on his face, and pressed it into the grass. He felt her arm on his back and was grateful.

'Don't worry,' she whispered.

'You must think me a fool,' came his voice from the grass 'Like John Fry. He couldn't see when he wasn't wanted.' He thought of John Fry, and said, 'I think I know now how he has felt all the years over Dolly.'

She wished she could think of something to say to help him.

'I think we're alike in some things,' she murmured.

Soon he sat up and smiled at her.

'Goodbye,' he said, rising, and walked away swiftly down the hillside.

'Then you'll come to tennis this afternoon?' she called after him, but he did not reply.

His footsteps through the plumy grasses released from anchorage many seeds of hawkbit and dandelion, which floated away in the sun-stained air. At the foot of the downs he turned round, thinking that Mary might be waving, and wanting not to disappoint her; but the hill-crest was bare. 'Goodbye downs,' he said and waved to them. A tiny arm rose up against the grassy edge of the sky, and then disappeared. He hastened on, for he did not want to be late for dinner with Jack. His father would probably be expecting him; but it was his last day.

Chapter 29

'Do have some more pudding,' Mrs. Temperley said again, and looked coaxingly at Willie.

'No thank you,' he replied again.

'Well, you've had nothing at all! Besides, we shan't be seeing you again for goodness knows how long. Come on, another helping!'

'Really, no thank you.'

'Well, I don't like the idea of your starving yourself,' said Mrs. Temperley, helping Jack to some more gooseberry pudding. 'I don't really. Are you sure? One spoonful, now?'

'No thanks, Mrs. Temperley,' he said slightly irritably.

'Very well. Just as you like, my dear.'

At last the meal was over, and Willie could retire with Jack to the loft over the disused stable, with their pipes of cherrywood purchased a few days ago for one penny in the general store at Rookhurst. The entrance to this sanctuary was guarded by an old door hidden with ivy, and the lock was so stiff with rust that only a stick used as a lever would turn the key. Inside the floor of beaten earth and stones was covered with furze-roots and logs of beech. In the middle stood an ancient weighing machine, an old friend, the abode of spiders, whose dusty webs everywhere were laden with the wings of moths, and the empty cases of flies.

They closed the door, and relocked it. A vertical ladder stretched into the dim loft above, which for years had been a retreat prized for its secrecy, its treasure of apples and old magazines. Had they not in far off days discovered here a rusty single-barrel without a trigger, and several bags of snipe-shot? It had been forbidden, but that had enhanced it as a place for hiding and for the discussion of plans.

Willie climbed up first, and looked around him. The same old mattress on the floor, the same feathers escaping from it, the same old oak furniture piled in the corner, the same stuffed birds on their loose perches slowly falling apart in a last moult, the same picture frames with their faded huntsmen, leaping cut-and-laid hedges after hounds in full cry.

Jack rose beside him and stood still. Faintly from the rusty grate came the wheezy clutter of the starlings on the chimney top, while the pattering of the sparrows' feet on the gutter sounded through the walls. Everything was the same; nothing changed here; it would remain so when he had gone away. In the gloom Jack whispered, 'I've got them all here, safely. No one saw.'

'Dear old Jack,' replied Willie in a relieved tone. 'You're sure no one saw?'

'Absolutely!'

'They're in that old corn-bin. In a tin, to keep the rats away.'

'Righto. How much was it?'

'Oh, that's nothing.'

'Come on, man, I must pay.'

'Oh no, I'll do that.'

But Willie persisted, and eventually Jack pocketed two shillings and threepence. They sat down on the feathery mattress.

'Tobacco?' asked Jack holding out a tin.

'Maresee,' Willie thanked him, with an accent that of olden time would have caused Rattlethrough to cry out as though in pain. 'What is it?'

'Guv'nor's.'

'Not that poisonous black twist I've seen lying about on the window ledges?'

'No. His special. I bagged it this morning. He said I could.'

'Bong,' approved Willie smelling it, 'there's no latterkeer in this. I don't like latterkeer.'

'No more do I,' agreed his friend, wondering what it was.

They lit their pipes and smoked rapidly, sometimes coughing. The blue smoke hung listlessly in the stagnant air of the loft. Outside the sparrows cheeped and scolded.

'What time to-night?' asked Jack.

'Ten o'clock,' murmured Willie, looking at an otter that grinned unmoving in the dimness. Poor mouldy beast, shut up there for ever! 'You'll have the ladder in position against the southern window?'

Jack nodded, and stared at the worm-eaten boards. 'I wish—'

'Go on.'

'Oh, it don't matter.'

'You wish what?'

'I wish you weren't so keen on her,' said Jack.

'Oh, shut up.'

'Don't get angry, Willie. I merely think, as your friend, that she isn't worth all your unhappiness. She doesn't understand you. She thinks you're morbid.'

'You've been talking to Mary, haven't you?'

'Well, we did mention it. She's your friend, too, if you'd only see it. A decent girl in my opinion.'

'Do you call it friendship to talk to anyone about me?' cried Willie, putting down his pipe.

'I don't talk to anyone. I said Mary. But if you want to know, I'll tell you that it's well-known, all about your being keen on Elsie, I mean. The Margents know, the Cerr-Nores, the Priddles, and the Radford girls, my sisters and mother, Bryers and Bony, Clemow and Hoys, Miss Nicholson—'

'I don't believe it,' said Willie in desperation.

'It's an honest fact, Willie.'

Jack went on, with the air of one who has made up his mind to be hurt, 'Honest, Willie, I do wish you would listen to me—'

Willie cried out, 'Jack you *can't* understand, really you can't.

To me she is, O — God, I wish I were dead. How do they all know, Jack?'

Jack puffed a lot of smoke, coughed, and looked at the rafters. 'Elsie told them, or they heard through her. Or her mother. Mrs. Norman calls it "calf-love".'

Willie stared at the worm-eaten boards of the floor.

'I believe in speaking out,' continued Jack. 'I'm not going to shut my mouth up to facts. Elsie's quite a nice girl'—Jack was now unconsciously quoting his mother—'but not good enough for you. She is incapable of appreciating you. Behind your back she laughs at you for being so keen on birds and things. An obsession, she called it. Do you think I like to hear a blasted girl laugh at my friend, a chap who I know jolly well is a million times too good for any girl, and who will jolly well get on in the world.'

'You don't understand,' said Willie, unhappily.

'I'm certain that you don't understand her properly, otherwise you wouldn't be so—so—so keen on her. Won't you believe me, old man?'

The ivy leaves touched the windows, a gathering of flies wove and interwove aimlessly under the bursting ceiling. Jack puffed, and Willie puffed, striking many matches, puffing a shower of sparks out of the fuming bowls of cherrywood. As time went on, and it became later and later for the tennis party, Willie grew more morose, until something Jack said made him fling his pipe at the wall, rise up with a sort of scream and rush away. Jack followed, and found him in tears by the old weighing machine.

'Jack, I'm sorry. O God, I can't bear it any more!'

'I understand, Willie.'

They shook hands.

'My God, Willie—'

Tears stood in Jack's eyes now. They smiled at each other.

'Dear old Jack,' laughed Willie, and began to cry again.

'It's that blasted tobacco,' he explained. 'I swear there's

latterkeer in it. Oo-ah! I believe I'm going to be sick.'

When he had been sick behind the rain-water hogshead by the ivy wall, Willie left the farmhouse, and went towards 'The Firs.'

He walked quietly up the path, hearing the thuds of rackets on balls coming from the tennis lawn behind the house. He crept forward, seeing Charlie Cerr-Nore, clad in new flannels, his auburn hair brushed back and oiled. Mary was playing, in the same blouse and blue skirt; but SHE was in snow-white clothes; her beautiful, beautiful hair in two long plaits, one in front, the other behind. Elsie, Elsie! O, why hadn't he changed? But his flannel trousers were so short; they ended quite three inches before his ankles. His last chance—all was ruined—London.

Sadly a greenfinch called by the crimson splashes of the gladioli, and the wind soughed in the pine trees. He heard someone coming, and prayed that his throat would not dry up if it were Elsie. He sat down in the hammock. A moment now. He looked up, and saw Mary.

'It's Willie! I'm so glad—I'll tell the others—'

'No, no! I'm going now.'

Mary stood looking at his face.

'I wish I had gone away to-day,' said Willie. 'I say, they won't come here, will they?'

He was disappointed when Mary said, 'No, they're playing on the hard-court as well. I came to get a handkerchief.'

'I'm going,' said Willie, sitting still, and listening to a voice that transfixed him with its 'Good shot, Charlie.'

'I'll catch the night train. Goodbye, Mary. Thanks for being decent.'

She stood with dark, wide, calm eyes before him. 'Won't your father be disappointed, Willie?'

'He doesn't want to see me.'

She sat at his feet. He looked so unhappy, sitting there with his big sad eyes that she longed to do something to comfort him, but what could she do? Without realising what she did, Mary leaned her head against his knee, and clasped it with her brown hand.

'Don't,' said Willie; and she shrank back, turning her head so that her sorrowful dark hair hid her face; she rose up, and went away, leaving him wretchedly staring after her.

He could not leave. He sat there in a dull anguish until Elsie, coming round by the trees, swishing her racket at flies, saw him and sat beside him in the hammock, which bulged and touched the ground beneath.

'Cheer up, Willie,' she smiled. 'Anyone would think you were going to a funeral. Why so late? And why not flannelled?'

'I thought you'd be enough without me.'

'What a mournful voice you speak in. What did you say to Mary that she went off so suddenly. She wouldn't speak to me as she went upstairs.'

He could make no reply.

'Cheer up, Willie,' she said; adding half chidingly, half coaxingly, 'Really, you know, you ought not to let yourself go so, or you'll be growing up with a morbid mind. Mother says that it is only the little minds that are morbid.'

Willie felt more hopeless at every word, which feeling was increased by the realisation that everyone must have been talking about his morbid mind. What had Charlie Nore been saying, too?

Elsie said, quietly and seriously: 'What you really need, Willie, is religion.'

He said nothing.

'You ought to go to a Roman Catholic Mass in Bruges Cathedral. It would soon change your outlook. Yes, you want religion.'

'Religion crucified Jesus.'

'How can you say such things!' declared Elsie, shocked.

'It's true,' he faltered.

'You're thoroughly morbid, that's your trouble.'

'I'm not morbid, Elsie,' he stammered. 'You don't understand.'

'Father says that those people who say that they are misunderstood are usually the ones to misunderstand.'

'Elsie, Elsie, can't you see that I am upset because I'm going away from you, and because it's near autumn now, Elsie, and the swallows will be going south.'

Elsie looked at him in surprise, and tossed her hair so that it dispread its gold masses over her shoulder and side. He nearly cried his pain at the beauty of it. Her hand gave his a friendly shake, and she said, 'I do understand, more than you understand yourself, if you only knew it. Now, be sensible Willie. I've known you for many years now. Try and be just friends, Willie. I know how you feel at going away, well enough, because I had to go away to Belgium, which is much farther away than London. Anyone would think that you were the only one who's ever had to go away. Besides, think of the sights you'll see! All those ripping theatres and restaurants. They're nearly as nice as those at Brussels, where mother and I used to go and eat such ripping confiserie. Besides, you'll have holidays.'

Encouraged by the intimacy of her tone, he asked her if she would meet him that night at half-past nine by the haystack in the field beyond the fir trees. 'Do come,' he begged. 'I've prepared a surprise. Please come.'

'Half-past nine! What an unearthly time. I shall have to bring Mary. Besides I doubt if mother would let us come.'

'Can't you come without telling them? And we don't want Mary!'

'What's the surprise? A fire and a kettle of tea, and a baked potato?'

'It's inside a building. It's my last evening. Elsie, come, do come.'

'But supposing mother and father find out?'

'Say you're going into the garden to see the moon.'

'But is there any moon?'

'Yes. The moon is a waxing moon now. It rises to-night, so my chart says, soon after eleven o'clock. '

'Your chart?'

'I made a chart of Rookhurst, putting in all the footpaths, the main rabbit-runs, stiles, footpaths, spinneys, streams, and where the more important nests were this year. Also a separate chart showing the stars at night. I can tell the time by the stars—not exactly, of course, but correct to within an hour or so.'

'How wonderful! Do you know, Willie, while you were telling me of that you looked quite different. Why can't you always be like that? Father says that useful work is a sure cure for morbidness. That's why he, as an artist, has succeeded.'

'I wish I could paint,' said Willie meaningly.

'Genius is rare.'

'Then I'd paint you.'

'Daddy's painted me enough already.'

'Your hair is like the sun on ripe corn.'

'Is it?' she replied, tossing her hair.

'I like your hair in plaits best,' he cried.

'I think I shall plait it again after tea. It gets in the way. expect tea's ready. I'm hungry. You'll stay, won't you?'

She would plait it after tea! Obviously for him! Suddenly exhilarated, expecting to see her face fall, Willie said that he had promised to have tea with a friend.

'Well, in that case I won't keep you.'

Oh, what a fool he was! Oh——

Damhell! Charlie was coming round the corner.

'Hullo Maddison. I am to inform you that tea is ready,' he said, bowing and smiling to Elsie. She got out of the hammock.

'Well, I'll say goodbye, Willie.'

'Goodbye.'

Mrs. Norman called 'Elsie!' and Elsie cried 'Here. Willie's here.'

'Good afternoon, Willie,' said Mrs. Norman joining them. 'Where have you been? Independible Willie Maddison! However, now you're here, come and have some tea.'

'I've got to go to a friend's Mrs. Norman, thank you very much all the same.'

'Well, come to supper? The young people are having just a small gramophone dance. Come along too, will you?'

'I've got to have supper with another friend,' said Willie. And lacerating himself further, he said. 'I'll say goodbye now. Goodbye.'

He gave a half-bow, and turned away, muttering through his teeth, 'Oh God, you fool, you fool.' Deliberately he shut his hand in the gate, so that blue grooves were left on his fingers.

Chapter 30

HE set out for an endless walk. He passed the quarry and looked in, but the cottage of Tom Sorrell was locked up, the kilns cold and deserted. A hare bounded from its chalky form in a tussock as he peered over one edge of the pit, and rushed up the opposite slope, disappearing into the wilderness of ancient teazles, thistles, and briars in the grass. Evidently the quarry had been deserted for some days, he thought, otherwise the hare would not have chosen it as a place to muse away the long hours of day.

He loitered among the dry grasses for a while, then decided to take one last look at the village and say goodbye to his friends in various cottages. As he walked along beside the stream he heard a faint thunder merging with the tranquillity of the summer eve. The old mill-wheel was working. He peered around the mud of the ebbing millpond, and saw the body of a dog lying on its side. Its legs were hidden in the ooze, but he saw part of the string that had tied them together. There was something familiar in the look of the head and the mud-logged tail. Pushing it with his stick he saw that it was Bill Nye's dog, Tiger. Who had done it? Then he remembered that Bill Nye was in the Infirmary. Tiger had been homeless, probably running around howling for its master. Tiger, Tiger old boy, why didn't I look after you, and give you a straw bed in the summer-house at the end of the garden? Too late now. With his hazel stick Willie sorrowfully touched the drowned head. 'Good-bye, Tiger,' he said, and walked on to the millhouse, which roared dully with the grind of the stones on the oaken floor-beams.

A flume broke over the hatch of the penstock, where the water fell on the wheel. Cool flushings leapt from trough to trough, and jets of silver spurted from the patched elm planking, refreshing continually the green of the mosses and the hart's-tongue ferns. Slowly revolved the wet shaggy-green wheel throwing fanwise from its trundling rim a shower of drops ever stealing the sunlight. Blue singing swallows passed through the spray, and to them all he thought farewell. Then in the maple branches above the mill alighted a flock of starlings already gathered for their autumnal expeditions from boggy meadow to upland pasture, upland pasture to fallow field. Immediately thousands of birds began to wheeze, whistle, chuckle, mimic, twitter, pipe, croak, rattle, whine, and troll a jumbled parody of all the birds' notes heard during summer. They flapped their wings, they swelled their throats, they raised their greasy crests, they puffed the feathers of their breasts, all the while squirting their communal song into the air. This was the first grand performance of the squitchedy din he had heard that year, although for months little groups had been practising upon the chimney tuns, on the roofs of cattle shippen, and on the tower of the church. Willie left as they began to preen their feathers, for he was standing directly under them, and had not forgotten what old Granfer Will'um, who used to sit outside the inn all day, had often told him: that a flea fell from a stare each time it shook its wings. Other things were falling as well, so he climbed down to the millhouse.

As he came to the open door the thunder of the runnerstone on the bedstone became greater. Old Andrew the miller, was leaning over the door, his hair and beard white with flour dust, and talking to Dolly. Dolly said that she was leaving Rookhurst very soon and going away. Willie asked her where she was going, but Dolly replied vaguely that she did not know—she could get work somewhere, she supposed. Bill Nye had told her in the Infirmary last Friday that he would like to go with her when he was better; one day, perhaps, they would go. Had Willie, she inquired, seen Bill Nye's puppy-dog, because he were worritted about it, and didn't want it to turn into a rough 'un.

Willie told her and went away; and she came after him.

'Willie,' she said, 'I want to tell you something, for you was always my friend. But promise to tell no one? I be going to marry Tom Sorrell.'

'I'm so glad, Dolly, I like Tom.'

'Do you, Will'um? But I shouldn't be calling you Will'um, should I? You'm a grown-up young gentleman now, ban't you?'

'I don't feel any different,' he answered. 'Please always call me Will'um. It sounds less soppy than "Willie." I know! Call me Bill.'

'You'll always be Li'l Will'um to me,' replied Dolly. 'But be ee glad really that I'm going to marry Tom Sorrell?'

'Yes, rather.'

'Don't ee tell old Biddy! Us be going to get married in Colham. Tom has got a job there in a builder's yard. And Bill Nye shall live with us when he's better.'

'Dolly, how splendid! I will write to you from London. But where shall I write to?'

It was arranged that she should write to his house, and the letter would be forwarded. They were standing in a lane. As they were shaking hands the glances of each other's bright eyes drew them together for a spontaneous shy clasp and kiss. With a small laugh Dolly squeezed his hand, then turned and ran round the corner. Willie felt such a sweetness in his breast that he went away swiftly, to walk over the fields to the Big Wheatfield, sometimes singing with happiness.

Returning sometime later along the Colham Road, he saw with a slight alarm Rattlethrough approaching with two small boys. Willie raised his cap, smiling with awkward shyness. Mr. Rapson raised his straw hat to him, and the small boys did likewise. He beamed upon Willie.

'Well, Maddison, this is a—er—surprise. I might say, yes, a pleasurable surprise. You have not left for London yet?'

'No Sir. I'm going to-morrow.'

'Ah, yes. You live here? A delightful country. I have been takin' my two small sons to see the old forest. It has been delightful, hasn't it?'

'Yes, Dad,' they replied together.

'I am hopin' they will become interested in natural history, Maddison. I feel very strongly about the value of nature study for education—the real education. Well, my boy, I won't keep you. I wish you every success. And if I was rather a . . . er . . . let me see . . . at my public school one would have said . . . er . . . terror . . . yes, if I seemed a terror, remember that generations of boys who .. . er . . . won't learn, are . . . er . . . rather terrible in mass!'

He smiled charmingly, and seemed so eager to be nice to him, that Willie felt a sudden tremendous gratitude and liking for him.

'Yes, Sir,' he said. 'I suppose masters have to repeat the same lessons for ever.'

'Already the Old Colhamean has an altered perspective! One changes, Maddison. Well, my dear boy, I am proud to think you were in my House. We shall not come first in the Harriers' Team Race next year without you, I fear. Do let me know how you get on from time to time, won't you?'

'Yes, Sir,' replied Willie. He would write as soon as he got to London!

'You see, one gets to know one's boys, although it may not appear so to the boys themselves; and when one is fond of them, they . . . er . . . er . . . they go out into the world, and one . . . er . . . one hears no more of them usually.'

'Yes, Sir, thank you. I will write.'

'And I shall reply; but forgive me if I delay sometimes—those, er—those piles of exercises to be taken home and gone through, don't you know, night after night. Our homework in fact!'

'Good lord, yes. I beg your pardon, Sir!'

Mr. Rapson laughed. His sons were staring admiringly at Willie.

'Well Maddison, I must be off. You should do well, my dear boy. The Head Master agreed with me when you left that you had the power to do brilliantly.'

'Me, Sir?' said Willie.

'Yes, you! You look astonished. Well, old Rattlethrough must not keep you any longer.'

They all laughed, and shook hands, and parted. Willie hastened away to tell Jack about his amazing encounter. Decent old Rattlethrough! He felt very happy, and saw Rattlethrough's smile, to which was added the inner glow given by Dolly's kiss.

'I've been looking for you,' said Jack. 'I've been up to your house. I say, your Guv'nor's got a ripping spread for you. When I asked if you were there he replied in that aloof voice of his that he didn't know, but he expected you were somewhere about. I saw a big green bottle of stuff on the table with gold foil round the neck. Don't you think you ought to go, and chuck coming to supper with us?'

'If you don't want me, I won't come.'

'Don't misunderstand me, Willie. I want you very much, you must know that. Only I thought—'

'But isn't this my last day? I am no longer a schoolboy, and as I'm grown up I can jolly well please myself. You know as well as I do that Father and I don't get on at all well. Oh, don't let's rake up those old things.'

'Righto. Sorry.'

'I shall have to leave you after supper, but I'll see you to-morrow morning before I go. Bony's going to be at Colham Station, so is Rupert, Mac, Yeates, and Swann.'

'It's rotten you're going,' lamented Jack moodily, for the twentieth time.

293

Chapter 31

AFTER supper at Skirr Farmhouse the minutes seemed to drag very slowly. The fiery colour of sunset merged into a purple hue that stained the field seen through the western casement as a child's mouth is stained by blackberries. Then the little shy maid, her right stocking furled about her boot, came into the room and smilingly placed a hand-lamp upon the side-table. In a soft burring voice she asked if she should light the lamp swung under the beam supporting the guns. This seemed to take a long time; at last the orange shine was steady behind the glass, and the door closed behind her.

Willie cleared his throat, coughed, and drained once more the dregs of his cocoa. The grandfather clock in the corner buzzed with irritating hastelessness, the buzz droned into a whirr, which in turn became absorbed in nine weary frangings. He said he ought really to be going. There were protestations from everyone, until he mentioned that he must see his father, which met with agreement.

The little maid sat in the kitchen through which he had to pass. She smiled at Willie, and asked him if he had heard how Bill Nye in the Grubber was a-getting on. Willie replied that he was much better, and as he walked into darkness he wondered if Bill Nye had inspired an affection as years ago Jim Holloman had in the young Dolly.

He decided that it was more romantic to reach her house by the fields, and quitted the roadway for the friendly meadow. After breaking through several hedgerows and falling into the brook in his haste, a yellow point of light before him told that he had held to the right direction. Steadily he went forward, his eyes intent on the beacon. He was taut and keen with the adventure. Slowly he crept forward, coming to the wire fence beyond the fir-trees. Very carefully he insinuated himself between the top and second strands, holding them lest they should twang. He would hear music and voices. He waited, so enjoying the night-feeling that he wanted to prolong it.

He felt his way, with hands and feet, round the rhododendron bushes, until the last of the shadow-line was reached. Dare he cross the area of lighted grass, then the gravel path? He crept away, to where he could get a good view of the room, and lay down on the grass. He must be careful or they would hear him, and perhaps think he was eavesdropping. The double doors were open. They had stopped dancing. Mr. Norman, in his blue velvet coat—Mrs. Norman—Elsie, in white with her hair up, sitting by Charlie. Young Mary and others. His sight became fixed on Elsie. Her hair up!

Mary was winding up the cabinet gramophone. Lovely things the Normans had; nothing like that in his own home. Horrid to be poor! Ah, what lovely 'cello music. He listened in a rapture, resting his cheek on the dewy grass, staring at the rectangle of light. When it was over her voice said:

'Let's have a jolly waltz now. Mary always likes those bits best, so do you, Daddy.'

'Ah, its music,' replied Mr. Norman. 'Not donkey music.'

'I think all lovely things are sad,' said Mary, so softly that he could scarcely hear. 'You should hear Diana Shelley play!'

'You and Willie would make a fine pair, I say. You'd be able to weep out your woes on each other's shoulders. Willie I'm sure would shed tears.'

Eavesdropping or not, Willie felt that he had to creep nearer lest anything be missed; it seemed that he had a heavy weight attached to his heart as he crawled over the dewy lawn.

'Put on that ripping *Come to the Ball* waltz,' said Elsie.

'I know where it is,' said Charlie.

He heard the slap of records being rapidly turned over, and

then the whirr of the gramophone being wound up. Then the music—very nice and jolly, thought Willie, wishing he had gone to supper, then he might be dancing with her now instead of Charlie.

He saw her smile at him. As they moved past the door he saw her hand on his shoulder lift and tweak his ear; and then Charlie trying to kiss her. She held back her smiling head, but O God, she still danced with him.

He pressed his face in the grass, and clutched the ground wildly. A hundred sleepless nights, a hundred fragile dreams, a hundred gray mornings of misery, and again, as many of joy and hope—and all the while he had been a damned, damned fool. What need was there to go now to London, what was there remaining but an empty life that the sooner ended, the better. If only he had a gun—

Sometime later, hiding in shadow behind a rhododendron bush, out of which a startled blackbird had flown squealing, he saw Mary coming over the lawn.

'Are you there, Willie?' she whispered.

'Yes,' he whispered back.

'I thought it was you when I heard the blackie. Are you coming in?'

'I can't!'

'Shall I tell Elsie?'

'She won't come.'

'She might. I'll tell her secretly. How long have you been here?'

'About an hour.'

'You're shivering with cold, you poor dear!'

'No, I'm all right,' he replied. If only he could stop shivering!

'I'll tell her,' said Mary. 'Wait there.'

'Mary!'

'What?'

'Don't tell the others,' he begged.

'No fear!'

She went back, and soon afterwards he saw her go out of the room followed by Elsie. Charlie put on *That Ragtime Cowboy Jo.*

Willie swung his arms, to stop the unmanly shiver. The wind had ceased, and the night was silent. She did not come, and the shiver returned. He crept round to the lighted window. Steps on the gravel! The shiver became a shudder over all his body.

'Where are you?' she said.

'Here,' he whispered.

'Isn't it dark? I can't see an inch in front of my nose. Where are we going?'

'Ah, you leave that to me. Elsie, I thought you wouldn't come!'

'It isn't very far, I hope. The grass is rather wet.'

'Oh, but you will love the sound of your feet in the grass. I felt coming here as though I were walking among the stars.'

'Pouff, you silly, there aren't any! Why, your sleeve is all wet. Where have you been?'

'I tried to jump the brook for the last time and fell in. I don't care.'

'You ought to care, then!'

Ah, she must care for him secretly. This was just like the lovely stories by Ian Hay—like *The Knight on Wheels.* Indeed in this romance Willie had long seen a parallel to his own case. It was all working out just like it! He began to thrill with joy.

They left the garden. This, at last, was the night of nights. Hadn't she left Charlie and all the others, just to see him? So lightly on his arm were her fingers resting. He wanted to shout aloud. How wonderful were their footsteps in time on the road, how warm was her arm when it touched his arm. He could see her lovely proud head against the afterglow of the sunset.

'I think your hair is lovely up,' he managed to say.

She withdrew her hand to pat it. 'Do you?' she said. 'I had

it done in the hairdresser's at Colham. We went in Daddy's new car after tea. I'm going to keep it up.'

'Elsie, give me your photo!'

'I haven't one, I'm afraid.'

'I'll pay to have it done! I shall have some money soon.'

'Don't be silly. We're not so hard up as all that. I'll think about it.'

'Oh, thank you!'

'Have you seen your father this evening?' she asked.

'No.'

'Well, I think you ought to be ashamed of yourself. You're absolutely heartless. Aren't you?'

He said nothing.

'You ought to go home this minute.'

Hearing the finality in her tone he realised that he must say something bold, quickly.

He said, 'I don't like Charlie.'

'Well, and why not? You are very rude to him. You forget he's my friend, who's going up to Oxford very shortly. Surely you aren't jealous of him because you're not going to the 'Varsity?'

Willie said nothing, fearful lest his voice break.

Yet she spoke rather as though she desired him to admit that he was jealous, he convinced himself. Remembering *The Knight on Wheels*, he believed that she was pretending; that it was the feminine contrariness shown when a girl secretly liked anyone. The instinct of the pursued to pretend indifference; the man was the hunter, and the woman was the hunted, and she enjoyed it.

Willie repeated boldly that he was jealous.

'Well then, I wish you wouldn't be. I think we'd better go back. This is silly.'

'We're nearly there. Please come, please. Will you please? Please do. It's going to be lovely, really it is.'

'Only for a little while then.'

298

He secretly congratulated himself at the success of his theory. The hunted was yielding, although she still feigned a casual reluctance. He wondered if he was expected to kiss her, but the idea was instantly evaded in his mind. O, never in the world had there been a goddess like her.

They reached Skirr Farm. Willie found the ladder in position, and clambered up.

'Am I expected to climb up there?' complained Elsie, in what seemed a very loud voice.

'Shus-s-sh,' he called down in agony, 'they'll hear!'

The window was open about half a foot, and all his heavings and strainings failed to move it. The sash must be hopelessly jambed. He strained again, but it was immovable.

'Here, I'm going home,' decided Elsie from below.

Willie's answer was to push with his shoulder at the centre of the window. The rotten woodwork yielded, and a chime of broken glass came from inside the room. Again and again he stabbed with his elbow, till the entrance was clear.

'Come on,' he whispered urgently. 'I've done it. I'll get in, and help you.'

Elsie came up the ladder protesting its imminent collapse at every rung. Willie said that it had borne him easily enough, and she replied that she was not a skeleton, a remark that precipitated him into an agony of self-consciousness. This precipitate was soon dissolved, however, when he lifted her safely to the floor without sagging completely at the knees. As they walked on the boards there was a sound as of nutshells being crushed.

'Who's been eating nuts up here?' she asked.

Willie lit a candle, and immediately a rat scampered away.

'Oh, look,' cried Elsie, clutching him; 'Oh, look! its green eyes are staring at us. They'll bite our throats.'

'I'll show them!' cried Willie, picking up a tied bundle of magazines and hurling it at the twin pricks of green. The missile crashed into a case of stuffed birds, and the candle went out, while other rats scurried away.

He groped for the candle desperately, for Elsie was sure she smelt something burning. The surprise that he had so longed for was a disaster. Willie rekindled the insignificant flame, by whose light, bending in the draughty night air, several cockroaches were seen to be crawling over the floor. Some already were squashed.

'I'm going,' decided Elsie, 'It's a terrible place you've brought me to. Oh, dear, I think I've got a bat in my hair. Take it out, take it out!!'

'It's only a moth,' he beseeched.

'I don't care, I want to go home.'

'Elsie, I swear it isn't a bat! Look, it's only a daddylonglegs.' On the floor the blood dripped from his cut elbow, but Elsie did not hear.

'I don't really care what it is,' she protested, calm again, 'but I know that I'm not going to stop here any more.'

'Oh, if only you would. Listen, I've got cakes, and sandwiches, and four pasties, a bottle of father's claret half filled up with water, some lemonade, six sausage rolls each, and—'

'I'm not hungry, thank you. I'm going home.'

Willie prayed hard to himself that he would not burst into tears. He made another appeal this time to the memory of happy days gone by, but Elsie was half-way out of the window, and complaining that she would fall.

The walk back was made in silence. Elsie was the first to speak, pressing his arm and saying that she was awfully sorry to spoil his picnic, but really she ought not to have come.

'Now if it had been somewhere sensible, Willie, it might have been different. Anywhere but up in that dirty, rat-eaten old loft. Whatever made you choose such a place.'

'It's a place sacred in my memory, because of old times,' he said, in a wavering and low voice.

She did not reply.

His heart started to romp. Several times, as the distance to her house became shorter and shorter and shorter, he opened his mouth to ask the dread question, but no sound issued forth. Once he tugged at her sleeve, and she inquired if he felt ill. They seemed to be rushing towards her gate, the light in a top window was describing irregular arcs in the darkness. A wind was moving in the hedges. Outside the gate he held her sleeve and from far away he heard an unfamiliar hoarse voice saying:

'Elsie, this can't go on any longer.'

O, never had she appeared so calm and remote from him as from her lips came the insistent 'What can't go on?'

'This—this terrible business. I—I, O, I've never been so bad before, so unhappy I mean. It can't go on, it can't! I can't stand any more.'

Again the calm, the merciless, the far-away repetition, 'What can't go on?'

'Oh, this between us. You know. This—this—'

'This what?'

She waited, quite still.

The black earth seemed spinning round him.

'This what? Tell me.'

'Elsie,' he gasped, 'Elsie, don't you know I love you?'

Would she never answer, would she never answer?

'Can't we just be friends, Willie?'

'Elsie, do you love me?'

'Only as a friend, Willie. I'm very sorry, but I can't help feeling nothing more for you.'

Just as mother had told her to say! Poor Willie, he was in a dreadful state.

'I'm sorry,' she repeated, softly. 'But I can't help it.'

'Don't be sorry,' he gasped, 'Don't be sorry. It's all my fault. Please don't tell anyone, will you? I—I—O, I always thought—I—dn't to tell anyone.'

'Now go to your father, there's a good boy.'

'I—I—you.'

'Remember, you're all he's got. I don't want to rub it in, but you haven't been the best of sons, have you? And he's such a dear, too. Promise me you'll go straight home?'

He was still spinning away in utter blackness, only his feet on the earth; and a tiny part of him seemed to be watching. If only he could have some terrible accident, jumping before a train, and dying under the wheels to save a child. He clutched the hope; it vanished, leaving him in the utter blackness of onrushing grief.

'Goodbye,' her voice was saying, far away in the darkness.

'Good luck,' she softly cried, from the other side of the gate.

Gone, gone, she was gone; he must rush after her, and implore her to love him. Finished, finished.

The wind was rising, but no stars shone. Then he noticed a speck of light in the road, and knelt down, and took it in the palm of his hand, speaking in a voice low and sad and tender, as though the wan shining were of himself. He placed it in the bottom of the hedge, and lay beside it, his face on his arm pressed into the earth. Patiently in the night the glow-worm wandered with its pale green fires, never heeding the slight form shaking among the grasses withered at the roadside.

Chapter 32

THE liquid call of a curlew made him raise his head and regard the sky through his tears. Stars were aflicker in the deep
spaces between luminous clouds. A dim light filled the lane,
and revealed the haystack in the field over the hedge. He
stood up, and looked towards the eastern horizon, where the
beeches on the ridge showed massy and black against the
tawny glow spreading up the sky. Slowly an umbered moon
lifted above the forest, like a shield forged in fire and slowly
cooling, a red-smoking dross about its face. The grasshoppers
began to risp in the hedges.

He walked down the lane. Time had no significance, his
home was of no account. Nothing mattered any more. Better
if the flames had consumed his heart that night years ago
when they had resolved the body of Jim into irreclaimable
ash, freeing his spirit for the sun and the corn. Was that stir
of wind in the hedge nothing more than wandering air? Why
was his back so icy and strange? He glanced over his shoulder,
seeing strange things in the light of the moon. An owl hooted
suddenly near him.

Without a backward look at the house, Willie went down
the road, his steps steady, quitting it for the fields when he
deemed he had gone beyond sound of footfall. He would walk
all night. His mind must become calm and clear as the bluish-
white star immediately over his head, lying centrally in the
silver stain of the Milky Way. The stars should be his night-
long companions. Though love was gone from his life, though
the fields he loved would know him no more, yet still he might
watch the sky. He would be proud, and know henceforward

the stars; he would be proud—but why were the tears running down his cheeks.

My heart is breaking, he thought, with a sudden feeling of calm.

Swiftly he went towards the Big Wheatfield, to the spinney that was an old friend. Once he paused, sensing rather than hearing the noise of footfalls pursuing. But only the wild cry of a curlew came to his ear, and he walked on, swiftly as before, guiding himself by the constellation of the Swan. To the north of the five stars he recognised the Lady of the Chair, seen from his pillow during many summer nights. Farther north was Perseus, who had rescued the daughter of Cassiopæia from the sea-monster sent by Neptune; Andromeda the beautiful was now for ever in heaven with her hero. It was from a birthday present book that he had learned to know the stars.

All the bright company were his friends for evermore. Arcturus as brilliant over the downs, lancing a ray of blue then flaring with sudden crimson. Aldebaran glowed low in the east, near Capella, a yellow star that was in the night sky throughout the year, never setting. He would purify his heart of human love and weakness, he would lift his heart even above the flowers and the birds. 'To the stars through difficulties.' By heaven, it was a grand idea!

'But you mustn't cry again, you fool,' he said aloud, and now the starry sky was but a high vain wilderness.

Along the path through the rustling corn to the spinney he ran, as though relief were waiting there among the friendly trees. He would keep vigil this night by the shelter; and in the morning he would go home with no expresssion on his face weary and stained with sleeplessness, but calm. He would walk past the Norman's house like that, while they were at breakfast. And he would bow, and pass on whistling!

The moon over the corn-sea was transmuted to pale gold, and through the summer vapours it loomed big and solemn.

Its serene loitering to the higher solitudes released it from earthly taint, and the lustre changed to shine. The trees of the spinney hid it from Willie's sight as he approached the ancient home of the crowstarvers. When once more he was walking into its direct gleam, he noticed that some grotesque thing was against the circle of the moon. The apparition did not move. Two horns curved upwards from its head, black in silhouette with monstrous ears below the lean face which was given a golden fringe of hair.

'Who's there?' he cried, his back icy.

'Good. I knew you'd come,' replied a satisfied voice.

'Jack? Dear old boy, how did you get here? Oh, I am so glad to see you. Where are you. I'm nearly dead. What's that awful thing up there? Oh, I have such a lot to tell you. Jack, Jack, don't desert me, ever, will you? Be my friend, Jack. If ever I needed a friend, it's now.'

'I've been running to get here first,' his friend panted. 'I followed you after you left at supper, but I lost you at Norman's. I hared off home, and found the windy broken and no food touched. I guessed something had happened. I went back to the Normans, and saw you there, and kept off. Did you hear me hoot like an owl?'

'Yes! I thought it was one, too!'

'Pouff, I'm nearly blown. I ran all the way round the field, to get here, first. With the grub too. Look at this blinking goat! It's Farmer Turney's.'

'What's it doing here?'

'It must have strayed here to find Bill Nye, who I bet used to milk it. Feel her, isn't she warm. Let's build a fire, what say? Well, I rushed back agen, and heard you talking outside her house. I guessed what happened. Dear old fellow, remember I'm always your friend, whatever happens. I know I'm a fool, but I'd die for you. Dam. Lend me a handkerchief, will you? I'm soppy to-night. We're both soppy."

They shook hands, and clasped one another.

'Good Lord, Willie, what's up with your arm?'

'Nothing, a scratch.'

'It's cut badly. How did it happen?'

'Window. Yours. Sorry. I'll pay.'

'Get out! I'll bind it up when we get a fire going, shall I?'

'Just as you like, Jack.'

'Right,' said Jack gently. 'I brought the grub. You don't mind, do you?'

'You've got the grub? Splendid. It's like old times.'

'Rather!'

'I'll milk this blinking goat! Damhell!'

'Hurray, that's the idea. Now you're talking!'

'We'll build a devil of a great big fire. The Colham Fire Brigade will send its chestnut-barrow to put it out. Hurray!'

'Hurray!' they shouted at the top of their voices.

'Get more sticks. Get some logs. We'll sleep in the shelter! Did you bring the wine?'

'One bottle.'

'Give it me. I'm wounded! I'm goin' to get dam hellfirey drunk to-night.'

'I feel drunk already. I've had some cider. Isn't it a ripping last night?'

'Yes, I'm HAPPY!' yelled Willie in his loudest voice. 'I don't care for any one. Can you hear me?'

'Yes, I can hear you,' bawled Jack, while about a dozen dogs in the village below commenced to bark.

They lit the fire, and soon the spinney lost its pale shade and seemed to dance in the flamelight. The cheerful warmth, the crackle of branches, the swirl of sparks, the wine and the food, the comforting tobacco, caused the wildest spirits in Willie. He milked the goat into Jack's cap, and they poured out a libation to the gods. Just as the Old Bird used to explain during Latin. Afterwards, when Jack put it on his head, white trickles crept down his ears and cheeks, which dried in the heat and gave him a mildewed appearance. They both vowed that they were

306

drunk, and incapable of standing on their legs. By way of demonstration they staggered about and rolled into one another, and into the goat, who resenting this intrusion upon its slumber, butted Willie gravely. By the swift accuracy of his flight it appeared that the grape fumes had not the hold upon his brain as he had hitherto declared. They rolled on the pine spindles, aching with laughter.

The moon was now a silver bubble in the vast pool of the sky. In flame and spark the bonfire blazed. More faggots were tossed on. A fox yapped at the light from the distant coppice, a hedgehog paused in its rustling search to listen. They tapped out the cherrywoods and lit a third bowlful, smoking with intervals of silence increasing. Once Jack yawned, and Willie thought of the soothing security of slumber. His tragedy seemed a dream, to-morrow appeared as something that could never become the present.

Again they went away for more sticks, again the fire blazed, and sunk into embers, and became flat and dull-red. Willie shivered and yawned again. His pipe was out. Midnight had long passed.

Jack went away for more firing, and came back with a handful of twigs. All else had been burnt. He stared at the fiery shell from which darted a tiny flame. Where was Willie? He called his name.

'Just a minute, Jack. I'm saying goodbye.'

Jack understood.

Alone at the edge of the corn, Willie was standing. 'I shall return one day,' he whispered, his eyes on a fiery red star above the beechwood. 'Jim, are you there? I shall not forget you. Goodbye, Big Wheatfield. Goodbye, spinney—Jim, Dolly, Bill Nye, and now Willie—goodbye. Brook, and meadows where the plovers nested, goodbye. And downs, goodbye. Oddmedodds, all broken up and scattered now—goodbye. Longpond—Heron Island—'

He leant against a tree, while an aerymouse passed round

his head as it flew along the edge of the spinney, returning
with a dark erratic flitter of its skin wings.

'Goodbye, aerymouse, too.'

When the ruddy star was clear again, he went back to his
waiting friend. Silently and with arms linked they passed
down the right-of-way, leaving behind the wind sighing in the
silver-swaying wheat.

EPIGRAPH

IN the following winter 10943 Private W. B. Maddison, serving in a territorial Infantry Battalion in the Ypres Salient, (whither a lie about his age had prematurely taken him) received a letter which he guarded in a bundle of other letters received from Mrs. Norman and his Father, stained and half-pulped with rain, in the breast pocket of his tunic.

COLHAM GRAMMAR SCHOOL,
(Founded 1562)
COLHAM,
29th October, 1914

MY DEAR MADDISON,

Many thanks for your most interesting letter.

The hardships will not be without their use, and when you are fit—why glorious. I speak having suffered in many a weary walk and climb and ride. Tasks of fatigue are wisely taken at intervals. I regularly take them now. This I mention to cheer you in your toil with thoughts of the ultimate gain and the pleasant memories.

Very many Old Colhameans have taken the post of honour. I am proud to think of your determination to serve your King and Country at the front by concealing your age. Such is the mettle of our pasture. We hope to make a roll of all such for undying memory.

Never was there a more righteous war—civilisation against military despotism.

None of us can survive with honour, unless there is victory. It is quite possible the war may be short. What sort of soldiers are made by scourging and spitting in the face? There can be no ideals. The cry of 'Fatherland' has no inspiration for men thus heated.

Please remember me most kindly to Temperley and to him and to you my kindest wishes. And when you lie in the field amid the panoply of war, seeking memories of the past ere sleep falls on you; think that my thoughts will be with you nightly in my solitary walk between 10 and 11 p.m. With regrets that I cannot be with you to share your fighting and hardships.

Kindest wishes
Very truly yours,
T. W. RORE.

P.S. 24-11-'14 This letter was accidentally delayed in the posting. Since it was written we learned that your battalion had gone overseas, and I was unaware of its destination. Now we have just heard, with the deepest sorrow, of Temperley's death. It will be hard to bear; but you will bear it. We must go on—the fallen will be more and more numerous, alas!—but our cause is the cause of liberty, humanity, and true Christianity. If we in England steel ourselves to punish, in charity; to use the knife instead of a palliative ointment, our sacrifice will not have been made in vain.

Dulce et decorum est pro patria mori.

T. W. R.

SEPTEMBER 1920—DECEMBER 1921

END OF BOOK TWO OF

The Flax of Dream